City
of
Ink

Also by Elsa Hart

The White Mirror
Jade Dragon Mountain

City of Ink

Elsa Hart

MINOTAUR BOOKS
New York

CITY OF INK. Copyright © 2018 by Elsa Hart. All rights reserved. Printed in the United States of America. For information, address St. Martin's Press, 175 Fifth Avenue, New York, N.Y. 10010

www.minotaurbooks.com

The Library of Congress Cataloging-in-Publication Data is available upon request.

ISBN 978-1-250-14279-5 (hardcover)
ISBN 978-1-250-14280-1 (ebook)

Our books may be purchased in bulk for promotional, educational, or business use. Please contact your local bookseller or the Macmillan Corporate and Premium Sales Department at 1-800-221-7945, extension 5442, or by email at MacmillanSpecialMarkets@macmillan.com.

First Edition: August 2018

10 9 8 7 6 5 4 3 2 1

To my father

City
of
Ink

Prologue

Summer, 1711

The courier rode out of camp in the yellow haze of a dust cloud. Wearing an expression of faint puzzlement, the man to whom he had delivered a letter watched him disappear amid the plumes of golden sand, before turning and reentering a spacious tent. Its interior was filled with a bright clutter of painted furniture, rugs, saddles, and sacks. These were all coated in a layer of cooking oil and dust, suggesting that the portable dwelling, fashioned from wool felt on a wooden frame, had not been disassembled in some time. At its center, around a blackened stove with a chimney, four men were engaged in a friendly disagreement over ingredients for a stew.

Waving away their curious glances, the man crossed to his pallet, sat down, and opened the letter. As he unfolded the paper, a small square of indigo leather fell from within. He picked it up and examined the rune stamped on its surface. It was a symbol he had not seen in all his travels. He turned his attention to the letter, which, to his relief, was easier to decipher. It was written in Chinese, and addressed to him.

There is, in the capital city of China, a small bookstore, accessible through a door covered in a white curtain. At this bookstore, customers can purchase the City Gazette, *a publication that provides news not only of happenings within the city walls,*

*but of various campaigns ranged outside of them. It is my habit
to purchase this Gazette, which is how I came to read, in a
recent edition, an account of a banquet held for our Chinese
ambassadors to the Mongols in Ordos. It contained a brief
description of the storyteller who entertained them there, including, in an appeal to the whimsical appetites of capital readers, a
selection of memorable details from the tales he told. Cursed
clockwork, poisoned wine, a demon in the snow. Your subjects
betray you, friend.*

*Knowing your dedication to strange adventures, I write to ask
for your help. If, when you have finished this letter, you are willing to undertake the task, here is what I propose. First, you must
retrieve a book . . .*

As he read, the man began to smile, his eyes to kindle and glow.
Winter had passed, and the dust storms of spring were giving way
to summer. If he departed within the week, he would reach the imperial seat of the Chinese empire before the leaves began to fall.

Chapter 1

Audacity is what distinguishes the great scholars from the merely successful ones. Twenty-two years ago, when the examiners asked me to arrange the chapters of *The Great Learning* into their most proper order, I will confess, I had no answer. So what did I do? I attacked the authenticity of the entire tome. Audacity, you see. Now I am the one who marks the essays."

The speaker was Bai Chengde, eminent scholar and frequenter of elite social gatherings. It was a warm afternoon in autumn, and he was a guest at a private literary party. Around him, intellectuals, artists, and officials mingled in walled courtyard gardens shaded by bamboo, elm, and cypress trees.

"My son is taking the examinations." With his rustic complexion and cotton robes, Hu Gongshan was out of place amid the affluent literati of Beijing. He had nodded respectfully for the duration of Bai's monologue, which had spanned three cups of wine and the whole of Bai's academic and professional accomplishments. "I am a factory manager. I make tiles, sir. I have done what I can, but my boy surpassed me in learning years ago. If you could offer any advice, that is, coming from such an esteemed scholar, it would be of great value." The words tumbled awkwardly into silence.

Bai was looking over Hu's shoulder in an unconcealed effort to catch the eye of someone more distinguished. "Advice? My advice is to avoid such obvious attempts to flatter examiners a week before the examinations begin. Corruption has no place in our city's most illustrious institution."

Hu looked stricken. "It—it was not my intention to flatter

you," he stammered. "The examinations identify the best men in the empire, those most qualified to govern. You are one of those men. I know you would never allow yourself to be manipulated by flattery."

The reply earned a cool nod of approval from the scholar. "I suppose this is your son?"

A young man had emerged from a nearby bamboo grove. "Yes," said Hu, his face alight with fatherly pride. "This is Erchen."

With a look of intense mortification, the youth bowed to Bai, and placed a hand on the other man's arm. "Father," he gasped. "He is an examiner. We cannot speak to him about the examinations." He turned a pale, exhausted face to Bai and held up a slim, somewhat battered volume with a creased paper cover. "Of course, we would be honored to hear your opinion of the text our host assigned for this afternoon's discussion."

Bai made a show of consulting his own volume, which bore the same title, but was elegantly bound in pristine white silk. "I wish I could enjoy books with no literary merit," he said with a rueful sigh. "Alas, such diversions are denied me. I am too accustomed to a higher standard. And, since your father asked me to give you advice, I will recommend that, with the examinations so near, you devote your energies to more elevated material."

Without acknowledging them further, Bai glided away to join a group of gentlemen dressed, as he was, in robes of pale gray and blue. These were colors of affected humility, but the silk was of the finest quality and fell to the season's most fashionable length. Amid the rustle and creak of branches swaying in the blustery weather, the scholars were alternating contentedly between criticizing the book they had been assigned to read and debating the efficacy of a mnemonic device popular among this year's examination candidates.

In an adjacent courtyard, a circle of spectators surrounded two men sitting opposite each other at a chessboard. One of them reached out his hand and, with fingers swollen around rings, picked up the cannon piece. The spectators pointed, shook their heads, and murmured suggestions.

"Don't distract me," growled the man. The words ran into each other. His hand, still holding the cannon, traveled over the board until, with abrupt decision, he slapped the piece down. Then he picked up a cup of wine, drank deeply, and returned it to its place beside a porcelain bottle at the corner of the table. He swayed, leaned back, and rubbed his stomach absently, exploring the texture of silk rounded by the soft hemisphere of a large belly.

His opponent might have been the same age, but was such a picture of health and vigor that he appeared much younger. From beneath brows smooth and dark as brushstrokes, his eyes assessed the board with more amusement than concentration. He slid his remaining knight into position, revealing a trap from which there was no escape. The game was over.

The audience relaxed, but the defeated player sprang suddenly to his feet. As he rose, he placed his fingertips beneath the edge of the table and lifted, flipping it into the air. The cup and bottle smashed to the ground. The pieces scattered and spun across the cobbled courtyard. There was a horrified silence.

The victor, who had watched the table's progress through the air without leaving his seat, stood up slowly and smiled. It was an attractive smile, languid and mobile, all the more beguiling for its hint of insincerity.

"Perhaps you did not intend your final move," he said. "Would you like to play it again? I recall the arrangement of the pieces." He surveyed the pieces—painted disks—that littered the garden. His broad smile thinned to one of subtle mockery.

The man who had lost didn't appear to be listening. He ignored the question and made his way on unsteady feet toward three women whose company had been purchased for the party. They were laughing and shaking spattered wine from their skirts. Their dangling earrings sparkled. Dainty red shoes peeked out from beneath silk hems.

From the doorway of a room bordering the courtyard, two men observed the action. "Hong is eight-tenths drunk," said one, a calligrapher known for his vast collection of bronze artifacts.

His companion was an elderly scholar who had made a name for himself with a series of essays on using dream analysis to predict examination results. "Hong is not a bad chess player even when he drinks," he said. "But I've never seen anyone beat Pan." He sighed and raised his own cup to his lips. "An examination candidate would make a bargain with a demon to acquire a mind like his."

The spectacle was over, and they turned their attention back to the room, which was dedicated to a collection of antiquities. The calligrapher bent over in front of a low table to admire a vase glazed a fathomless blue, with a white dragon wrapped around its widest section. "For a man without a degree, I will admit that Hong has good taste."

"His wife is the one with the taste," replied the scholar. "Madam Hong is a connoisseur of beauty. In addition, I have heard, to being beautiful herself." He chuckled. "I was told she read *The Bitter Plum* and declared it insufficiently intellectual for our gathering."

The calligrapher was examining a bronze vessel, holding it by handles as thin as twine. "She was right. A pity Hong does not allow her to curate his bookshelves, in addition to his antiques. I have never been to a party with less stimulating discussion, our own conversation excepted, of course."

After draining his cup, the scholar craned his neck to see if any of the delicacies remained on the tables outside. "Fortunately," he said, "this party will end early. It is about to rain."

The scholar's predictive powers were borne out. Within the hour, black clouds advanced upon the city. Gusting winds gained strength. Slim trees shuddered in their pots, and golden-yellow leaves fluttered to the ground, where raindrops pinned them down. It was not yet evening, but the storm brought an illusion of night. Through the darkness, jagged bolts of lightning scarred the inky sky, and thunder mimicked the evening drums. Guests sent for covered sedan chairs to convey them home, while servants rushed to collect silk cushions from the courtyards.

In one of the mansion's secluded gardens, three men stood in a pavilion, obscured by swaying branches and a veil of rain that poured down the tile roof and formed agitated puddles at the edges of the marble floor. A sudden flash of blue light tore the darkness apart. There was a crash, as if all the walls of the city had shattered at once.

"It's a warning," one hissed. "We're going to be found out. I thought I saw someone there, hidden." He pointed toward a dense thicket of bamboo.

"We won't be found out."

"But aren't you listening? This storm means disaster, destruction. We never should have—"

"Leave the study of omens to scholars and priests." The third man, who had been standing at the edge of the pavilion with his back to the other two, turned around and bestowed on them a languid smile. "Apply your mind to more practical considerations. There are advantages to darkness and fire."

Chapter 2

Two days after Hong's party, Wei Yonghen hurried through the streets of the Outer City. He was late. Of the thirteen doors in Beijing's outer wall, only twelve had opened that morning. By chance, he had chosen to enter through the one that was closed. Crammed in the middle of an impatient crowd, he had waited over an hour before the soldiers in charge of the towering red door announced that it was to be renovated and repainted, and would remain closed all day.

"It's because of Prince Yinzao's return," a sweating rug seller close to Wei had murmured. "He will enter the city through this gate."

A merchant standing nearby had sighed. "I should have known. My family has been reminding me of it for months. They made me promise to bring them to the welcome parade."

Without waiting to hear any more discussion, Wei had extricated himself from the crowd and hurried south to the next gate. As soon as he was inside the city, he had started to run, splashing through puddles and skidding across the ubiquitous mud slicks of Beijing's marshy southern boroughs. His thoughts were full of concern that he would not be able to secure employment and would have no money to bring home. His wife would sigh. The friends with whom he played cards in the village square would be embarrassed for him. Perhaps his bad luck would continue, and when his daughter was old enough to marry, she would have no dowry.

He was out of breath when he entered the Black Tile Factory. To his relief, he recognized the man who stood near the center of the courtyard issuing commands to laborers powdered with clay dust and streaked with coal. Wei smiled and bowed, willing Hu Gongshan to remember that they had drunk wine together, before Hu had been promoted to manager.

"We have enough men already," said Hu, when Wei reached him. "We can't take any more." His tone, though not unkind, was firm.

Wei tried to appear confident, even as his hopes faltered. "But I heard that you needed extra workers this week."

"We did, but now we have enough."

"If I come back tomorrow—"

"These men are all hired for the next ten days. I'd give you work if I could, but I can't. I'm not the owner."

"I would have arrived earlier," said Wei. "Xibian Gate is closed today. Please. I walked all night."

"Look." Hu gestured at the teeming courtyard. There were almost a hundred workers within the high stone walls. Most were clustered around the kilns, shoveling coal, stoking flames, or unloading finished tiles that clinked against each other like bells as they were stacked onto carts. The rest were dispersed across the flat courtyard, preparing the clay, cutting it to tiles of standard size and shape, and arranging them in rows to dry. "We're full," Hu said. "I can't pay you to stand around."

Wei thought of the previous evening, when he had watched his wife pack dumplings for him to eat on his journey. He pictured returning home with coins and placing them, one by one, into her hand. "You and I go back, don't we?" he said to Hu. "Isn't there space for one more?"

He waited, but Hu's attention had shifted to the factory entrance. Wei turned, following the direction of his look. A man stood at the open door. He wore black robes with dusty hems. His beard was brown and gray like a sparrow's wing, and his face, it seemed to Wei, was dominated by an enormous nose. Wei had only seen foreigners of this type a few times in his life, and then only at festivals near the palace walls.

The stranger scanned the courtyard until his eyes fell on Hu. He approached, and bowed. "I have come to buy—" He pointed to the stacks of tiles at the edge of the courtyard. "—for the roof," he finished. Though he spoke Chinese with a Beijing accent, his pronunciation was unusual, and his words were separated by minute hesitations.

"You want to buy roof tiles?" asked Hu.

"Tiles, yes," said the man. "I did not know the word."

"I apologize," said Hu. "The owner hasn't come in today."

"I see," said the man. "Would it be possible to make arrangements without the owner? There is some urgency—"

Hu's brow creased as he struggled to comprehend the foreigner's odd delivery. Perceiving Hu's distraction, Wei seized his chance. "I'll find a task," he said. "If I'm not doing good work by the time you finish speaking with this visitor, you can send me away."

Relenting, Hu nodded and waved Wei toward the center of the yard. Before Hu could change his mind, Wei slipped quickly into the obscuring smoke and dust. Most of the workers ignored him. Some grunted greetings. He assessed his surroundings and found, to his relief, a slumped mound of clay almost as tall as he was. Before it could be cut into pieces and shaped into tiles, it needed to be compressed, the air beaten from it. As Wei prepared to claim the task, he realized, to his dismay, why the clay had not been receiving any attention. There were no tools. Every mallet, shovel, frame, wire, broom, and blade was in use.

He knew he couldn't remain idle. One of the others would notice and report him to Hu, or Hu himself would notice and send him home. He searched with growing desperation for another occupation, until his eye alighted on a small building in a remote corner of the complex.

Wei had been inside it, years ago, when it had been a workroom. Since then it had been converted to an administrative office, but Wei remembered the jumble of materials and broken tools that had been stored there in the past. If he was lucky, he might find some object in that building that he could use to justify his presence at the factory. Even a piece of wire would be enough.

The administrative office was forbidden to day laborers. But, he reasoned with himself, he only needed to slip inside for a few moments. A quick glance told him that Hu was still talking to the foreigner. If he was quick, Wei could be out of the office, and hard at work, by the time Hu noticed him again. Almost without realizing he had made the decision, Wei began walking toward the building.

There was an unattended kiln not far from it. Wei slipped behind the kiln, which was tall enough to hide him while he assessed the door to the office. It was closed. The windows were also shut tight. His heart was pounding as he placed a hand on the side of the kiln to steady himself. Warmth spread through his trembling fingers. He turned his attention back to the door. There was no sign of movement from within. He dropped his hand and darted to the veranda, expecting to hear someone shout at him. No one did. He climbed the stairs and put an ear to the door. There was no sound from inside, no step, no flutter of paper, no creak of furniture. The building was silent.

As he touched the handle, he hesitated, and withdrew his fingers from the cold brass loop. He wiped his sweating hand on his shirt and reached out again. It was only a minor transgression, he told himself. The worst that could happen was that he would be sent away, and that was going to happen anyway if he didn't find some way to be useful.

With a decisive motion, he pushed the door open. No shout of censure came from within, or from without. He slipped quickly inside, closed the door behind him, and sagged with relief. Shut away from the bright day, he was suddenly blind. Impressions of sunlight swam through the gloom in front of him, translucent circles expanding and contracting across his vision.

He blinked rapidly, willing his eyes to adjust. The shapes around him gained form and solidity. He saw a desk, and a chair, and a cabinet bed in the corner. He watched it materialize, its edges and details emerging from the fractured shadows. Then he saw, unmistakably, the shape of a boot, and the draped and crumpled folds of a robe. Fear assailed him, clutching his shoulders with sharp talons. There was someone on the bed.

Wei remained where he was, pinned by miserable uncertainty. He could feel the pulse and flutter of his heartbeat in his neck. One footstep, one creak of the floor, could wake the sleeper, and then what would happen? He turned his head toward the door that led to the storage room.

He heard his own cry break the silence of the room. There was someone else there, lying on the floor. He saw, but could not understand the whole of what was before him. Robes of golden orange, a bare arm thrown across a face, as if to shield the eyes, long hair spread across the floor, and streaks of something dark, on the skin, on the silk, and pools, pools on the floor like oil.

Wei clutched his hands to his head. He stepped backward until he felt the door, then turned and fumbled to find the handle. He pulled and, half tripping over the threshold, stumbled outside. His knees buckled and he fell in the dirt.

He heard a shout, but the syllables sounded out of order. The open door seemed to him a hungry animal trying to suck him back into its jaws. Energy skittered through his spine, telling him to run, run. He stood up. Hu and the stranger were almost upon him.

"What were you doing in there?" Hu repeated angrily. The foreigner looked with curiosity over Wei's shoulder to the open door.

Wei sank to the ground again in a desperate bow. "I—I'm sorry," he said. "I didn't do anything. I just went to find tools. They were there, both of them, just as they are."

"Who is there? What do you mean?"

Wei tasted salt on his lips, and realized that terror had made him weep. "I didn't do anything. I just wanted to work." His voice broke. He stood up and watched, clasping his hands at his chest, as Hu climbed the stairs.

The workers were beginning to dart uneasy glances in the direction of the office. Wei knew they were looking at him. It made him feel alone, conspicuous, and envious of their distance from the horror to which he was now bound. Hu was inside the room now. Some moments passed, and Wei could not hear what was said. The man in black robes, who had followed Hu inside, came out first, his pale face now ashen. With the fingers of his right hand, he touched his forehead, his chest, and each shoulder, then looked down from his height at Wei.

"You will have to summon someone. A—" He hesitated. "I do not know the correct term," he said. "A soldier. An officer." He cast about with the frustration of someone who knew precisely what he wanted to say, but not the word to put thought into expression. "A person," he said finally, "of authority."

Chapter 3

Li Du scanned the books stacked in front of him on the desk until his gaze came to rest on a thick volume. It was near the top of a pile, high enough that he was obliged to stand in order to retrieve it. This accomplished, he lowered himself back into his chair, opened the book to the page he had in mind, and ran a fingertip lightly down the lines of text. *It will do*, he thought, and set his paperweight, a long, narrow block of scuffed jade, across the pages to hold them flat. He withdrew a clean sheet of paper from a drawer.

It was still early in the morning. Outside Li Du's closed office door, the clerks of the North Borough Office were gossiping over their breakfast, which they had purchased from the bean cake peddler who rattled daily into the courtyard, dampening the crisp morning air with fragrant steam. Li Du did not try to make out what the clerks were saying. He rarely did. Each morning brought the same rumors of promotions and demotions within the ministries, the same complaints about the onerous demands of the day ahead, and, at this time of year, the same speculations about the upcoming civil examinations. Two of the clerks were registered to take the tests, earning them simultaneous sympathy and goading from their coworkers.

The North Borough Office was tasked with maintaining order in a small, designated area of Beijing's Outer City. The daily activities of the office's staff of eight clerks, supervised by a chief inspector, consisted mainly of routine responsibilities such as arranging assistance for the poor; resolving minor disputes between neighbors; investigating local crimes, usually not more serious than petty theft; and delivering speeches on moral behavior to North Borough residents. The job of writing these speeches belonged to Li Du ever since he had been hired as an assistant to the chief inspector almost two years earlier.

As he prepared to write, Li Du allowed the noise from the courtyard to sink like sediment through his thoughts and join the other distractions he kept out of the way, in the depths of his mind. The set topic for this month's speech was "The Necessity of Respecting Academies and Honoring Scholars." Li Du reflected that it was a deliberate reminder to those inclined to complain about the examination candidates inundating the capital that among the anxious, volatile crowds were the men who would become advisors to the emperor and presidents of ministries, men who would influence the future.

He poured a few drops of water onto his ink stone, a shallow dish carved in the shape of an eggplant. It was not a design he would have chosen, but it had come with the desk, which had come with the room, along with shelves and cabinets that looked too big for the cramped space. Behind the desk was a window that opened into the narrow area between the outside of the building and the outer wall of the complex. Light entered through this window, delivered by the day like an afterthought. It fell sluggishly over Li Du's shoulder, enabling him to work while maintaining the privacy of a closed door between himself and the central courtyard.

As he lifted the lid of a small wooden box, Li Du had a thought that caused him to replace it with a frown. He stood up and went to one of the shelves. With practiced fingers, he teased a scroll from its place without disturbing the teetering mountain of scrolls around it. A quick perusal confirmed his worry, and he put the scroll back with a little tut of frustration. The passage he had selected for the speech was the same one he had quoted in the speech he had written two months ago. A choice was before him. He could search for a fresh analogy, or he could acknowledge that none of the dutiful citizens who attended the lecture would be paying close enough attention to notice the repetition. As he hesitated, a sense of futility pressing on him, he was only vaguely aware of the clang of the courtyard door and the proud step of a horse on the flagstone.

With a sigh, he returned to his chair, removed the paperweight from the book, and began to turn the pages in search of new inspiration. He had just settled on a passage elucidating the lofty and enduring qualities of bamboo when he heard footsteps on the veranda. A moment later, his door was flung open. The sudden draft sent a chorus of whispers through the papers neatly arranged on the desk and shelves. Because he couldn't see above the piles of books and papers on his desk, he didn't know who stood on the threshold, poised to enter. Before he could speak, the door was pulled closed again. The footsteps retreated.

A mistake, Li Du thought, dismissing it. The clerks rarely visited his office. When they did, it was usually to find a book or consult a record. In the early days of his employment, he had inspired intense speculation among them. They knew he held a high degree that would almost certainly have secured him a more prestigious position, had his career not been interrupted by a sentence of exile. Li Du was uncertain of how much they knew about the reason for the punishment, but appreciated their tactful avoidance of the subject. They *had* questioned him as to the reason for his pardon, but he had volunteered nothing beyond his gratitude for the Emperor's mercy. They knew he had obtained the job through a family connection to the chief inspector, and that he eschewed opportunities to mingle with the chief inspector's coterie of friends, preferring to absorb himself in endless bureaucratic tasks. As the months passed, their interest waned. Eventually, they concluded that he was merely an eccentric in need of funds, and left him alone.

Once again, Li Du lifted the lid of the wooden box. He drew from it an ink cake that was worn down to a small stub. Of the patterns that had decorated it, only a talon and a tip of a bird's wing remained, the fine details of the feathers rubbed almost smooth. Dust motes, disturbed by the door being opened, swirled in the light from the window as he ground the ink against the stone. When enough had pooled in the shallow well, he cleaned his hands, selected a brush, and began to write. His spectacles slid down his nose, and he used his knuckles to push them back into place. They were new to him, and an encumbrance.

Spectacles excepted, Li Du was approaching the end of middle age without significant alteration in his appearance since the beginning of it. Life in the capital city could bloat a man, but in the two years since his return from exile, it had not done so to Li Du. He remained trim and compact, his hair only lightly silvered. Though his brow was often creased, the lines were not yet permanent. He wore a blue robe in a color not quite deep enough to conceal the ink stains that mottled the cuffs.

"Maybe he's gone to the ministry archives again. You haven't seen him today?" The words came from the veranda. Li Du recognized the voice of Mi, the eldest of the clerks. A moment later, his door opened again. This time, before it could shut, Li Du coughed.

"Oh," said Mi. "Are you here?"

"I am," Li Du answered.

Mi crossed the office in a few strides and peered down at Li Du over the wall of stacked books on the desk. He was a young man whose face was just settled enough to enable an interested observer to predict what he would look like as an old one. He had passed the examinations three years earlier, but like many men who had their degrees, he was still waiting for the slowly ticking bureaucracy to give him an official assignment. Certain of his right to an impressive posting, but uncertain of when it would come, he attacked each day with an impatience fueled by a growing sense of insecurity. "You're invisible behind all these books and papers," he said. "The chief inspector needs you at once."

Li Du glanced at the wall that divided his office from that of his superior. Mi, following the direction of his look, appeared exasperated. "Not in his office. He isn't there. They fetched him directly from his breakfast table."

"Who fetched him?"

"The soldiers who were summoned to the scene of the crime."

"A crime? What crime?"

Mi retrieved Li Du's hat and satchel from where they rested on a chair and gestured with them for Li Du to hurry. "You have to go to the Black Tile Factory right away. The messenger says it's murder."

Chapter 4

Li Du hurried south with his satchel slung over his shoulder. He kept to the edge of the street, away from the horses and sedan chairs that crowded its center. In the past, before his exile, he had occasionally walked by the Black Tile Factory on his way to picnics and literary gatherings in Taoranting, the park built to beautify the pits left by clay excavations. The ragged ditches had been turned into lakes, which were pleasant, if not as blue as those nearer to the palace. Elevated pavilions offered a view above the smoke of the kilns.

It was a view filled with rooftops, sloping surfaces that seemed to cover the whole city in one massive, scaled hide, scored with roads and alleys. Under early autumn's blue sky, the rooftops dried to a dusty gray. In the rain, they darkened beneath a glaze of water that fell in curtains to the ground. The uniformity of this vast expanse came from millions of identical tiles, the manufacture of which was the responsibility of the Black Tile Factory. In a city constantly under construction and repair, the kilns were always hot.

This morning, four guards stood outside the door to the factory complex. They were soldiers of the Green Standard, one of several constabulary forces in the capital. Two were armed with bows, their arrows prickling from quivers at their backs like spines. The other two had swords. They were talking among themselves, which drew Li Du's attention to distinguishing features that were usually, and intentionally, subjugated by strict training and matching uniforms. One soldier was gesticulating. Another was prefacing his remarks with a squint. When they saw that Li Du intended to speak to them, they reverted to a more familiar, threatening rigidity.

"You can't go in," said one.

"I was sent for by the chief inspector," Li Du said. "I'm his assistant."

"In that case, you'd better hurry. He's already here. The doctor, too."

Li Du entered a wide courtyard. The air was thick with smoke and grit and noise. Whatever had occurred, the factory had not ceased its work. Fires glowed at the mouths of kilns. Stooped laborers carried coal and clay on circuitous paths through rows of tiles arranged on the ground to dry. At first glance, nothing seemed out of the ordinary, but as he watched, Li Du saw that the workers kept turning their heads toward the same place, a building in the far corner of the courtyard from where he stood. He started walking toward it when he saw its door open. A figure emerged, paused, then strode purposefully toward the courtyard entrance. He recognized the smoke-blurred form of Chief Inspector Sun.

Li Du prepared to speak, but Sun walked past him.

"Guard!" Sun shouted at the door. One of the soldiers stepped inside and waited at attention.

"I need two of you to go to the home of the factory owner. It's just down the alley to the east. The name is Hong Wenbin. Bring him here. Tell him only that there has been an incident at the factory."

The soldiers started to turn. "And send someone to look for my assistant," Sun added.

Li Du spoke. "Chief Inspector."

Sun spun around. "Li Du. Didn't notice you there. I'm going to need you to write everything down. Every detail. It's a bad scene."

A mid-level civil servant whose career had stagnated after an undistinguished term as magistrate in a southeastern province, Chief Inspector Sun ran the North Borough Office with an air of relief that he hadn't fallen any further down the ladder. In middle

age, he retained the history of a stiff, handsome frame, now padded by moderate indulgence. His full cheeks had fallen into jowls,
carrying with them a short beard that now barely clung to the lowest
outskirts of his face.

"A bad scene," Sun repeated. "Not what you expect in the
capital."

Li Du glanced toward the corner building, which had assumed
an ominous, waiting silence. "What happened?"

"There are two dead people in there, and it wasn't an accident.
He's a ministry official, and she's the wife of the factory owner.
We'll have to be careful with this one. Doctor Wan has already
begun a preliminary examination."

Li Du followed Sun through the open door into the building.
As soon as he crossed the threshold, he halted, frozen by the strange
violence of the scene.

His eyes went first to the body of the woman. Her robes of
golden-orange silk caught the light from the open door and window, their bright color drawing the eye like a flame in the dark. She
was lying on her back. One of her arms was at her side, the hand
concealed by fabric. The other was outstretched, the opening of the
sleeve puddled at her elbow, exposing a pale forearm and fingers
streaked with blood. From the tips of her fingers, Li Du's gaze
moved across the floor, noting vaguely the papers scattered across
it like stepping-stones, and to the bed, on which rested the body
of a man. He was also supine, his head resting on a dark cushion.
The cause of his death announced itself in a grinning wound across
his throat.

Doctor Wan, a gray, wispy man, moved across the room toward
Li Du and Sun like a cobweb caught by a draft. He nodded to Li
Du, and knelt beside the woman. "This was the mortal blow," he
said, speaking to Sun. Gently, he lifted her bloodied collar to
expose a deep wound.

Sun drew in a long breath and let it out slowly, as if he wanted
to prolong the time before he had to speak. "What about the
weapon?" he asked finally.

"I'll need to examine all the wounds thoroughly," said Doctor Wan. "But I would speculate that it was a knife with a short blade. I haven't found any weapon here that could have done it."

With a short exclamation, Sun shifted suddenly from where he was standing at the foot of the bed. A gray rat scurried between his boots and disappeared out the door.

Doctor Wan scanned the room with a frown. "I found one dead in the corner. It seems the place has been poorly kept."

Following the doctor's look, Li Du assessed the room. Even with the door and window thrown open, the corners were dim, and the air was heavy with the odor of death. In addition to the bed, the room contained a large desk, and numerous open shelves were arranged against the walls. They bore a disorderly assortment of papers of inconsistent size and color. On the desk, an unwashed brush rested on a stand, its bristles stiff with dried ink. The ink stone was also dirty. The documents that littered the floor had apparently fallen from teetering piles on the desk. They were mixed with shards of porcelain—all that remained of a small vase or bottle that had been knocked down.

"What about the storage room?" Sun indicated an opening into an adjoining space.

"I haven't looked inside," said Doctor Wan. He had returned his attention to the body and was holding the woman's wrist with a furrowed expression of concentration.

At Sun's request, Li Du made his way to the adjoining room. It was obvious that the space was rarely entered. Tangled piles of wire and crates of broken tiles filled the corners, draped in dust and cobwebs. His brief search yielded nothing. The edges of broken tiles were wickedly sharp, but none could have delivered the stabbing wounds to the woman. He returned to the other room. "No knives," he said.

"Footprints?" asked Sun.

"None other than my own. I'll make a note of it."

Sun looked relieved as he saw Li Du's stylus move rapidly and with confidence down the open page of his notebook. Sun disliked writing, and relied on Li Du to compose the letters, reports, and speeches that were required of the office. As for Sun, he spent the majority of his time promoting goodwill between local gentry and merchants, a task usually accomplished over generous meals and expensive wine. His methods were not ineffective, and Li Du gave him due credit for the atmosphere of calm security that generally permeated the neighborhoods surrounding the North Borough Office.

Sun peered over the shoulder of the doctor, who had taken out a small measuring stick and was holding it to the wound over the woman's heart. "Madam Hong," said Sun. "Wife of Hong, who owns this factory."

It was difficult for Li Du to picture exactly what Madam Hong had looked like in life. She wore powder on her face, but the expressions that had accompanied her struggle for survival had carved deep lines through the white, making her appear older than Li Du estimated she was. Her hair was spread in a loose, dark pennant across the floor, several pins scattered within the strands. Even with the evidence of violence that altered her, she had a face that the citizens of the city would have called beautiful. Li Du wrote, in neat, clear handwriting, the measurements of the wounds as the doctor listed them.

When they had finished, Doctor Wan straightened his thin form carefully and stepped toward the body on the bed. Sun had said he was an official, but his dark robes were informal, and did not immediately indicate his rank.

"According to the manager," said Sun, "his name is Pan Yongfa, and he was employed by the Ministry of Rites."

"Was it the manager who discovered the bodies?" asked Li Du, writing.

"No. One of the laborers came to search for equipment in the storage room. His story seems to place him above suspicion. He arrived at the factory from outside the city, went straight to the room, emerged a moment later, and nearly fainted on the step."

Li Du wrote quickly. "And the time of death?" he asked.

"During the night," said Doctor Wan. "Certainly after midnight, before dawn." He pointed to the man's hands, which were bloodied but otherwise unmarked. "She has defensive wounds, but he does not. I would suggest, therefore, that he died first." The doctor remained looking at the man, a thoughtful expression on his face.

Sun nodded. "He looks as if he barely moved."

"It's possible," said the doctor, "that he was asleep."

Li Du turned away from the bodies and allowed his gaze to rest on the papers scattered across the floor. At a distance, they appeared to be contracts and commissions, fallen in the struggle between the woman and her killer. But one piece of paper stood out from the rest. It was small, and crumpled as if it had been clutched in a fist. He picked it up and held it at arm's length to examine it without his spectacles. The note was written in a neat hand, precise, educated, on quality paper. Though stained with dried blood, the words remained legible.

The moon shines on my beloved in the old pavilion, green with moss. Meet me in the office of the black tile kilns tonight.

"What do you have there?"

Li Du gave the note to Sun, who read it. "Well," he said, passing the note to Doctor Wan. "That settles the question of why they were here. Either they planned to meet at the same time a thief decided to rob the kiln, or they were caught by someone who knew about their tryst. Either way, we're looking for a murderer, unless—" His next thought appeared to cheer him. "Could it have been a lovers' quarrel? He killed her, then himself?"

In which case, thought Li Du, *there would be no one to find, and little left to do.* Sun was not a lazy man, but he believed that the more complicated a situation, and the more steps necessary to resolve it, the greater the chances of inviting trouble.

Doctor Wan pointed, tracing the shape of the cut across the man's throat. "No," he said. "The manual states that a man who cuts his own throat will be found with his eyes closed, and his

features fixed in a sad expression. You see that his eyes are open."
His perusal moved to the dead man's limbs, crawled along the outstretched arm, assessing the musculature beneath the loose black
silk sleeve. "It is straight," he said. "If he had committed the act
himself, the elbow would be slightly bent. The body, you understand, must work hard to overcome the mind's resistance to self-
destruction."

A shadow fell across the floor, and they turned to see a soldier.
"Hong is at home, sir," he said to Sun. "But he is so drunk he cannot stand. What do you want us to do?"

Sun's expression was gloomy. "A bad case," he muttered. He
continued in a stronger voice, "Revive him, and make sure he stays
where he is. I will interview the manager now. As soon as I'm
finished, I'll come speak to Hong myself."

At Sun's request, a place to conduct interviews had been prepared
in a corner of the premises shaded by the overhanging branches of
a maple tree that grew on the other side of the wall. The kiln manager apologized for the primitive arrangements as he watched the
chief inspector shift uncomfortably on the lumpy surface of a sack
of coal.

"You are the manager here," said Sun, once he had settled himself. "Your name is Hu Gongshan. Is that correct?"

"Yes."

"Tell me how you were able to identify both bodies."

Despite the trepidation that was apparent in his furrowed brow,
Hu emanated stern, paternal stability. "I have only been the manager for eight months, but I've worked here for almost ten years. I
have seen Madam Hong on several occasions and was able to recognize her at once."

"And Pan?"

Li Du noticed that Hu hesitated for a moment before replying.
"Pan worked for the Ministry of Rites. I beg your forbearance.

My understanding of his place within the ministry is limited to the work he commissioned from us. He was the one the ministry sent to negotiate contracts for roof repairs."

"So he was here often?"

"Yes."

"When was the last time you saw him?"

Hu glanced at Li Du's notebook. "Yesterday," he said. "In the afternoon."

Sun's eyebrows went up. "Yesterday afternoon? Was he here to—what was it you said he did—negotiate a contract?"

"No. He said he was here on ministry business, but I don't know what it was. He said he needed to review our records."

"Can you be more specific?"

As if sensing incredulity from the chief inspector, Hu hastened to explain. "It wasn't unusual. He often came to verify expenses and inspect our work. That was one of his responsibilities. But my own duties are to make sure the kilns are correctly maintained. I have little experience with contracts."

"I see," said Sun. "So Pan was here in the afternoon. If he was reviewing paperwork, I assume he did so in the office?"

"Yes."

"Alone?"

"Yes. He requested refreshments to be brought to him there."

"And did he stay through to the evening?"

"No. He left in the afternoon, not long after the bells tolled the hour of the monkey."

Sun frowned. "So he left the factory. Did he say anything about returning?"

"Nothing."

"And what was his demeanor?"

Hu turned his head to the center of the courtyard, as if to observe his own memory. "As I told you, I didn't speak to him at any length. But he seemed—" Hu paused. "He seemed in high spirits, but he usually did."

"What about Madam Hong? Did you see her yesterday?"

"Oh, no." Hu shook his head. "She only ventured outside the family residence for neighborhood festivals. I hadn't seen her in weeks."

Sun leaned over to watch Li Du write, and gave a short nod of approval. "Every detail," he whispered. He turned back to Hu. "What time did you leave the factory yesterday?"

"Early. Before twilight. There were no fires to maintain, and therefore no reason for anyone to stay the night. I confess I was very tired. You must know about the renovation of the examination yard roof? We've had to produce more tiles than we expected."

Sun looked at the courtyard, and the neatly stacked mountains of tiles. "But what about all these?"

"We can't use them. The tiles of the examination hall are in an older style. They come from another province. But since we have no time to send for more, we are replicating them the best we can."

"And were you the last to leave?"

"No. I left the foreman in charge. Zou was responsible for making sure the entrance was locked."

"We will need to speak to him."

From among the laborers, Hu summoned a man who took his time responding, seemingly reluctant to turn away from his work. Zou Anlin was wiry in build and wore his gray cotton sleeves rolled up to his elbows, exposing clay-crusted, sinewy forearms. Though he was not an old man, deep wrinkles formed tracks that sloped from the outer corners of his eyes, across his cheekbones, and down almost to his jaw. He knelt in front of Sun, bowed, and remained kneeling until Sun told him he could stand.

"Hu informs us that you were the last to leave the factory last night."

Zou dipped his head. "Yes."

"At what time was that?"

"The night watch had just begun. I heard the drums."

"Was anyone here when you departed?"

"No. I'm sure there wasn't. And I locked the doors." His dark eyes darted to Hu. "I am sure I locked the doors."

"If the night watch had started already when you left, how did you get home through the guarded alley gates?"

"I have a room at the Sichuan lodge. I'm a Sichuan man."

Sun's curt nod communicated his understanding. Throughout the city there were lodges built to house men from the provinces who traveled to the capital for work or pleasure. A man from Yunnan could be assured of a place to stay among others who spoke his language and could help him. The Sichuan lodge was only a stone's throw from the Black Tile Factory.

"Who was the first to come in this morning?" This question was addressed to Hu and Zou together.

"I was," said Zou.

Sun raised his eyebrows. "You were the last to leave, and the first to arrive. Is there anyone who can vouch for your whereabouts during the night?"

For a moment, Zou stared at the chief inspector, his face frozen in fearful comprehension. Then he began to nod vigorously. "There is," he burst out, "there is someone. I share a room with six of my countrymen. Old Gao suffers terribly from rheumatism. He was up all night. If you ask him, he will tell you I never left my bed."

Sun watched Li Du make a note, then turned back to Zou. "We will speak to him. When you arrived, then, in the morning, did you notice anything out of the ordinary?"

"No."

"The entrance was locked?"

"Yes. I unlocked it."

"You didn't go into the office?"

"No, sir. What business could I have there? I inspected the tiles that had been drying yesterday in the sun to determine whether they could be put in the kilns. By the time I was finished, the laborers were starting to arrive. The only strange thing that happened all morning, before Wei found the bodies, was that foreigner coming to the factory."

"What foreigner?"

Zou looked at Hu. "He spoke to you."

Chief Inspector Sun turned a stern eye to the kiln master. "You should know that the activities of foreigners are of the first importance to any investigation. Who was this foreigner, and what was he doing here?"

"I apologize," said Hu. "The only reason I failed to mention it was that, though the man himself was unusual, there was nothing unusual about his visit. He only wanted to commission a repair. The roof of a place called the South Church, in the Inner City."

Li Du looked up from his notebook, surprised. "A Jesuit?"

Hu nodded. "He said the storm the other night had damaged the roof. He asked if we could come soon and fix it."

"Did he tell you his name?" asked Sun.

After a pause, Hu shook his head apologetically. "He might have, but it was not a Chinese name. I can't remember it now. I can tell you his hair was brown and gray, and his eyes were green, like a spring leaf."

A breeze moved through the maple tree, making the yellow-tinted shadows shudder on the dusty ground. Sun stood up. "We're going to speak to the factory owner," he said. "I have one more question for you. In your opinion, is Hong a violent man? Inclined to jealousy?"

Again, Hu took his time with the question. He turned and looked across the courtyard at the open door of the office. When he returned his gaze to Sun, his eyes appeared filled with sadness. "I don't believe he is a violent man. In his right mind, Hong would never commit such an act. But—"

"But if he had been drinking wine?" prompted Sun.

"I will not be the only one to tell you," said Hu. "When he drank, no one could guess what he would do."

Chapter 5

Hong Wenbin's manor was enclosed by a gray brick wall. The main entrance was a recessed door, painted red and flanked by two white stone lions. Next to each lion stood a soldier, which gave the impression of two tamed beasts sitting obediently beside their owners. In answer to Sun's query, the soldiers reported that Hong was conscious and awaiting the chief inspector's arrival. At Sun's knock, the red door opened, and he and Li Du were ushered in by a servant whose shock was evident in lines etched above his elevated eyebrows. He led them deep into the manor, along winding paths through courtyard gardens, until they reached a marble veranda crowded with painted pillars and birdcages inhabited by thrushes and small blue parrots.

The servant opened a door to a spacious parlor, where they found Hong slumped in a chair, his elbows on his knees, his face in his hands. Hearing them enter, he stood up, performed an unsteady bow, and regarded them with pink-clouded eyes set in a swollen face. "Please sit," he said in a hoarse voice. He waited for them to take their places in elegant chairs covered in red brocade before sinking back into his own chair.

While two maids with tear-streaked faces served tea, Li Du took in their surroundings. The room had been decorated by an astute collector with expensive taste. A fine copy of *Spring Morning in the Han Palace* dominated one wall. Li Du's eyes traveled over the horizontal scroll, which depicted the private inner courtyards of the palace on a misty spring morning. It was a luxurious fantasy of genteel pleasures, with elegant ladies, flowering trees, and strutting peacocks rendered in precise lines and sumptuous colors. Li Du surveyed the rest of the room, the shelves of which were full almost to the point of being cluttered. Whoever had chosen the ornaments possessed, in addition to a discerning eye, a tendency toward excess.

"Have you been told why I am here?" asked Chief Inspector Sun, when the maids had gone.

A small convulsion rippled the silk stretched over Hong's ample stomach and traveled upward. His chest heaved as if he was going to be sick. With an effort that made him shudder, he controlled himself, and exhaled a cloud of malodorous breath. "I have been told almost nothing," he wheezed. He recovered, and continued in a clearer voice. "Last night, I went out to enjoy the company of friends. This morning, I was pulled from my bed by soldiers and weeping servants, who tell me that my wife is lying dead in my factory. My *own wife*, and that is all they will say. I want to know what happened. I *demand* to know!"

"I understand you must be upset. Under different circumstances, I would be here to answer your questions," said Sun. The words were conciliatory, but there was a cold current in his tone that Li Du rarely heard within the relaxed atmosphere of the North Borough Office. Sun continued. "Given the nature of the crime that took place last night, not a hundred paces from where we now sit, I must insist that we begin with the questions *I* have for *you*. Where were you between the time the drums set the night watch, and the time the bells announced the morning?"

Sweat broke out on Hong's forehead. After a tense pause, he capitulated. "I went to Qi's restaurant."

"I know Qi's," said Sun. "It's in the neighborhood, just across from the sentry post at the Xiping Alley Gate."

Hong nodded, compressing the folds of flesh beneath his chin. "I am acquainted with the soldiers who are stationed there during the day. Sometimes, after the night watch comes to relieve them, they go to Qi's. I was there with them last night."

"When did you return home?"

Wariness crept into Hong's voice. "I don't know. It was late."

"Did anyone walk with you?"

Hong rubbed his eyes. His large fingers pressed deeply into the sockets. "I was alone," he said. "I think I was alone."

"Do you think you were alone, or do you know you were?"

Hong reached for his cup with a trembling hand. He grimaced as the hot liquid touched his lips, and returned the cup to the table in front of him. "I don't remember."

"There must have been a servant at the door to let you in."

The statement made Hong pause. "I don't come in through the main entrance at night. I use the door in the alley."

"And what—"

"No!" Hong lurched forward and slapped his palm on the table. "This has gone on too long. What are you insinuating? That I had something to do with the death of my wife? How did she die?"

"Your wife was murdered."

Hong retreated slowly back into his chair. His palm left a damp mark on the lacquered wood. "Murdered," he whispered. "But you cannot be saying that you suspect me? I didn't do it. I had no reason to kill her."

Sun regarded Hong in silence for a long moment. "When was the last time you spoke to your wife?" he asked finally.

Hong appeared at a loss. "The last time?"

"Did you see her yesterday?"

"Of course I saw her, but the day was just like any other day—" His voice caught. "I must write to my sons. Forgive me, but I cannot think. What was your question?"

"When did you last speak to your wife?"

Hong's eyes wandered the room. "We spoke after the midday meal."

"What did you discuss?"

"Nothing out of the ordinary. I told her about progress on the examination hall roof. She told me about a bowl she intended to buy. I can hear her voice. *Decorated with pine trees and cranes,* she said. *At thirty taels,* I told her, *it had better come from the Emperor's own private kilns."* Hong's eyes were misted with tears. "But I intended to let her have it. How can this have happened? It cannot be possible."

"Then you were on good terms with your wife?"

"Of course we were on good terms. What is this about? Do you think I am lying to you?"

Chief Inspector Sun cleared his throat. "Wine can steal a man's reason, and his memory. You say you left the restaurant last night alone, which means that no one can account for what you did on your way home, not even you. Consider my position, when I ask myself whether I can believe what you say."

Hong had picked up his cup again. Now he set it down so hard Li Du thought it would shatter. "So I don't remember. When does a man remember his walk home when he is drunk and thinking of bed? But I will tell you what I *would* remember. I would remember murdering my wife."

Li Du glanced sideways at Sun. He knew the chief inspector well enough to see that, though he maintained his professional demeanor, he was beginning to feel out of his depth. In the usual course of his work, Chief Inspector Sun rarely faced anything more dire than a disagreement between a merchant and a customer over the terms of a contract, or a complaint about a poorly maintained road. Violent crime was unusual within the walls of Beijing. Not only were civilians forbidden to carry weapons, but there were guards posted at every gate in the city, from the great gates of the outer wall to small latticework alley gates scattered throughout the boroughs. Deaths resulting from occasional robberies or tavern brawls were handled with practiced efficiency by Green Standard or Gendarmerie soldiers, and stories of lives lost to cruelties and abuses within families often remained, by tacit consent, within families.

Sun cleared his throat. "Your wife was not the only person killed last night," he said. "She was found with a man, a love letter on the floor between them. Did you know your wife had a lover?"

It took Hong a moment to comprehend Sun's words. When understanding dawned, he started up from his chair, his face suffused with rage. He remained that way, half standing, clutching the arms of the chair to support himself. Then, slowly, he sank back down. With obvious effort, he tried to compose his features. It was too late. He had revealed that while his wife's death had upset him, the suggestion that she had been unfaithful infuriated him.

"The man's name was Pan Yongfa," said Sun.

"Pan?" Hong looked as if some force was pushing him apart from the inside. His eyes bulged, and the tendons on either side of his neck looked as if they were going to burst from his skin. His swollen fingers clenched and unclenched at his knees. "That is impossible."

"I understand you knew him."

"Of course I knew him. And he was here, in my own home, not three days ago!" Hong stopped, closed his eyes, and pressed his hands to his temples. "It is too much. I don't believe any of it." He opened his eyes and stared fiercely at Sun. "You've made a mistake. You've gotten it wrong. My wife isn't dead. Has anyone looked for her? She likes to arrange flowers in the east courtyard. Has anyone looked there? Well? Has anyone looked for her?"

"I am sorry," said Sun. "But the identification was made with certainty by your manager, Hu Gongshan. Unless he is an untrustworthy man—"

Hong seemed to deflate. "No," he murmured. "No. Hu is reliable. But what you are implying about me is absurd. A man does not forget that he has done murder, no matter how much wine he drinks. I have no vision of this crime in my mind. Was there blood? You see there is no blood on my hands. Ask my servants. They will tell you there was none on my clothes."

"We will conduct a thorough investigation, of course," said Sun. "And I urge you to cooperate fully with the North Borough magistrate when he summons you. Rage is a natural response in a man confronted by his wife's betrayal. You should know that there are statutes to protect a husband who temporarily loses his reason."

Hong started to protest, then changed his mind. His pallor was pale and uneven, like paper disintegrating in water. "What should I do?" he asked.

"Make arrangements for your sons and your wife's family to mourn her. They live outside the city?"

"In Jiangxi," muttered Hong.

Sun nodded and stood up. "Write to them. Make offerings at the temples. When Magistrate Yin summons you, answer his questions wisely."

Li Du closed his notebook. "You mentioned that Pan was recently here," he said, prompting both men to turn to him with startled expressions. It was the first time he had spoken. He realized that his presence had been all but forgotten.

"Yes," said Hong. "The day before yesterday. I invited him to my literary party."

"Was your wife in attendance?" asked Sun.

"I would never have permitted my wife to appear at a gentlemen's gathering," said Hong. "She was a respectable woman." Hong's cheeks reddened, and he choked a little over his words. "At least, I believed her to be so."

Chapter 6

When the emperors of the Ming moved their seat of power to Beijing, the Chinese aristocracy built their mansions in the area surrounding the Forbidden City. Opulent architecture met natural splendor, creating an enclosed world of green hills, clear lakes, island pavilions, and gleaming glazed tiles. These neighborhoods, which came to be called the Inner City, were bordered to the north, east, and west by the capital's massive outer wall, and to the south by a sodden rectangle of muddy land, bereft of charming architecture, scenic vistas, or influential families, known as the Outer City.

With the fall of the Ming, and the invasion of the capital by Manchu horsemen, came a new dynasty. Among the early decrees issued by the first young emperor of the Qing was the transfer of the Inner City to the eight Manchu military units known as the Banners. The conquered Chinese were ousted from their mansions and relocated to the undeveloped boroughs to the south. Over the next sixty years, the humiliated elite worked hard to elevate their new surroundings to a higher standard, and to develop, despite the geographical deficiencies and distance from the palace, a bustling urban atmosphere within the Outer City.

It was into this mood of transformation that Li Du had been born, twenty years after the Qing came to power. His grandparents had been less resentful of the forced relocation than relieved that it had occurred as peacefully as it did. The violence of the dynastic transition had been centered in the empire's southern provinces, where the heirs of the Ming had fought to retain some vestige of power. In the north, the primary concern, as Li Du's grandparents had seen it, was not that they would lose their lives, but that they would never grow used to the bizarre Manchu military attire, manners, and hairstyles. They had bemoaned the inevitable effacement of centuries of Chinese culture.

Their fears had proved unfounded. The Qing emperors were enthusiastic scholars who did not see Chinese and Manchu culture as mutually exclusive. Eager to legitimize themselves in the eyes of Chinese intellectuals, they employed hundreds of Chinese scholars to tutor them. Li Du's own father had been hired as a calligraphy instructor to the children of princes, and had traveled daily to the wide avenues and clear air of the Inner City from the Outer City's narrow, pitted lanes.

It was along these narrow, pitted lanes that Li Du and Sun made their way back to the North Borough Office. They had remained at Hong's manor long enough for Sun to ascertain from the servants that Madam Hong had gone to bed as usual on the previous evening, after having sat for a while with Hong's grandmother in the east garden. The Hong family's presence in Beijing was a small one, and the grandmother, having outlived Hong's parents, was the only remaining member of the older generation. Hong's two grown sons owned and operated a tile factory in Jiangxi Province.

"The news is beginning to attract attention," said Li Du as they passed the Black Tile Factory. A small crowd had gathered outside. Gentlemen in cloud-colored silk robes, on their way to stroll the pavilions at Taoranting, stood speculating amongst themselves. Servants, tidy and self-important, watched and listened. They would justify their late returns from the markets by reporting all they had seen and heard to their mistresses. A few peasants with baskets on their backs lingered apprehensively, weighing their curiosity about what had happened against the chance that proximity to it would put them in danger's path.

"Hurry, before they can start asking questions," said Sun, quickening his pace. Despite the fact that the chief inspector was a head taller than he was, Li Du had no trouble keeping up. Preferring to feel the ground beneath his boots, he generally eschewed sedan chairs and horses. As his errands often took him from one side of the city to the other, he was used to walking fast.

When they had left the factory behind, Sun slowed to a more comfortable gait. "We'll stop at Qi's," he said. "It's just ahead. If Hong was there last night, he would have walked right past the factory gate on his way home."

"Do you think he is guilty?" Li Du asked.

"Yes," Sun answered, after a short deliberation. "What I don't know is whether he's telling the truth when he says he doesn't remember doing it. It is clear from the state he was in this morning that he was as drunk as a man could be." Sun screwed up his face in the effort of thinking. "And then there is the question of how the law will apply. Drunk or not, a man cannot be expected to retain his reason when he is confronted with his wife's infidelity." Appearing to give up, Sun relaxed and shook his head. "It's up to Magistrate Yin to decide what to do."

Sun's superior, Magistrate Yin, was one of the city magistrates responsible for administering the five boroughs of the Outer City. Like all important government buildings, their offices were located in the Inner City. This meant that they relied heavily on their chief inspectors, stationed at offices within the boroughs, to monitor daily activity and make regular reports. Once Sun had completed the initial steps of the investigation, responsibility would shift from the North Borough Office to Magistrate Yin's extensive and well-trained staff.

The entrance to Qi's courtyard establishment was concealed by a tangle of unpruned vines. Li Du held aside the straggly vegetation and let Sun pass before him. In the shadows of the empty courtyard, seating was arranged around a central ash tree. A canopy of branches sheltered low tables and stools. An odor of tobacco and excrement hovered between the earthen floor and the dry, curled autumn leaves above. Qi, an elderly man with sleepy eyes and hands wet with oil, emerged from the kitchen. At the sight of

Sun's official attire, he dropped into a low bow, and apologized that he was not yet prepared to serve lunch.

"We haven't come for a meal," said Sun. "I would like you to tell me whether Hong Wenbin, the owner of the Black Tile Factory, was a customer of yours last night."

"Hong? Yes, yes, he was here."

"We understand that he consumed too much of your wine."

Qi nodded guardedly. "My wine? Well, yes. He did insist on more cups than most men could drink in one night, but how could I refuse? He is a loyal customer. And his house is so near. I thought, what is the harm?"

"How late did he stay?"

"Very late. The soldiers had gone to sleep. It was the middle of the night."

"And he left alone? There was no one with him?"

"Yes, he was alone. He was happy in his own company, sir, if you take my meaning. He was singing and reciting poems. I was worried the night watch would take him in for making so much noise. I don't drink wine myself, sir. I don't like its effect." His eyes flickered anxiously over Sun's expression, endeavoring to read it. "I hope nothing has happened."

"Two people were murdered last night at the Black Tile Factory."

"Murdered?" Qi looked shocked. "In the North Borough? Was it a robbery? Should I warn my customers not to walk alone?"

Sun spoke reassuringly. "It has all the appearances of an isolated incident. Did you notice anything unusual in Hong's behavior last night?"

"Unusual, sir?" Qi chewed his lower lip. "No, nothing unusual. He was playing cards."

"And did he at any point behave aggressively, or express violent intentions?"

"Well, sir, he *could* be like that, sometimes. He did not like to lose at games. But last night there were no incidents at all."

"What were the subjects of conversation, before the singing and recitations began?"

"They didn't talk very much while they were playing. But when they did talk, I suppose it was about the examinations. That's all anyone is talking about, isn't it? It's the same every examination year. Yes, I remember now. Hong was talking about the work the factory was doing to repair the examination yard."

"Did Hong, at any time last night, mention his wife?"

Qi's wrinkled eyelids lifted, and he stared up at the chief inspector, unable to conceal his curiosity. He swallowed. "Madam Hong? No, sir."

Sun glanced toward the kitchen and sniffed. He closed his eyes for a moment, and an involuntary expression of appreciation passed across his face. "Black chicken soup today?" he asked.

"Yes, sir. It is almost ready. Would you like to wait? Or I could have a portion brought to the North Borough Office if you wish."

"I don't have the time," said Sun, with obvious regret. His appreciation of well-seasoned broths was known to all his staff. Li Du, glancing around the courtyard scattered with chewed bones, did not share Sun's enthusiasm.

They left the restaurant and returned to the North Borough Office, where they observed a sedan chair decorated with beads and tassels waiting outside the gate. On entering the courtyard, they were informed by Mi that the scholar Bai Chengde was awaiting Chief Inspector Sun in the reception room.

Sun scowled. "I forgot that we had scheduled a meeting with him today. What is the complaint of the hour? Puddles in the roads? Noise from overcrowded inns? Graffiti?"

"Concerns about pollution in the air around Taoranting," said Mi. "Shall I attempt to put him off?"

"No. He'll just add our office to his list of grievances," said Sun. "Take me to him."

Bai must have sensed their return, for he appeared at the door of the reception room and approached over the cobbled courtyard, leaning on a walking stick. He wore a dark blue robe trimmed with pale fur that most would consider too hot for a warm autumn day. "Chief Inspector Sun," he said in a reedy voice, "your clerks have informed me of the tragedy at the Black Tile Factory. The woman's husband, I understand. What a painful thing to happen in our own neighborhood, and among educated individuals! It is a shock. Truly, it is a shock. I hope, though, that you do not intend to cancel our meeting?"

"Of course not," said Sun stiffly. He was looking hungrily at the remains of bean cakes on the small plates waiting to be washed beside a bucket of water.

Bai's attention, meanwhile, had shifted to Li Du. Suddenly his eyes brightened in recognition. "But you are none other than Li Du! Of course I knew you had come back to the capital, but I had no idea you were in my own neighborhood! How long has it been since you returned?"

"Two years."

"So long! How is it I have not seen you at the literary clubs?"

"I have not been to them."

"Not been to them! But you were always the wit of the group. Charming everyone with your memorized poems and innovative interpretations. And now you have come to advise the chief inspector, and I thought I was the important scholar of the North Borough. I must defend my territory," he concluded with a dry chuckle.

"Not at all," said Li Du. "I am employed here as a secretary."

"A secretary?" Bai lifted a hand to his heart in exaggerated surprise. "But how can that be so? Am I misremembering? Your examination score placed you among the top twenty of your year. A most impressive set of essays. Of course, you've walked an unlikely path since then, eh? Exiled, then pardoned. Years in the southwest territories among the uncivilized of the empire. You must tell me about it, one of these days. I will invite you to see my gardens."

Sun looked at Li Du as if he expected him to reply. But Li Du bowed his head deferentially. Bai sighed and turned his attention back to Sun.

"I was at a party at Hong's house, you know, only the other day. A tiresome affair. It was supposed to be a discussion of that old novel, *The Bitter Plum*. Between you and me, it's just the kind of text chosen by a man who cannot judge quality. But Hong was determined to be a literary man. Determined. And now we see that you can't teach a merchant to be an intellectual, not really."

Something stirred in Li Du's mind, a memory of a day a long time ago, in the library, with raindrops plinking on the roof, and an open book with faded pages, illuminated by gray light through the window. *The Bitter Plum*, a story of romance and adventure.

"I understand Pan was at the party also," said Sun.

"Yes, yes, he was. I didn't know him well, but I must admit that I am not entirely surprised to hear he fell into immoral behavior. There was something in his affect, you know, a certain unseemly arrogance. But what young man isn't arrogant when the world is before him? It is a sad story. But yes, if you are ready, I am ready. I have carved time from my own schedule to come. The examinations are in only ten days, and the questions this year, I can assure you, are of the highest quality. We'll challenge the minds of the rising generation of officials as they have never been challenged before. Only the greatest will advance to lend their intelligence to the government of the empire."

He started back to the reception room. Sun, looking harassed, addressed Mi in a whisper. "Have a horse ready for me to go to the offices of the magistrate as soon as this is over."

Li Du thought of the stack of papers and books on his desk. "Am I to accompany you?"

"No. Use the day to finish composing this month's lecture to the borough. But tomorrow morning, I want you to go to the South Church. You know how to speak to the foreigners. Find the man who visited the factory this morning and ask him to account for his presence. A thorough investigation never ignores a foreigner, especially one who roams so far from where he belongs."

Chapter 7

*U*pon his return from exile, Li Du had refused offers of accommodation from his relatives. Politely, and to their evident relief, he had declared an intention to live alone. Solitary travel, he said, had inclined him toward a meditative existence. He had given the same explanation to the clerics responsible for the maintenance of Water Moon Temple, and they had agreed to rent him a room. The situation proved satisfactory for all involved. The clerics had a quiet tenant and a reliable supplement to the meager income they received from incense sales and charitable gifts. Li Du had regular meals, a sufficient supply of coal when winter froze the city, and privacy.

But privacy was never guaranteed in the imperial capital, and this evening, Li Du entered the first courtyard to find one of the clerics sitting on the veranda outside Li Du's door. Recognizing the always voluble Chan, Li Du altered his course and made his way past the incense cauldron into the Hall of Buddhas Past, Present, and Future. The setting sun threw heavy light across the floor, mocking the tiny candle flames with its might. Li Du stepped quietly, in deference to the silent visitors who had come to pray and make offerings, and exited on the other side into the temple's second courtyard.

Behind one of the small side halls were three drooping clotheslines. Li Du's pale robes were easy to identify amid the red and yellow that belonged to the clerics. The cotton, after a day of sun and city dust, was stiff to the touch. Li Du gathered his clothes and held them bundled in his arms. He remained there, comforted by the cool shadows and drifting aromas of clean cloth and incense.

Ever since he had seen them, the two corpses in the Black Tile Factory had exerted gruesome authority over his thoughts. Li Du's assignments for the day, while numerous, had required little concentration, leaving his mind free to wander. He saw again and again the open, staring eyes of Madam Hong, the outstretched limbs and crumpled waves of orange silk evocative of movement, yet motionless. And he saw again Pan's neck, torn open with a single, unhesitating purpose.

Chief Inspector Sun had not returned to the North Borough Office from the Inner City, and in the warm, slow hours of the afternoon, Li Du had found himself thinking about what the chief inspector had said to Hong. *There are statutes to protect a husband.* Li Du knew of the statute to which Sun referred, though crimes of that nature were rare among the wealthy. In his two years at the North Borough Office, Li Du had never needed to consult the violent crimes section of the penal code. Today, he had done so for the first time.

The provision appeared in Article 285. *When a wife or concubine commits adultery, and her husband, or a close relative of her husband, catches her at the place and in the act of adultery, and immediately kills them both, there will be no punishment.*

Sun was right. If Hong had stumbled into his factory that evening, found his wife there entwined in a lover's embrace, and killed them both in a frenzy of rage, it was possible that the law would excuse him. But was that what had happened? Had it truly been love—or desire—that had brought the victims together under cover of night? Had another purpose drawn them to the dark factory? And, if so, did someone other than Hong have a motive to kill them? Li Du had closed the heavy volume of statutes and returned it to its place. The task of answering these questions did not belong to him, and the corners of his mind reserved for pursuing secret truths had already been claimed by questions that did.

Taking care not to allow a clean sash or sleeve to drag in the dirt, Li Du made his way back to the temple's main courtyard, and the final, harsh streaks of golden sun. Chan had not moved and, resigned to conversation, Li Du greeted him.

"Put those clean robes away before they are stained," said Chan, gesturing with a thin, blackened hand at the white cotton. He was sitting amid a collection of plates piled high with powder. Beside him was a basket bristling with thin sticks. In front of him, he had positioned a block coated in thick black paste.

Li Du entered his room, deposited the clean laundry onto his bed, and started to close the door. Chan's voice stopped him. "It will be dark soon. Are you going to sit inside shuffling papers in the gloom until dinner? I know you are. You clerks and your papers. Come back and see what I found in the market today."

With a rueful glance at the space that was neat, and quiet, and his own, Li Du stepped outside. "I see you are making incense," he said. He knelt. One plate was heaped with sawdust, another with sandalwood powder. He pointed to a third. "Agarwood," he said. "That is a rare ingredient."

"Not so rare as this one," said Chan, indicating another powder. "Can you identify it?"

Intrigued, Li Du examined it. The powder was white, tinted with opal iridescence. He leaned closer, inhaled, and gave an involuntary shudder. A bitter odor filled his nostrils and burned all the way down his throat to his chest. He drew back and reflexively covered his nose with one hand. Temporarily overcome, he shook his head, blinking tears from his eyes.

"They call it dragonbrain camphor," said Chan. "Or 'icicle flakes'—touch your fingers to it."

Li Du took a pinch of the powder. It coated his fingertips with the same sensation, simultaneously hot and freezing, that it had inflicted on his throat, only more acute.

"You'll want to wash your hands," said Chan. "And be careful not to touch your eyes, or you'll burn them. It comes from the southern islands. We hardly ever find it at the markets these days, and when it appears, all the temples rush to buy it before it is all sold out. It's expensive, but we'll make a good profit from these incense sticks. The examination candidates want to burn whatever will please the gods the most, and what god would not be pleased with such a rare fragrance? With the vendor rent for the temple market in our courtyard next month, we'll have enough money for a new image of Guanyin by the end of the year."

Chan pattered on about his various schemes to raise more money for the temple. Li Du half listened, watching the thin fingers deftly roll the sticks one by one through the dark paste and dip them once more into powder. Darkness fell and Chan lit a lantern. Illumination within the temple walls was placed without design, and was dictated each night by the activities of the monks. Light puddled beneath swaying lanterns, shone through latticework panes, and glowed from the tips of incense sticks above an unseen cauldron. Where there was no light, doors and rooms disappeared into black emptiness.

Li Du helped Chan put away his supplies and prepare for dinner. His mind was wandering through pages, as it always did at the end of the day, through ministry records and statutes, and, added to them now, the words scrawled across a bloodied slip of paper. *The moon shines on my beloved in the old pavilion, green with moss.*

Chapter 8

Li Du rose early the next morning and arrived at the gate of the South Church well before the bells tolled the hour of the snake. Lacking instruction to the contrary, the builders who had been tasked with erecting a temple to an unfamiliar god had modeled the stronghold of the Jesuits after the temples they knew. A high wall enclosed a wide courtyard, on either side of which were two long, single-story buildings in the Chinese style. Only the church itself had been designed according to the priests' specifications. Instead of a roof sloping low over a polished veranda, a flat edifice of stone towered skyward. To Li Du, it had always seemed stretched out of proportion, perpetually strained in its vertical quest.

This morning, he found the church altered. The smooth vertical lines were broken. A corner of the main body of the roof had fallen in, destroying the symmetry of the façade, and leaving a jagged indentation like a wound. In the courtyard beneath it, shattered stone and tile had been consolidated into a heap. A man in a black robe was trying to sweep away grit and debris into the pile, but a gusting wind carried dry leaves and glittering dust away from his broom and pulled his long white beard into tangles.

Li Du crossed the courtyard, pausing for a moment at its center to look at the three stone stelae arranged there. Two he remembered from his last visit, but that had been almost a year ago. The third was new since then, and far more splendid than its companions. It stood on the back of a stone turtle. Attached to the top was a miniature roof of glazed yellow tiles.

"Li Du! Is that my old friend Li Du?"

The words, spoken in Latin, came from a figure who stood in the doorway of the church, waving a cane with teetering enthusiasm. Fearing the man would tumble down the stairs, Li Du hurried forward. He had known Father Calmette for more than twenty years, ever since the French Jesuit had first arrived in Beijing. Unlike most of the others who had come, Father Calmette had never once returned to his native country. Now an old man with round pink cheeks framed by curling white hair and a snowy beard, he spoke the language of his hosts with proud fluency, and seemed to have every intention of ending his days in China.

"It *is* Li Du," said Father Calmette, switching to Chinese. His weak voice, infused with an inherent cheerfulness, turned chiding. "But how I recognized you, I cannot say, since we never see you anymore! It's been two years since you returned from your exile in the lonely mountains, and you haven't visited above three times. How I miss those days when I would find you drinking tea in the antiques market, professing opinions on poems and paintings."

"I think often of those pleasant hours," said Li Du. "But my work at the North Borough Office keeps me very busy. Are you well? What tasks has the palace set you this month?"

"Too many!" said Father Calmette happily. "We are treated just like your own palace scholars. Up at all hours of the night to chart stars at the whims of princes. No sooner is one clock made than a more elaborate one is requested. One of the Emperor's own consorts wishes to learn to play the organ, but a decision cannot be made as to the propriety of such an endeavor. Meanwhile the Emperor would like a new map of the city, and the thirteenth prince has commissioned the fashioning of a scepter that Father Gaillard fears would be blasphemous to craft. But all this in service of our mission. You saw the newest addition to our courtyard?"

Li Du nodded. "An Emperor's affirmation is the greatest honor a temple can receive."

Father Calmette nodded enthusiastically. "I understand better why the yellow tiles are only allowed to be used for the rooftops of the palace. To see them here in our own courtyard is like seeing the Emperor himself come to visit every day. He wrote the inscription, you know. *He had no beginning, and will have no end. He has produced all things from the beginning, and it is He that governs them and is their true Lord.* You can read it there on the stone. How can the Dominicans say we have failed to communicate the message of the church to this city, when the Emperor himself writes poetry in honor of the Lord?"

Beijing has many gods, thought Li Du. But he had never challenged Father Calmette's optimism, and he didn't now. Together, they entered the church. Limited to the resources and craftsmen of a city that was not their own, the Jesuits had been unable to reproduce the arches and columns that gave depth to their houses of worship. To compensate, they had turned to illusion. Every surface of the church's interior was painted. False columns supported false walls. False sunlight pooled on floors of false rooms. Only the cascade of shattered tile and broken stone compromised the deception.

Father Calmette heaved a sigh. "Observe what the storm has done to our church. And we only completed construction last year. But what are broken tiles compared to the very grave matter that brings you here? Yes, yes, I have guessed why you have come."

A man was just emerging from a door near the altar. He came forward, stepping gingerly over shards of stained glass and broken tile. "Father Aveneau," said Father Calmette. "We must be very grateful, for out of all the officials and soldiers and secretaries in the city, they have sent us Li Du, one of the first scholars I ever met in the capital. He was a librarian in the palace library, a magnificent library, now sadly forbidden to outsiders. Such a collection of books and community of scholars I have not seen since I was last in Rome." Sighing at the memory, Father Calmette touched the other man's shoulder and addressed Li Du. "This is Father Aveneau, whom you have not met, and who was, through unfortunate circumstances, brought into proximity with a terrible act of violence yesterday morning."

Father Aveneau was younger than Father Calmette, hollow-cheeked, with large, deep-set eyes that were a shade of cloudy gray-green, like flawed jade. His brown beard was streaked with strands of white. Seeing that he was preparing to bend his knees to the floor in a formal bow, Li Du spoke quickly. "It is not necessary. I am only the secretary at the North Borough Office. I have been sent to take a statement from you about your presence at the Black Tile Factory yesterday. It is only a formality."

Father Aveneau straightened. "When I told Father Calmette what had happened, he said that we should expect someone. I am prepared to answer any questions you have, but I doubt I will be able to tell you any more than you have undoubtedly learned from the manager, and from the poor laborer who made the discovery." He spoke in careful Chinese, inserting small pauses between his words.

Li Du pulled out his notebook. Shafts of blue and green light from the glass windows played across its cover. "I will begin by writing down your full name, in your own language and in mine."

"Of course. My name is Louis Aveneau. I am recently gone—" He halted, and corrected himself. "I am recently arrived from France—"

Father Calmette interrupted. "He and I hail from the same part of that country, the fair city of Lyon, where silk is made using our own European methods."

Li Du wrote the name in neat Latin letters. Watching him, Father Aveneau commented, "You are educated in our language."

"Father Calmette was one of my teachers," Li Du said, bringing a smile to the older priest's face. "If I may ask you to explain to me in your own words, what brought you to the Black Tile Factory yesterday morning?"

"As you can see, our roof sustained damage during the recent storm. I went to the factory to commission new tiles."

"Can you describe what happened from when you arrived there until you departed?"

Father Aveneau drew in a deep breath. "I was conveyed to the factory by a sedan chair. When I entered, I spoke to the manager. Our conversation was hampered by my limited understanding of your language, and by his accent, which I believe was less refined than those to which I am accustomed. I had only just begun to explain my purpose when I perceived that the manager was no longer attending to my words. I searched for what had arrested his attention. He was staring at a building on the other side of the courtyard. Its door had been flung open, and a man—one of the laborers—seemed to have been propelled from within. He was on his knees in the dirt, obviously very distressed."

"What happened then?"

"The manager—Hu—apologized, and hurried to see what was wrong. I followed."

"Did you go into the room?"

"I did. I will not soon forget what I saw within."

"Did you recognize either of the two victims?"

"I could not see the woman's face, but as I am not acquainted with any women in this city, I am sure I would not have known her."

"And the man?"

"I did not recognize him, but his face did look familiar. Perhaps I had encountered him. It is difficult to know. I might have recognized him if I had seen him living, but as it was, no, I cannot say. Did he reside near our church?"

Li Du looked up from his notebook. Father Aveneau was watching him. "He lived in the Outer City," Li Du said. "But he was employed by the Ministry of Rites. Perhaps you saw him there."

"Ah, yes. That is possible."

"While you were in the room, did you shift any item out of place? Did you remove any object?"

"Certainly not. I left as soon as I understood what had occurred. The man who discovered the bodies—I do not know his name— was very upset. I instructed him to find assistance, thinking the chore would facilitate his recovery."

"And then?"

"Then I departed. I did not think there was any reason to stay. Under the circumstances, it was no longer appropriate to discuss the repair of our roof, however anxious we are to protect the frescos now exposed to wind and rain."

Li Du considered this. "I understand your sense of urgency," he said slowly. "But I am surprised you went directly to the factory, rather than submitting a maintenance request through one of the ministries, or through the Gendarmerie."

"Ah," said Father Calmette, breaking in. "I can explain that. We have a young man employed here as one of our clerks. The day after the storm, we were lamenting the damage to the roof. I must say, Li Du, that while my affection for this city will never abate, I have learned in my years here that building construction is not always effected in the most efficient manner. This is understandable. There is always so much of it happening. We were indulging, I confess, in complaints unworthy of guests who have received such lavish hospitality in a foreign place. The young clerk I mentioned—his name is Hu Erchen—overheard us, and informed us that his father is the manager at the Black Tile Factory. It was at his suggestion that we sent Father Aveneau to commission the tiles, hoping to speed the repair."

"Hu's son works for you here?"

"He does. We call him by his given name, Erchen. Would you like to speak to him?"

Li Du considered the question briefly, then nodded. "I believe the chief inspector would want me to talk to anyone with a connection to the factory," he said.

"Certainly, certainly," said Father Calmette. "But I will warn you. The poor boy is one of your exam candidates this year. He is usually more articulate than you will find him today."

The three of them left the church and entered one of the side buildings. Li Du was relieved to be ushered into a room cheerfully cluttered with books, globes, brushes, and candles burned down to solid pools of wax in bronze candlesticks. A profusion of papers were stacked like cliff faces against the walls.

The room appeared to be empty. Closer scrutiny revealed a still figure slumped over one of the desks. Father Calmette shook his head, wearing a concerned expression, and advanced quietly. Li Du saw that it was a young man in blue robes, with a hat that had fallen from his head and rested on the desk. His cheek was pressed to the paper in front of him, and he was asleep.

At Father Calmette's touch on his shoulder, the head shot up, revealing a cheek smeared with ink. The young face was gaunt and drained from exhaustion. Words bubbled from him. "When I see the green vase at the end of the hallway, I read the inscription on the base, and it contains the fourth chapter of the Doctrine of the Mean, which says—" He began to rifle the papers on his desk in desperation. "Which says," he whispered. "Which says—" He lifted wild eyes to meet Li Du's. "Is it today?"

"No," Li Du said gently. "There are still nine days until the examinations."

The young man moaned and dropped his head into his hands. Then, suddenly realizing that Li Du was his elder, and probably his superior, he scrambled to his feet. "Sir," he said. "My apologies." He bowed to Father Calmette and Father Aveneau, clearly confused.

"There is no apology necessary," Li Du said. "I took the exams myself, once upon a time."

The young man's expression was easy to read. At that point, he wanted nothing more than to be in Li Du's position, in the position of anyone who had passed the exams, no matter what their current circumstances.

"This is Li Du," said Father Calmette. "He came from the North Borough Office to speak to Father Aveneau."

Hu Erchen looked up with worried eyes. "About the murders?"

Li Du nodded. "Yes. You are the son of Hu, the manager at the Black Tile Factory?"

"Yes."

"I assume your father has told you what happened."

Erchen nodded. "He says they think it was Hong who killed them, the owner of the factory."

"And does your father believe it?"

"I don't know. I—the story is so awful. Of what happened. I keep thinking it was one of my dreams, or something a fortune-teller told me. My mind is so full of texts. But it's true? Madam Hong and Pan are dead?"

Li Du nodded. "Did you know them?"

Erchen shook his head, then nodded, then shook it again. "I've seen Madam Hong. And Pan—I've met him. But I didn't *know* them."

Li Du hesitated, unwilling to scare the young man unnecessarily. "Since you have a connection to the factory, I must ask, only as a formality, where you were the night before last."

"I—" Erchen blinked, and Li Du watched his face turn even paler. "I was at home, studying. I am always at home studying if I am not here. But I—I can't really remember. All the nights have begun to seem like the same night, one long night, until the examinations. I'm sorry. I can't think very well."

"I have not forgotten what it is like to be in your position," said Li Du. "Be at ease. Your answers were clear enough."

"Perhaps," said Father Calmette kindly, "you have stayed here long enough for today. You have attended to your duties very well. If Li Du is satisfied with your answers, I suspect you would like to devote the afternoon to your own studies?"

"Yes," breathed Erchen. "Yes, yes, I would. Thank you. Thank you." He bowed and made his way out of the room, his thin shoulders hunched and his hat askew, the full satchel misshapen by sharp corners of books.

When he was gone, Father Calmette began to organize the papers scattered across his desk. "I am concerned about that young man," he said. "I have seen many examination candidates over the years, but none have—what is your saying? None have *ground through the ink stone* with as much ferocity as that one." His rheumy blue eyes indicated the door through which Erchen had passed. "Don't you think so, Father Aveneau?"

Father Aveneau, who did not appear to have been listening, asked Father Calmette to repeat what he had said.

"I was saying that we are concerned about Erchen."

"Erchen? Oh, yes."

"When he is not working," went on Father Calmette, "he speaks of dreams and omens."

"All the candidates are anxious," said Li Du mildly. "Six thousand have come to take the exams, and no more than two hundred and fifty can pass."

"So few?"

"Those who pass are guaranteed an official position, and there are only so many official positions to be given."

"How fortunate the three of us have reached a time in our lives when we can read what we want to read without fear that someone will make us recite what we have learned," said Father Calmette, resting a contented gaze at a shelf piled high with books. "But I have not asked you about your spectacles! Have they been of use to you?"

"Of great use," said Li Du. He opened his bag and drew out the small wooden box in which he kept them. A little over a year ago, he had been persuaded to assist the Jesuits with a Chinese translation of Aesop's Fables. At the conclusion of the project, Father Calmette had presented Li Du with the spectacles, having noticed Li Du's tendency to stand up at his desk and look down at the pages from a distance.

"They do not strain your eyes? Here. Read something for me now and allow me to observe."

Obediently, Li Du put on the spectacles. Then, casting about for something to read, he picked up one of the pages from the corner of the desk. "'Beijing is composed of two cities,'" he read. "'The first, in which stands the Emperor's palace, is called the city of the Manchu. The second is the city of the Chinese.'"

He stopped abruptly. "I apologize. I did not mean to read a personal letter."

Father Calmette chuckled. "A personal letter? What an idea! You must know that all our letters are read by the censors. Read on, and you will see."

Li Du heard a sharp intake of breath and glanced at Father Aveneau. If the priest had not been attentive before, he was now. His strange green eyes were fixed on the paper Li Du held. Li Du looked back at Father Calmette, who gestured for him to continue.

"'The two cities join one another,'" he read. "'And each is four leagues round.'" The phrase *four leagues* had been struck through with a thin line, and beside it was written, in Chinese, a simple command to "remove specific distances."

"We are never sure what we will be instructed to change," said Father Calmette. "Which is why we must send draft upon draft to your censors, and recopy draft after draft until one is deemed acceptable. Four leagues? What harm, I wonder, is there in conveying to our patrons and superiors the length and breadth of these remarkable walls?"

Li Du continued to scan the letter, in part because it was interesting to see the arrangement of Beijing explained by a foreigner, and in part because he wondered what was making Father Aveneau watch him so intensely.

All the great streets which are drawn by a line from one gate to another have a body of guards in them. These soldiers, who have the power to take all persons who make the least disturbance into custody, stand night and day with their swords drawn. The smaller streets, which come into the greater, have gates made in the form of a lattice through which all persons who pass along are seen. The lattice gates are shut at night, by the soldiers, and opened for none but those who can give a good account of themselves. No person is permitted to ramble about in the night.

"We must not forget that we are committed to teach at the Observatory today," said Father Aveneau.

"Ah! Of course!" Father Calmette tapped the side of his head lightly with one finger and gave a self-deprecating smile. "A lesson in armillary spheres. But do not think less of me, Li Du. I may not remember the hour, but I can still chart the heavens. You must promise to visit more often. Do not let another year go by. And in regard to your present task, I pray: 'In everything we do, O Lord, give us a desire to seek out the truth.'"

Chapter 9

L i Du bought a bowl of noodles from a street stall outside Xuanwu, one of three gates set in the wall that divided the Inner from the Outer City. He ate quickly but appreciatively, and continued south into the bustling streets of Liulichang, a neighborhood so popular that it regularly tempted Bannermen out of their luxurious Inner City homes, down to the Outer City in search of entertainment. Its central thoroughfare was a confusion of horses, mules, carts, sedan chairs, and the occasional camel. Outside shops and at alley intersections, there was a perpetual swelling and ebbing of crowds, gambling on games of cups and balls, consulting fortune-tellers, or purchasing potions from doctors eager to describe the promised effects of their tinctures.

Of the numerous bookstores that, in addition to antiques, characterized the commercial atmosphere, Wu's was the smallest. The door was covered by a single panel of white cloth, which was always clean, and had the word *book* painted at its center in blue. It was squeezed between an antique store, from which spilled piles of burnished relics, and a tea shop that displayed its stock, dried and pressed into disks the size of plates, in stately rows on shelves.

Li Du had to squeeze through a knot of customers in order to enter. They were all unmistakably exam candidates, pinched, drained-looking men who seemed to be following each other, each wanting to know what the others thought it was important to buy, and each too study-addled to remember what they had come in to purchase themselves. Through the milling hats and shoulders, Li

Du signaled a greeting to the bookseller, Wu Yingfen, who sat behind a desk piled high with neat stacks of papers and volumes.

"Li Du!" called Wu. "Are you here for the *Gazette?*"

"I need a book," Li Du said, but his inherently quiet voice apparently failed to reach Wu, who cupped a hand behind an ear and shook his head. Li Du pointed toward the shelves.

Wu's mouth opened in an *ah* of understanding. He smiled and raised an eyebrow, his expression promising gentle mischief. "Gentlemen!" he called out. He lifted three thin, identical volumes up in the air. "I have just received three copies of the thirty-second reigning year examination questions, complete with the winning answers! These are *the last*—"

There was a rush to the desk. Li Du braced himself against the force of movement that threatened to knock him over. Amid the cacophony of claims and arguments, he made his way to the now accessible shelves. He found what he was looking for between a collection of ghost stories—the third of five volumes—and an edition of a popular parody. He waited for the frenzy to die down, then took the book to the front of the store.

"Thank you," he said to Wu.

"They're losing their minds," said the bookstore owner. "If they aren't trying to memorize another five books in the days they have remaining, they're drinking too much and acting like fools at salacious operas. If I wasn't doing such good business, I'd close the store and go visit my brother in the country."

Li Du doubted it. Wu was as attached to his store as a bird to its nest. On the rare occasions that Li Du saw him out of it, the bookseller seemed highly conscious of his exposure to the unpredictable currents of the city. Within his store, he was at ease. Now he picked up the book Li Du had selected and raised his eyebrows. "I've never known you to take an interest in frivolous novels," he said.

"Is it really so frivolous? I heard that it was recently discussed at a literary gathering."

Wu directed a disbelieving look at the cover. "Not a high-minded gathering, I assume. A literary discussion of a book intended only for diversion? What could there be to discuss?" He shrugged and set the book down. "But there are radishes and cabbages—people have their preferences. If you find something of interest in this tangle of capers and crimes, please tell me. Perhaps I missed an allusion."

He placed his hand on a neat pile of slim volumes beside him. Their covers were yellow, and *Gazette* was printed in red on the front. "I assume you would also like one of these?" At Li Du's nod, Wu slid a copy across the desk. "The only exciting news this month is the return of Prince Yinzao."

"From the north? He has been gone a long time."

"Almost nine years," said Wu. "Out of favor, rumor has it, but perhaps back in it now? There are grand festivities and parades planned for his welcome."

"Are there?" Li Du did not follow closely the numerous celebrations connected to the Emperor's twenty-two princes, which multiplied the holidays on the city calendar so significantly that it sometimes felt as if there were more festival days than regular days.

"Between that and the examinations, the city will be quite busy," said Wu. Perceiving Li Du's lack of interest, Wu added, "And there is a discussion of the storm. You know that lightning struck the foreign church?"

"I have seen the damage. At least there was no fire."

Both men glanced at the shelves with a book lover's unease at the thought of flame. Li Du opened his satchel, removed several copper coins from their string, and gave them to Wu. "Is it correct?"

"It's too much for a favorite customer," said Wu, and handed one of them back. "Someone has been asking for you."

"Who?" Li Du was only mildly curious. Former acquaintances sometimes sought him out, eager to learn what had happened to him during his exile, and what exactly he had done to inspire the Emperor to end it. Some wanted to increase their social currency with gossip; others hoped he had some influence at court that could be useful to them, or some weakness that they might exploit. His answer was the same one he had given the clerks at the North Borough Office. *The Emperor is merciful.*

"I had never seen him before," said Wu. "I don't think he was Chinese or Manchu. Ah, I can see that piques your interest."

Li Du met Wu's inquisitive look without a change in his own expression. "Are you sure I was the one he wanted to find? What did he say?"

"He asked if I knew the librarian called Li Du. I told him the Li Du I know is a secretary at the North Borough Office, and that he could look you up in the register if he wanted." Wu indicated the copy he had on his desk of the book listing all public employees, their occupations, and their places of residence. "Someone you met during your travels, perhaps."

"Perhaps," Li Du said. "Did he say anything else?"

"He said he was personal friends with the author of this book." Wu tapped the cover of a yellowed tome.

Li Du looked at it. "The author of that book is unknown."

"That is exactly what I told him."

"It was also written three hundred years ago."

"I told him that, too. It's a good thing the fellow didn't seem to be visiting in the hope of passing the examinations. Do you know who it might be?"

Li Du rubbed the back of his neck and tried to look disinterested. "I can't think of anyone," he said finally. He thanked Wu and left the store. Under the hot sun, the muddy edges of puddles had become cracked and pale. Li Du had to move at a shuffle with pedestrians and riders packed between the balustrades of marble bridges. Sedan chairs, lacquered and decorated with swinging silk tassels, lumbered through the crowds, cotton robes clinging to the sweating shoulders of the sedan bearers.

A bright red spot amid the brown and gray clutter of leaves and mud caught his attention and made him stop. He stared at the tiny pool at the edge of the street, his thoughts suddenly saturated with the seeping color. His gaze shifted upward to where the decapitated body of a rat dangled at knee height from a length of twine strung beside the door of a dumpling stall. The proprietor, following Li Du's look, indicated a roughly painted sign above the little body. *A warning to all rodents who conspire to enter my shop.* He pointed invitingly at the dumplings sizzling in a pan. Li Du swallowed, shook his head, and hurried away. Feeling tired, he adjusted his hat and shifted his heavy satchel to a more comfortable place on his shoulders. It was the hour of the goat, and the day was far from over.

Chapter 10

As usual, Li Du was able to enter the North Borough Office quietly. The soldiers posted outside glanced at him with brief, apathetic recognition, and the outer door stood open wide enough for him to slip through without provoking its worn, creaking hinges. Within the outer wall, three buildings faced a barren courtyard. To the left stood the long, drafty hall occupied by the clerks and their desks. Directly ahead was a reception hall with a faded countenance and a somnolent droop to its tiered roof. Li Du bore right across the courtyard to the third building, which contained his little office, appended like a closet to that of the chief inspector.

There was no indication that Sun was present. A quick consultation with the dense agenda printed neatly in Li Du's own hand informed him that the chief inspector was scheduled to meet that afternoon with merchants from Shanxi about expanding their temple to the horse god. The addition would necessitate the demolition of an adjacent temple that, they argued, was so neglected that it had become more of an insult than an honor to the god for whom it had been built. The merchants wanted Sun to take their proposal to the Ministry of Rites. This meant they would be treating him to an afternoon of Shanxi delicacies and entertainment. Li Du returned the agenda to its shelf. It seemed the murders at the Black Tile Factory had not affected daily operations. He took a deep breath and went to his desk.

As he had done almost daily for the past two years, he deposited his satchel on a wobbly stool in the corner and perused the stack of papers that had made their way from Sun's office to his own. Today, he found a collection of invitations awaiting the chief inspector's reply, a request from a local temple for a poem that would lend official consequence to a commemorative plaque, and a letter from a retired scholar asking for any available information on the history of the North Borough's oldest trees, to be used in his forthcoming *Guide to the Ancient Sights of the Capital*.

By the time Li Du had finished, the last of the phoenix-printed ink cake was gone, his ink stone was covered in a drying coat of black, and his fingers were stiff. He had completed in two hours enough paperwork to account for two days, which meant he could devote what remained of the afternoon to the question that never stopped pulling at the edges of his mind. It was the question that had kept him in the capital as lonely days turned to lonely weeks and months.

He stood up, went to a cabinet, and opened one of its numerous black-lacquered drawers. From its deepest recess, he withdrew the thin sheaf of documents he had taken from the Ministry of Punishments a week earlier and had not yet made time to read. If he didn't return it to the ministry soon, he risked the discovery of its absence from a cobwebbed corner of the Hall of Records, or worse, the discovery of its presence in his office. He had just taken a seat and set the papers in front of him when there was a knock on his door. Before he could speak, or move, it opened.

"Are those the notes from the Black Tile Factory? May I look?" The question came from Yuan, a round-faced clerk with perpetually flushed cheeks and buoyant affect. Yuan had failed his first attempt at the examinations, but had upheld his reputation as the light-hearted joker of the office by confidently asserting that he had done it on purpose. The questions, he insisted, had not given him the opportunity to demonstrate the full range of his intellect, and he could only hope this year's prompts would meet his high standard. He liked to brag that he was not even studying, but Li Du had noted the dark circles beneath the young clerk's eyes, and the persistent flutter that had recently manifested in his right eyelid.

"They are not," Li Du replied, quickly placing a book on top of the pages in front of him. "I haven't started to write the report. The chief inspector has barely begun his investigation."

As Yuan approached the desk, Li Du saw that he was not alone. Mi was behind him. Li Du kept his expression blank, but couldn't help resting a hand protectively on the book he had placed over the ministry documents. "But will there be much of an investigation?" asked Yuan, with cheerful curiosity. "Everyone is saying Hong Wenbin is guilty. Didn't he confess when the chief inspector interviewed him?"

Li Du shook his head. "He confessed to being inebriated, not to committing murder. He insists he didn't kill them."

"That's probably because he hasn't yet realized that the law protects him," said Mi, in a condescending tone. "As soon as someone explains Article Two-Eighty-Five, and he understands that he is safe, I doubt it will take him long to admit to everything. He may even enjoy confessing."

"Enjoy it?" asked Yuan, raising his brows inquiringly.

Mi shrugged. "It would give him back some of the pride he lost when he found his wife with a lover."

Yuan considered this, then shook his head. "If Hong is clever, he won't confess too hastily. Think about the parties involved. His wife's family won't be able to make a case against him, not when there is such clear evidence of her disloyalty. But her lover's family—that's different. I hear he was a high-ranking ministry official. His family could say that the law should not protect a drunkard who murdered their son. If they do, Magistrate Yin will have to find a way to appease them." He turned to Li Du. "What was it like to be there in the room with the bodies? Is it true that they died in a lovers' embrace, and that she didn't have her robes on? Was she as beautiful as they say?"

Li Du had listened to the exchange between Mi and Yuan with growing anxiety. Unwilling to remove his hand from where it rested between the incriminating documents and the curious clerks, he had kept it where it was. He imagined he saw Mi's eyes flick down

to the corner of the page peeking out from the book that covered
it. Now, Yuan's question drew him unwillingly back to the blood-
spattered room at the Black Tile Factory. He saw the still body of
the woman on the floor, helpless to resist a city that would dismiss
her death as the deserved fate of an adulteress. "There was no embrace," he said, with quiet condemnation. "It is not even certain that
they were lovers."

"Whether it's a simple case or a complicated one," said Mi, "I
would not want to be chosen to write the report. I hope, for the
sake of our office, that Magistrate Yin takes the case away quickly."

Yuan nodded in fervent agreement. "A wise clerk stays far away
from murders," he said. "Think of Xi."

Li Du understood the reference. Xi, who had been employed
as a clerk at the North Borough Office before Li Du's return to the
capital, had attained almost legendary status among the clerks as
a cautionary tale, and was still a frequent topic of conversation.
Ambitious and envied, Xi had passed the examinations with a high
score and received a coveted assignment as an assistant to a provincial magistrate in Guangzhou. Wanting to prove himself, Xi
had volunteered to write the report of a case involving the murder
of an incense seller outside a temple. But Xi had made several small
clerical errors in his assembly of the evidence, which would likely
have gone unnoticed, had not the murderer been sentenced to
death.

The Emperor required every case resulting in a sentence of execution to be sent to him for review, whether the crime occurred
in an elite neighborhood of the capital, or in a province on the other
side of the empire. Xi's report had been duly sent to the capital,
where the Emperor had personally identified the mistakes, and
chastised Xi for laziness and incompetence. The incident had ended
Xi's career, and his former coworkers still cringed whenever they
remembered how, prior to his downfall, they had coveted his
position.

Sensing that Yuan was about to renew his questions, Li Du
spoke quickly. "If neither of you is busy," he said, indicating the un-

even piles on his desk, "I have several assignments I could easily relinquish. I'm sure Scholar Lao would appreciate additional information about these trees of historical interest, and—" He stopped, seeing that he had achieved the desired effect. Both clerks were retreating to the door with muttered references to the numerous assignments awaiting them at their own desks.

When they had gone, Li Du exhaled slowly, and removed a damp palm from where it had pressed down on the book he had used to conceal the ministry records. He spent the ensuing hours reading, only faintly aware of the rattle of the outer door as the clerks went home. When he finally looked up, he could hear the servants in the courtyard preparing to sweep the offices. The sky was lavender and the air through the window was cool. He looked at the pages. They contained nothing of use to him. The information was as broken as the strands of cobweb that clung to the edges of the paper. With a sigh, he cleaned his brushes, blinking to keep his eyelids from closing.

As he picked up his satchel, he hesitated, aware of the heavy exhaustion that had fallen over him. Twice he started out the door, and twice he stopped. Finally, he set down his satchel again and went into Sun's office. There, he opened the box of evidence retrieved from the Black Tile Factory and took out a small envelope made of oilcloth. He removed the paper it protected and smoothed it out on Sun's empty desk. It was the note that had been found near the body of Madam Hong.

After reading it again, he returned it to its place and went back to his office. He took from his bag the book he had purchased from Wu's store. Holding the cover to the last of the light from the window, he read the title embossed in gold. *The Bitter Plum.* He opened it and began to skim the elegant lines of text, his finger hovering just above the words. Time went by, and he turned the pages. He removed his spectacles and rubbed the backs of his ears, where the smooth metal bit into his skin. Finally, just as it had become almost too dark to see, he lowered his finger and touched a sentence. He tapped it several times. He had been right. *Well,* he thought, as he gathered his belongings, put on his hat, and left the office with a rattle and scrape of the old door, *that changes the situation.*

Twilight had fallen, and the stone walls of the city were turning black against the dimming sky. Li Du walked briskly through narrow lanes that echoed with the clatter of hooves. Riders emerged without warning from connecting alleys, their features indistinct in the gathering gloom. They passed without acknowledgment, hurrying to their destinations.

There was a reason for the urgency shared each evening by noble and commoner alike. With the coming of night, the city closed. The thirteen great doors of the outer wall were hauled shut by straining soldiers, sealing the capital from external threats. But danger from without was not the only concern. There were also walls to separate the Inner City from the Outer City and divide the boroughs. Hundreds of wooden doors, guarded by soldiers, barred the alleys. Citizens and residents who wished to spend the night in their own beds had until the drum towers announced the first watch of night to reach their neighborhoods. After that, movement was almost impossible. Anonymous movement was the prerogative only of gods and ghosts.

Li Du followed his usual path up through the center of the North Borough, which required him to cross only one wide, busy intersection. In a city that discouraged public gatherings, street intersections were among the few public spaces expansive enough to accommodate groups. Caishikou was one of the largest. It was the site of a regular vegetable market, but that was not its only purpose. In the early days of winter, when frost began to creep at the edges of ponds, Caishikou became the execution ground, where crowds roared with approbation as the executioners swung their heavy swords.

The space was bordered on one side by a canal. A group of mounted soldiers occupied the bridge. Li Du waited for them to cross, looking down at the water. There had been no executions since the previous winter, but small ripples, restless spirits, capped with lantern light, lapped sadly against white stone. When the riders were gone, he crossed into the wide-open space. A group of young men exited the courtyard of a nearby tavern. Their voices were loud, animated by social competition and liberated by wine.

"They won't ask that question."

"But the fortune-teller said—"

"The fortune-teller can't tell you what will be on the test. What a stupid thing to ask!"

"Shh. Which way is the inn?"

This was met with laughter, sharp and aggressive. "Look at this country man who has come to the city."

"I'll wager a coin he gets lost in the examination yard."

"Shh. Hurry, before the drums."

Li Du watched them cross the square and alight like birds around a street vendor on the other side of it. After his return to Beijing, Li Du had learned that, during his exile, a group of candidates had accused the examination officials of corruption. Sleepless, furious, impassioned, they had fashioned effigies of examiners, marched from the book market to Caishikou, and beheaded the dolls in mock executions. For this act of defiance they had themselves been put to death.

A sedan chair passed so close that Li Du could smell the musk and incense that perfumed its inhabitant. The bearers were breathing hard in their effort to deliver their charge in time to return home themselves. Reminded of the advancing hour, Li Du continued on across the intersection and into an area of dense, narrow alleys. The doors of the homes on either side of him were all shut.

He reached the final sentry post before Water Moon Temple, aware of the silent attention of the soldiers preparing to close the alley door. During the day, ministry and palace officials reigned, their robes proclaiming their status as the decision makers of the empire. But at night, the soldiers were in power. Their judgments decided the fate of nocturnal wanderers. That night, Li Du was in time to avoid an extended negotiation. He had only just passed between the guards and turned onto the temple alley when he heard the first beat of the drums.

As their final strike faded, Li Du discerned a different sound that made him stop and turn. The alley was divided by lanterns into pools of light and dark. He was certain he had heard a footstep, but he saw no one. He stood still, searching for movement. He could turn now and hurry to the door of the temple, but he was unwilling to put his back toward the presence that waited and watched from the shadows.

"Who is there?"

A figure detached itself from the dark recesses of an old, unused shrine to an obscure deity, and stepped forward into the light. Dark, voluminous clothing obscured his build, but his face was as Li Du remembered it.

"Your street is too quiet in the evening," said Hamza. "I've had only cats for company, and I've heard all their stories before."

Chapter 11

In the second courtyard of Water Moon Temple, outside the hall of Guanyin, stood a modest stage used for performances on holidays. Li Du and Hamza occupied one corner, a bottle of wine and a small lantern between them. It was an old lantern. Candlelight shone through the torn silk, casting ladder-like shadows across the bamboo mat that covered the stage. The courtyard was empty, as were the halls, but for the day's lingering incense.

Hamza was sitting comfortably with his back against a painted column, his legs stretched out in front of him. "And after Seratsering and I saw the lost Capuchin back to Lhasa, and set him safely on his journey home to his olive trees, we two traveled together, until she chose to apprentice herself to a Tungus shamaness. We plan to meet again in three years on Turtle Mountain, which, you understand, is not a real turtle, but merely the remains of one that turned to stone an eon ago. After I parted from her, I journeyed for a time with a caravan of Russian traders. Perhaps you have noticed my costume?"

Li Du assessed his friend critically. Hamza was attired in a brown, belted tunic that fell to the tops of high leather boots. A voluminous gray hat rested at a jaunty angle across his forehead. It was easy to believe he had journeyed the long miles from Nerchinsk to Beijing, protecting carts piled high with pelts, and was now preparing to return, having traded them for Chinese silks. "The Russians have their own lodge and church in the Inner City," said Li Du. "You would fit in very well there."

Hamza looked pleased. "I have never told you that my mother's family hails from the mountains between the Black and the Caspian seas. I explained this to the guards at your city gates, when they asked me."

Li Du accepted Hamza's statement with gently lifted eyebrows. Since he had met Hamza three years earlier, in a trading town at the border of the empire, Li Du had heard him assert at least twenty versions of his past. Hamza's appearance offered little indication of his ancestry, or of the number of years he had lived in the world. His name, he had admitted once to Li Du, was borrowed, and age seemed, for him, to be a collection of mannerisms that he could command so as to appear closer to twenty or to forty, as he wanted. His bright, dark eyes took in their surroundings with restless interest, and he wore a short beard, which he kept meticulously groomed. He was, by profession, a storyteller.

"Then you are introducing yourself as a trader from Russia?" asked Li Du.

"For the present," said Hamza.

"I was not even aware that you spoke Russian."

Hamza took a sip of wine. "A teacher might, perhaps, point out a fault or two in my accent, but I have always found that it is not so important to speak a language well when no one near you speaks it at all. In any case, you Chinese and Manchu don't listen very closely to tongues other than your own."

Unruffled by the criticism, though he himself had a good command of Manchu, Latin, French, and the Tibetan languages of the tea trade routes, Li Du nodded. "You make a reasonable point," he acknowledged. "In fact, the Jesuits had to help broker a treaty between—" He paused deliberately. "Between *your* country and ours. They were the only ones who spoke all the languages required to write it."

"Is there a treaty?" asked Hamza mildly. "That is very good to know. I have been counting on the assumption that we are not at war."

Li Du refilled their cups. "Let me be sure I understand. You chose to enter Beijing under the assumed identity of a Russian trader, knowing neither the language of that land, nor whether it is currently at war with this one?"

Hamza was unruffled. "A storyteller must have some skill at improvisation," he said. "I was simply taking advantage of an opportunity to practice. But aren't you pleased that I have come? Your letter nearly failed to reach me. The courier found me just as I was preparing to depart Ordos."

"I am pleased indeed, and grateful to you for making the journey. Did you—"

Hamza interrupted. "I did." He straightened his shoulders and affected a lofty expression. "But do not rush my tale. As I was saying, I received your letter as I was preparing to leave Ordos, and devoted myself at once to the task you set me. After making provisions for a desert journey, I set out west across the Shamo, those indifferent and sand-choked wastes that lurk just outside the reach of your Great Wall. On the first day, I met herders and cattle. On the second, I met traders and camels. By the third, I met only a few wild asses, who clung to the shade of a dry pinewood. And by the ninth day of my journey, I met only a single falcon with feathers of white and rose gold, the color of a pale sunset reflected in a mirror.

"At last I came to Etzina, the Black City, whose ruined ramparts contain but one door, through which they say the Mongol Khara Bator escaped his besieged domain in the hours before it fell. Following your instruction, I climbed the hill behind the silent city, passed the empty watchtower, and found the small temple beyond. It exhaled breath of juniper and smoke, which spoke of living inhabitants, though its exterior was as bleak and quiet as the desert."

In the flickering light of the lantern, Li Du was drawn back to nights around the fire, deep in the mountains, when Hamza had entertained the caravan with tales.

"I went inside," Hamza continued, "and passed beneath the quiet scrutiny of sculpted gods to a door behind the altar. There I encountered a monk with a face at once smiling and solemn. He was sitting just outside, in a comfortable chair, reading a book.

When I asked its title, he told me it was called *The Pearl and the Palm*. When I asked what story it told, he informed me that it was a dictionary. I hid my disappointment, for I was aware that I was in the company of those who, like you, have a reverence for ink and paper.

"Goodwill thus established, I presented to the monk the small token you had entrusted to me, and told him your name. He remembered you. Over a cup of tea, he told me of the day, nine years ago, when he and the other monks had watched you approach, with your mule and your cart, like a peddler to their door. You told them that you had, until recently, been a librarian, and that you knew of the secret cave in the ruins of Etzina, where paper would never rot and ink would never fade. You asked, humbly, that they allow you to entrust your books to them. You had been sentenced to exile and could not carry them with you. It was a small collection, the monk informed me, but a fine one. When I told him what book you had sent me to retrieve, he sighed, and confessed that he would mourn its loss, for he had enjoyed many hours contemplating it."

Hamza pulled from his satchel an object. For a moment, the scent of juniper hung in the air. He gave it to Li Du, who removed layers of coarse silk and oilcloth from the volume they protected. There was no title on its paper cover, which was golden brown and bound with white thread. Li Du took his spectacles from the purse at his belt and put them on. Ignoring Hamza's incredulous look, he opened the book carefully. "A Song edition of *The Commentary on the Book of Rites*," he said, almost in a whisper. "Printed in Lin'an. I was never a true collector, but this book, discarded by one who did not recognize it, is among the greatest treasures a collector could own. And it has not aged or altered in the nine years since I last saw it."

"Nothing in those caves can age," said Hamza. "I have seen the caverns, hidden within the stone, where books and scrolls of every size and shape and language rest in timeless sleep. Indeed, I suspect the monks who keep the books are themselves many hundreds of years old, preserved by the desiccated air.

"After passing a night in the temple, and promising to bring the monks any rare volumes I encounter on my adventures, I departed. I made the long journey to the gates of this city, which I entered this very morning. Once more following your instruction, I located the bookstore with the white curtain and blue sign, and asked the owner for your address. A true bookseller, he regarded me with a shrewdness that made me think he could perceive by some extra sense the value of the book I carried with me."

Hamza drew in a breath, and concluded. "Now I am here, and have brought you what you asked me to bring. In return, I expect you to tell me why you wanted it." He looked around, squinting in an effort to assess his surroundings outside the pool of lantern light. "And why are you living in a temple? I expected an imperial librarian to be ensconced within the palace walls."

"I am not an imperial librarian," said Li Du. "I am not, at present, a librarian at all. I am a secretary."

Hamza looked incredulous. "That's what the bookseller told me, but I didn't believe him. A secretary?"

Li Du nodded, and raised a hand to forestall further questions. "One story is enough for such a late hour. My account can wait." He gave a small smile. "It *is* good to see a friend. And since a room has been found for you here, I hope you will remain a guest in the city for at least some days."

For a moment Hamza looked as if he would argue. Then, after a short assessment of Li Du's expression, he appeared to change his mind. He yawned. "Certainly," he said. "For I have every intention of enjoying myself."

Chapter 12

Li Du entered Sun's office the next morning to find the chief inspector sitting at his desk, absorbed in the perusal of a document. As he read, his eyebrows suddenly drew together so forcefully that only the deep furrow between them prevented mutual attack. "This is too much!" he exclaimed. He looked up, saw Li Du, and beckoned for him to sit in a sturdy chair across the desk from him.

"Yesterday's reports," Sun declared. "Apparently an examination candidate staying in the East Borough drank tea of nightshade because he thought it might improve his memory."

Li Du raised his eyebrows. "I hope it didn't kill him."

"It would have, had the doctor arrived any later. As it is, he is recovering, and still plans to take the tests. What confounds me is that he might well pass them." Sun let out a huff of exasperation so strong that it lifted the page in front of him. "These scholars can all recite the classics, but what of *practical knowledge?* What of *sense?* I'll tell you—I didn't do so badly on the exams myself, but nothing I'd studied prepared me to collect taxes in the provinces. If my mind had been less full of poetry, I might have fared better. And if these candidates would close their books and get some sleep, they might be less likely to poison themselves."

The complaint was a common one, often expressed by examination candidates themselves who, after earning their hard-won degrees, received magistracies in the provinces and found their previous education left them woefully unprepared. Li Du, recalling the delirious days leading up to the examinations, was inclined to be sympathetic. "Most of the candidates will be more sensible once the tests are over," he said. "The atmosphere in the capital can be unsettling at examination time. Unfortunately, there are many who are willing to take advantage of heightened nerves to make a profit."

Sun conceded the point with a glower. "Charlatans on every corner," he said. "Trying to relieve fools of their money. I expect some fraudulent fortune-teller sold him that potion. At least he didn't wait until he was inside the examination yard before he drank it."

Li Du nodded. Such tragedies were not unprecedented. The examinations consisted of three sessions, each lasting three days and two nights. During those periods, no one was allowed in or out of the examination yard. There were no exceptions. If a student became ill while writing his essays, he had no recourse. Of the four thousand students who had taken the tests with Li Du, two had died at their desks.

Chief Inspector Sun slid the report he had been reading to the corner of his desk. "Regarding the murders at the Black Tile Factory," he said, "we are awaiting a report from Doctor Wan. No doubt he will have his conclusions to us before long. In the meantime"—he indicated a listing pile of documents—"there are the usual tasks to complete."

Li Du looked at the pile that seemed to replenish itself daily. The safe course of action would be to pick up the pile, carry it to his office, and pass another day as he passed most of them, quiet and unnoticed. But how much harm could it do to draw a mere moment's attention to himself? He hesitated. "Actually," he said, "I wanted to mention that I had an idea."

Sun looked startled. "Is this to do with the foreigners at the South Church? Did you discover something there?"

"No. I did speak to Father Aveneau, the man who visited the factory on the morning the bodies were discovered, but his account agreed with what the manager, Hu Gongshan, already told us. I saw for myself that the roof of the church was badly damaged."

"In that case, where did you come by an idea?"

"I was thinking about the note we found at the scene."

"The note," said Sun. "Ah yes, you mean the love letter."

"It *looked* like a love letter," said Li Du. "*The moon shines on my beloved in the old pavilion, green with moss.* Do those words sound familiar to you?"

Sun considered for a moment, then shrugged. "Moons, moss, pavilions? They are common words in literature."

"They are taken from a novel entitled *The Bitter Plum.*"

"That *does* sound familiar," said Sun, the furrow returning to his forehead.

"That is because it was mentioned to us the day before yesterday, outside this very room."

"*The Bitter Plum,*" said Sun, his expression clearing. "The book discussed at Hong's party."

Li Du handed Sun the volume he had purchased the previous day. "I have marked the page."

Sun opened the book. He read silently for a moment, then leaned back a little in his chair and scratched the side of his beard. "*The moon shines on my beloved,*" he said. "The very same words." He closed it and looked up. "But there is nothing strange about that. Pan Yongfa was at the party. Naturally, when he arranged to meet his lover, he would quote a book he had just read. It is a pretty sentiment."

"That is what I would have thought, too," said Li Du. "Were it not for the context."

"What do you mean, the context?"

Li Du indicated the book still open in front of Sun. "The line is not about lovers. It is taken from a scene in which a blackmailer is rejoicing because he has been paid sixty taels. He takes the ingots to a hidden pavilion to count them. The moon, shining into the pavilion, is reflected in the polished silver. The villain uses the words to address his spoils: *The moon shines on my beloved.*"

Sun stared at Li Du. "What exactly are you suggesting?"

"I am wondering if the allusion could have been intentional. Of all the lines to choose, *this* line, from *this* book. What if Pan Yongfa and Madam Hong were not lovers surprised by a jealous husband? What if something else brought them to that room? What if Hong simply walked home drunk that night, and had nothing at all to do with the crime?"

To Li Du's surprise, Sun let out a bark of laughter. "You know," he said, his shoulders shaking a little, "when I agreed to give you a position in my office, my sister advised me not to do it. *Why?* I asked her. *Because,* she told me, *my former husband has a tendency to make simple matters complicated.* I always thought she was merely being spiteful."

"It is not my intention to introduce unnecessary complications," said Li Du, roused to defensiveness by the unexpected mention of his former wife. "I only wanted to point out a detail that could alter our perception of the case."

A trace of mirth lingered in Sun's expression. "Secret messages? Blackmail?" He grew serious. "Your idea suggests premeditation, corruption, conspiracy, all crimes far outside the jurisdiction of this office."

"But shouldn't the magistrate be informed?"

"The magistrate is not interested in idle speculation. Let me tell you something you do not yet know. Early this morning, an item was delivered to this office by two soldiers, a knife with a short blade covered in dried blood. It was found concealed in a pile of rubbish beside the door Hong used to enter his home that night."

Li Du considered the new information. "Have you confronted Hong?"

"Hong has already been taken into custody. His story remains unchanged, but I expect we will have a confession soon." Observing Li Du, who sat quietly before him, his hat slightly askew, Sun seemed to repent his bluntness. "I was not idle yesterday," he said with a hint of contrition. "I have met with the commissioner of the Ministry of Rites and questioned him thoroughly about Pan Yongfa. He was, by all accounts, an upstanding official. He scored highly on the examinations and was given a temporary assignment in the capital. He had been here three years. His job, as we have already been given to understand, included management of construction contracts between the ministry and the Black Tile Factory. According to everyone with whom I spoke, he was diligent, reliable, and efficient, with a successful career ahead of him. There is no suggestion of anything unusual."

"And Madam Hong?"

"He must have met her in the course of his business with her husband. I suspect he conveyed to her the note asking to meet that evening when he came to the factory in the afternoon."

"Did you discover what his official reason was for going there?"

Sun nodded. "Ministry audit," he said. "He was there to review previous contracts. As I said, he must have sent her the note then. Unless she was the one who sent it to him—the handwriting is inconclusive."

"Where did he go between leaving the factory and returning to it?"

"He returned to the ministry, where he continued work as usual. He left, alone, well before the night watch was set. He would have had more than enough time before the alley gates closed to return to this neighborhood and wait in some concealed place near the factory for his assignation with Madam Hong. She, of course, lived so close that she would not have had to pass through any gates. She must have gone to bed, and slipped out through a side door of the manor once everyone else was asleep. Naturally, we are interviewing the soldiers at all the North Borough inspection points. So far, none have reported a single suspicious attempt to pass through a gate after dark. You see that I am being thorough. But it would require more than literary interpretation, now, to change the course of the investigation."

From outside the office walls came the sound of bells and chimes, some near, others distant, tumbling over one another in their enthusiasm to report the hour of the day.

Sun heaved himself from his chair. "I'm expected at Dragon King Temple. I'll be finished by the hour of the horse. We'll meet on Seven Hearts Street after lunch."

"Seven Hearts Street?"

"It's in the West Borough," said Sun. "It falls to us perform the unpleasant duty of interviewing the concubine of a murdered man."

Chapter 13

For his sojourn in the capital, Pan Yongfa had selected a small but luxurious residence. Its entrance was framed in stone, carved in relief to form patterns of tiny, interlocking mazes. A polished plaque affixed to the lintel proclaimed the inhabitant to be the holder of a high degree. Li Du, late to meet the chief inspector, hurried through the door into an outer courtyard, where he found two soldiers stationed amid a forest of potted plants.

"You're the secretary?" asked one.

Li Du said that he was, and the other soldier gestured to a circular gate that opened to a second courtyard. "The chief inspector is already here. Go through to the third courtyard. It's the building on the right."

Passing into the second courtyard, Li Du headed for the gate on the opposite side. He had almost reached it when he heard women's voices coming from an open latticework window in a building on his left.

"But I'm frightened to talk to the officials." The voice belonged to a young woman, who ended the declaration with a hiccuping sob.

Another woman answered, her voice calm and superior. "You'll have to tell them. If the master of the Black Tile Factory is a thief, the law won't forgive him."

"But the chief inspector looked so stern. And did you see the soldiers? They make me so nervous that I can't think. I'm sure I won't be able to talk."

Li Du had learned not to ignore opportunities to make use of his unassuming appearance. He hesitated only a moment before adjusting his hat so that it sat a little more crookedly on his head, climbing the stairs to the smooth veranda, and knocking on the door.

The woman who answered had an erect, authoritative bearing. She wore robes of pale blue silk. Her face was lightly powdered, and she wore a modest silver ornament in her hair, which was styled with elegant practicality. Li Du guessed her to be a senior maid.

"Sir," she said, and bowed.

"My apologies for interrupting you," he said. He turned and indicated the courtyard with a look of helplessness. "I am the chief inspector's assistant, and I am not sure where I should go."

She bowed again. "He is with our mistress."

From behind her, the maid who had been crying appeared. She was no more than a girl. Blue shadows under her eyes glistened with moisture. She was holding a slim porcelain vase in one hand and a dusting cloth in the other.

"Yes," said Li Du. "Can you direct me to them?"

The elder maid paused thoughtfully, assessing him. "Of course, sir," she said. "But I wonder, if you can spare a moment, whether you might listen to this girl? She is afraid to speak to your superior, but I think she might know something important."

"I would be most grateful to hear it," said Li Du. "She is brave to come forward. I know that I, myself, am often at a loss for words when soldiers are staring at me."

The girl gave a wan, tearful smile. "I wouldn't have hidden anything from the authorities, sir, but I think it will be easier to explain to you. I saw something strange on the morning our master left, the morning he didn't come back."

"What did you see?"

The girl looked to her companion for approval. "Speak clearly," said the senior maid. "Don't cry."

The young maid took a long, shuddering breath. "That morning, our master called to me from his office. He had torn his jacket. He asked me to take it away and bring him a new one. When I came back, I saw him putting silver ingots into a bag. It surprised me. He didn't usually carry more than a string or two of copper coins."

"How much silver was it?"

"I don't know the exact amount, as I couldn't see what he had already put in the bag. But I'm sure it was more than fifty taels."

"Fifty?" Li Du raised his brows at the hefty sum. "Can you describe the bag to me?"

She thought for a moment. "It was made of leather, and it was a light color. It cinched at the top with a blue string."

Li Du made a mental note of the description. "And did he tell you why he was taking the silver with him?"

"No. He only laughed at me because I was so surprised. Sir, when I heard that he was dead, I forgot all about it. But then, later—" She broke off and began to cry again.

The older maid turned to Li Du. "The circumstances of our master's death did not remain a secret from us for long. We know that he was killed by Hong Wenbin because he was drunk, and he found our master with his wife. And we know that he isn't going to be punished for it, because the law says a man can kill his wife and a man if he finds them together. I know it's true, because it happened just that way once in my own village." Her voice trembled with repressed emotion.

"If Hong is guilty," said Li Du, "the law might protect him, yes."

The maids exchanged glances. Then the younger one sniffed and spoke again. "I remembered the silver later," she said. "And I thought it was strange that it wasn't brought back to us. We received the bag he was carrying with him that day, but there was no smaller bag with the silver inside it. It was gone."

"We thought you should know," said the elder maid, "because if Hong Wenbin stole the silver, then the law wouldn't protect him, would it? He'd be punished for killing our master, wouldn't he?"

"This could prove a most important detail," said Li Du. "You were right to share it. I must assume your master was a good man, to have inspired such fealty in his household." Both maids looked at him, their devotion clear in their eyes. "I will do all I can to bring his killer to justice," he said. "Now, if you will be so kind as to direct me, I will speak to your mistress."

Li Du found Sun sitting opposite a woman. Sun, clearly uncomfortable and overlarge in the delicate chair that supported him, welcomed Li Du with exasperated relief. He indicated first the chair beside him, then, with an expression that reminded Li Du of a traveler warning his companion of a sheer cliff ahead, nodded in the direction of the woman. "This is Lady Ai."

The woman did not turn to look at Li Du, so it was not until he had taken a seat beside Sun that he was able to see her features. His first impression was of a face that had been unused to grief, to which grief now clung with the tenacity of a predator. Blue-black hair, gleaming like silk, was pinned up away from her smooth brow and round cheeks. Her ears were slightly large, and would have added unique charm to a merry expression. But whatever predisposition to merriment she might have possessed was now extinguished. When she looked at him, it was as if the bright, welcoming room was suddenly draped in gray veils through which they regarded each other.

"You should not be here," she said quietly. Her lips barely moved. "No one should be here."

Looking as if he agreed with her, Sun shifted in his chair, which creaked, as uneasy with its occupant as he was with it. "We will not intrude on you long," he said. "My questions are simple, but I am afraid they are necessary." He turned to Li Du. "You are prepared to write?"

While Li Du hastily drew out his notebook and pencil, Sun cleared his throat. "You were saying, before my clerk arrived, that you were unaware of any clandestine affair between your husband and Madam Hong."

"That is true." Her words were cold and lifeless, like pebbles dropped in water.

"He never mentioned her."

"Never."

"And you didn't know that he had gone to meet her on the night he died?"

"No."

"When was the last time you saw your husband?"

Lady Ai closed her eyes. "I see him still."

Sun, looking as if he wanted to sink through the floor, muttered an ineloquent apology. "I must ask you to be specific," he said. "When was the last time you saw him alive?"

She was silent. Sun repeated the question.

"I saw him that morning," she said.

"Before he went to the ministry."

"Yes."

"Did you expect him to return that night?"

"I did not know if he would be home. My husband often stayed late at the ministry. Sometimes he spent the night in the Inner City."

"It is an indelicate question, but I must ask. To your knowledge, did he enjoy visiting women?"

After a long moment, Lady Ai lifted her head a fraction, and regarded first Li Du, then Sun, with dry eyes. Her hands, corpse-like, remained immobile in her lap. "He admired women. He went regularly to the theaters."

"But you did not know what he planned to do that night?"

"No."

Sun lapsed into silence. Li Du guessed that the chief inspector was searching not for a question, but for how to pose the question he wanted to ask. "It would be helpful," said Sun, after a while, "to speak to someone in whom your husband might have confided. A close friend, perhaps."

Lady Ai's eyes remained dull. "You will want to speak to Ji, then."

"Ji," said Sun. "A coworker?"

"Ji Daolong. He is the owner of the Glazed Tile Factory at Mentougou. He and my husband were children together in Anhui."

"Mentougou is some distance from the city. Is there anyone nearer to us? A fellow official at the ministry, perhaps?"

"No. I don't know of anyone."

"Did your husband often speak to you about his work at the ministry, or, specifically, with the Black Tile Factory?"

"Not often. Sometimes."

"Had he mentioned anything unusual recently?"

"I don't understand."

"I mean the question to be very broad. Every detail is important to ascertaining what happened that night. I wonder, perhaps, did he quarrel with someone? Did he have enemies?"

For the first time, Lady Ai's face showed engagement in the question that had been asked. It was barely perceptible, only a faint kindling behind her eyes. "What purpose could that question serve? Do you mean to diminish my husband? To protect Hong, you will say that my husband was a troublemaker? You will say that he was immoral?" She stopped, her lips trembling.

"Not at all," said Sun, gruff and awkward in his attempt to soothe. "Without a confession, we must investigate every possibility. If you know something, it is essential that you tell us."

Her shoulders, which had tensed, now eased, and she seemed once more to withdraw into another place. After a silence, she sighed. "He worked very hard. He was so clever and so diligent that I felt sometimes the ministry asked too much of him."

"Why do you say that?"

"He did mention one name. Is Bai known to you?"

"Bai Chengde, the scholar?"

She answered with a minute, apathetic nod.

"In what context did your husband mention him?"

"It was a few days ago. He was very tired, more tired than I usually see him. When I asked him why, he said that he was very busy with an unscheduled audit. That's when he mentioned that man's name. He said it was his fault, and he—he cursed scholars who care too much about their walls being white."

A shadow slid across the ornaments on the wall across from the door. There was a human quality to the movement, and Li Du wondered whether a maid or servant had been on the veranda, trying to eavesdrop on what was said. He turned his attention back to Sun, who had just drawn in a deep breath. "Four days ago, your husband attended a literary gathering at Hong's house."

"Yes."

"Did he say anything about that evening?"

Lady Ai opened her mouth to speak, then closed it. She held herself very still. As Li Du watched, a tear slid down her cheek. She let it fall, not seeming to notice. "He enjoyed himself," she said finally. "He was entertained."

"Entertained?"

Lady Ai struggled to maintain her composure. Her next words were choked. "He was amused. He found it funny that Hong tried so hard to make intellectuals like him. My husband said that Hong chose a book he thought was an ancient classic, but mistook the title, and chose a cheap novel by accident. Pan laughed when he told me." Her voice broke.

"I have no more questions," said Sun. "You have been gracious to permit our intrusion." His voice was uncharacteristically gentle. It recalled to Li Du a distant memory of a shadowed courtyard, and Sun speaking to his sister, not long after she and Li Du were married. She had been homesick. He shook himself from the memory to see Sun standing up.

"I—I have one question," he said, tapping his pencil lightly on the page of his notebook.

Sun shot him a look, but did not protest.

"When your husband left for the ministry that morning, he had a large quantity of silver with him. It would be a great help to us if you could share what he intended to do with it."

Lady Ai gave him a look of incomprehension. "He didn't speak of it," she said finally. "So I cannot tell you how he meant to use it. But I don't want it returned, not now. Give it to a temple. I—I—"

It was as if a string that had been holding her upright was suddenly cut. As she bowed forward, she clutched her arms around her stomach and began to sob. Sun stood, a look of embarrassment on his face, just as the two maids to whom Li Du had spoken rushed in. They fell to their knees on either side of their mistress and began to whisper soothing words. Murmuring excuses, Sun made his way to the door. Li Du, following just after him, had a final sight of the three women, the hems of their robes overlapping, apparently oblivious to their guests' departure.

"I thought I'd never get out," said Sun, when they were on the street. He drew in a deep, appreciative breath and exhaled slowly. "Such a storm of grief could topple trees and crumble bricks to dust. I hope the poor woman does not do herself harm."

"Will she leave the city soon?"

"She will have to wait for a letter from his family. Either they will send avenging brothers here from Anhui to demand recompense for Pan's death, which will mean certain headaches for the magistrate's office, and for us, or they will tell her to return home with the body of their son. She is, you should note for the records, his second concubine."

"I see. His wife and first concubine remained in Anhui?"

"Yes. The wife is mistress of the house there. An extensive family, I am told, including two sons born to Lady Ai. She is fortunate to have sons; she will certainly retain a place in the household." After a pause, Sun added, "I spoke to the servants about her activities on the night of the murder. She was at home when the night watch began and the gates closed, and she was at home when the bells rang and the gates opened. Any route from this neighborhood to that of the Black Tile Factory would involve passing through— how many gates would you say?"

Li Du considered. "The wall between the boroughs, and at least nine alley gates."

"If not more," said Sun, nodding. "Impossible to do without being stopped. What was the meaning of your question about the silver?"

Li Du gave a full account of his conversation with the maids. As Sun listened, his expression became more grave. His pace slowed, as it tended to do when he was thinking and walking simultaneously.

"It has an unsavory feel," said Sun. "I still think your blackmail theory takes it too far, but I'm not one to ignore facts. I'd like to know what became of that bag."

They had almost reached a popular intersection, where it would usually have been possible to hire sedan chairs. Today it was blocked by a barricade of stacked boards and Banner soldiers.

"This is why I was late," Li Du explained. "The street is being cleaned in preparation for the return of the prince. There is to be a procession."

"Of course there is," muttered Sun. "There's always a procession somewhere in the city."

Despite the closed street, Sun was able to procure transportation, and they were soon bumping and jostling through the narrow, packed streets that connected the West and North Boroughs. Over the hubbub outside, the bells struck the hour of the monkey. As soon as they reentered the office courtyard, Li Du heard chair legs scraping, footsteps, and fluttering papers. A moment later, the clerks were all vying for Sun's attention, proffering contracts, reports, and letters in need of review or signature. Sun fended them off with promises to attend to each issue one at a time, then, ordering Li Du to join him, shut the door of his office firmly in their faces.

"This Ji Daolong," he said, when the door was closed. "Do you know anything about him?"

Li Du shook his head. "I think that the glazed tile kilns used to be within the city walls, but they were moved out to the western hills more than fifty years ago."

Sun dropped heavily into his chair. He plucked a sheet from the top of the pile on his desk and perused it. "The Fa family wants permission to build another temple," he said. He sighed and slid the paper to the bottom of the pile. "I don't have time for a full day's journey to Mentougou. I'm delegating the task to you."

"To interview Ji?"

"Yes. If he and Pan were close friends, Pan might have told him about the affair. If we can confirm it, our job will be simpler."

"And if not?"

"As I said, I find your blackmail theory far-fetched. If you uncover evidence to support it at Mentougou, bring it to me, and I will take it to Magistrate Yin. But remember, please, that this is not scholar's work. Don't tie knots in a case that is almost straightened out. By the time you return, I expect we'll have obtained Hong's confession."

Chapter 14

Morning brought a thin mist that blurred the corners of rooftops and settled over the surfaces of lakes. As the first bells began to toll, Li Du and Hamza left the temple, and made their way on foot to the West Borough. Around them, alley gates rattled open as tired soldiers fumbled with latches. Smoke and steam billowed from carts pulled by vendors on their way to markets and busy streets. By the time Li Du had procured two horses, the great doors at Guangning were open, the day's crowds were streaming in, and warm light was beginning to dispel the haze.

"I have spent only a day in your city," said Hamza as he ate the last of the steamed rolls from the bag they had intended to save for the afternoon, "but I was beginning to worry that the world outside its walls had disappeared. I am relieved to find it still here."

They had crossed the moat and were riding at an easy pace along a wide dirt road. Li Du twisted in his saddle to look back over his shoulder. The city, from their current vantage point, was a faceless gray wall, its only visible feature a hulking watchtower at the southwest corner. "We are not far from the northern frontier," he said, returning his attention to the path ahead. "It is not by chance that the city resembles a fortress."

"I don't blame the capital for wanting its walls to appear insurmountable from the *outside*," Hamza replied, examining the empty bag that had contained the rolls. With a rueful expression, he pocketed it. "But the unfortunate consequence is that they also seem insurmountable from the *inside*. A person does not enjoy being trapped. And I do not like those towers always looking down at me."

Li Du understood. He had spent the past two years trying to ignore the message communicated by the ever-present towers. *Someone is watching. Someone is listening.* "Is it so different from other capitals you have visited?" he asked.

"No," Hamza conceded. "Most of them have been the same. In cities built to house emperors, danger is admixed into the very bricks."

And tiles, Li Du thought, his mind going to the murders.

"But you understand," went on Hamza, "it is not the danger that disconcerts me. I am drawn to danger. It is only that I have grown accustomed to facing it in more open spaces. When Sera and I journeyed to the kingdom of Nyimagon, we rode for two weeks without encountering a single barrier to our progress. No mountain, forest, or ocean mandated a change of course. Not even a hill, a tree, or a pond to impede us. And certainly no walls. It was not until we came across a strange sight—a snake whose movements carved letters into the desert sand—that we halted. It was a decision we later regretted."

"What happened?"

"You have asked the one question it most pleases me to hear," said Hamza with a bright smile. "I will tell you."

As Hamza told his story, the last of the mist burned away, and the day turned clear and blue. There was not a wisp of cloud in the sky. On either side of the path, fields of wheat and millet sunned themselves, rippling faintly in the breeze like the fur of a sleeping cat. Ahead, the western hills rolled across the horizon in watercolor shapes of purple and gray.

"And that is how Sera-tsering and I came finally to the city of Guge, only to find it swallowed by sand. Its spires, which had once stood the height of ten elephants, reached only to our knees. Wandering among them was an old woman, who greeted us and said that she had once been the city's queen. For a year and a day, she said, she had been searching for a magical jewel buried in the dust, a jewel that could melt the sand, and restore Guge to its former glory." Hamza paused, awaiting the question.

"Did you find it?" asked Li Du dutifully.

"Sera did—in the eye of a stone lizard. But by then we knew that the woman was a cruel sorceress, and that to give it to her would have led to the ruin of more cities. The destruction might even have reached east all the way to the wall of your own empire. We escaped the sorceress, and took the jewel to a monastery beside a blue lake, in which, they say, a dragon lives." Hamza paused. "Surely it is time for lunch?"

They had begun to pass scattered houses, protected by walls. From their vantage points atop their horses, they could just see fluttering cotton hung from clotheslines in the courtyards. Li Du pointed ahead. "In the center of this village is a restaurant that makes fine noodles."

Hamza twisted in his saddle to look at his friend. "You seem to know this path well. You have ridden it before?"

"I have."

The storyteller's gaze remained on his friend for a long moment before he turned back to the road. "You were not so reserved when I knew you as the little patchwork scholar of the mountains," he said. "What has this city done to make you so quiet?"

Li Du gave a small, self-deprecating smile. "The city is not to blame. On the contrary, I have been given ample opportunities to reenter something close to the life I once knew." He hesitated, thinking of the courtyard conversations he had avoided, the invitations he had ignored, and the family ties he had neglected. "I have gone to some trouble to be left alone," he said finally. "I've become unused to answering questions."

"I noticed," said Hamza. "And I will tell you that nothing good ever came of being invisible. I have a story to illustrate this point—" He stopped himself. "But it will keep. You have answered one question. Now answer another. Why do you know this road?"

"I know it," Li Du said slowly, "because I occasionally teach calligraphy to the children of a family outside Mentougou."

Hamza gave an approving nod. "Good. Now that we have cured you of your reticence, I have several other small questions. They are as follows. First, why aren't you in your library? Second, and related to the first, why is a man who saved the life of an emperor employed as a humble secretary? Third, why did you send me through the sandy deserts to fetch for you a single, priceless volume? Fourth, have you discovered the answer to—"

"We are here," interrupted Li Du, drawing his horse to a stop outside a building with a cheerfully listing patio. At the base of a dusty set of stone stairs, a huge cauldron sat over a fire, savory clouds advertising its contents. From inside the courtyard came the regular sound of a knife cutting rice dough into noodles, as steady as a ticking clock.

Hamza abandoned his demands with a mutinous scowl, but was soon distracted by the food and company. Though they finished their soup quickly, they remained behind long enough for Hamza to conclude, for the benefit of rapt customers, his account of a puzzle involving ravens, which was solved at last by a clever vizier in the court of a king.

Chapter 15

The Glazed Tile Factory was built on a green hill, at the base of which was a village. After they had made arrangements at the Mentougou inn and settled their horses in its stable, Li Du and Hamza walked up a winding path to a wall draped like a necklace over the hilltop. The servant manning the gate escorted them up and over the crest of the hill to the other side.

Like its counterpart within the capital, the factory bustled with laborers at work processing clay, cutting tiles, and tending fires. But unlike the Black Tile Factory, which was tightly constrained by the city that surrounded it, the Glazed Tile Factory seemed to have grown out of the hill. Where the Black Tile Factory gave an impression of gray solidity, the Glazed Tile Factory was a place of color. Miniature mountains of tiles gleamed yellow and green. Mythical creatures, ready to be fitted to roof ridges, presided in glassy coats of glaze.

The servant brought them to an airy room in a building nestled in the dappled shade of an elm, away from the smoke and clamor. The interior was furnished like an office, but its original function appeared to have been abandoned in favor of other activities. Tools, their handles and blades obscured by chipped layers of dried clay, were arranged on shelves built for books. The floor was patterned by the bristle marks of a broom scraped through clay dust. One corner of the room was occupied by a man bent over a spinning potter's wheel. His right hand was concealed within the vessel that rotated at the wheel's center. His left moved steadily up the clay, controlling its liquid shape with steady fingertips.

"Master Ji," said the servant. Receiving no response, he repeated the name.

The man did not look up from his work. "Has Lao made the fire too hot again?"

"There are two officials from the capital here to see you."

The object on the wheel, which had taken the form of a vase, wobbled and collapsed. The man raised his head and fastened anxious eyes on Li Du and Hamza. Observing Ji Daolong for the first time, Li Du could not help but note the stark contrast between the two factory owners. Where Hong had embraced the businessman's access to society's elite, Ji was clearly a man of his craft. His lean torso was offset by powerful arms and shoulders. His hands and arms were gloved in watery clay. The silver hair at his temples was singed from frequent dealings with fire. Li Du guessed his age to be around fifty.

"I didn't expect a ministry representative so soon," said Ji, before Li Du could introduce himself. He stood up, washed his hands in a basin of water, strode to a desk, and began shuffling papers. "I had intended to be more prepared for your arrival, but there have been so many contracts this season that I have not had the time. I must beg your patience. If I could have one more week to—"

"I think you misunderstand," said Li Du. "I have come, with my assistant, from the North Borough Office. I was sent by Chief Inspector Sun to interview you in connection with a criminal investigation."

"Investigation?" Ji stared. "What crime has been committed?"

Li Du hesitated. It seemed that Ji had not been told of his friend's death. Ji, comprehending that his visitors had not come to review contracts, left the papers on the desk and began to clear two chairs of clutter. He instructed the servant hovering at the door to prepare and serve tea, and invited Li Du and Hamza to sit.

"You were expecting someone from a ministry," said Li Du, taking the chair that was proffered. Hamza, ignoring the other chair, began a leisurely inspection of the room.

Ji sat down on the stool by the potter's wheel. "The Ministry of

Rites has scheduled an audit of their construction contracts, but I was not expecting a representative until next week. I intended, by that time, to have the contracts in their proper order. In my anxiety, I gave you a disrespectful welcome, for which I apologize." He glanced uncertainly at Hamza, who was perusing a small collection of porcelain vases displayed on a table, then turned back to Li Du. "You say that a crime has been committed?"

Li Du leaned forward, holding Ji's gaze with his own. It was a gesture of sympathy that allowed him to watch the other man's reaction closely. "I am sorry to inform you that your friend, Pan Yongfa, is dead."

"Dead." Ji echoed the word with apparent bewilderment. Then his eyes widened. "Pan is dead? But how? When?"

"His body was discovered three days ago in the office of the Black Tile Factory."

"You must mean there was an accident. A fire?"

"His death was not an accident."

"Are you saying he was—Pan was—"

Li Du nodded. "It is a case of murder."

"I cannot believe it." Ji's fingers beat a nervous tap on his knees. "How did it happen?"

Because Sun had instructed him that there was no reason to withhold the basic details of the crime, Li Du provided a succinct account of the discovery of the bodies. He concluded by informing Ji that Hong had been arrested.

When he finished, Ji let out a long breath. "I see," he said. "I see." He looked down at his hands, staring at the white tracings that had settled into the lines of his palms. "Pan may have washed the clay dust from his hands, but he was an Anhui man. His family will want him brought home."

Two servants arrived carrying tea trays, and a period of silence followed while cups were arranged and filled. When they were gone, Li Du spoke. "While the circumstances suggest that Hong is the culprit, there has been no confession. Because of this, the chief inspector wishes to make broad inquiries. He sent me here to speak with you because, according to Pan's concubine, Lady Ai, you and he were close friends."

Li Du perceived a fleeting hint of displeasure in Ji's expression. "Close friends?" Ji shook his head. "In her distress, Lady Ai must have misrepresented the strength of our connection. Pan was an Anhui man, and Anhui men support each other when they are far from home. But we have not been close friends since I left Anhui—nearly thirty years ago. Pan was still a boy, and I was barely old enough to be called a man."

Li Du withdrew his notebook and stylus from his satchel as Ji continued. "Our families were friends. I was already an apprentice at my father's kiln when Pan began coming over to watch us work. I taught him to throw bowls. He was only a small child, but he had a good sense for clay. I thought he would run a kiln of his own one day. But his family knew he was clever, and decided he was destined for the exams. He disappeared into the classroom, and I eventually traveled here to work for my uncle." Ji glanced through the window at laborers stacking tiles. "When my uncle died, I became the owner."

"You must have seen Pan when he came to take the examinations."

Ji considered this. "I don't recall that I did. He had already passed them when I saw him next. I went back to Anhui to be with my mother, who was ailing, and to mourn her when she died. I saw him then."

"And soon after that, Pan was assigned to the capital."

Ji picked up a fist-sized ball of clay and began to roll it into a sphere between his palms. "About three years ago. He came to visit. I set him up with a few connections, but he didn't need much from me. He was an official with a coveted job in the capital."

"Then you didn't see him often over the past three years?"

Ji shook his head. "We dined together occasionally, when I had business in the city."

"You visited his home?"

"Once or twice. But Pan preferred to meet at a restaurant called The Green Door, in the opera district. It makes a good Anhui dish."

"When was the last time you saw him?"

Ji hesitated. "I did see him a few days ago. How many was it? Five, I think. There was a party." A thought seemed to occur to him, and his eyes widened. "Of course, that is more significant now. It was at the home of Hong Wenbin."

"You mean the literary party," said Li Du.

"Yes."

"Then you know Hong well?"

Ji shook his head vigorously at this. "Only professionally. Roofs need black tiles to keep out the rain, and they need glazed tiles to make them beautiful. We often collaborate on contracts. I was only invited to his social gatherings when the invitation list was extensive. There must have been forty or fifty guests that day."

"There was a book assigned for discussion," said Li Du. "I have forgotten the title. Do you remember?"

"Yes, a book." Ji's tone was vague. "I didn't read it. As I said, I've been very busy this season. I wouldn't have attended the party at all, except that I was in the capital that day, and thought my absence might be taken as an offense. Was it something about a pear?"

"It was called *The Bitter Plum*."

"A plum, of course. I remember now. The title reminded me of the master who taught me my craft. He told me that a man who works with glaze should be able to produce every color that appears in the flesh of a fruit, capturing both hue and translucence." He looked as though he would continue, but then, seeming to recall the grave subject of the conversation, lapsed into silence, waiting for Li Du's next question.

"Then the last time you saw Pan was at that party," said Li Du. "Did you and he speak?"

"Only briefly. We exchanged pleasantries."

"Did he mention anything unusual, or confide anything to you?"

Ji considered the question before he answered. "No," he said finally. "He was enjoying himself. It was a pleasant afternoon, until the storm."

"What is your opinion of Hong?"

"Hong? He is more a businessman than a craftsman. Even though we both make tiles, we do not have much in common."

"Have you ever seen him behave violently?"

"Hong drinks too much. Everyone he knows has seen him behave violently."

"Then you would believe him capable of this crime?"

Ji replied quickly. "Certainly I would. Hong was jealous of all his possessions, his beautiful wife among them."

"You knew Madam Hong?"

"I met her at a New Year celebration some years ago, and have seen her at one or two parades in the capital."

"What did you know about her, other than that she was beautiful?"

Ji took his time with the question. "It would not surprise me to learn she had secrets." He set down the sphere of clay and picked up a porcelain bowl from the shelf behind him. He turned it, causing a flash of light to travel slowly around its interior. "When glaze is fired at a low heat, it does not become one with the clay beneath it. Madam Hong gave the same impression. Her face and her thoughts were not as closely connected as they are for some people." Ji looked at the bowl, the outside of which bore, in sepia and rose enamel, an illustration of wild geese among reeds. "I also know that she had fine taste in art," he said. "Hong displayed their collections proudly, but it was Madam Hong who found the treasures."

"And Pan never spoke of her to you?"

"No, but as I have said, we were not that close. I would not have expected him to confide something so personal to me. I don't know why he would have pursued a married woman when there are many beautiful actresses and concubines in the capital, not to mention his own Lady Ai. But again, I did not know him well."

"Were you in the city two nights ago?"

"No. I was here, working. The renovation of the examination complex has demanded more time than anyone anticipated. The tiles are only now ready to be taken from their kiln. I'll be overseeing their placement the day before the exams begin, though I would not have chosen to complete the work so near the deadline."

"I was told by Hong's manager that the tiles required were not the standard size."

"Just so." Ji's expression warmed a little. "You must have been speaking with Hu. He's a good man for the job. I would hire him here, if the Black Tile Factory closes."

Li Du became aware of a gentle clattering sound coming from one corner. He turned to see Hamza standing over a basket, shifting its contents between his fingers. When Hamza noticed that he had attracted attention, he withdrew an object and held it to the light. It was a round piece of ceramic, not much larger than a pebble, glazed a soft white.

Ji stood up. "A project of mine," he said as he crossed the room to where Hamza stood. "In every dynasty, emperors have challenged master glazers to produce colors to their specifications. The color you are holding was requested by the Xuanzong Emperor, who believed that the humblest colors were the most beautiful. He asked for a vase the color of steam from a rice pot, when the sky behind it is cold and blue."

Hamza looked delighted. "But that is exactly expressed," he said. "A marvelous accomplishment."

"My family did not earn renown by making thousands of black and yellow roof tiles," said Ji. "My ancestors made tiles for the emperors of the past in the great southern capital. Climb to the top of a hill in Nanjing, and you will see rainbows and gardens of color, protected from wind and rain and time. They will not fade. Such splendor is not known here."

Li Du had also risen, and was scanning the shelves near where Hamza and Ji stood. On them were bowls and boxes of various size and color, containing rocks and powders. He was about to speak, when the sound of a footstep announced someone at the door. They all turned to see a laborer whose face was smudged with soot. He bowed apologetically and addressed Ji. "We are concerned about the temperature of the fire in the eighth kiln."

Ji's face tensed. He addressed himself to Li Du. "With the greatest respect, if you are satisfied with my answers, I beg you to let me attend to this matter. The early stages of firing are critical."

Li Du said he had no more questions to ask at present. They left the room together, Ji locking it behind them with a heavy padlock. Ji made his excuses and hurried ahead, leaving Li Du and Hamza to follow at a more measured pace. They crested the hill, and saw Ji come to a halt at an earthen kiln with a roaring fire at its mouth. The kiln master began to shout instructions at the laborers, who were feeding branches into the flame. Smoke and sparks surrounded them, causing the workers to turn away and wipe their streaming eyes. Ji, seemingly impervious to heat, kept his attention on the fire. He turned only once to watch Li Du and Hamza go, his expression unreadable through the smoke.

The sun was low when they arrived at the outskirts of the village. "I think he was hiding something," said Hamza. "Why did he lock the room behind us when we departed?"

"Because," Li Du answered, "the contents of those bowls and boxes were more valuable than an equal amount of gold."

Hamza appeared interested. "But they looked like bowls of powder and humble rocks."

"They don't reveal their color until they are made into glaze," Li Du replied. "But I have seen illustrations and read descriptions. Those were rare agates, so rare that they are reserved, like the finest fruits and silks, exclusively for imperial use."

"Ah," said Hamza. "The obvious conclusion is that he is a prince in disguise."

"Alternatively," said Li Du mildly, "he has a supplier willing to circumvent the rules."

They had entered the village square, in which the residents were just concluding a celebration of the birthday of the local deity. A

stage on which a play had just been performed was being disman-
tled, the potted chrysanthemums carried away. They had almost
reached the inn when a shouted greeting from the edge of the
square stopped them.

They turned to see a man crossing the square toward them at a
rapid stride, evading with easy movements, in spite of his significant height, the villagers, monks, and acrobats moving through the
space. He was soon close enough for Li Du to recognize the rigid
features, which were softened by a gentle steadiness of expression.

"Finally," said the man. "I have caught you when the sun is setting, and it is too late for you to say you must hurry back to your
business in the city. You will come to my house for dinner. My wife
will be overjoyed, and would not forgive me if I permitted you to
refuse."

Chapter 16

L i Du!" The cry came from behind a green hedge of silkworm thorn, from which emerged not one, but three children, who repeated Li Du's name in a chirping chorus. Two boys, close in age, ran across the garden with reckless enthusiasm, followed by a younger girl who could not have been more than five years old. All three were dirt-smudged and bedecked in leaves that had caught in their clothes and hair.

They teetered to a halt in front of Li Du, who regarded them with a serious expression.

"What," asked Li Du sternly, "were you doing tearing up the hedges of this beautiful garden?"

"We were escaping the ghosts," answered the little girl.

"Through the secret tunnels," said the smaller of the two boys, who seemed to think further explanation was required. "The ghosts don't *know* about the secret tunnels, so they can't follow us."

Li Du accepted the answer with equanimity. Hamza cocked his head thoughtfully. "Running is a fine way to start," he said. "But often, the best way to stop a ghost from chasing you is to turn around and ask it what it wants."

As the children considered this, Hamza directed a questioning look at his friend. "These are my pupils," said Li Du. He turned back to the children and addressed them in the tone of a disciplinarian. Their sparkling eyes and smiles made it clear that the affect didn't convince any of them. "I hope," he said, "that when you saw the acrobats on stage today, you studied their movements, and are prepared to apply your observations of form to your next calligraphy lesson?"

With obvious effort, giggles were repressed, and three heads nodded dutifully. But, liberated by the permissive atmosphere of celebration, the children could not contain their delight for long. In eager voices, they began to tell their guests about the day's adventures.

"Li Du, you should have told us you were coming." The words came from a woman who entered the courtyard through a keyhole door, on the other side of which another vibrant garden was illuminated by the sinking sun. She looked at the children, took in their muddy clothes and red cheeks, and smiled with rueful maternal indulgence. She herself was neatly attired in a robe of pale gray with a pattern of white flowers, cinched at the waist by a woven red belt. Over her shoulders she wore a blue shawl, and her hair was pinned up with flower pins in a matching blue. Though her face was youthful, hard years had marked their passage at the corners of her mouth, and several streaks of gray shone in her hair. Her curiosity when she beheld Hamza was almost instantly replaced by a delighted smile. "You must be the storyteller!" she said.

"My reputation," said Hamza, bowing, "has spread to many lands."

"Li Du has told us all about you," she said. "I knew you at once."

The children, who were of the age to know an adventurer of their imaginations when they saw one incarnated, stole shy, fascinated glances at Hamza. The woman returned her attention to Li Du. "There is no lesson scheduled until the end of the month," she said. "What brings you to Mentougou?"

Hamza spoke first. "A crime," he announced.

As if she had stepped into shadow, the radiance vanished from the woman's face. Her eyes, full of worry, fixed on Li Du's face.

"There is no danger here," he said quickly. "The incident took place within the walls of the capital, at the Black Tile Factory. I was sent to speak to the master of the Glazed Tile Factory, who has some connection with the parties involved."

"I see," she said. "I hope Ji Daolong is not in any trouble? The children are always sneaking over the walls of the factory to collect shards with colored glaze on them. They seem far more fascinated by broken chips than with any of the fine vases in our own home." Though she smiled, her face was drained of its previous brightness.

"Very wise," said Hamza, who seemed eager to make up for the worry he had inspired. "Broken pieces are certainly more interesting than intact objects. I once found a relic in the desert, a chip of an ancient blade, which set me on a quest of three years to try to find the rest of it. Yet, when I had finally collected all the shards and restored the blade to its original form, I was disappointed to see that it was only a dull sword with no significant magical properties. The adventures I had while gathering the pieces—in them reposed the true value of the treasure."

They were joined at this point by the man who had hailed them in the village square. He wore rough clothing that emitted a faint smell of sun-warmed hay and leather. His gaze moved across the faces of his children and came to rest on the woman with unselfconscious affection.

Li Du turned to Hamza. "I have not yet formally introduced you," he said. "This is Cao Mei, and her husband, Cao Yun." Waving away formalities, Yun ushered them to an inner courtyard, where four servants were setting out dishes on a long table. At the center were two large bowls of rice as bright as snow. As the number of dishes increased and savory aromas mingled, Hamza inhaled deeply and appreciatively. Green peppers gleamed in oil. Crisp-fried mint leaves covered plates heaped with spiced meat. Plump mushrooms cushioned slivered red peppers. Hamza sighed. "I have not seen such a magnificent table since I was invited to the feast of a princess celebrating her victory over a monster that had terrorized a kingdom," he said. "And that food, which I believe incorporated choice pieces of the monster, did not appeal nearly so much as this."

The little girl mouthed the word *monster* to one of her brothers, her eyes wide.

"It tasted best in the stew," said Hamza.

"The village celebrations merit a special dinner," said Mei. "Lacking monsters, we have made do with mushrooms," she added with a smile. She nodded to the children, for whom places had been set. "We will all eat together, and you will be very respectful of our guests, even though Li Du is never as strict with you as he should be."

There were nods and solemn promises, and the dinner began. Hamza, after tasting and praising each dish, turned to Li Du. "How did you become a tutor in this house?"

"That is a long story," Li Du said. "But to share its most important point, Mei and Yun were the first to offer me hospitality on my return to Beijing and, by fortunate coincidence, they had three talented children in need of a calligraphy instructor." Li Du infused the words with subtle finality and was relieved when Hamza did not ask further questions.

Yun surveyed his table, his family, and his guests with kindly, contented eyes. "What brought you to Mentougou today?" he asked Li Du.

It was Mei who answered. Mei frowned rarely, but when she did, the expression formed deep lines, testifying to a time in her life when her burdens had been heavier. "Li Du is investigating a crime committed in the capital," she said. "He came to speak with Ji Daolong."

Yun's expression became concerned. "Can you tell us more, or is the matter confidential?"

Li Du was aware of the children's rapt attention. "It is not confidential," he said. "But the details are not for the ears of children. The matter should be resolved soon, but until it is, perhaps it would be best if they stopped climbing the walls into the Glazed Tile Factory."

The children received a stern lecture. Once promises of obedience had been extracted from them, Mei turned to Li Du. "You are tired," she said. "And we have kept you from resting your mind. Why are we discussing anxious subjects, when it is a day of celebration, and we have a storyteller among us?"

The words elicited trembling excitement from those present under the age of ten, who had been, it now seemed, waiting with barely contained impatience to question Hamza.

"Have you really been a pirate?"

"Did you really travel with the wild horse caravans?"

"Is it true that you know magic?"

Hamza smiled and straightened his shoulders. His chin tilted downward in the aristocratic posture that had become so familiar to Li Du during their travels. "Scholar," said Hamza. "How can you bear to teach children with such ungoverned imaginations? What exaggerations have you been spreading about your friend, who is a very serious man?" Hamza looked apologetically at the children. "I am, by profession, a calculator of taxes," he said. "Perhaps after dinner we can practice equations?"

His eager audience protested vehemently. Hamza's eyes glinted. "Now that I turn my mind to it, I recall that I *have* sailed in a pirate ship," he said. "A *flying* pirate ship," he added. "I have also traveled with horse caravans that trade in jewels of hidden power. As for magic, I may have some experience with it."

As the light faded, the candles and the eyes of the children grew brighter. The plates were refilled, the servants hovered delightedly in the doorways, and the day turned to night.

A light drizzle began to fall as Li Du and Hamza made their way back to the inn.

"Mei speaks with an accent I have not heard," said Hamza.

"She comes from Jiangsu, in the distant south," Li Du replied. "Her father traveled north and settled in the capital. She remained in the south with the man to whom she was betrothed."

"Yun?"

Li Du shook his head and explained. "Mei has endured more pain than many. Yun is her second husband. She never speaks of her first marriage, but I know it was an unhappy one. Her father told me once, after many cups of wine, that of all his children, Mei was the one he had failed. He blamed himself for marrying his daughter to an unkind man. Perhaps it was not so terrible that her husband died, and yet to become a widow so soon after becoming a wife, and to lose her father not long after—" Li Du's voice trailed into silence. "For all her grief," he went on after a moment, "she has found happiness. I have never seen such a loving partnership between husband and wife."

The silence that followed was broken at last by Hamza. "When we traveled together with the caravan of Kalden Dorjee, you spoke to me of a man called Shu, who was your teacher."

Li Du started to speak, but found he could not. Hamza went on. "He taught you how to eliminate moisture from air, to mend pages with needle and thread, to banish the little creatures that eat words, hidden deep in shadowed shelves."

Li Du's mind returned to the last time he had spoken to Hamza about his past. They had been sitting beside the crumbling court-yard wall of a dusty inn, deep in the western mountains. Li Du had been holding a battered bowl gingerly between fingers stiff from cold, and lacerated by wooden saddles and kindling. He had told Hamza about the man whose crime had been the reason for Li Du's exile, and also the reason for his return.

"Yes." Li Du took off his hat and wiped the rain from his eyes. "Mei is Shu's daughter."

Chapter 17

The rain stopped and the sky cleared. Moonlight fell through the needles of a potted pine onto a stone table, on which stood two bottles. A third was propped above a brazier of glowing coals. As the only guests at the inn, Li Du and Hamza had the courtyard to themselves. They sat at the table opposite each other, Li Du studying his empty cup.

"When I met you," said Hamza, "you missed your library so much that you walked its hallways in your dreams. It has been two years since you returned home. I was sure I would find you back in those hallways, arranging and rearranging books, humming to yourself, a contented bear in a cave."

Li Du lifted one of the bottles and shook it. Finding it empty, he picked up the other one and, with a hand that was not quite steady, filled first Hamza's cup, then his own. "Another Li Du, perhaps," he said. "In another library."

"It is a great sacrifice on my part," said Hamza, "not to pursue this idea of numerous versions of the scholar Li Du. It brings to mind a story I once heard of a prism with unusual properties of multiplication. But witness my restraint, as I limit myself to the most obvious question. Why is *this* Li Du not in his library?"

Li Du took a long sip of wine. "Because it was closed. That section of the palace is no longer accessible to librarians or scholars from outside the palace walls. Even if I occupied the same position I used to, I would not be allowed there. I doubt it's even a library anymore."

"But why was it closed?"

Li Du took another sip, then lifted a hand and waved it in a vaguely explanatory gesture. "For reasons," he said. "*Official* reasons."

"My dear librarian," said Hamza. "I speak many languages, but the language of bureaucrats is not among them. Make your answer more interesting, please. What *official* reasons?"

"Too many doors," Li Du said. "Too many rooms. Too many dark corners. And all too near the Emperor. The library was an ideal place for secret meetings. Too ideal. A repetition of the events of the forty-first reigning year could not be risked. In that year, the library played host to nine conspirators who planned to kill the Emperor and restore the Ming heir to power."

"They were obviously unsuccessful," said Hamza.

Li Du traced a finger across the table, turning the spiky shadows of pine needles into a maze. "They came very close. By the time the final would-be assassin was struck down, only a single courtyard wall separated him from the garden in which the Emperor strolled."

A light breeze made the shadows quiver, and Li Du turned his attention away from them. "The ensuing investigation did not last long. It led to the arrest of my teacher, Shu. And it ended—" Li Du picked up his cup again. "It ended at his public execution."

"And you were sentenced to exile," said Hamza. "For your friendship with him."

Li Du did not appear to have heard Hamza's words. "Shu never denied the accusation," he said. "He confessed to treason."

Hamza reached down to the brazier, lifted the warm bottle, and filled their cups again. "And you believed him, or convinced yourself that you did, until the spy we met in the snow told you that you, along with everyone else who accepted his guilt, had been misled. He told you Shu was innocent. So you decided to return, and prove that your teacher did not commit the crime for which he died."

Li Du nodded, remembering the cold night on the far western border of the empire, and the voice that had hissed through the cutting mountain wind. *Shu was innocent.* At the time, Li Du had considered the possibility that he had lost his mind, that the whispering voice had not been that of a man, but of a ghost, telling Li Du what he had always, secretly, known. *Shu was innocent.*

Returning to the present, he watched steam blur the air above his cup. "I needed access to ministry records. I needed to know what the city knows: who has been found innocent, and who has been found guilty; who has lived, and who has died; who has power, and who defers to it. So I did what it is sometimes necessary to do in Beijing. I made use of a family connection. I obtained a job at the office of Chief Inspector Sun in the North Borough."

"Is he a close relative?" asked Hamza.

Li Du did not look up. "No," he said. "I wanted to avoid those relatives who would feel personally invested in my reintroduction to society, and those relatives who would pay close attention to my behavior." He tripped slightly over his next words. "Chief Inspector Sun is the brother of An, my—She was my wife."

"Your wife?" Hamza's lips thinned to a line as he pressed them together in an obvious effort to control the torrent of questions now occurring to him. "Your *wife*," he repeated.

"She is no longer my wife," Li Du said. "She obtained permission to leave me after I was sentenced to exile. She has a new family now, and lives in the east."

Hamza began to ask a question. To Li Du's surprise and relief, he stopped himself. With an expression of supreme self-sacrifice, he motioned for Li Du to continue with his account. Nodding thanks, Li Du went on. "I explained to Sun that I was in need of a job, and asked him to take me on as his assistant. I believe I convinced him that I was an eccentric, reclusive scholar."

"My friend," said Hamza. "You *are* an eccentric, reclusive scholar."

Li Du's answering smile was faint. "The situation has benefitted both of us. Sun obtained an assistant willing to do the paperwork he detests, and I obtained a position that gave me frequent excuses to run errands to the ministries. Each time I went to de-

liver a message, consult a case record, or review a statute, I searched
for records connected to Shu's trial." He stopped to rub his tired
eyes. "I had to be very careful," he said. "It took me a year to find the
relevant records, and it has taken me a year to read them, a few
borrowed pages at a time."

"And?"

"I read the transcript of Shu's interrogation. I read reports on
his family and friends. I read my own interrogation and sentence."
He paused, his mind filling with confused recollections of the past
two years. How many invisible hours had he claimed in dim record rooms, when there had been no one to notice his absence from
where he was supposed to be, or his presence where he wasn't? How
many files had he slipped quietly from their places? How many
pages had he quietly turned? His fingertips had grown accustomed,
as they had once been, to the varied texture of paper, his eyes to
the infinite spectrum of black ink. No longer a librarian, but a lone
voyager through the city's archives, he had held tight to the thin
thread of relevance that led him from one record to another, as if
through a dark maze.

Some turns had led him to information that was new to him.
Others had augmented his understanding of what he already
knew—it was within this maze that he had read, with silent com-
passion, the official report submitted to the Emperor from a Jiangsu
magistrate, detailing the tragic circumstances of the death of Mei's
first husband. Still others had taken him to painful reminders of
all that he wanted to forget, and never would. He had been confronted with the record of the dissolution of his marriage, at the
request of his wife's family, and the subsequent record of permission being granted for her to remarry.

Recalling himself to the moment, he saw that Hamza was looking at him, waiting for him to continue. He drew in a deep breath.
"I found a great deal more than I expected," he said. "But none of
it proved to be of use. Nothing led me anywhere, until finally, I
found an account of the decision to close the library to outside
scholars. The reason given was the attempted assassination, the

very one Shu had been accused of planning. I learned that, two nights before the attempt, the conspirators met for a final time."

"Ah," said Hamza. "In the library."

"Yes. This information came from the testimony of a man called Han Zongwan. He claimed that, unknown to the conspirators, he was in the library that night, and witnessed the meeting. He had not reported it because, unable to hear their words, he had been given no reason to think the meeting was not innocent. Later, news spread that there had been an attempt on the Emperor's life, and that only eight of nine conspirators had been apprehended. A furious search began for the ninth man. Han Zongwan, upon learning the names of the would-be assassins, finally understood the significance of what he had seen. He was able to identify the ninth man, the one for whom everyone was searching."

"Shu," said Hamza.

Li Du nodded. "According to Han Zongwan, he saw Shu's face distinctly."

"But who is this Han Zongwan?" asked Hamza. "Was he also a librarian? Did you know him?"

Li Du's mouth twisted slightly. "He was a librarian, and he wasn't. I knew him, and I didn't."

"I am the storyteller," said Hamza. "Do not taunt *me* with riddles. Explain your contradictions."

"Han Zongwan's testimony exists in the form of a letter, written and signed by him. As soon as I saw it, I knew who he was. I know that handwriting as well as I know my own. The letter of Han Zongwan was written by Shu himself."

"Shu wrote a letter accusing himself of the crime?"

"Yes."

"But why?"

Li Du dropped his eyes to the shadows on the table. "I returned to Beijing with the belief in Shu's innocence," he said. "Which I thought meant that he was not in the library with the conspirators that night. I was wrong. He *was* in the library. I think it was Shu, not the fictional Han Zongwan, who witnessed the meeting, and who saw the ninth man. I think Shu wrote the letter in order to conclude the investigation before the identity of that man could be discovered. I think Shu implicated himself in order to protect that man."

"Possible, perhaps," said Hamza. "But what could have induced him to make such a sacrifice?"

It was the question Li Du pondered during sleepless hours of the night, while listening to the clerics chanting sutras in the temple halls. He didn't have an answer.

"It is clear to me," Hamza went on, "as clear, as I have heard you say, as scallions on tofu, that if this ninth conspirator exists, you must find him and speak with him."

"That was also my conclusion," said Li Du. "I devoted months to the search. Unfortunately, every path I followed led to one of those gray walls you say are too abundant within the capital."

Hamza, inspired by wine to a literal interpretation, shook his head. "No wonder you didn't find him, wandering through alleys and walking into walls."

Li Du's voice remained grave, but there was an amused twinkle in his eye. "The paths to which I refer are not made of dirt and stone, but of paper and ink. Each of the eight assassins who died on the night of the attack had deep ties to the Ming, some better obscured than others. But I was looking for something else they had in common. I was looking for a person. Finally, six months ago, I found him. His name is *Feng Liang*."

"Ah," said Hamza, leaning forward in anticipation. In the dark, the enunciation of the name seemed to conjure a presence at the table with them. Li Du nodded. "The first mention of him I read was in the employment record of one of the conspirators, who had served for a year on the Council of Princes and High Officials. Feng Liang was on the list of officials who were also members at that time. His name remained in my memory, but I would never have thought to pursue it, had I not encountered it again in the records of a second conspirator, a man who had published a well-received poem on the subject of his pilgrimage to Mount Tai in the company of a good friend. The friend was named—"

"Feng Liang," finished Hamza.

"Yes. But I was so tangled in the documentation that the coincidence did not attract more than a moment of my attention. This changed when I encountered Feng Liang's name in the records associated with a third conspirator, who had for some years occupied a place on the Examiner Selection Committee, along with six other scholars, among them Feng Liang. It was then that I began to search for his name in connection with each of the conspirators. With the exception of Shu, he knew them all.

"So I began to investigate Feng himself. He was born in Gansu to a scholarly family. He came to the capital to take the exams, attained high scores, and chose to remain in Beijing. He served on various advisory and academic committees within the palace, and tutored several of the princes. Over the past nine years, he has retreated into a solitary existence, which is not an unusual decision for a scholar of his age. To the casual observer, he is a successful man who has decided to spend the rest of his life working on his collection of books in peace and quiet."

"In that case," said Hamza, "why couldn't you go and speak to him?"

"I tried, but was unsuccessful. First I wrote to him, but received no answer. Then I went to his manor, but was not admitted. He leaves only to attend meetings of the Examiner Selection Committee, on which he still serves, and occasionally to peruse the palace book market. This is held in a public square dense with soldiers, and is not the place to discuss treason, no matter how many years ago it occurred. That is when I had the idea to approach him directly with a book of immense worth. The trouble was that I had nothing here of sufficient value to tempt him. Now, thanks to you, I do."

Hamza bowed his head in acknowledgment of Li Du's gratitude. "So you wish to ask two questions of the reclusive Feng.

First, was he in the library that night? Second, does he know why Shu died? Tell me, if you learn that Feng was involved in the conspiracy, what will you do?"

"I don't want vengeance," said Li Du. "I don't want any more deaths. I only want to understand."

Hamza considered this for some moments. "The wine is gone," he said finally, turning the final bottle upside down. He looked up at the sky. "And what if he knows nothing, after all? Will you stop?"

"What do you mean?"

"You do not have to live like a mouse in a temple." Hamza gestured into the darkness, toward the hill topped by the glazed tile kiln. "You are now a valued employee of the North Borough Office. Once a month, on sunlit afternoons, you teach Shu's grandchildren the proper order of brushstrokes and consistency of ink. Are you tempted, now, to let the past fall away?"

Li Du thought back to his arrival in Beijing two years earlier. The decision to return had been clear, but the experience of it had been more difficult than he had anticipated. He had known that his house had been sold, and that his wife had left. He was not surprised when he learned that his aunts and uncles and cousins, with whom he had never been close, had long ago closed the gap left by his absence. But he had not known that the library would be gone, and in those early weeks, he had been overwhelmed and lost. Then he had received a letter from Shu's daughter, inviting him to visit. Mei and Cao Yun had been the first to offer him friendship, and he had seen, in their family, the happiness that had once belonged to Shu.

Returning through a wine-blurred mist to the inn courtyard, he shook his head. "You misunderstand why I come to Mentougou," he said. "It is not a reprieve from my task. It is a reminder of it."

Chapter 18

Li Du arrived at the North Borough Office on the following afternoon to find Chief Inspector Sun pacing in his office, wearing only pants and a thin cotton robe. The room was redolent of ginger and garlic. The floor was papered with sodden documents spread out to dry.

"Noodles," said Sun.

Li Du nodded. "Brought from Qi's restaurant?"

Sun took a seat at his desk, looking profoundly aggrieved. "You know how generous Qi is with his portions. Of course the entire contents of the bowl were emptied just as I was preparing to go see Magistrate Yin. I've sent Ding to bring a change of robes from my residence. How was your journey to Mentougou?"

Sun nodded distractedly through Li Du's account of his interview with Ji Daolong. "So the owner of the Glazed Tile Factory could offer no real insight into the unexpected death of his childhood friend," he said, when Li Du had finished. "But, after all, we did not have high hopes that he would."

"No," said Li Du. "I was surprised, though, at how little he knew, given how close Lady Ai believed them to be."

Sun stared broodingly at his desk, which gleamed with the oily residue of soup. "Magistrate Yin has summoned me to his offices because he believes Hong's confession is imminent. As soon as we obtain that confession, this matter will be resolved, and we will be able to return our attention to more welcome tasks."

Li Du knew that the welcome tasks to which Sun referred were official meetings accompanied by expensive food, with the space between them occupied by the usual administrative busywork. Repetition never bored the chief inspector. Rather, it reassured him. With an effort, Li Du repressed an urge to bring up the quote from *The Bitter Plum* again. He was Sun's assistant, not his supervisor. "I wondered," he said, "if you happened to see my request to leave early today in order to attend my aunt's birthday celebration. I understand if, given the situation, you would prefer me to remain here, but—"

"Of course you must attend," said Sun. His face broke into a genuine smile, the one he wore when the world seemed to him to be operating as it should. "I am happy to see you making more of an effort to reacquaint yourself with your relations. When you spend all your hours here, or in that old temple, I worry you might have wandered alone for too long away from civilization. I will—"

He was interrupted by a clatter of hooves. "At last," he said. He stood up, crossed the room, and, clearly self-conscious of his thin robe, opened the door a crack so that he could see outside. Then he gestured urgently for Li Du to join him. Li Du saw Ding, a clerk whose naturally gaunt features had become decidedly haggard with the approach of the examinations, which he was registered to take for the first time. Ding stood at the center of the courtyard, pale and out of breath, carrying robes of dark silk draped over his outstretched arms. But he was not the only one who had just entered. Behind him were two mounted soldiers. A third man sat slumped on a horse between them, his bowed head obscuring his face.

"Gendarmerie soldiers," muttered Sun. "Go outside, send Ding into my office, and stay with them until I am presentable."

Li Du obeyed. The Gendarmerie was arguably the most powerful law enforcement entity in the capital. While their soldiers were concentrated mostly in the Inner City, their jurisdiction also extended into the Outer City. Li Du greeted the soldiers, who now stood on the cobblestones, their charge between them. The man wore rough laborer's clothes. His hair was stiff with clay dust. His lips were pressed tightly together, making the skin around them bloodless and white. Li Du recognized him at once. It was Zou Anlin, the overseer at the Black Tile Factory.

"Is this the office investigating the recent murder at the Black Tile Factory?" asked the shorter soldier, whose authoritative bearing proclaimed him the higher ranking of the two. The other stood quietly, his stern presence alone serving to affirm and amplify what his partner said.

"It is," said Li Du. "And I know who this man is. Why have you brought him here?"

At that moment, the door of Sun's office opened. Sun stepped onto the veranda, looking much more the part of the competent administrator in robes of deep blue that fell to a richly embroidered hem. But for the aroma of broth wafting from his open door, the mishap might not have happened. He summoned them all to the reception room. Ding emerged from the office, still recovering from his rushed errand, and hurried across the courtyard to join Mi, Yuan, and the other clerks where they had gathered at the open door of their building.

The two soldiers, while respectful, held themselves somewhat aloof. Unlike the Green Standard soldiers who were available for use by the chief inspectors of the Outer City boroughs, the soldiers of the Gendarmerie reported to their own commandant, whose authority in matters of city security far outweighed Sun's. "We were patrolling the Outer City alleys after being relieved from our posts at You'an Gate," explained the soldier. "At the market, we were approached by a vendor who said that a laborer from the Black Tile Factory had just tried to exchange a large amount of silver for copper coins. We identified the man. A search of his possessions yielded this. It did not take us long to convince him to admit that he stole it."

The soldier made a sign to his companion, who stepped forward and set down on a table a bag of pale leather, drawn closed with a blue string. It settled, heavy and clinking, across the empty surface. The soldier loosened the string and allowed the soft leather to fall open. Li Du and Sun leaned over it. Inside, silver ingots gleamed.

It was Li Du who looked up first, and caught for a moment the expression of frustrated longing on Zou's thin, pinched features.

"We are taking him to the Gendarmerie to await trial for theft," said the soldier. "But as we have all been informed of the murders, we brought him here first, in case you have questions for him."

"A courtesy I greatly appreciate," said Sun. He examined the contents of the bag. "It looks like sixty taels to me."

"Fifty-eight," said the soldier.

Li Du took his turn to look. The sizes and shapes of the ingots made their values easy to ascertain. There were four large ingots worth ten taels each, and a collection of small one-tael pieces. It was not a vast sum, but it could feed six monks for a year. To a poor laborer, it would appear a fortune.

"A bag of this description containing approximately this much silver was seen in the possession of the male victim," said Sun. He addressed Zou. "What explanation can you offer?"

Zou cringed, the longing gone from a face that now looked simply frightened. "I found it," he said in a voice that was almost a croak.

"Where did you find it?" asked Sun.

The words came in a rush. "That morning, when I arrived at the factory, I did go into the office. I went inside, and I saw them."

"You saw the bodies," said Sun.

"Yes. I saw them dead. I will tell you the truth now. I found the bodies first. I found them in the morning. Blood all over them. Blood all over the room. I am a poor man, and a weak man. I repent my deed. I saw the silver, and I took it. But I tell you, they were dead already. They had been dead for hours."

"What do you mean, you saw the silver?"

Zou clutched his arms as if he was cold. His voice was full of penitence. "I was so afraid. It was barely light outside. I thought whoever killed them might still be somewhere among the kilns. So I stayed in the room, terrified that I, too, would be attacked. Then it began to grow lighter. I could see their faces, and all the blood. I turned away, and that's when I saw the bag on the floor. You must believe that I am not, by nature, a thief, but I was so frightened that I was not myself. I opened it, and there before me was more wealth than I have ever seen before. You must understand, I was at the mercy of temptation. I have always been a poor man. I told myself, *What harm could it do them now?*"

"So you took it," said Sun. "Did you take anything else? Did you alter anything within the room?"

Zou shook his head vigorously. "Nothing."

"Well?" asked the shorter soldier. "Do you believe his story, or should we inform the commandant that this man should be charged with murder as well as theft?"

"Murder?" Zou's eyes were wide. "No, I'm not a murderer." He turned a beseeching expression to Li Du and Sun. "I beg you to explain to them. I took the silver. I accept that I must be punished. I will reform. But I cannot have murdered them. Ask the monk who tends the shrine at the lodge. Ask the cook in the kitchen. I ate with my countrymen, as I do every night. And Old Gao can tell you I never left my bed."

The soldiers looked to Chief Inspector Sun for confirmation. "It's true," he said slowly. "The murders took place during the night. This man has an alibi from sundown to sunup."

"You're sure?"

Sun nodded. "We've confirmed it."

The shorter soldier shrugged, pulled the strings of the bag closed, and picked it up. "That is fortunate for him. In that case, I will inform my superior not to charge him with murder. He will await trial for theft in the Gendarmerie cells."

Chapter 19

Hamza was waiting for Li Du at the place they had prearranged, a pagoda situated in a desolate corner of the East Borough. Upon reaching the top of the dilapidated, winding staircase, Li Du found the storyteller absorbed in contemplation of a column that had once been painted with a pattern of phoenixes. Though reduced to faded impressions of their former selves, the birds were still perceptible, frozen in ghostly orbits.

"I cannot read this language," said Hamza, pointing to a line of graffiti over a bird's wing. "What lost civilization has left its messages on your empire's ruins?"

"It's not a lost civilization," Li Du replied, when he had caught his breath. "It's Korean. This pagoda, despite its current state of disrepair, is listed as an attraction in the Korean guidebook to this city. No one knows why, but the result is that every emissary and traveler from that country asks to visit it."

From their vantage point in the top room of the pagoda, they saw little that could be called scenic. Brown marshes stretched between courtyard walls and alleys, shadowed by the great square watchtower that rose from the city's southeast corner. "A dubious attraction," said Hamza. "I myself intend to visit the golden tortoises of Rainbow Bridge. A bridge with such a name cannot fail to be impressive. Are there many golden tortoises?"

Li Du suspected that Hamza would be crestfallen to discover that the golden tortoises were inanimate. "The bridge offers a fine view of the imperial lakes," he offered as he started back down the stairs. "I used to cross it daily on my way to the library." *The library.* The word produced its usual silent echo in Li Du's mind.

Hamza followed him. "Did the chief inspector believe you were going to celebrate your aunt's birthday?"

Since Hamza's arrival, Li Du had tried to keep the intended visit to Feng Liang tucked safely within his thoughts, where it would not influence his expression, or inspire a comment that could rouse the suspicions of Sun or one of the clerks. Now, as he drew closer to the conversation that could end his search for the answers he had come to Beijing to uncover, he found himself almost unable to remember the North Borough Office, or to recall the role he played there. "Sun has been encouraging me to become reacquainted with my relations," he said in a distracted tone. "He believed me because it pleased him to think I was taking his advice."

They exited the pagoda onto a lane eroded by rain and the wheels of laden carts. Li Du halted. "I should go alone," he said. "I am not certain it will be safe."

Hamza stopped too, and turned to him with his dark eyebrows raised and his arms crossed over his chest. "That is why I am coming with you. Do you think he will receive us?"

Li Du patted his satchel, reassuring himself that the *Commentary* was still there. "If he is truly a book collector, he won't be able to refuse."

From the outside, Feng Liang's manor seemed uninhabited. Wisteria cascaded over the walls into the street, living vines entwined with dead ones. Brittle leaves littered the stone manes of lions positioned on either side of the entrance. Li Du's knock on the faded red door was met with silence.

"It is possible only spirits live here," said Hamza. He patted one of the vines, sending a tremor up through the tangle and producing a dry, rattling hiss.

Catching movement out of the corner of his eye, Li Du turned in time to see a man in a plain blue robe retreat into the doorway of a small temple on the other side of the lane. Li Du wondered if it was only his imagination that leant an air of furtiveness to the slim figure stepping backwards out of sight. With a creak and a whisper of vines, the door of the manor swung inward, interrupting his speculations.

A servant stood before them. Tall and broad-shouldered, he conveyed an impression of immovability in his gray robes, like the rock face of a mountain gorge steadfastly resisting the erosive power of a river.

Li Du tilted his head back to meet the servant's eyes. "We are here to speak to Feng Liang."

The man bowed. It was a polite bow, but not one that implied servility. "If you are from the Examiner Selection Committee, you may give your message to me, and I will convey it to my master. Feng Liang does not admit visitors to his private residence."

"We are not from Examiner Selection Committee," said Li Du. "We are here because we have a book he may be interested in purchasing for his collection."

"Then I must ask you, respectfully, to depart," replied the servant. "Feng Liang gives his business only to the most exclusive dealers in rare volumes, not to unknown peddlers." He stepped back, preparing to close the door.

Li Du spoke quickly. "Tell your master that we have brought a Song edition of *The Commentary on the Book of Rites.* If he is not interested, we will trouble him no further. I am confident we will have no difficulty finding another buyer. We will wait here for his answer."

The servant hesitated. Then, with another perfunctory bow, he departed. Standing once again in front of the closed door, Li Du and Hamza exchanged glances. "I'd say he is more of a guard than a servant," said Hamza in a hushed tone. "I understand better why you required a treasure before you could approach this place. Your quarry takes his seclusion seriously."

"If an easier way had presented itself, I would not have asked you to undertake such an arduous errand," Li Du replied.

"Perhaps," said Hamza. "Though you might have made the journey to retrieve the book yourself. I think you must have missed my company. Why do you keep looking over your shoulder?"

"Hm?" Li Du returned his attention to Hamza. "I saw a man go into that temple. For a moment, I had the impression that he was watching us."

Frowning, Hamza crossed the lane to the temple, and peered inside. After a moment, he returned. "There *is* a man there, but he is lighting candles at the altar with every appearance of devotion."

The manor door opened. The same servant appeared, his stance and expression unchanged from when they had first seen him. "I will escort you to Feng Liang," he said, and stepped aside so that they could enter. They followed him through an outer courtyard, which contained no plants other than wisteria that smothered the walls, and weeds that bristled between worn cobblestones. The long halls on either side appeared unused. Rusted padlocks hung from rusted handles, below which ran verandas coated in dust and grit. The air held an odor of sweet decay, which Li Du traced to a tall date tree outside the walls. Its fruit had fallen onto the flagstones, where it was slowly rotting. In the center of the second courtyard, a maid tended a stove while two more servants in gray sat on either side of a bucket of water, cleaning and preparing chicken intestines.

They continued into a third courtyard, which was dominated by a two-story building. An exception to the general theme of disuse, it had a clean veranda, and freshly painted doors with polished handles and hinges. The servant led them inside, through a sparsely furnished parlor, and up a staircase to another room. Upon entering, Li Du could not prevent his gaze from lingering on the book cabinets arranged and labeled with obsessive precision. Colored according to subject matter, each label boasted an exhaustive list of titles and editions. Within the open cabinets, books in boxes of rich silk returned Li Du's look with the contented superiority of treasures fully cognizant of their worth.

An elderly man awaited them beside a table of black lacquer inlaid with gold. He was frail, his face stretched taut over a sharp brow and high cheekbones. His robes were parchment white. The sash tied low at his hips emphasized his diminutive frame. Despite the warm weather, a gray fox fur rested across his shoulders. He assessed their features without recognition.

"I am Feng Liang." He had a raspy, whispering voice that sounded like snow being brushed from a marble balustrade. "My servant tells me you have a Song edition of the *Commentary*. Is it with you now?"

"It is," Li Du replied. From his satchel, he withdrew the book Hamza had brought to Beijing. It was wrapped tightly in silk. A few grains of desert sand still clung to it. He could feel them pressing into his fingertips.

The old man regarded the package with undisguised skepticism. "You understand I must examine it carefully," he said. "To satisfy myself that it is not a forgery."

"Of course," said Li Du.

They sat down at the table. The servant, obeying instructions from Feng, procured a folded piece of pristine white silk, which he proceeded to smooth over the table in front of his master, before stepping back into the shadows of the book cabinets.

"May I?" asked Feng.

Li Du handed him the book. Feng unwound the cloth from it and set the volume on the length of silk before him. He examined the cover before carefully lifting it. His expression remained skeptical. *But his hands betray him*, Li Du thought, seeing them tremble as they caressed the edge of the first page, assessing its thickness and texture.

"A Lin'an edition," Feng murmured. He leaned forward until his nose almost touched the paper, and inhaled. "Fragrant ink, thinly applied. Correct script. Elegant, archaically bold." He straightened and continued his examination in silence. After a while, he looked up, pinning Li Du with his eyes. "Where did you obtain this?"

"It was given to me a long time ago."

"You are a collector?"

"No, but I was a librarian once."

"Were you? Tell me, then, in your opinion, what wood is best for the building of book cabinets?"

Li Du was startled, but the answer came easily. "Dealwood from Kiangsi, cypress from Sichuan, or gingko."

"Why not rosewood?"

"Because it absorbs moisture."

"What is the best way to prevent white ants?"

"A paste of pulverized charcoal."

"How many lines per page are there in the Song edition of the Seventeen Histories?"

"Nine, and eighteen characters to the line."

"And in a Tang edition of the Thirteen Classics?"

"There are no existing Tang editions of the Thirteen Classics."

Feng Liang gave a thin smile, and sighed. "But what would we sacrifice to obtain one? I hope you will forgive an old recluse his little tests. I thought you might be a common thief. I do not wish to own a stolen book, though in this case, I would almost make an exception." He had not taken his eyes from the text. Now he lifted them to Li Du. "Please know that you have my deepest sympathy. I will not ask what dire circumstances could induce you to part with such a book as this. I will only ask your price."

"The book is not for sale."

Feng had dropped his eyes once more to the volume. Now he raised them again. "Please, let us not treat this object as if it were a common market trinket. There is no need to haggle. I will pay what you ask, but I must have it." There was a tremor in his voice.

Li Du regarded the other man with quiet gravity. "I brought the book because it was the only way to gain admittance to your home. I have questions I believe only you can answer. If you agree to do so, the *Commentary* is yours."

The old man stared. He seemed baffled. "What subject could merit such a charade, performed for an infirm recluse who lives with only his books for company? What answers do you think I have that would be worth such a treasure?"

Li Du hesitated. "This man is my associate," he said, indicating Hamza. "He knows all that I know. Unless you can say the same of your attendant, I suggest you dismiss him. The matter I wish to discuss is private."

There was a period of silence while Feng Liang considered this, studying Li Du's face, wearing a look of wary curiosity on his own. Finally, he addressed his servant. "We old men have long histories," he said. "Filled with small indiscretions we would prefer to forget. I will hear what my visitors have to say alone. Do not go far. I will call if I require assistance."

The servant bowed and departed. The three of them listened, without speaking, to his steps across the floor, and to the straining creak of wood as he descended the stairs. After a while, silence returned.

"I would like to know to whom I am speaking," said Feng.

"My name is Li Du. This is Hamza—"

"A storyteller by vocation," Hamza supplied.

Feng's eyes flickered in Hamza's direction, but his attention remained on Li Du. "I do not know you," he said. "What is it you think you know about me?"

Li Du took a steadying breath, knowing that every word he spoke mattered. He had no leverage over the man who now fixed him with a look of penetrating intelligence. He had to rely on the power that came from asserting with confidence what he only guessed to be true. "In the forty-first reigning year, an attempt was made on the life of the Emperor," he began.

"That is known to everyone in the capital," said Feng. "They were Ming conspirators who wanted to restore the throne to the Ming prince hidden in the south. They were captured and executed."

"Not all of them," said Li Du. "*You* escaped."

"I?"

Without taking his eyes from the other man, Li Du nodded once. "I know you were one of them."

Dense creases formed on Feng's forehead as he lifted his gray eyebrows. "You are mistaken. What led you to such a conclusion?"

"I consulted records," said Li Du, undeterred by Feng's denial. "Hundreds of records, in search of a connection between the conspirators. You were that connection. You knew them all."

When Feng did not reply, Li Du continued, his words coming faster. "I am here on behalf of an innocent man. I am here because I want to know why Shu died for a crime he did not commit." He stopped, a little out of breath. "I want to know why Shu died in your place."

"*Li Du.*" Feng uttered the name in a long exhale. "The exiled librarian. Of course. You were Shu's friend." Dawning comprehension seemed to ease the tension from his face.

"Yes," was all Li Du could manage.

"But what are you saying?" asked Feng. "That Shu was falsely accused?"

"I think he gave his life to protect one of the conspirators."

"And you think I was that person."

Li Du made an effort to speak, and found he could not. He had a growing sense that something was wrong. The eyes of the man looking at him were filled not with guilt, or anger, but with an expression closer to pity. Li Du was relieved and grateful when the sound of Hamza's voice filled the silence. "My friend is not here for vengeance," said the storyteller, echoing the words Li Du had spoken to him at the inn. "He is here for the truth. What harm can it do you now to give it to him?"

Once more, Feng lapsed into a long silence. The wrinkled eyelids shuttered, and his face went still. Just as Li Du was beginning to think the old man might not intend to speak again, he did. "Shu was your teacher, wasn't he?"

"Yes," said Li Du. "My teacher, and my friend."

"I understand," said Feng. "Imagine, then, what it was like to lose seven friends, where you lost but one." His eyes opened wider, and his gaze roamed the shelves surrounding them. "Having survived the pain of such a loss, is it any surprise that I choose to remain here alone with my books, and allow the threads that bound me to the companions of my younger years to fray and separate?" Feng placed his fingertips on the white silk beneath the book, resting them there so that his fingers formed a cage around the volume. Slowly, he slid the silk and its precious burden across the table to Li Du. "As loath as I am to relinquish it, I cannot take this volume from you, for you offered it in exchange for answers I cannot give."

"I don't understand," whispered Li Du.

"I wasn't one of them," said Feng. "I swear it to you. I knew nothing of the conspiracy until it became public knowledge, and if Shu was indeed innocent, your words today are the first intimation I've had of it." He lifted his fingers from the silk, leaving the book in front of Li Du on the table.

Li Du barely glanced at it. "But if you knew them, if you were friends with them, why weren't you exiled, as I was?"

"I was not in the capital," said Feng. "If you consult these records you speak of further, I am sure you could find proof of it. I was with my family in Gansu, and had been for several months before the attempt was made. I was there when I received the news of it. One never knows which way the imperial eye will turn. As it happened, it never fixed on me. I am no traitor, though I admit I wept for my friends."

"Did you know what they intended?"

"I never suspected it."

"And Shu?"

Feng shook his head. "I saw his name on the list of the accused. That is all." He sighed. "I stayed away for more than a year. When I at last returned, I found myself changed. I no longer took pleasure in the city, as I once had. I wanted only to be left alone, and I found comfort only in my books."

Disappointment swept through Li Du. He had come to the center of the labyrinth, and found only another wall.

Chapter 20

Your book," said Hamza. They were some distance from the manor, and had stopped within sight of a textile market. Occupying a wide intersection, it overflowed into the surrounding alleys, enlivening them with brilliant bolts of cloth, rolls of thread, and browsing customers.

Li Du took the book, wrapped once more in its silk, and returned it wordlessly to his satchel. "I think you would have left it behind, had I not retrieved it," Hamza continued. "And for all the pathos of the solitary, haunted collector, I am not certain he would have stopped you. Did you see the way his hands shook when he touched it, and seized when he tried to let it go?"

Recognizing that Hamza was trying to distract him, Li Du made an attempt to emerge from the corrosive cloud that was settling over him, fraying thoughts and fading memories. He heard his own voice as if from a distance. "Devoted collectors, when they see a book they want, cannot rest until they possess it. They are known to pawn the clothes on their backs, if necessary."

"I would not want to desire anything so much," declared Hamza. He seemed relieved that Li Du had spoken. "I am reminded," he went on, "of a time I endeavored to cross a vast bog. I was a less experienced traveler than I am now. Unwisely, I began the journey on a sunny morning. With delight, I followed paths of yellow asphodel, cloudy cottongrass, and pink sundew that spread its glistening tentacles across the ground before me. But daylight soon departed, and took the paths with it. The air grew cold. Dim spirits, composed of blue light, appeared above the dark grasses and unseen pools, beckoning for me to follow them. I thought I must freeze or drown, until one of these spirits came near enough for conversation.

"I set myself the task of discovering what, beyond leading me to my death, this spirit desired. After a time, it revealed to me that it had long wished to meet the moon, whose glow it tried so ceaselessly to imitate. *Ah, I said, but this is a fortunate coincidence, for I am a personal friend of the moon.* I persuaded the spirit to, against the instincts of its kind, guide me safely through the bog. In return, I promised it an introduction to the moon."

Li Du, who had only been half listening, caught the look of concern on Hamza's face. He tried to look curious. "What happened when you could not give it what it wanted?"

Hamza's face brightened. "I may have tricked many a monster and demon who meant me harm, but I never make hollow promises. I *am* acquainted with the moon, and I *did* make the introduction. But that is a story for another time." His tone grew serious. "What will you do now?"

They began to walk again. As they entered the market, patterned silks and brocades stood out in vivid relief against the grays and browns of the East Borough. At the far side of the intersection, several sedan chairs waited for business, their bearers dozing in their seats. "I will return to my place of employment," said Li Du, indicating the sedan chairs. "And you will visit the Rainbow Bridge, if that is still your intention."

Hamza frowned. "But what will do you regarding your—" His voice dropped to a whisper. "—your investigation?"

Li Du stared unseeingly at the colors surrounding them. "Maybe the truth is lost," he murmured. "Maybe Shu—" He couldn't finish the sentence.

"Nonsense," said Hamza. "Someone knows."

Li Du saw in his mind the room in the library where the conspirators had met, and the empty table at its center. "I begin to think that everyone who knows is dead."

A golden cast moved across Hamza's features, followed by blue and purple, as he was lit through gossamer scarves caught in a breeze above them. He smiled. "It is not impossible to ask questions of those who have passed into other worlds."

Li Du returned the smile with the most genuine one he could produce. "In your wanderings today," he said before he turned to the borough office, "do not forget that when the drums set the night watch, the gates of the city close. It is not a rule to take lightly. The guards will not allow you through after dark, and they will not respond well to being asked for favors."

Chief Inspector Sun had not yet returned from the Inner City. Unchallenged by the clerks, Li Du went to his desk, put on his spectacles, and immersed himself in the assignments that had accumulated over the past several days. The bulk of the documents on his desk were minor complaints submitted to the office by local families and businesses. Li Du's only responsibility was to review the complaints for clerical errors. Those containing errors would be returned to the parties that had issued them with instructions to make the corrections before resubmitting the complaint.

The body of the plea must be limited to three lines and no more than one hundred and forty-four words, he wrote in the margin of one complaint. *In a case concerning landed property, a copy of the deed must be included,* he wrote in another. When he had finished reviewing the twentieth complaint, a sizeable stack remained. He removed his spectacles and rubbed his eyes. He could hear voices from the other side of the courtyard. The clerks were concluding their work for the day. Plans were being made for dinner and entertainment. Brush handles were clicking against stone as their owners tapped water from the rinsed bristles. Li Du stood up, put a portion of tea leaves into his cup, and went outside in search of hot water.

Mi was standing beside the brazier, perusing a document. "The water isn't boiled yet," he said absently to Li Du.

Yuan emerged from the office, carrying his own cup, and took a seat on the edge of the veranda. "What is it you're reading?" he asked Mi.

It was the end of the day, and they were both bored. Mi shrugged. "The Ministry of Punishments has updated the list of exiles for the borough offices to compare to housing records. No new names here, though."

Yuan lifted dreamy eyes to the sky. Then he placed a finger between his black felt hat and his forehead and scratched vigorously. "I envy the exiles," he sighed. "Because they have no rank, they are free not to wear hats. If I were an exile, my paintings of bamboo would become famous. *How brilliant*, people would say. *He paints bamboo because, like the exile, it bends without breaking.* I would walk through the mountains with an attractive walking stick. Behind me, my attendant would walk with my zither. Sometimes the wind would strum a tune across its strings, inspiring me to write a poem—"

"You lose a great deal when your connection to other people is severed. I do not think you would find the experience as pleasurable as you imagine." The words were spoken before Li Du could consider them.

The two clerks turned to him with startled curiosity. It was a tone Li Du had never used in the North Borough Office before. "I apologize," said Yuan. "You never speak of your exile. We weren't even sure that it was true. Is it also true that your sentence was lifted because you performed a service for the Emperor?"

Feeling his invisibility beginning to crack, Li Du was preparing a vague denial when a pounding at the door claimed their attention. The three of them crossed the courtyard to the entrance, as the guard stationed there admitted a mounted messenger. Remaining on his horse, which dipped its head and flipped its mane impatiently, the messenger handed a rolled missive to Li Du. He opened it and began to read.

"What is it?" asked Mi. The surprise on Li Du's face must have been evident, given the urgent tone of the question.

"It's from the chief inspector. He went to the magistrate's office to interview Hong Wenbin."

"We know," said Yuan. "They were going to try to convince him to confess. Is he refusing?"

Li Du had rolled up the scroll again and was staring at the kettle of water that had just begun to boil.

"Well?" demanded Mi. "What did Hong say?"

"He didn't say anything," murmured Li Du. "Hong is dead."

Chapter 21

Magistrate Yin himself addressed the employees of the North Borough Office on the following morning. His robes proclaimed his rank with an embroidered square affixed to his chest. A silver pheasant, crowned with a proud swoop of blue, rose from a rainbow-colored wave toward a red sun. For Magistrate Yin, an uncomfortable-looking man whose demeanor conveyed no natural authority, the trappings of status were of particular advantage. Flanked by soldiers, he stood on the edge of the veranda outside Chief Inspector Sun's office door, squinting into the morning glare.

"Gossip will not be tolerated," he said. The silence in the courtyard absorbed his voice rather than enhancing it. "I have come here, in person, despite the numerous demands on my time, to communicate the facts to you. I expect an end to frivolous speculation and idle chatter on the subject of the sordid incident at the Black Tile Factory. As the edict instructs, it is your duty, as officials, to *cultivate peace and concord in your neighborhoods in order to illustrate harmony and benignity.* Should any report to the contrary reach me, I will hold every clerk here responsible. Most of you hope to advance to ministry positions or magistracies. I would advise you not to disappoint me at this tender time in your careers."

Li Du observed the clerks striving to outdo each other in their performances of dutiful attention. Their shoulders were drawn back, their faces solemn, and their eyes filled with affirmation of the magistrate's words. Chief Inspector Sun was standing just behind the magistrate, staring at the courtyard cobblestones with an attitude of grim endurance.

"As I am sure you have all heard by now, the primary suspect in the case, Hong Wenbin, took his own life yesterday afternoon. Taking into account the nearly conclusive evidence against him, his suicide may be considered a clear admission of guilt. The investigation of the death of Madam Hong and Pan is concluded. My office will take over the responsibility of ensuring a peaceful reconciliation between the families involved."

Magistrate Yin paused and surveyed his audience. His lips were pursed, as if he wanted to scold someone but could not decide where to direct his criticism. Failing to identify a target, he addressed the group again. "This unusual and wasteful episode of violence in our peaceful capital was caused, in part, by excessive consumption of wine. Let this serve as a reminder of the dangers of dissipation and excess. Chief Inspector Sun has been instructed to make this the subject of next month's lecture on moral behavior."

Sun straightened to attention as the magistrate's head rotated on its thin neck to look at him. "Yes, sir," said Sun.

Nodding in approval of his own handling of the situation, Magistrate Yin began a slow descent from the veranda into the courtyard. He was obliged to lift the hem of his robe slightly, and Li Du wondered if he kept his hems long in order to emphasize the point that it was not his job to trudge through puddles in the Outer City.

Watching him, Li Du felt a quiet, disheartening sense of finality. For Magistrate Yin, Hong's death was a convenient end to a case that might have proved troublesome. Sun had given Li Du a succinct account of what had happened. The chief inspector had gone to see Magistrate Yin on the previous day. Up to that point, Hong had continued to insist that he had not committed murder. Magistrate Yin, convinced of his guilt, felt that Hong simply needed further reassurance that the law would protect him. He and Sun had formulated a strategy to elicit a confession, then sent a soldier to retrieve Hong from his cell. The soldier had found Hong hanging from a roof beam by his own sash. No one was reported to have entered the cell since the guards had checked it on the previous evening, at which point Hong was alive. There was no evidence of harm to the body beyond the harm that Hong had, apparently, inflicted on himself. The investigation of the Black Tile Factory murders had reached its conclusion.

"Magistrate Yin." The magistrate was almost to the courtyard door when Li Du's voice stopped him. He turned, his nostrils flared in disapproval.

Li Du dropped into a low bow. "I apologize, sir. I have been assisting the chief inspector with the case. I wish to ask, humbly, by what day you expect the report of our investigation to be delivered to you?"

"Ah," said the magistrate. Li Du saw him search for an authoritative answer to a question he had not expected to be asked. "If they are ready, you may give your notes to me now. My clerks will revise and recopy them for the official record of the incident."

Maintaining an expression of the utmost deference, Li Du went on carefully. "If I had only a few additional days, I could ensure that the information is clearly presented, and confirm its accuracy. I would not wish to be the cause of any accusation of incompetence directed at this office, or yours, should some essential detail be left out, or some erroneous one included."

Magistrate Yin's attention turned briefly inward as he debated what would be easiest, and most advantageous to him. "Four days, then." He addressed Sun, who had joined them. "You understand I want no undue allocation of resources to a closed case. The eyes of the palace are on the boroughs as the examinations approach. There will be additional Green Standard soldiers assigned temporarily to the most crowded intersections. I want you present at their training this afternoon. In addition, the review of the sentry post locations is behind schedule, and the outer wall of the Altar of Agriculture needs repainting. Contact the Ministry of Rites about it. And, most important, keep the examination candidates who are staying in the North Borough under control. We don't want any incidents this year."

Chief Inspector Sun looked at Li Du over the papers and ornaments that had repopulated his desk since the misadventure with Qi's noodle soup. "Is the door closed?"

It was. Sun let out a long breath, and allowed his big, round shoulders to slump a little. "Magistrate Yin is not a bad administrator," he said. "But he likes problems that solve themselves. He always has. Present him with a solution that is tidy, and he accepts it. Hong's suicide is a very neat solution."

"Did you tell the magistrate about the note and the silver?"

"I did. He assured me that all such minor details would be examined by his clerks before the record of the case is finalized." Sun heaved a sigh. "Magistrate Yin wants to believe that the murder suspect killed himself, and that he did so because he was overcome with regret at what he had done. He wants to believe it, and he does believe it."

"And you don't?"

"I saw the body," said Sun. "It looked like suicide. But—" He lapsed into silence. Li Du, recognizing that Sun was collecting his thoughts in preparation for a longer speech, waited. "My vantage point within the administration is not a lofty one," said Sun finally. "I am not embarrassed to admit it. I enjoy my work. I have seen a great deal of this city. I am not talking about streets and buildings. I'm talking about the inner workings of it. And I will tell you this. For someone with the necessary resources, it is not difficult to make a man in a prison cell die."

"Do you think that is what happened?" asked Li Du. "That whoever killed Pan and Madam Hong arranged for her husband's death in order to bring an end to the investigation?"

Sun picked up one of the papers from his desk. Li Du guessed he was only pretending to read it. "The ministry reminds us to direct the request for the paint to the imperial household," he muttered. With an effort, he returned his attention to Li Du. "I don't know," he said. "But it doesn't matter. The conclusion of this case lies with the magistrate's office."

"Except that we still have to provide the report," said Li Du.

Sun set the letter from the ministry aside. "Yes? What do you mean?"

"I mean that, for the next four days, the case is still here in North Borough Office."

"But you cannot think it possible to uncover our own solution to this problem in four days, all under the guise of writing a report?"

"It's possible to try."

Sun's eyebrows shot up. He was looking at Li Du as if he wasn't sure whether to take him seriously. "You understand that I am a subordinate of the magistrate. I can't reopen the investigation without his permission."

"You won't be reopening it. You'll be doing exactly the tasks the magistrate has assigned you, and I'll be doing what you delegate authority to me to do—completing the report."

Understanding began to dawn on Sun. "I assume," he said, "that merely in order to clarify your notes, you may be obliged to revisit the scene of the crime, in addition to resolving any points of confusion in the accounts given to us by those involved?"

"That was my assumption," said Li Du.

"And," Sun continued slowly, "should this report contain a compelling alternative explanation for the murders, and for Hong's death, the magistrate would presumably have to acknowledge it."

Li Du remained silent, waiting for Sun to decide whether to accept Li Du's plan. "You have set yourself a difficult task," said Sun. "I suggest you approach it with caution."

Chapter 22

It was another unseasonably warm day, and the narrow strips of shadow at the bases of walls were crowded with pedestrians seeking shade. As Li Du approached the Black Tile Factory, the number of people around him dwindled, most choosing alternate routes to avoid the thick gray air and choking coal smoke. He found the entrance to the factory open and unguarded, and received neither challenge nor welcome as he passed through the chaotic courtyard to the administrative office.

His knock received no reply, but he could hear movement inside. He opened the door in time to see someone scrambling from the floor to his feet, caught up in voluminous black robes. A pair of startled green eyes met his.

"Father Aveneau," said Li Du. "What are you doing?"

Quickly regaining his composure, Father Aveneau smiled, as if to suggest that they were more closely acquainted than they actually were. "I was just on my way to open the door," he said.

"You were searching for something?"

There was a short pause. Then Father Aveneau nodded. "That is precisely what I was doing." From the corner of the desk, he picked up a slim folder made from worn black vellum. "I came to retrieve this."

Li Du stepped deeper into the room, leaving the door open to let in the light. "What is it, and how did it come to be here?"

"It is simply a small collection of documents that I often carry with me," said Aveneau. "I noticed yesterday that it was missing. After a thorough search of the offices at the church, I remembered that I was carrying it that morning—the morning I came here—and had not seen it since. It occurred to me that I might have set it down, and in my distress, forgotten to pick it up again. I decided this morning to return and search for it."

Li Du cast his eyes over the room, visualizing it as it had been the day the bodies were discovered. "We made a thorough examination," he said. "I'm surprised neither the chief inspector, Doctor Wan, nor I myself noticed it."

"It had fallen," said Father Aveneau. "It was here, tucked between the desk and the wall. I had just drawn it out when you came in. If I hadn't looked for it, I'm not sure it would ever have been discovered, at least not without the desk being removed from the room."

Aveneau spoke in Latin. It was the first time Li Du had heard him communicate in a language other than Chinese. The change produced a significant alteration in his affect. His eyes, which had in the past conveyed the daunted hesitation of a man uncertain of his own meaning, now suggested that the mind animating them possessed a calm intelligence. It was a reminder, Li Du thought, never to judge a person's intellectual capacity too quickly when they are speaking in a language other than their own.

"Did you consider coming to the North Borough Office first?"

"I reasoned," said Father Aveneau smoothly, "that if you had found it, you would have mentioned it to me when you came to the South Church, the contents being so clearly indicative of their owner." He held the folder out to Li Du. "Please see for yourself."

Li Du took it. The leather was protecting a number of sheets of paper. The first few contained a neat list of Chinese words transcribed using the Latin alphabet. About half were accompanied by a translation of the word into French. It was a basic vocabulary, a list obviously intended to help a foreigner conduct business within the city.

"My command of your language remains uneven," explained Father Aveneau. "It is a modest glossary. The other pages are devoted to my equally modest exercises in illustration."

Turning the pages, Li Du saw that the remainder of them were covered in sketches. He examined the faint outlines of bridges and pagodas with interest. "This is compelling work," he said, closing the folder and handing it back to Father Aveneau.

"Merely a record," said Aveneau, taking it. "As I was told by the young painter Zou Yigui, the skill of reproducing what we see belongs to a craftsman, not an artist. All the same, I am glad to have them back." He paused, seemed about to speak again, then changed his mind and was silent.

"Father Aveneau," said Li Du. "If you know something about this case that you haven't shared, I urge you to speak to me now."

Aveneau's eyes were bright and wary, their leaf green color intensified by the purple crescents below them. "What could I know? I had never seen this factory before that day. My visit was prompted by a lightning strike, an occurrence both easily verified and entirely outside the control of man. What I mean is that I have no connection to this place, and no information to give you regarding the terrible event that occurred here."

Li Du wasn't convinced. "Your presence that morning may have been a coincidence, but I am not sure that you can say the same of your presence here today, the first day since the discovery of the bodies that there have been no soldiers posted at the entrance to the factory."

Father Aveneau began to speak. Li Du cut him off, soft-spoken but firm. "I know that it would be a risk to trust me," he said. "I understand the position of the Jesuits at court is precarious. But it is better to volunteer honesty to a sympathetic listener than to be compelled to it by an unsympathetic one. I value the presence of the Jesuits in the capital, and would not put you in the way of harm. If you know something, if you are involved in what occurred here, I ask again that you confide in me."

Aveneau attempted a smile, but it was little more than a compression of his lips. "I appreciate your sympathy to our order. Father Calmette has assured me of it. We consider it a privilege to be allowed to remain, a privilege we strive to deserve. Neither myself, nor any of my brethren, would consider withholding information from the authorities."

They were at an impasse. Father Aveneau, after deferentially asking permission, took his leave, claiming that he was obliged to host a demonstration of the self-chiming clock at the South Church. Li Du gave an inward sigh as he watched the Jesuit go. He was almost certain that the folder had not been in the room when he had been there last. Something else had prompted Aveneau's return. He hoped, for the sake of all the Jesuit fathers, that whatever it was Aveneau was hiding, it wasn't murder.

Alone in the room, Li Du took in the changes it had undergone since he had last seen it. The floor had been scrubbed, but only in the places where it had been stained with blood, so that those areas stood out from the surrounding surface. The cloth and cushions had been removed from the bed, leaving a bare slab of cheap wood beneath the carved and lacquered canopy.

He sat down at the desk and began to go through the jumble of papers piled on top of it and stuffed into its drawers. They were, almost without exception, contracts for the supply of roof tiles. The majority of the projects were for the Ministry of Rites, which was responsible for the building and maintenance of public temples, or the Ministry of Works, which was in charge of most other government-funded construction projects. The remaining contracts were either with private families, or the Imperial Household Agency, a separate entity that handled the personal expenditures of the Emperor and his relatives. They were the kind of papers that filled the city, stamped with the usual array of seals from different offices, representing level upon level of approval and adjustment. A diligent assessment yielded nothing that seemed unusual.

Li Du had been sitting at the desk for some time. He removed his spectacles and rubbed the sore bridge of his nose. When Pan Yongfa had sat in this same chair and looked at the same papers, had he felt the same weariness? Or had he seen something important within them that Li Du had not? Li Du stood up and went outside.

A group of laborers was clustered around the open mouth of a kiln, removing finished tiles from within. Among them, Li Du recognized Wei Yonghen, the man who had discovered the bodies. Li Du approached, and politely asked Wei to speak with him for a moment. Together, they moved away from the group, Wei nodding and bowing and trying surreptitiously to wipe the ash from his hands onto his grimy robe.

"The man who was just here," said Li Du. "Did he speak to anyone when he came in?"

Wei looked over Li Du's shoulder with trepidation, as if he was worried Li Du would make him return to the administrative office. "No, sir. I did notice him, but he walked across the courtyard and straight to the door of the office without speaking to anyone. We—" He gestured to the other laborers, who were observing the exchange warily. "—we were trying to decide whether one of us should offer him some tea, or ask him if he needed anything, when you yourself arrived. I am very sorry if we should have done something different."

"I am not chastising you," said Li Du. "Indeed, I am impressed to see the kilns lit and the new tiles being arranged so neatly into carts. It must be difficult to continue work, after all that has happened."

Wei's thin shoulders sagged in relief. "Oh it is, sir. To think that when I came here that day, I thought there were so many others that I wouldn't be given work." Again, his eyes flickered in the direction of the office. "But the day *after* it happened, a fourth of the hired men didn't return. And now we learn the owner has killed himself. And Zou Anlin was arrested as a thief! Even fewer came back this morning. They're afraid of spirits, as well as soldiers. Well, sir, we're doing all we can, and Hu Gongshan is a good manager."

"I was hoping to speak to Hu, if he is here."

"He's at the examination yard, sir, overseeing the installation of tiles."

"Then I will speak to him there, but perhaps you can help me. I am writing the official report of the case, and I need more details about Pan's business here at the factory. The office is filled with contracts and commissions. Unfortunately, they do not appear to have been kept in the clearest order."

Wei looked apologetic. "I don't know anything about papers," he said.

One of the other laborers had been listening, and now moved closer. "Excuse me, sir," he said, "but I could not help overhearing. If you have questions about Pan Yongfa, Hu Gongshan won't be able to answer them."

Li Du turned to him enquiringly. "What do you mean?"

"Well," said the laborer, "they never spoke. Or rather, hardly ever. Not recently, at least."

This struck Li Du as curious. "How can that be, if Hu was the kiln manager, and Pan was often here to review contracts? Was there some disagreement between them?"

Wei, looking slightly stricken by the thought that he might have facilitated some betrayal of a man he respected, tried to quiet his companion. "I'm sure there wasn't, sir! He is a good kiln manager, the best I've ever worked for, and a good man, too. We all think so."

Li Du kept his attention on the other laborer. "A clear picture of the situation is essential to an accurate report," he said gently. "It would be best for you to describe the relationship between Hu and Pan in the most honest way that you can."

The laborer nodded. Beneath the smudges of clay, his face was open and earnest. "Hu would never have disrespected an official. He is always ready to show inspectors the precautions we take against fire, and he is patient whenever there are complaints about the smoke and ash. It's just that, when *Pan* came to the factory, Hu always assigned someone else to see to what he needed. And it always seemed—"

Li Du waited patiently as the man searched for the words. The laborer gathered his thoughts. Then, as if he had found within himself a well of poetic inspiration, he spoke. "When a man walks on a path and sees a snake ahead of him, he goes a wide distance around it, just to be safe. When Pan came here, Hu was like the man who sees a snake on the path. He never went close to Pan. He just kept clear of him. He kept well clear."

Chapter 23

The southeast corner of the Inner City, in which the examination yard was situated, had taken on a carnival atmosphere.
Temporary shops, no more than skeletal wooden frames, listed under
the weight of their wares. Garlands of brushes, their handles
rattling and clicking as the breeze caught them, hung above quilts,
candles, ink stones, pots, and charms of every color and shape, all
promising good luck. Fluttering signs competed for attention:
*Examination Supplies for the Optimus! Famous Writing Brushes for
the Three Examinations! Protect Your Pages with Xu's Impermeable
Oilcloth!*

The examination yard was forbidden to candidates. Until the
morning the examination began, they could only look at the walls
surrounding it. When they did finally enter, they would be locked
inside for three days, confined to one of six thousand wooden cells.
The cells were roofless, exposed to the scrutiny of guards from
watchtowers and examiners from the sheltered comfort of elevated
pavilions. Looking at the entrance, open now only to inspectors and
to an army of laborers cleaning and renovating the cells, Li Du was
aware of a hollow feeling in his stomach unrelated to the anxieties
of recent days. He had not forgotten how frightening it had been
to face those great doors for the first time.

Looking at the crowds around him, he found it easy to distinguish the candidates from the numerous servants and family members who had accompanied them to the capital. What surprised
him was how familiar they all seemed. He might have stepped back

in time to his own examination year. Names long since forgotten returned to him as he made his way through the crowds. There was Jia, pale and unkempt, holding fifteen brushes in his hands in an agony of indecision while the shopkeeper urged him to buy them all and choose later. There was Ren, all smiles as a courtesan led him away to a discreet location. And there, surely, was Dui from the countryside, hungry and desperate, having spent in two days all the money he had brought with him for his stay in the capital. Li Du expected at any moment to see Xin, obsessively planning what food he would bring with him, Shi, fixated on a nightmare that his essays had caught fire, or Liu, making everyone around him nervous with his drawling complaints about corruption and favoritism.

Ignoring offers to predict his future, give him a night of pleasure, or double his money with a simple game of chance, Li Du circumambulated the wall, trying to stay upright as he was jostled from all sides. Just when he was beginning to despair of locating the kiln master, it occurred to him to lift his gaze above the crowds. There, he saw the smooth line of the sloping roof that adorned the wall broken by two figures standing on simple scaffolding. They were catching tiles that appeared to be flying up into their waiting hands.

Li Du made his way to them through the bustle. He found Hu Gongshan at the base of the wall, lifting tiles one by one from a cart and tossing them up to the laborers on the roof. The curved gray tiles rose through the air, following the same path each time, slowing and seeming to hover just at the level of the rooftop until they were caught. Hu's movements appeared effortless, but Li Du knew the tiles were heavy. The ability to achieve that precise trajectory every time required skill few people had.

As soon as Hu recognized Li Du, he stopped his work, wiped the sweat from his brow with a dirty sleeve, and dropped into a low bow. "Whatever you require, I will cooperate in every way," he said.

He appeared so certain that Li Du had come with news of some new disaster that Li Du felt compelled to reassure him. "You see the chief inspector has only sent his assistant," he said with a small smile. "I have come simply to clarify certain details of the case, and will not keep you long from your work, which I understand must be completed with all expediency." He nodded at the tiles, which had resumed their flight in the hands of another worker.

Hu relaxed slightly. "All has been confusion since that morning," he said. "I must keep the men working, but it is no surprise that many are afraid to return."

"Are you in charge of the factory?"

"Only until one of Hong's sons arrives," said Hu. "But both of them are grown and have positions in distant provinces. I am not an educated man. I understand clay and fire and rooftops, but I know little of contracts and commissions. And Hong did not keep his papers in good order. I am only barely succeeding in making sure that every commitment is addressed."

Li Du nodded. "I have just been at the factory trying to make sense of them."

This information did not seem to have an effect on Hu, who was lost in his own thoughts. "Seven days ago, who could have expected this?"

"Seven days?" Li Du made a quick count in his head.

Hu shook himself out of his reverie. "Seven days ago, there was a party at Hong's manor. I was thinking of that day."

Li Du tried not to let his surprise be too evident. "You were also at the literary party?"

Hu glanced down at his rough clothing with a look of embarrassment. "It *was* too fine for me," he said. "Hong would never have issued me an invitation, but I asked him if I could come. You see, I wanted to bring my son, so that he could be introduced to a higher class of citizen. I have heard it is important for examination candidates to make a good impression on examiners."

If Hu knew that the chances of any individual passing the examinations were slim, he showed no sign of applying that statistic to his own son. Li Du read in his eyes the absolute conviction that his boy would succeed. "You said just now you were thinking of that party. What made it come to mind?"

"Well, it was so elegant," said Hu. He stopped. His brow creased as he struggled to express what he meant. "I'd never been in company so refined, everyone speaking so quietly, reciting poems, all the colors as pleasing as colors in a screen. It's one thing to be out in the city, where you see—you understand—you see hard things. But in a place like that, well, you can't picture blood and death, can you?"

"Then the party did not presage murder," said Li Du. "Except, perhaps, for the content of the book. *The Bitter Plum* does not lack violence."

Hu looked down. "I am ashamed to admit that the language and style of that book were too advanced for me. My son read it easily. I saw him discussing it, as smooth as any scholar. He can finish a book faster than I can tile a roof, and when he's done, he knows every word. He'll be a brilliant magistrate one day. Take my word for it. There will be stories about him."

"I understand that Pan was an accomplished scholar," said Li Du. "He received the highest degree, with honors, at an unusually young age. Given how often you must have seen him at the factory, I imagine it occurred to you to introduce him to your son?"

A cord of tension was suddenly visible on the side of Hu's neck. Hu's expression darkened. "They were introduced once," he said.

"Did you speak to Pan at the party?"

"No, I didn't, and neither did my son. I didn't even notice Pan was there. There were many courtyards, and many guests."

Li Du persevered. "What about the day of Pan's death?"

"There was nothing unusual about it. Hong wasn't at the factory that day, so when Pan arrived, he came to me. He said he was going to review contracts in the office—ministry business. I told him he was welcome to whatever he needed, and asked him if he required anything from me. He requested some refreshment. But that was all the interaction we had. I instructed Zou to bring him wine and roasted soybeans."

"Zou Anlin? The man who was arrested for stealing silver from the scene of the crime?"

Hu nodded. "I shouldn't have hired him. I had a sense he was dishonest, but what with the unusual demands of the season, I failed to employ the usual degree of caution. I trust the silver will be returned to its rightful owner?"

"I'm sure it will be," said Li Du. "Returning to Pan's movements on the day he died, did you notice whether there were any messages delivered to him while he was at the office? Is it possible that Madam Hong visited him there?"

Hu shook his head firmly. "She couldn't have visited without my seeing her come in."

"When Pan departed, did he give any indication of his intention to return?"

"He didn't say anything about it to me."

Li Du was blunt. "It is possible that another motive existed for Pan's murder. What I need to know is whether there is something about him that has not yet been revealed to us, something that may help uncover what has been hidden. I have been told that you avoided his company. I ask you to tell me why."

Hu was silent for a long moment. "I'm not the kind of man who lies to the authorities," he said finally. "I did avoid Pan. I didn't like him, and I didn't trust him. He—"

Hu was interrupted by a commotion at the gate closest to them. There were shouts coming from inside the examination yard. Over the noise of those moving toward the scene or away from it, Li Du thought he heard the hiss of a blade being drawn from a sheath.

A man burst from the gate and ran headlong into the crowd. A soldier followed in close pursuit, sword drawn, but he stopped at the boundary created by the ring of spectators. The chase was no longer necessary. The man, in his desperate attempt to separate himself from the soldier following him, had run into three armed soldiers standing in the crowd. With his arms trapped in their grips, he was dragged back to the gate, his face a mask of horror.

Li Du could not hear what he said, but he shook his head wildly, sobbing and trying to free his arms, as if he wanted to use them to plead his case.

Two more soldiers emerged from the yard, another man between them. The man's head drooped in despairing capitulation. As Li Du watched, the crowd knotted around the scene. By the time it shifted again, the soldiers and their captives were gone.

"Cheaters," said a voice nearby. It belonged to a peddler who had come from the site, pulling his cart behind him.

"What were they doing?" asked Hu.

"Trying to bury answers inside," answered the peddler. "Old trick. I haven't heard of it being attempted since the twenty-eighth reigning year. I expect they thought they could get away with it because of the construction." He squinted at Hu, his eyesight obviously poor, and nodded a wrinkled chin at the laborers still tossing and catching tiles. "They were dressed up like workers."

Hu was frowning. "What will happen to them?"

"They'll be lucky if they aren't executed," said the peddler. "I don't know why they'd risk it. There are enough soldiers around here to spot an old scheme like that one."

Li Du knew. The examination yard was a point on the path to power that could not be bypassed. No matter how many literary gatherings a merchant hosted, or how many paintings he acquired, he could never attain the status conferred by a degree. Those few candidates whose names appeared on the list would be on their way to claiming some small part of the gold and glamor visible, every day, on the streets of the capital.

The peddler turned weak eyes to Li Du. "You a candidate? Can I interest you in one of the items in my cart? I have ink stones that keep ink from drying out. I have brushes so fine the answers all but write themselves. And here—this is something very special. Take a sniff of this powder, and it will block the smell of the latrines for half a day. You can't beat that for helping concentration, can you? I've heard the stench is terrible in there." He looked at Li Du hopefully.

Hu, whom the peddler had thus far ignored, picked up one of the brushes and examined it thoughtfully. It was made of white porcelain, decorated in blue with encouraging maxims. "How much for this one?" he asked.

The man's eyebrows lifted. "So you're going to move up in the world?" he said. "You won't find a straighter path than the one you can paint for yourself with that brush. That brush will write you all the way to a ministry job. And if you buy a stick of ink, too, I'll throw in this charm at no charge." He plucked a tiny, carved wooden tortoise from a basket in the cart full of identical carvings.

Hu produced several coins. "Ah," said the peddler. "That would be enough for one of the more humble brushes, but your fine taste has led you directly to the most valuable item in my cart."

After a short bargaining session, Hu agreed to a price and handed over an additional coin. "My son's brushes are old," he explained to Li Du. "I wouldn't want his marks to suffer just because the bristles blurred his calligraphy. He has as fine and controlled a hand as any scholar."

"You have obviously worked hard on behalf of your son," said Li Du, eyeing the brush. "I took the exams once myself. I know they are as difficult for the families of the candidates as they are for the candidates themselves. If I may—" He approached the cart, selected a different brush, and examined it. Made of black lacquered wood, it featured a simple design, in inlaid silver, of a carp borne up on a curl of water. He handed it to Hu. "May I suggest this one, instead? It is lighter, and will not tire his hand as quickly. The peddler will give it to you for the same price."

The peddler looked as if he would argue, then changed his mind, recognizing Li Du as a man who was knowledgeable about the worth of brushes. It was a fair price for a brush of significantly higher quality than the other one. Hu thanked Li Du, paid for the brush, then stood turning it over in his hands, admiring it. "It has a lucky feel," he said.

"The design refers to the carp that jumped over a waterfall and became a dragon," said Li Du. He thought of Hamza, and made a mental note to tell him the story.

Hu smiled. "Just as my son will pass the exams and become an official." After a moment's silent indecision, he spoke again. "I will tell you why I avoided Pan. About a year ago, my son met Pan by chance at the Black Tile Factory. He—my son—told Pan he was studying for the exams, and Pan offered to take my son to the opera. Now, my son is a moral man and a serious student, but I allowed him to go because I knew that Pan had passed with distinction, and I thought his friendship would help my son in his career. But when Erchen—my son—returned home the next morning, he confessed something to me. He said that Pan had told him he could help him cheat, that he had a scheme to smuggle answers into the exam yard, and that Erchen could benefit from it. I am telling you this because I know you will believe me when I say that my son never even considered accepting Pan's offer. As I told you, he is a moral and honorable young man. But a newborn calf does not know to be afraid of the tiger, and I feared Pan's influence. After Erchen told me about Pan's proposition, I forbade him from ever speaking to Pan again. I would not allow my son to be lured into the same terrible fate of the two men we just saw dragged away."

"But you never said anything to Pan?"

A shadow of guilt crossed Hu's features. "Pan was a powerful official. How could I speak to him on the subject, or accuse him, with only my son's story as proof? I knew that would lead to trouble. I am sorry that I did not mention it before, but I did not feel it necessary. You asked me what I knew about Pan, and now I have told you. Pan was not a man to be trusted. I am certain of that."

Chapter 24

That evening, Li Du and Hamza dined at a restaurant that specialized in a spicy stew from Sichuan. Because it was new, and claimed to be the only restaurant in the capital serving that particular dish, it had attracted a large crowd. More eager to be seen at the popular restaurant by their coworkers and competitors than they were to ingest its food, most of the patrons were eyeing the opaque red broth warily, or recoiling from the tingling assault on their noses as they lifted their chopsticks toward their lips.

Hamza extracted a broth-soaked wedge of lotus root from the depths of the bowl between them. "Murder, blackmail, theft, adultery," he said. "There are as many crimes associated with the Black Tile Factory as there are peppers in this soup."

They spoke quietly to ensure that the clamor of conversations and clinking dishes around them remained louder than their voices. Li Du had apprised Hamza of Magistrate Yin's visit to the North Borough Office that morning, and of the official closure of the case. "I would add bribery to your list of infractions," he said, almost in a whisper. "No one could have walked into Magistrate Yin's office, gained access to its prison, and attacked Hong without being caught. I agree with Chief Inspector Sun. If Hong's death *wasn't* a suicide, then we are looking for someone with the resources to have identified a guard willing to dirty his hands, and to have paid that guard enough to do it."

"Then you should question the guards."

Li Du shook his head. "There must be a hundred soldiers with access to the complex in which the magistrate's offices are located."

Hamza considered. "There is another possibility."

"That the murderer works for the magistrate," said Li Du. "I thought of that also. If I can obtain a list of officials working within the complex, and compare it to the list of guests at Hong's literary gathering, there might—"

"I was thinking of sorcery," said Hamza, interrupting him. "A murderer could have effected Hong's murder from outside the walls of the prison using some spell or curse."

"If we admit that possibility," said Li Du, "the investigation becomes rather more complicated."

"And more interesting," said Hamza. "You look at me as if I am joking, but it is your own city that is to blame for the idea. I met a peddler today who, thinking I was an examination candidate, offered to sell me a potion that would make me dream the winning answers to the essay questions. I thought I might at least test its power. Is it still possible to register for these examinations?"

"If it is not your intention to spend your life working your way up through magistracies and ministries," said Li Du mildly, "then it would seem unfair for you to claim a spot on the list of passing candidates from one of the scholars who desires it more than anything."

This gave Hamza pause. "You are right," he said. "As for the matter at the factory, it is simple. The murderer now believes the case is closed, and will pay no attention to the quiet little assistant who is writing the report. All you must do is uncover the truth without alerting a wealthy and powerful killer to the fact that you are conducting an investigation."

"Within four days," added Li Du. He began to lift a bite of rice from his bowl, but stopped halfway and put his chopsticks down again, the food forgotten as he worked to follow his own thoughts. "The note that brought Pan and Madam Hong to the factory office that night was inspired by the book discussed at Hong's literary gathering. Whether it was written by Pan, Madam Hong, or the murderer, I am certain that someone who was at that party was involved."

"In that case," said Hamza, "you should follow the strategy you just mentioned. Return to the list of guests. Interview them all."

"Unfortunately, there were almost fifty guests in attendance. The report will be due before I could speak to five of them. I don't even know if any would agree to speak to me at all. Without Chief Inspector Sun or a retinue of soldiers lending weight to my visit, I am merely an assistant from an inconsequential borough office writing a report."

Hamza waved a dismissive hand. "You have faced more difficult challenges. Surely you recall the time you restored the pearl that was taken from the diadem of the Queen of the Seven Islands?"

Li Du's small eyebrows lifted in a silent invitation for Hamza to explain himself. "There was also the time you thwarted the ghost bandits of Tiger Gorge," Hamza continued. "That was not an easy task."

"None of these events occurred," said Li Du.

"Ask the Mongols that guided me and Sera-tsering over the steppes," said Hamza. "They will tell you all about the exploits of Li Du, and I doubt even I could talk them out of retelling the tales now."

Li Du's eyes smiled gently beneath heavy lids. Then he stood up and slipped his chopsticks into their case. They paid for the meal and exited the restaurant into a twilit alley. Lantern light and muddled conversations hovered over courtyards hidden by walls. The air was savory, thickened by cooking oil and dust, carrying a heavy hint of manure and temple incense. There were not many people left on the streets. Hunched peasants pulled the day's empty carts toward the outer wall, while others pulled the evening's laden ones, ready to serve spice-encrusted meats to hungry customers. Those revelers who remained much longer where they were would be trapped by the closing gates, committed to the night's entertainments until the doors opened at dawn.

As they made their way back toward Water Moon Temple, Li

Du recounted his finding of Father Aveneau at the scene of the crime, and subsequent conversations with Wei and Hu.

"The Jesuit is hiding something," said Hamza, when Li Du had finished.

"Certainly," Li Du agreed. His pace quickened. He always walked faster when he was thinking, and slowed down when he started to talk. "But there is no way a foreigner could have gone from the South Church to the Black Tile Factory at night without being stopped. And what motive could Father Aveneau possibly have to kill a woman he has never met, and a ministry official with whom he had no business? I cannot believe he could be the murderer. Also, he wasn't at the party."

"But the manager, Hu, was."

"Hu is, so far, the only person to whom I have spoken who admits that he did not like Pan, and who lived near enough to the factory to access it at night without passing a sentry post. But the fact that he was unable to read *The Bitter Plum*—if that is true—means that he did not write the blackmail note. He does not seem like a man who would commit murder. To me, what is more interesting in his statement today is the suggestion that Pan was not the upstanding official I imagined him to be. If Pan was indeed corrupt, possibilities suggest themselves, though I cannot see how Madam Hong fits into them."

"It is as if there were two versions of the same story," said Hamza, with a dreamy look at the alley lanterns that were gaining strength as the sky darkened. "Consider, first, the lovers. A man lies on a bed, his blood soaking the silk cushions. Near him lies a woman. She wears a dress of golden silk. Her gleaming hair is tumbled, black as ink, around her face. Her heart is pierced. Above her stands her husband, whose love, confronted with her betrayal, turned to rage. Is that an accurate description, based on what you saw in that room?"

"It is."

"Then let us consider a different murder," said Hamza. "The scene changes. Look again at the faces of the victims. There is no recent passion in their expressions, no flushed cheek, no kiss-swollen lips. It was not love that drew them to that room, but silver and secrets. And it was not jealous fury that tore their lives from them. The spectral husband fades, and is replaced by a colder shadow."

They had entered a narrow alley. The walls on either side of them were almost black, the sky behind them soft and dim, like a petal drained of color. Since his return to Beijing, Li Du had become more aware of its walls, within which the thoughts and anxieties of hundreds of thousands of people were compressed. After two years of searching within those walls for memories and secrets, he had only encountered patterns too faint to follow, soon lost.

"The scholar, Bai," he said. "According to Lady Ai, Bai instigated the audit of the ministry contracts, an action for which Pan had cause to be angry at him. In addition, Bai has been petitioning to shut down the Black Tile Factory for months. He thinks the smoke and coal are staining the walls and polluting the parks at Taoranting. He was at Hong's party, and he is exactly the kind of well-connected man who could arrange a death in prison. These connections are tenuous and unexplained, which gives me all the more reason to think he might supply information we do not yet have."

They reached the door of Water Moon Temple. There was no one nearby, though the hollow echo of horse hooves was just audible from a nearby alley. Inside, they found the clerics lighting incense sticks and sweeping the cobblestones. Chan approached them, his arms outstretched, his face a picture of worry and frustration. "Rats," he said. "We have rats. I saw another one, stealing a slice of orange out of a basket at the feet of Guanyin's statue. What if the visitor who had left the offering had seen? No patron wants to leave an expensive piece of fruit for a god and have it be eaten by a pest! A letter came for you." He produced a slim, folded piece of paper. As Li Du took it, Chan turned around and left them, clicking his tongue against his teeth and muttering that they were lucky the rats hadn't nibbled all the words away.

Li Du opened the letter and read it without bothering to find his spectacles, then folded it again. "Well?" asked Hamza, who had been watching with evident curiosity. "I would like to know who deserves credit for writing a letter that so clearly improved your spirits. And I submit to you that it was written by a woman."

"It is not what you think," said Li Du. "It was written by a mutual acquaintance, suggesting a meeting tomorrow morning."

Hamza looked disappointed. "A mutual acquaintance? But the only person I know in this city, other than yourself and the good clerics who have agreed to host me here, is Feng."

The corners of Li Du's eyes crinkled as he smiled. "With all the stories you have invented about my past, I hope you still remember the ones that you did not conjure from nothing. Consider a town at the foot of a mountain, a model of the heavens made of jewels, and an astronomer who had a daughter. You cannot have forgotten Lady Chen."

Chapter 25

Early the next morning, Li Du and Hamza joined the officials streaming through Xuanwu Gate. Once inside the Inner City, they separated themselves from the current flowing toward the ministries and made their way north along a wide avenue. This was the privileged domain of the Banners, where elevated pavilions offered views over the city walls to the western hills, and glittering blue lakes provided relief from the constraints of urban living. When they reached the district of the Yellow Banner, Li Du led them into the maze of alleys that defined the tranquil enclaves of its residents.

Hamza touched the wall beside him, which was as white as a swan's wing. "How is it so clean?" he asked in wonder. "Do the wealthy have their walls repainted every morning?"

"The walls of a mansion are a statement to the neighborhood," Li Du explained. He lowered his voice. "My cousin used to favor crimson. He didn't know that the choice was earning him a reputation for being as tasteless as he is wealthy."

"As I recall from my own brief dealings with him in Dayan, he has a certain skill at giving that impression," said Hamza.

"So he does," said Li Du. His cousin, Tulishen, had been serving as magistrate of Dayan at the time Li Du and Hamza had met in that remote trading town. Family ambition, wealth, and willingness to exploit connections had earned Tulishen a prestigious career and an honorary Manchu title to replace his former name, but he was a petty man who had allowed his enjoyment of privilege to be compromised by fear of losing it.

"It was Lady Chen," Li Du went on, "who perceived that the ostentatious color of the walls was a miscalculation. She had them painted white, and within a month, Tulishen was receiving invitations to parties that had previously been closed to him."

Hamza's expression turned speculative. "If I had a mansion, I would cover its walls in enchanted paint, and passersby would perceive it to be whatever color pleased them most. Then I would not have to concern myself with these conventions."

They arrived at a door set within an entrance of green glazed brick. Li Du's knock was answered almost immediately by a trim, bright-eyed servant who led them through a series of courtyards to a garden bustling with activity. Maids, neatly dressed in pink and gray silk, were untangling garlands of rice-paper flowers from willow branches, while male servants were carrying away bronze incense burners and crystal lanterns that scattered reflected light over the cobblestone paths. A lute with a broken string rested on top of a folded silk tapestry.

Lady Chen came forward to greet them. Her slow progress—she zealously affected the small steps of a fashionable urban lady, though her own feet had never been bound—gave Li Du time to reacquaint himself with her unique beauty. A tall woman, she held herself with the commanding grace of a lone tree on a mountain promontory. Her robes were the color of a moonlit sky at midnight, and her hair was ornamented with silver beads.

"Forgive me," she said when she reached him. "You are too busy to be summoned for social calls." She turned a welcoming expression to Hamza. "Do you also work for the chief insp—" She stopped, her eyes moving in quick assessment of his features. "But I know you. Li Du, why did you not tell me the storyteller had come to Beijing?"

"I am at fault," Li Du said. "The only excuse I can offer is that recent duties in the North Borough have demanded more of my attention than the usual permits and property disputes."

"You refer to the murders at the Black Tile Factory." Lady Chen's lips were set in a faintly challenging smile. "Are you surprised that I know so much?"

To please her, Li Du lifted his eyebrows and blinked. "I am astonished."

Her smile widened. "Do not pretend," she said. "I can see that I have not impressed you."

"In truth, Lady Chen, I have stopped being surprised by how much you know." Li Du rubbed the back of his neck. "But I am curious to hear how the information came to you."

Lady Chen considered. "News passes through the walls of this city more easily than people do. I heard it from one of my maids, who heard it from one of our servants, who heard it at the vegetable market from the Zhao family servant, but beyond that the thread is too long and tangled to follow. By now it is being widely discussed. Everyone wants to know the blood-soaked details of the lovers surprised by the wine-drunk husband. That is why I have asked you to come."

"Lady Chen, I—"

She interrupted him. "Do not make unflattering assumptions. I did not bring you here to pry information from you in order to elevate my status among the gossips. Let us go where we can speak privately."

They followed her to another garden, in the center of which was a wide pond bisected by a flat bridge. They crossed, the water mirroring their passage in muddled greens and blues. On the other side, nestled in a grove of pear trees with ruby red leaves, was a small building. Lady Chen unlocked the door and invited them to enter.

"The room was a recent gift to me," she said, noting Li Du's admiring glance at the shelves that lined the walls. They were filled with books of diverse age and size. Most had silk covers, but some were bound in leather. A few were studded with metal and gemstones. The only ornaments in the room, besides the books themselves, were a small collection of astronomical instruments, polished and stately, and a painting of a mountain.

"A gift from my cousin?" he asked.

"From his mother," Lady Chen replied. "She has developed an affection for her son's humble concubine."

An affection, thought Li Du, *carefully cultivated by Lady Chen herself.* Living in a house with Tulishen's mother, wife, and two additional concubines, with no children of her own to secure her place in the family, Lady Chen had approached her rise to power within the household with all the focus and discipline of a scholar mastering the classics, or a general leading a campaign, two other activities of which Li Du believed her entirely capable.

She was watching him now, as if she could read his thoughts. "Please sit," she said, indicating a comfortable arrangement of chairs around a table with a green marble top. No sooner had they taken their places than three maids arrived with tea and trays filled with small dishes. Hamza immediately leaned forward over a plate of lotus-root cakes and inhaled the fragrance of osmanthus flower with obvious appreciation.

Lady Chen turned to him with open curiosity. "If I recall correctly," she said, "you were born in a valley above a river called Manas, down which deities travel on the backs of saddled fish."

"Your memory, madam, is faultless."

"The words of a skilled storyteller are not easily forgotten."

Her flattery found its mark, and Hamza beamed. "Nor is a mountain spirit. So, Lady Chen of Snowflake Village is now Lady Chen of Beijing. How do you like this walled city?"

It was a question Li Du had not asked her. He waited, curious how she would answer. They had met three years ago, in a small town on the empire's southwest border, where Li Du, an exile at the time, had come to register his presence with the local magistrate. The magistrate, he discovered, was his relation, Tulishen. Lady Chen was his concubine. A local woman facing the prospect of being discarded when Tulishen returned to Beijing, she had been determined to remain a part of the household.

Lady Chen's smile answered Hamza's question before her words did. "This city suits me well. I was not happy to remain on the periphery of this world. But what brings you here?"

"I have intended to visit for many years," said Hamza. "But whenever I approached the walls of this great capital, I was like a spider whose silken rope is broken by a breeze. Always I was carried off course." He inclined his beard in Li Du's direction. "It was the invitation of a friend that finally brought me through the gates. Now I indulge in the idle amusements of a carefree traveler while—" He directed a questioning look at Li Du, but it was Lady Chen who finished the sentence.

"While our friend the scholar plays the role of the humble secretary," she said. "A performance I have never found convincing, though the reason for the charade still eludes me." She turned to Li Du, and he felt, just faintly, her keen eyes linger on his cheek, a little thinner than usual, and his eyelids, drooping more heavily than they had done in the past. "But you are tired," she said. "I will not tease you today."

Her voice was low and comforting. Li Du felt some of the anxiety ease from his shoulders, and he realized suddenly that he was hungry.

"Eat," said Lady Chen. "And let me tell you what I have heard."

As they served themselves, she began. "Madam Hong and a ministry official were found dead in the office of the Black Tile Factory. The kiln master Hong had been drinking nearby. It is the conclusion of the chief inspector that the husband surprised the lovers together, and killed them both. That is accurate?"

Li Du ate a piece of eggplant and found himself reaching for another. "Yes."

"And you believe that it happened that way?"

Li Du's hesitation was enough for Lady Chen. "I knew I was right to summon you," she said.

Li Du set down his chopsticks. "Are you saying that you have evidence relevant to the case?"

"Not the kind of evidence that I could present to the chief

inspector," she said. "But I hope you will understand. You see, I cannot claim to have known Madam Hong, but I'd met her on several occasions. Her clothes were always new and fine. She would not step on a path unless a rug protected her feet from the ground." Lady Chen hesitated, concentrating on her next words. "She was the kind of woman who was always looking at herself from the outside. She wanted her life to look like a painting."

"I understand," said Li Du.

"I don't think you do," said Lady Chen. She refilled their teacups, and Li Du could see the red leaves outside the window reflected in the gold bracelets on her wrists. She set the teapot down. "What woman in this city, who values above all silk that has never been worn, and jewels that have no scratches, would choose to meet her lover in a shabby office hut covered in coal dust, for a stolen hour in the middle of the night?"

"If it was the only way?" Li Du asked.

She gave a soft laugh. "It is never the only way."

"Then what you are saying," said Li Du, "is that you don't believe it was adultery that brought her to that room."

Her smile subsided. "No," she said. "I don't. And isn't it true that, if she was innocent of adultery, Hong's actions are no longer *justified* by the law?"

Beginning to understand, Li Du nodded. "It is true, but—"

Lady Chen interrupted. "The law may forgive a man for murdering an adulterous wife, but if Madam Hong was not an adulteress, the law would not forgive Hong. If you can prove she was not unfaithful, you destroy the shield he holds up to protect himself."

"Yes, but—"

"If you do nothing, Hong will escape punishment."

"Lady Chen, Hong is dead."

"Dead?" Lady Chen's surprise temporarily deprived her of her customary command over her own expression. Without it, her unusual features—large eyes and an angular nose—became more pronounced. "How did he die?"

"It appears he committed suicide, an act that is being taken as a confession."

Her exuberance faded. "In that case, I have wasted your time. Unless—" Her eyes snapped up and fixed on Li Du's face. "You say it *appears* he committed suicide. What do you mean? Do you— can it be that you think he might have been murdered?"

Li Du met her look, and she read the answer in his eyes.

"Three murders, then," she said softly. "Whom do you suspect?"

With some difficulty, feeling that he knew simultaneously too much and too little about the case, Li Du gave a brief account of the investigation. She listened carefully, absorbing the story with evident fascination.

"My intention to do more than write the report is not common knowledge," he concluded. "I know I may trust your discretion."

"Always," said Lady Chen. "Though I would advise you not to believe anyone, other than myself, who makes you such a promise. Most of the secrets I know were shared with me by people who say their discretion can be trusted. If what you believe is true, you must proceed with caution. You will tell me the answer when you have discovered it?"

"I am not certain I will find the answer," Li Du replied.

Lady Chen brushed her fingers through the air as if she were guiding away an insect that buzzed too close. "You are a capable man," she said. "You will uncover the truth. You have succeeded in the past under equally challenging circumstances."

"That is just what I told him," Hamza exclaimed.

Li Du took a deep breath and stood up. "Then we will take our leave, and resume work."

"I hope you will come back soon," said Lady Chen, also rising. "And you?" she asked Hamza. "With what idle amusements will you occupy yourself today?"

"I confess I do not know," replied Hamza, looking slightly dispirited. "My usual approach to exploring a city that is new to me is to wander its streets in search of marvels. But in the hours I have spent lost in *this* city's narrow alleys, I have seen little besides blank walls and locked doors. I even went so far as to consult a guidebook." He directed a faintly accusatory look at Li Du. "In addition to the famous turtles of Rainbow Bridge, which, to my disappointment, proved to be statues, the book suggests I visit notable graves, sigh over ruins, and admire old trees. I mean no disrespect to this great capital, but I had expected to spend more time navigating the gilded corridors of the palace, examining the Emperor's collection of magical objects, and sailing on the imperial lakes, counting the fish that gleam like jewels in crystal waters."

Lady Chen brushed a hand through the air dismissively. "You will receive no pity from me," she said with mock censure. "If I can find enough to entertain and interest me within the walls of my own home, where propriety keeps me generally confined, I am certain you can find adventure in the capital without the help of guidebooks. Have you been to the elephant stables?"

Hamza's eyes kindled. "Elephant stables?"

Satisfied by the effect her words had produced, Lady Chen smiled. "I will escort you out."

With a rueful look at the food that remained on the plates, Hamza followed Lady Chen and Li Du outside. They did not return to the garden in which she had welcomed them, but followed a different and more direct path to the mansion's outer door. They were nearing it when Li Du became aware of the pinging, metallic clamor of hammers on nails, and a voice raised in anger.

"I must have silence!"

Lady Chen changed course, moving toward a small door that opened into a courtyard at the mansion's edge. Paused in the doorway, the three of them observed a middle-aged man in the center of the courtyard bellowing at two pale servants. "Go tell the carpenters to stop their work!" Li Du recognized the man. He was Li Yujin, one of Tulishen's sons.

"He is taking the exams for the fifth time," whispered Lady Chen. "If he had spent the past four months studying, instead of carousing at the theaters in Liulichang, he would not be so anxious now."

"The temple to the thunder god must be almost complete," Li Du said, referring to the construction that was taking place just outside the mansion.

Lady Chen sighed. "I hope so. There will be no quiet in this house until it is, and I am not referring to the sound of hammers and nails."

For the past six months, Tulishen had spoken of little else besides the temple he was financing. His fixation on the project was due in part to the fact that it had attracted the attention of the returning prince, who had offered to compose a poem for it upon its completion. The patronage of a prince was an almost unimaginable distinction that would elevate Tulishen to new social heights, and Tulishen had promised to have the temple ready for Prince Yinzao's inspection on the day of the prince's long-awaited return to the capital.

The ire of Tulishen's son was reaching a crescendo, and Lady Chen turned to her guests with an apologetic smile. "I must go. I will encourage him to climb to the pavilion for a calming view of the western hills." She bid farewell to Hamza, and told him she hoped he would accompany Li Du again to her home before he resumed his travels. Then she addressed Li Du. "Be careful. You are shadowed by danger, and I can see that you know it."

Chapter 26

Away from the cooling breezes off the lakes, the glaring sun heated the walls and turned the narrow alleys into ovens. By the time Li Du and Hamza reached the border of the Outer City, after navigating several detours around construction sites and alleys blocked off for imperial use, Li Du's throat was parched and he was conscious of the weight and warmth of his felt hat.

They paused at an intersection crowded with sweaty horses and mules. Shoppers evaluated antiques displayed on mats and carts. Hamza, his skin glistening in the heat, declared that he would accompany Li Du to his next destination, the home of the scholar Bai.

Li Du negated the idea. "It's not the same situation as the Glazed Tile Factory. There are different levels of scrutiny. Visiting a factory in a village outside the city walls is different from paying a call on a respected official who knows I am in no position to have an assistant, especially not one dressed as a trader."

"Then we can do it the way it is done in the tale of the judge. I am your cousin who is visiting, and you have invited me to accompany you on your errands."

Li Du shook his head. "Secretaries do not have the freedom to take visiting relatives to work with them, a fact of which Bai is well aware. Not only is he knowledgeable, but he pays particular attention to such formalities."

"Allow me to remind you," said Hamza, planting his booted feet and crossing his arms across his chest, "that you tempted me here with a promise of intrigue and adventure. I did not come to spend

all my time making sketches of marble bridges, or composing poetry in parks, or engaging in whatever other genteel pastimes are
pursued by ordinary tourists."

As he listened to Hamza, Li Du's gaze moved over the market
stalls nearby. A peasant sat beside a basket of wilted greens. Beside
him on one side, another fanned flies away from a table of meat
scraps, beneath which a thin dog chewed on a bone. On the other
side, a woman sat on a blanket, on which she had arranged a collection of mineral powders and roots.

An idea occurred to him. "There are six large markets held in
the Inner City on this day of the month," he said, once Hamza had
lapsed into obstinate silence. "If you desire a task, I have one to give
you."

Hamza's eyes narrowed in suspicion. "Am I to purchase your
vegetables for the week?"

"I had something else in mind," said Li Du. "Rare and precious
stones."

The crossed arms unfolded. "That is more to my taste."

"I thought it might be. Do you remember the stones we saw in
Ji's workshop well enough to describe what they look like? They
are called by many different names."

Hamza nodded. "Rough and gray on the outside, the size of my
fist; when broken, filled with many colors. Not only one red, but
all the reds of autumn leaves; not one yellow, but all the many yel-
lows expressed by flame; not one white, but all the whites of clouds;
not one blue, but all the blues of sky and sea."

"Then I would ask you to make a search of the six markets."

"Ah," said Hamza. "You want to know where Ji purchased his
agates."

"Yes, and how much he spent. If they are as rare and precious
as I suspect, then Ji is in possession of more wealth than can be
explained by his profession. Given that the case is one of murder
and missing silver, that seems a detail worth pursuing. Is the task
sufficiently intriguing?"

"It will do," said Hamza. "I am an expert navigator of markets. I can tell real from false, and I can discern where there are shelves behind curtains that exist only for those who know to ask for them. If these rocks exist, I will find them."

Li Du glanced at their surroundings. "You said you wanted to see the elephant stables," he said. "They are not far from here, and they are open to the public. I will look for you there in the afternoon?"

Hamza agreed with enthusiasm to this suggestion. After setting the hour of the rooster as a tentative time to meet, they parted ways.

Bai's home, smaller and less ostentatious than Tulishen's, asserted that beauty was best expressed in cleanliness and precision. The courtyards were tightly cobbled in river stones, their patterns unbroken by a single weed or fallen leaf. Every door that opened onto a polished veranda was either fully open or fully closed. Even the sunshine on the potted plants seemed evenly distributed by a fastidious curator.

Li Du was received in an airy pavilion shaded by trees. Bai was sitting at a desk, paper before him and brush in hand. He invited Li Du to sit on an attractive bench upholstered in spotless silk, but as Li Du approached it, he saw Bai's gaze fix on the dusty hem of Li Du's robes, then travel to his ink-stained sleeves.

"Perhaps," said Bai, "we would be more comfortable here." He set his brush on its rest, and led Li Du to a plain ebony table with matching chairs.

"I apologize for interrupting you," said Li Du as they took their seats across from each other. "I hope I am not disturbing your preparations for the examinations."

"Preparations?" Bai's smile lifted the corners of his silky white mustache. "The only preparation that remains for the examiners is to brace ourselves for the disappointment we will feel when we read answers submitted by inferior candidates. No, the task you have interrupted is only a minor one. Yet again, I am asked to submit a line of poetry to be carved into a stone outside a temple. It adds credibility, you know, the attention of a famous scholar."

"A generous gift of your time," said Li Du.

Bai gave a world-weary sigh. "Why they insist on building new temples instead of repairing the old ones, I cannot tell you. It is disgraceful that so many have been allowed to fall into disrepair. It is one thing to visit a dilapidated temple on a mountain—there is poetry in isolation and decay. But in the capital of the empire, a neglected temple is like a decaying tooth in the smile of an otherwise lovely woman." The scholar paused to appreciate his own simile before shifting his attention to Li Du with a look of tepid curiosity. "What brings you to my home?"

Li Du withdrew the notebook and stylus from his satchel and set them on the table. "Chief Inspector Sun has asked me to complete the report on his investigation of the murders at the Black Tile Factory. I was hoping you might assist me in clarifying several details related to the crime."

"An unsavory affair," said Bai with a slight shudder. "I confess I am disappointed. I thought you might have come to discuss the reinvigoration of your career. A man of your credentials, really, there is no need for you to be reduced to such humble employment. Remind me—in what year did you receive your degree?"

"In Kangxi twenty-seven."

"Kangxi twenty-seven," Bai echoed with a smile. "A good year. You specialized in the Li-chi, didn't you? *Discuss the uses of ritual and music to bring order to society.* A question that requires a candidate to demonstrate the completeness of his knowledge, while also inviting a touch of creativity." The smile faded. "Your exile hindered your advancement, no doubt, but many of history's finest poets drew inspiration from times of loneliness and adversity."

Li Du listened, his expression studiously blank. Bai gave a small shrug. "If you decide to renew your efforts, I will do all I can for you, of course. It pains me to think of you entering your twilight years being sent on errands. So, you are here to speak to me about the unfortunate events at the Black Tile Factory. I have, of course, been informed of the story's conclusion, and I will tell you I am not surprised. Hong Wenbin was not a man in full possession of his reason."

"You knew him well?"

"Of course not."

"But you did attend the party he hosted shortly before the murders occurred."

Bai nodded. "I had misgivings, but I consider it my duty to support literary pursuits in the North Borough, even the mundane ones. It was a tiresome way to spend an afternoon. I regretted my decision to forego the monthly meeting of the Club to Debate Alternate Word Origins."

Li Du remembered a time when he had been a member of at least ten such clubs, some genuinely interesting, others merely pretentious. "It would be helpful to include in the report some insights into Hong's state of mind. Did his behavior at the party suggest that he suspected the affair between Pan and his wife?"

Bai considered the question briefly before negating it. "Hong was upset when Pan defeated him at a game of chess, but no more upset than he was after every loss. He was, without a doubt, inebriated." Bai gave another sigh. "The trouble comes from opening our elite, educated communities to common businessmen. Hong was so desperate for approval, and so incapable of earning it, that he became unhinged. That is what drove him to excessive drinking, and to violence. Violence against others and, in the end, against himself." The scholar lifted pained eyes to Li Du. "Do you have any other questions?"

Li Du glanced down at his notebook. "In regard to the victims, I assume you were not acquainted with Madam Hong."

"Naturally not," said Bai.

"But your name *was* mentioned in connection with the murdered man, Pan Yongfa."

"Was it?"

Li Du lifted his eyes, and saw that Bai appeared genuinely taken aback. "According to his concubine, Lady Ai, Pan was upset about the audit that he claimed had been instigated by you. As the Ministry of Rites official responsible for contracts with the kiln, he had been assigned the brunt of the work."

"Ah," said Bai, his expression clearing. "Of course. My actions were in the interest of the neighborhood, and I make no apology for them. Recall that, in the past, there were kilns in Liulichang. They were closed due to excessive smoke, and Liulichang is now one of the most popular and attractive areas in the Outer City. It is time for the rest of the boroughs to rise to the same standard. Have you seen the black stains that threaten to coat the marble pavilions at Taoranting? It is unacceptable."

Li Du allowed his gaze to take in their pristine surroundings. "Your campaigns for the beauty of the city are well known in the North Borough Office, but how would an audit further your goal?"

"I will explain," said Bai. "Because my petitions were not receiving sufficient attention, I was forced to devise a new strategy. I had been told that the Black Tile Factory kept its documents in a state of utter disorganization, owing to Hong Wenbin's poor leadership. There were numerous complaints from city businesses about delayed roof repairs, misplaced contracts, and so on. It was my hope that if the disgraceful state of affairs was made public, it would accelerate the relocation of the factory. That is why I suggested the audit not only to my contacts in the Ministry of Rites, but also to those in the Imperial Household Agency. I am pleased that both entities took my advice."

"The closure of the factory is almost guaranteed now," said Li Du. "Given the death of its owner."

"I hope that is true," said Bai. "Though of course I would not have wished for it to come about in such a sordid way."

Li Du nodded his understanding. "Then you did not know Pan Yongfa personally?"

"I had met him," said Bai. "He was often at parties."

"Did you speak to him at Hong's gathering?"

"Not exactly."

"What do you mean?"

Bai thought for a moment. "It was only a small thing. I hadn't recalled it until now. I didn't converse with Pan, but I did overhear him in conversation. It had nothing to do with his affair with Hong's wife, but yes, I did find it strange at the time."

"Strange in what way?"

Bai settled into the memory with the pleasure of those who like to speak about themselves. "It was toward the end of the afternoon. I left Hu—I assume you have met Hu Gongshan?"

"The manager," said Li Du.

"Yes. His son is an examination candidate. I believe Hu Gongshan had procured an invitation to the party solely in order to speak with me. The poor man hoped to convince me to mentor his son, right there, in the middle of a party, wearing clothes hardly appropriate for the event! I extricated myself as quickly as I could. But no sooner had I done so than my ears were assaulted with Hong's drunken verse. I would have left the gathering, but it was starting to rain, and I did not want to be soaked going home. So I strolled away from the others, along a covered walkway, in an attempt to regain a state of equilibrium with my environment. It was then that I heard voices near to where I was walking. They were coming from the other side of a stand of bamboo. I could just barely make out three figures standing in a small pavilion."

"Did you recognize them?"

"I am certain one was Pan Yongfa. I glimpsed his face, and heard him speak. But the others had their backs to me, and what with the obscuring bamboo and the rain, I could not see them."

"Were you able to hear what they were saying?"

"Nothing clearly, though it seemed to me they were arguing. I only caught a few words. First *Narcissus Temple*. And after that, something about not being on time. And finally, I believe it was Pan who mentioned tunnels."

"Tunnels?"

"Yes. *I cannot get it to you in time; I will deliver it through the tunnels*, or words to that effect." Bai nodded at Li Du's look of puzzlement. "It was nonsense, of course. I have never heard of a Narcissus

Temple, or of any tunnels. All I thought at the time was that the covert meeting under cover of rainfall confirmed the impression I had always had of Pan Yongfa."

"What was your impression of him?"

"That he was not as charming as everyone seemed to believe he was. I am a good judge of character. As a scholar and a moral man, I can sense corruption, and I cannot abide it. In my opinion, immorality hung about that man like an oppressive fragrance. If I were to speculate, I would say it was he who led Madam Hong to her fall from respectability." After a pause, he added, almost as an afterthought, "and to her death."

With this assertion, Bai stood up. "I hope I have been of some help, but I would advise you not to spend too much time writing a report of a case the facts of which are so tragically straightforward. I will tell you what I tell my students. Do not waste time on irrelevant details. One cannot write the whole truth, even with an ink pot as deep as the sea."

Li Du stood also. Thanking Bai for his time, he started toward the opening onto the veranda, passing the desk on his way. He paused beside it. However grating he found the examiner's pomposity, he could not help but admire the scholarly accoutrements arranged across its surface. He ran an appreciative eye over the clean brushes, carved paperweights, and sheets of ornamented paper, until his gaze came to rest on a rectangular ink stone, carved in the classical proportions of the late Tang. It was lavender gray tinged with the iridescent green unique to Duanzhou slate.

Looking at it, Li Du was drawn into a memory of a winter afternoon some fifteen years ago, when Shu had been so taken with a poem written by one of his granddaughters that he had decided to present her with an ink stone of her own. The proud grandfather had sat the little girl at his own desk and explained the properties of a quality stone. *All good ink stones are hard enough to grind the ink to a fine consistency, yet smooth enough not to damage your brush,* he had said. *But it is a rare stone that grinds ink without making a sound. Do you know how it does it?* Shu had paused for the anticipation of his listeners to reach its full strength. *It does it by convincing the ink stick to be friends with the water, so that they agree to mix without arguing. You don't want an argument on your desk when you are trying to compose a poem!* And Shu had chuckled to himself at the image of the embattled writing materials.

A hand intruded into Li Du's vision, reaching across the desk to pick up a volume and move it to another corner. He looked up, realizing he had been lost for too long in his reverie, and saw that Bai was watching him with a small frown. "You look fatigued," said the scholar. "Perhaps you should stay and drink a cup of tea. I am curious to know more about the years you spent outside the capital." Without waiting for an answer, he summoned a servant.

The servant who promptly appeared was a young man with an angular face and a serious set to his mouth. Upon seeing Li Du, he stopped short and stared at him for a moment with large, intent eyes that called to mind a bird of prey. Li Du was certain that within those eyes he could see surprise and recognition. He was sure he didn't know the man, but as they continued to stare at each other, he felt that he had seen him before. Then the servant dropped into a bow. When he rose from it, his expression contained only polite deference.

Li Du refused Bai's offer of tea, thanked the scholar again for his patience, and made his way back across the manor's elegant courtyards. He was conscious of his own footsteps, which sounded to his own ears like an intrusion on the studied serenity of the space. He almost expected one of the trees to chastise him. When he reached the manor's exit, he found the threshold occupied by a maid sweeping dust from the stone. *Even the brooms in this house are as neat as calligraphy brushes,* he thought, observing the clean, even bristles.

If he had turned, he might have glimpsed the old scholar engage in an urgent, whispered conversation with the falcon-eyed servant. By the time Li Du had left the manor, Bai was pacing the floor of his studio, glancing occasionally in the direction Li Du had gone with an expression of dawning alarm.

Chapter 27

It was late morning, and the dawn bustle had ended. Ministry officials were at their desks, markets were depleted of fresh fish, and breakfast vendors were resting as the leftover dumplings hardened in their trays. The sky had clouded over. As Li Du neared the North Borough Office, a light rain began to fall, tamping down the dust and making the air smell of damp, sun-warmed stone. Seeing an open restaurant, Li Du hurried to it and ducked inside.

The windowless interior was barely bigger than a hallway. It contained only one other customer, a burly Manchu who sat hunched over a cup at a table near the back of the room. Between him and Li Du, an elderly woman with sleeves cinched tight around thin wrists sat beside a pan of small dumplings sizzling in oil. "It comes with the food," she said, when Li Du asked for a cup of tea.

"In that case," said Li Du amenably, "I will have a plate of dumplings."

He took a seat at a sticky table. A man in an apron emerged from the back of the restaurant and presented him with a chipped bowl half full of lukewarm tea. The three tea leaves floating on its surface looked wan and apologetic. Li Du sipped it anyway, and, setting his thoughts against the backdrop of rain that curtained the restaurant's narrow entrance, reviewed what Bai had told him.

It was the mention of tunnels that confounded him. There were no tunnels in Beijing. Of that, he was certain. The ground beneath the city was so wet that any depression made in it was soon filled with water seeping in from every side. Any attempt to make a tunnel would only produce a new puddle, pond, or canal. Evidence of this was abundant. The lakes of Taoranting park, surrounded by balustrades and ornamented with pavilions, were an attempt to beautify the water pits left behind by excavated clay. If there were tunnels beneath the city, or ever had been, the scale of infrastructure required to build them would have made their existence impossible to conceal.

If I cannot get it to you in time, I will deliver it through the tunnels. Could Pan have been referring to secret passages? Those were plentiful enough within the mansions and ministries, and certainly within the palace. But of what use was this speculation with no knowledge of what Pan might have been intending to transport, or to whom he had been speaking? Li Du let his mind drift. He watched the raindrops bouncing in from the street, studding the floor near the entrance.

Six dumplings, greasy and hard, plinked as they struck ceramic. Li Du looked behind him and saw a plate being carried to the customer who sat at the back of the restaurant, slightly blurred by accumulated smoke. Another series of plinks, and Li Du was handed a plate of his own. Flies hovered over the small bowl of crushed pepper paste at the center of the table. A dark crust had formed around its rim.

According to Bai, Pan had also mentioned a place. *Narcissus Temple.* Could that be the location of the mysterious tunnels? Li Du had never heard of a temple by that name, but if it existed, there would be a record of it. Had he been within the quiet, cool halls of the library, Li Du would have been able to find the location of the temple with the same easy efficiency with which Hu installed a row of tiles. Librarians didn't forget the locations of books within their libraries.

His thoughts were interrupted by the squeaking scrape of a stool being drawn back. The Manchu, his meal finished, departed, leaving Li Du alone in the restaurant. He turned back to his cooling dumplings and forced himself to eat two of them. He glanced back. The woman who had served him his plate was poking the dying fire with a stick, sending little puffs of ash into the smoky air. He stood up, paid for his food, and slipped out into the rain.

The courtyard of the North Borough Office was gray and quiet. Chief Inspector Sun's door was closed. Li Du navigated a path around the puddles that were expanding across the uneven cobblestones. As he stood on the veranda outside his door, trying to squeeze water from the sodden hem of his robe, a voice called out from the entrance through which he had just come. A messenger had arrived. From the other side of the courtyard, Li Du heard footsteps in the clerks' office. A moment later, Mi emerged. Directing a look of displeasure at the rain, he beckoned from the covered veranda for the messenger to dismount and come to him.

Noticing Li Du, Mi called across the courtyard to him. "We haven't seen you since yesterday morning. What have you been doing?"

Li Du gave up trying to wring moisture from his robe and straightened. "I've been obliged to conduct several additional interviews in order to make the report as thorough as possible."

Mi had cupped a hand to his ear. "You're making more work for yourself," he called. "Magistrate Yin would have his own clerks write the report if he expected it to be scrutinized." He turned his attention to the messenger splashing toward him through the puddles, one hand clamped down on the flap of his satchel to keep it from flying open and exposing the paper to rain. Once he was under the roof, he bowed and presented Mi with a packet of papers. This done, he removed his hat, shook the water from it, and was returning to the entrance when Li Du hailed him. "If you can spare the time to wait, I have a message to send."

The messenger dipped his head deferentially. Li Du entered his office, walked quickly to his desk, took out a piece of paper, and hastily ground just enough ink to effect what he intended. He composed a short message, then sealed and addressed it. He hurried across the courtyard to where the messenger was waiting on the veranda outside the clerks' office, and explained that the letter should be directed to the Office of Temple Histories, within the palace. The messenger slipped it into his bag, bowed, and departed.

Mi, who had gone inside with the day's missives, emerged once again onto the veranda. "For you," he said, holding a single, hefty document out to Li Du. "The doctor's report on the autopsy."

The paper exuded a gentle fragrance of angelica root. Li Du took it to his office, sat down, and put on his spectacles. The report began with the usual formalities, making it clear that the doctor undertook to be accurate and truthful, understanding that his work would be judged not only according to the laws and statutes of the city, but also those of the gods and spirits in the netherworld, who would not tolerate wrongdoing.

The second section of the report detailed the wounds received by Madam Hong. As the doctor had suspected during his initial evaluation at the scene of the crime, Madam Hong's injuries had been sustained during a short, violent struggle with an assailant. Cuts on her arms indicated that she had tried to protect herself before receiving the mortal blow, a stab wound to the heart. This wound, in addition to the others, had been administered by the blade of a small, well-sharpened knife, almost certainly the one found at the door of the suspect, Hong Wenbin. A bruise on Madam Hong's hip suggested that she had struck the corner of the desk in her efforts to elude her attacker, which also accounted for the objects—a small bottle, in addition to various papers—that had fallen from its surface to the floor. A more general analysis yielded no relevant information except that Madam Hong had been a strong, healthy woman at the time of her death. She had not, it was briefly noted, been with child.

Li Du turned to the analysis of Pan's body. *In the case of the second victim*, the doctor had written, *certain indications merit further consideration.* As he read, Li Du began unconsciously to lean closer to the page, as if his growing sense of surprise and confusion could be addressed by proximity to the words. When he was finished,

Li Du remained for a moment as he was, staring down at the doctor's measured, slightly ponderous handwriting. Then he closed his eyes, nodded his head forward, and rested his temples on his fingertips. After a short while, he opened his eyes. He removed his spectacles, located his hat, and pulled it, still damp, onto his head. Holding the report, he walked the short distance along the veranda to the chief inspector's office.

Sun was affixing a seal to a letter when Li Du entered. "Yes?" he asked. "What is it? What do you have there?"

"This is the doctor's report," said Li Du. "I'll explain it to you on the way."

"On the way where?"

"To the offices of the Gendarmerie."

Chapter 28

Unlike the Banners, a Manchu institution incorporated into a Chinese city, or the city magistrates, a Chinese institution incorporated into Manchu rule, the Gendarmerie was an agency created solely for the purposes of maintaining order in the capital. As such, they were uniquely suited to the task. Consisting of some twenty thousand soldiers and a civilian staff, the Gendarmerie had assumed primary responsibility for everything from guarding the gates of the outer wall to clearing the city streets after heavy snowfalls.

Upon arriving at the institution's Inner City headquarters, Sun and Li Du presented their credentials to the crisply attired guards who asked for them. A short while later, they were ensconced in a small, well-appointed office that adjoined the institution's prison complex, where thieves and brawlers awaited punishments that generally ranged in severity from five strokes with a light bamboo stick to a period of penal servitude in a distant region. Harsher sentences of permanent exile or execution were reserved for more serious crimes, which were rare on the closely watched streets of the capital.

It was not long before a Gendarmerie official entered the room, looking as if he had stepped out of a painting commissioned to show the capital at its best. His robes bore no trace of a wrinkle or a spatter of mud, and his shaved forehead was so smooth that it would be easy to assume natural baldness, were it not for the thick ebony braid down his back. He moved with the easy grace of an athlete, and regarded them with the focused attention of an intellectual.

"I am Chief Inspector Sun, from the North Borough," said Sun, who appeared slightly dazzled. "This is my assistant, Li Du."

"Thank you, yes. I have been informed of your names. I am He Jingxiu." The perfunctory introduction, and the tone in which it was uttered, said clearly that He Jingxiu was not a man with time to waste on pleasantries, and that to require them of him would be to frustrate the course of justice. He turned to indicate a man who had just been escorted into the room by two guards. "This is Zou Anlin, formerly an overseer at the Black Tile Factory. I understand you wish to question him."

Li Du regarded the prisoner. Zou Anlin did not appear to have suffered excessively from his confinement. His hands and hair were clean of the clay dust that had coated them when Li Du had last seen him. His pallor was healthy, his expression almost complacent, though Li Du did not fail to observe Zou's start of unease when he recognized them.

He Jingxiu consulted a document. "I see that his crime was mitigated by the return of the stolen property. He has been sentenced to five strokes of the heavy cane. Have you come with an additional complaint?"

"It is possible," said Sun, with a glance at Li Du. "As I'm sure you know, this man was caught stealing a bag of silver from the scene of another, far more heinous crime."

"The murders at the Black Tile Factory," said He Jingxiu. "I understand the culprit died while in the custody of your borough magistrate," he added, censure evident in his voice.

Sun hesitated. A brief internal debate played out across his features before he indicated Li Du with a short nod. "In the course of compiling the official report," he explained, "my assistant has encountered several small details that require clarification. If it is acceptable, I will allow him to pose the questions."

Making no objection, He Jingxiu turned an inquiring look to

Li Du, who cleared his throat quietly before addressing Zou. "According to your confession, you entered the office at the Black Tile Factory on the morning after the murders. Upon discovering the bodies, you intended to report the crime, until you saw the silver. You decided to take it for yourself, and remain silent. Is that still your story?"

Zou looked down, his shoulders curved inward in apparent shame. "It is, sir, and I accept my punishment with gratitude. I am not a thief at heart, sir. I regret what I did." Li Du saw Zou's eyes lift and dart across the faces in the room, trying to assess the effect of his words.

"The murders took place during the night," Li Du went on. "As you were the last to leave the kilns in the evening, and the first to arrive the next morning, you would have been a suspect, had you not been able to provide an alibi for the hours between sunset and sunrise."

Zou began to nod vehemently. "I didn't leave my room at the Sichuan lodge. Not once."

"That is true," Li Du affirmed. "It was verified by the man who occupies the cot beside yours." He turned to address the others. "The man is elderly, and suffers from rheumatism. He says he was awake all that night, and that Zou remained asleep in his bed." Li Du turned back to Zou. "When was the last time you saw Pan Yongfa?"

"When I saw his body there in the office, sir."

"And when was the last time you saw him alive?"

Zou's reply did not come at once. "I saw him the day before," he said finally. "But everyone at the factory did."

"Perhaps," said Li Du. "But you were the only one who spoke with him alone in the office that afternoon. According to the kiln manager, Hu Gongshan, Pan asked for refreshments. It was you who served them to him. You brought him a small bottle filled with wine, and a dish of roasted soybeans. Is that correct?"

Zou's lips were compressed in a tight line. He barely opened them to reply. "Yes."

"Did you and Pan converse during that time?"

"No," Zou burst out. "He was an official. I would not have presumed to address him. I was only bringing him what he wanted. I gave him the food, and I left."

"And you didn't know he intended to return to the factory that evening?"

"Of course I didn't."

"Why did you enter the office on the following morning?"

Zou looked confused. "I—I was the first one to the factory."

"But you had no business in the office," said Li Du. "You made a point of that when the chief inspector first interviewed you. At that time, you insisted you hadn't gone into the office at all. Of course, that was before you were caught with the silver, and had to change your story." As he spoke, Li Du withdrew the doctor's report from his bag, and put on his spectacles.

"What document is that?" The question came from He Jingxiu.

"These are the findings of Doctor Wan, who, upon examining the body of Pan Yongfa, noticed a curious discrepancy. His report says that the wound to Pan's throat did not bleed as profusely as the doctor would have expected."

"Which suggests that the victim was already dead when the wound was inflicted," said He Jingxiu, his eyes now fixed on Li Du with increasing interest.

"It is a possibility," said Li Du. "But the doctor could find no evidence of another mortal injury to Pan Yongfa, or any sign that he had ingested poison."

"In that case," said He Jingxiu, "another doctor should be consulted, in case there is evidence of a poison unknown to Doctor Wan."

"That may not be necessary," said Chief Inspector Sun, motioning for Li Du to continue, his expansive face suffused with pride in his assistant.

"Doctor Wan may not have come to a conclusion," Li Du went on, "but he did provide a thorough account of what he observed. He mentions a slight blue cast of the lips and nailbed, present on

Pan's body but not on Madam Hong's. When I read his description, I was reminded of an incident reported in the *City Gazette* last winter. Two men, old friends, had died within hours of one another, both seemingly without explicable cause. The coroners there, too, noted a blue tinge to the lips and nails, but it was not until the testimony of a third friend that their deaths were explained. The men had been trying to compound their own medicine—a tincture of aconite—and had dramatically misunderstood the dosage. When mixed correctly, it can be very effective, but in quantities exceeding a drop or two, quite deadly." Li Du paused. "Aconite is used to treat—"

"Rheumatism," Sun declared, unable to contain himself. "The very same malady that afflicts the bunkmate of Zou Anlin."

"I suggest," said Li Du, "that if we were to ask the elderly man why his rheumatism kept him awake all that night, he would tell us that he had misplaced the bottle of aconite tincture that he usually kept to relieve his pain. But he would be wrong. He did not misplace the bottle. It was taken from the room by someone who knew that in a high dose, it could be deadly."

Zou's pinched face swiveled on his thin neck as he directed a panicked, beseeching look at the faces around him. "I don't know what any of this is about," he said, his voice almost a moan. "I'm only a poor laborer. I saw the silver, and I couldn't resist the temptation to take it for myself. But I never harmed anyone. They were dead when I found them."

Li Du spoke calmly and clearly. "Your crime was not an impulsive action, but a careful plan. You knew Pan had the silver with him that day. You had reason to believe he intended to return with it to the factory that night. You wanted it, but you didn't want to risk an attempt to overpower a younger, stronger man. So you used the time between Pan's visit to the kilns that afternoon and his return that night. You hurried the short distance to the Sichuan lodge, stole the bottle of aconite, and took it with you to the factory. Just before you left that evening, you refilled the bottle of wine you had served to Pan earlier in the day. This time, you added the poison. You hoped Pan would recognize the bottle, help himself to its contents, and succumb, leaving the silver for you to take on the following morning. What you did not anticipate was the presence of Madam Hong, and of another killer at the factory that night."

This time, Zou did not protest, but turned on Li Du a look of such burning resentment that the skin around his eyes seemed to wrinkle and retreat from their heat. The look of rage turned quickly to one of fear when he took in the implacable faces of the Gendarmerie guards.

He Jingxiu gave a short nod and turned to Chief Inspector Sun. "I had not realized you employed such competent assistants in the boroughs," he said. "It seems the charge against this man must be amended from theft to murder."

Sun and Li Du stood outside the gates of the Gendarmerie while a sedan chair was summoned to return the chief inspector to the North Borough Office. "I'll have to start paying more attention to the *City Gazette*," said Sun. "And I'll speak to Doctor Wan about improving his knowledge of poisons, not that I expect to encounter such an unlikely confluence of crimes again. Did you put all that together simply from seeing the doctor's report?"

"There were other signs," said Li Du. Now that the confrontation was over, he felt an uneasy awareness of having acted outside the constraints he usually placed on himself. The acute, curious glances of the Gendarmerie officials were unsettling. They had noticed him, and would remember him.

"What signs?" asked Sun.

"The broken wine bottle," Li Du replied. "And the rat."

"The rat?" Sun was momentarily perplexed. "Ah yes, the rat," he said, understanding. "The one the doctor found dead in the corner of the room. You think it drank the poisoned wine that spilled on the floor when the bottle fell?"

Li Du nodded. "The doctor's report suggested an interpretation. I considered it, and the pieces simply fell into place."

Sun's brow furrowed. "The question is what to do now. Though this addition to our knowledge of what occurred that night is undeniably significant, it does not suggest that Hong was innocent."

Li Du had anticipated this. "You mean that Hong might have stumbled onto the scene and attacked them just as before."

"Exactly," said Sun. "He wouldn't have known Pan was dead. He might have thought him asleep, cut his throat, and attacked Madam Hong. From Magistrate Yin's perspective, this won't change anything."

"I suppose not," said Li Du. "Though I would like to know why Madam Hong would remain in a room with a dead man."

"It is a good question," Sun said, considering it. "But the magistrate won't reopen the case just to answer it. He has his eye on a promotion to the Ministry of Punishments."

"And no one on the verge of a promotion wants complications," said Li Du. He saw the look of surprise on Sun's face, and realized he had spoken aloud what the chief inspector had tactfully left unsaid. He was about to offer an apology when he saw that Sun's face had tensed in a clear effort to gather his thoughts in preparation for speech. Li Du waited in silence.

Sun spoke at last. "I hope you do not misunderstand," he said. "I, too, wish to know the truth." He hesitated. "This city has its own rules," he went on slowly. "Not the rules laid out in the statutes, you understand, but *its own rules*. Only those who understand them best have the power to manipulate them, but to aspire to be such a man is dangerous. I myself have never desired it. My advice to you, as your employer and your friend, is to continue writing the report you have been given permission to write. You have shown an aptitude for uncovering truth. Use it, and hope, as I do, that it leads to further revelations. But do not go too far, because if you do, I am not certain I will be able to save you."

Chapter 29

In a city that preferred its citizens to have officially sanctioned reasons to be wherever they were, there were limited places to linger while waiting to meet a friend. Parks were, for the most part, accessible only by imperial invitation. Libraries were privately owned. There were no public squares. The elephant stables, located in the Inner City, were an exception to this rule, and had become a favorite destination for residents and travelers alike.

The elephants, gifts to the Emperor of China from lands to the south, were housed in six buildings, which were divided into eight stalls, separated by brick walls. Li Du entered through the open ironbound door into a cavernous space lit by skylights. One of the elephant keepers bowed to him, then returned to the task of shoveling manure into buckets, to be sold at markets as a luxury hair treatment to improve shine and luster.

It was long past the tentative time they had set to meet, and as Li Du moved from one building to the next, he began to think Hamza must have returned to Water Moon Temple. Then he spotted the storyteller standing very still in front of one of the stalls. Hamza's head was tilted back as he stared, transfixed, at an elephant. The elephant, busy with its own contemplations, was swishing its trunk across the floor of its enclosure, sweeping hay from side to side. As Li Du greeted Hamza, it raised its head, flapped its papery ears, and granted them a moment of its attention with one bright eye.

"What do they do here?" asked Hamza.

"They lend majesty to royal processions," Li Du replied. "When they are not so employed, they live in these stables, and are given more care and indulgence than are most citizens."

Hamza spoke without taking his eyes off the elephant. "I met a storyteller from Japan once, who told me about the elephants of the Emperor of China, how they are taught to bow to him, how they bathe in the city moat in summertime, and how they are granted noble titles for distinguished service. I, myself, prefer to see them depicted in gold and silver threads, or sculpted from metal and stone, or painted, not alive and kept in stables. And yet I would not have missed an opportunity to visit them, and thank them, for they have inspired more tales than could ever fit within the covers of a book."

A short silence followed, during which Li Du half listened to the conversations around them. There were between twenty and thirty Bannermen with them in the building, distributed across its capacious interior. Most were discussing familiar subjects: grain stipends, military drills, weddings, funerals, and of course, examinations. Others were simply watching the animals. Li Du sometimes wondered if the Bannermen who often visited the stables were those who perceived in the eyes of the elephants wilder, more open spaces than the city that confined them. Trained as soldiers, and descended from the mounted warriors of the steppe, there were those among the Manchu and Mongol Bannermen who chafed at urban life, despite being born and raised in the capital.

"I searched the markets for Ji's agates," said Hamza, interrupting Li Du's thoughts.

"And?"

"And they cannot be bought. The first market I went to had no peddlers of rocks and gemstones at all. The second had one such peddler, but she told me she had never seen a rock of the description I gave. The peddler at the third market insisted that he had agates, but held before me a piece of quartz. The one at the fourth market insisted she had seen me in a dream, and made suggestions that were tempting, but unrelated to my query. At the fifth market I was hungry, and forgot my errand."

"And the sixth?"

"The sixth and last market was the one that gave me an answer. The peddler, a man so sturdy of feature that he appeared hewn from rock himself, listened carefully to the description I gave, and told me there are only two ways to obtain such agates. The first would be to journey to their place of origin and chip them from the mountains myself. The second, to become a prince, for such rare stones cannot be bought or sold by anyone outside the imperial household. They are considered too precious for commoners."

"Which leaves us to wonder how the master of the Glazed Tile Factory came into possession of those we saw on his shelf," said Li Du. "And whether it has any connection to the death of Madam Hong."

His words caused Hamza to turn his attention away from the elephant. "Only of Madam Hong?"

With a glance at the Bannermen nearest to them, Li Du suggested quietly that they continue their conversation outside. Hamza turned a last, regretful look at the elephant. To his delight, the elephant nodded its head in apparent dismissal. Hamza followed Li Du out onto a wide avenue, and directed a pitying smile at a group of horses as they trotted past, bearing several officials in court dress. "I used to think horses more grand than I do now," he said. "Observe their thin legs and polished hides. If they stood beside the gray majesty of the elephants, they would not hold themselves in such a superior way."

As they walked, Li Du gave Hamza an account of all that had happened that day, beginning with his conversation with Bai, and ending with Zou's confession.

Hamza listened attentively, interrupting only to congratulate Li Du on the deductions that particularly impressed him. "But how did Zou know that Pan would return to the factory that night?" he asked, when Li Du had finished his summary.

Li Du thought back to the interrogation of Zou that had followed his admission of guilt. Quaking with fear, Zou had begged for lenience, and promised to answer truthfully any question put to him. "Because Pan told him," Li Du explained. "When Zou went into the office to serve Pan food and wine, he found Pan looking at the open bag of ingots. According to Zou, Pan smiled at him, and said he could see Zou was the kind of man who liked the shine of silver. He said he had business in the office that night that required privacy, and offered to pay Zou two taels if he would leave the factory entrance open. Zou agreed."

Hamza nodded his understanding. "But Zou wanted more, and to that end, he left a poisoned bottle of wine for Pan to drink."

"Yes. Pan had remarked on the wine's pleasant taste, which is what gave Zou the idea. He knew where to find poison. Old Gao, with whom he shared a room at the Sichuan lodge, had told him about the dangers of taking too much of his medicine."

Hamza was thoughtful. "Then Zou didn't know anything about Madam Hong?" he asked.

"No. Pan had only said he had business in the office. Zou didn't care what the business was. He just hoped Pan would still have the silver with him that night. Imagine Zou's shock when he entered the office in the morning, hoping to find Pan dead of seemingly natural causes, and the silver lying ready for him to take. Instead, he found a room soaked in blood, and two bodies instead of one."

"And yet his greed survived his shock," said Hamza. "He retained the presence of mind to take the silver, as he had planned."

"He thought he was safe," said Li Du. "After all, *he* didn't cut Pan's throat, or stab Madam Hong. For all he knew, Pan hadn't taken the poison at all. Unfortunately for Zou, there is clear evidence that he did."

"The wound that did not bleed enough," murmured Hamza. "And the blue lips that spoke of aconite."

Li Du thought back to the Gendarmerie office, where Zou, toying anxiously with the cuffs of his sleeves, had made a final, desperate attempt to persuade them that he was not truly a murderer. *If I hadn't done what I did, Pan Yongfa would still have been there, dead. Someone else meant for him to die that night. He was fated to die.*

They both were. From the expressions on the faces of the Gendar-merie officials, his pleas had failed to convince.

"Our object, then, is changed," said Hamza. "We are now searching for a killer who attacked two people, but whose blade ended only one life. We are looking for the murderer of Madam Hong."

Li Du's silence affirmed the storyteller's statement. "Tunnels and temples," Hamza went on musingly. "Speaking of temples, this one has an unusual shape."

They were passing the South Church. Over the wall, Li Du could see the roof, still caved in, slumped on one side like a wounded shoulder. Feeling a pang of guilt for his neglected friendship with Father Calmette, Li Du suggested they stop inside and ask the priest if there had been any progress with the repairs.

The courtyard was empty. The round windows on the church façade were dark. Li Du and Hamza ascended the quiet steps to-ward the imposing doors, which were unlocked. The air inside smelled of frankincense and rose, faint and chilled by stone. Once they had stepped over the threshold, the windows that from the out-side had been featureless were transformed into brilliant fragments of blue and green.

"It is like being beneath the sea," whispered Hamza. "Beneath a capsized ship." Li Du looked up at the vaulted ceiling, and imagined himself suspended in dark water. He shivered in silent agreement. Without the presence of worshippers or of lighted can-dles, or Father Calmette's indefatigable optimism, the space was very quiet. Though the church, with the exception of its damaged roof, enclosed them with protective welcome, there was a hint of forlorn pride to the grand, empty interior.

They left the church and crossed the courtyard to the offices. But these, too, were empty. "They must be inside the palace," said Li Du. "Or at the Observatory." There was nothing unusual about this. The Emperor had always preferred the Jesuits to be beneath the golden tiles of his personal domain. It reinforced their role as his advisors, rather than independent actors capable of building their own communities within the city.

As usual, the offices of the Jesuits were cluttered with the accumulated results of their dauntless curiosity. There were books open to half-colored sketches of birds, maps so crowded with labels that the lands they identified were obscured, globes of assorted sizes, dried specimens of apothecary plants, vials filled with potions, and varied alchemical and astronomical tools. Hamza walked to a table and began to examine the inner parts of a clock that were arranged on its surface. In addition to the more utilitarian gears and springs, there was an array of jeweled flowers ready to be animated by mechanical trickery.

Li Du walked to another clock that rested alone on a marble pedestal. "They say this is the first clock built for the Wanli Emperor by Matteo Ricci," he said.

Hamza joined him. "I know the tale. Long ago, and yet not so long ago, there was a man who wished he could visit the Emperor on the other side of the world. He wrote a courteous letter asking the Emperor to grant him an audience, but two years went by with no reply. *Surely*, thought the man, *the business of court life distracted him from his correspondence.* So again he wrote, again he waited, and again he received no answer.

"Years passed, and he filled the silence from the empire across the world with his vision of a place of abundant knowledge and sights unknown to him, of philosophies and languages and histories that, fitted with his own understanding, would turn questions into answers, uncertainty into complete knowledge. But without an invitation, he could not go to that place.

"So he wrote again, and offered to share with the Emperor all that he knew. *I can tell you*, he wrote, *the formula to calculate the movement of stars. I can speak to you of the history of my own kingdom. I can reveal to you the existence of God and of heaven. And I can teach you how to make a clock that chimes on its own, with no need of human hand to ring a bell and announce the hour.*

"The Emperor, pacing through the offices within his palace,

had these letters read to him, but they were like colorful insects one passes on a springtime hunt, of interest in the moment, but soon forgotten once larger animals came into view.

"This continued for twenty years, and silver appeared in Matteo's hair as he set his pen to paper again and again. In the continued silence, twenty years of imagination flourished, and finally, he could bear it no longer. He set to sea to find the Emperor. He had many adventures on that journey, and faced many perils, including the sea monster—"

Li Du cleared his throat.

"Of which I will tell you another time," Hamza finished. "At last, Matteo reached the wall of this very city, and asked the soldiers there to take him to the Emperor. But everyone knows that visitors cannot simply ask to see the Emperor. The guards assumed that the dusty man who spoke Chinese in the garbled tones of an imbecile must be mad. And Matteo was cast into prison. There, in the dripping cell, he believed that the time granted him had run out.

"As it happened, it was time that saved him. One day, the Emperor, at work in his study, heard the sound of bells as his loyal servants struck the hour across the city. And in that moment, the Emperor wondered whether someday they would fail him. He was the ruler of a dying dynasty, and knew that men could not be trusted.

"So the Emperor went to his advisors, and he asked them about the man who had once written to him from a distant country, the man who had offered him a self-chiming clock that would speak to him of time with no intermediary."

Hamza's words inspired a faint worry in Li Du. He tried to remember how long it had been since the bells had tolled the hour of the rooster. The light in the room was dimming.

"The advisors, who were tasked to know of every person in the prisons of the city, told the Emperor that the man who had written to him of the clock was within his very walls. And that is how Matteo Ricci came to have an audience with the Emperor of China.

The Emperor was patient with him, and taught him to behave in a civilized manner. And even though the clocks ticked the Wanli Emperor to his doom, the friendship formed between the Jesuits and the palace survived the fall of that dynasty, and lived into this one."

But not too close a friendship, thought Li Du, in the silence that followed. The Jesuits had never been granted freedom of movement in and out of the city. His glance fell to the surface of a nearby desk, and on the red seal of the Censor's Office stamped onto a paper there. Even their words didn't have free passage.

He put on his spectacles and picked up the letter. The handwriting was even and precise, with the red stamp made over it to show that its contents had been read and approved. The paper was thick and crisp, the ink fresh. He imagined it reaching its destination, distant Rome or France, by which time the ink would be blurred, the paper rough at the edges, wrinkled and stained with salt water.

"'The Emperor,'" he read from the top page, startling Hamza from his inspection of Ricci's clock, "'sent to enquire our names, our several capacities, and the talents we possessed. The tranquility which the empire enjoyed by his prudent conduct, since his two last journeys into Tartary, the Relation of which we had perused in Paris, gave us the opportunity of answering that the French admired his majesty's genius and conduct, and entertained the highest idea of his valor and magnificence.'"

"Ah," said Hamza. "A letter that knows it is being read by the censors. Imagine what it would say without awareness of the watchful eye? *The Emperor inspired terror in us by demanding to know what we could do, as if in expectation of our ability to perform magic. We flattered him as best we could in order to distract him from asking us to turn water to wine, a miracle of which he seems to believe us capable, and which he is most curious to see effected. We fear our mission is failing, and that we are no longer truly welcome here.*"

Chapter 30

In the chamber at the top of the drum tower, the tip of an incense coil dropped to the tray beneath it in a tiny heap of ash. Another hour, marked on the coil with a red line, had burned away, and the drummers took their positions to announce the coming of night. Li Du heard a rumble that might have been thunder, an evening storm blowing in after a day of fitful rain, except that instead of diminishing, the sound continued in a repeated rhythm that spoke of human discipline, not nature's mystery. They had left the church too late. It was the hour of the dog, and the gates were closing.

Xuanwu closed with a rattle of hinges just as they came in sight of it. Li Du watched soldiers take their places in front of the door. Their movements were relaxed, unhurried as they followed a routine that almost never required improvisation. Over time, the mere presence of soldiers had become enough to deter most citizens from attempting to break curfew.

Li Du called quietly to Hamza, who was a few paces ahead of him, to stop. "We can't get through," he said, when he had caught up to the storyteller.

Hamza looked up. "The sky is still so light that I can only see one star. The soldiers will allow two more to pass before the door bars are in place."

"Not without asking us our business," Li Du said. "And as there is no way to predict the course of such a conversation, I would rather avoid it. I suggest we return to the South Church. Even if the Jesuits are still absent, we can assume we are welcome to stay there."

Hamza dismissed the suggestion with an exaggerated shudder. "I will not spend the night in a cavern of cold stone. Such an accommodation may be acceptable on a mountain, but not in a city full of light and food and silk cushions. Where else can we go?"

Li Du considered. "There is another gate. Zhengyang is used by so many ministry officials that it often stays open later than the others at the end of the day. We won't be able to get all the way to Water Moon Temple, but at least we'll be back in the Outer City. We'll have to find a place to stay on the alley of theaters and pleasure houses."

"A dire prospect," said Hamza with mock sincerity. "Perhaps we should return to the empty church after all, and sustain ourselves on cold vegetables from its courtyard garden." His words did not reach Li Du, who had set off at a fast pace, heading east. Hamza hastened to join him.

Li Du's prediction proved to be correct, and they were jostled through Zhengyang Gate with a group of about twenty beleaguered officials muttering at the soldiers to let the hardworking men of the city go home to their dinners. The neighborhood into which they were funneled was assuming its evening guise. Book and antique shops, their doors shut tight and flat against the alley walls, were almost invisible. The morning's peasants and merchants, carrying baskets heaped with vegetables, were replaced by groups of men swaying down alleys, laughing and gesticulating. Because of the curfew, those who did not live nearby would be frequenting neighborhood establishments until dawn. Women with heavily powdered faces waited in the shadows, calling to revelers who looked capable of paying.

The single star Hamza had seen above became many. "We'll have to find somewhere to stay," said Li Du without enthusiasm. He had never liked crowded places. He liked them least in the gloom and glow of night, when confusing shadows made it harder to see faces, and to distinguish friends from strangers.

"I count four signs for inns on this alley alone," said Hamza cheerfully.

Li Du straightened his hat, which had slid to one side, and they started down the bustling lane. As Li Du expected, Hamza's optimism proved to be unwarranted. At each inn, they were informed by harried servants that there were no rooms available. "I doubt," said Li Du, after their fourth attempt, "that we will be able to find a bed, pallet, or couch in this neighborhood that has not been claimed by an examination candidate or an accompanying family member."

He was debating which way to turn when he noticed a restaurant across the alley from where they stood. Its name, The Green Door, was painted on a wooden sign above the entrance. With an effort, he shut out the din around him and tried to remember why the name was familiar.

Hamza stopped a few paces ahead of Li Du to read the advertisements pasted to the alley wall. "Famous cold noodles," he said. "Just down the alley to the right."

Li Du pointed. "I have another suggestion. If we are going to be here all night, quite possibly without sleep, we may as well make use of the time. Do you remember, in our conversation with Ji Daolong, he mentioned this establishment? He said that Pan dined often at The Green Door. Perhaps this is an opportunity to glean some information."

Hamza acquiesced, on the condition that they could order food in addition to asking questions. They had to wait for a group of armed and mounted Bannermen to pass before it was safe to cross. The horses, sleek and gleaming in the lantern light, emitted the same repressed strength as their riders. They had been trained for war, and the narrow alley seemed too narrow to accommodate them. Pedestrians backed up against the walls, pressing close together to stay clear.

Li Du and Hamza crossed in the wake of the Bannermen, just before it filled with people again, and entered the restaurant. The place was not busy, most of its patrons having dined there on their way home from the Inner City, and departed before the gates closed. Its specialty was a dish of duck and vegetables. Steam from cooking rice filled the air and condensed in drops of water that studded the leaves of courtyard plants.

While Hamza took a seat at a table, Li Du made his way to the fire, where a bald man with expansive cheeks, shining with heat and grease, was turning three ducks on a spit. Speaking just loud enough for the man to hear him over the crackle of flame and shouted orders of food and drink, Li Du explained that he was an official of the North Borough Office, and that he had come with questions about a man who, until his death, had been a regular customer.

"I heard about it," said the man, who proved to be the owner. He had an affable demeanor. "Sad news. Jealous husband, wasn't it?"

"I was told he came here often."

"Very often. I'd say he was here more days than he wasn't."

"Did he ever speak with you about his life, or his work at the ministry?"

"For most of my customers, life *is* work at the ministry. But he didn't talk to me about that. Of course he didn't. I would never presume to address my customers on familiar terms, even the ones who are here all the time. I would not be so impertinent. This is what I know how to do." He indicated the golden skin of the roasting ducks.

"When was the last time you saw Pan?"

The owner began to slice pieces of meat onto a plate. He considered the question for some time. "Which day was the big thunderstorm?"

"Eight days ago."

"It was after that," said the owner. "Must have been, yes, I think it has been seven days. I didn't hear he was dead until yesterday."

Seven days, thought Li Du. *That means Pan was here on the evening he died.* Out loud he asked whether Pan had dined alone.

The owner mopped his brow with a stained sleeve to which several feathers adhered. "He was alone, yes."

Something in his tone caught Li Du's interest. "Was there something unusual about that night?"

"Well, now that you ask, I think he met a friend of his."

"But you just said he ate alone."

"He did, he did." The owner's hands were occupied, but he gestured with his chin toward the open door of the courtyard. "But when he left, I saw him speaking with someone at the door."

"Did you see who it was, or hear what was said?"

"It was a young man, but I can't tell you his rank. It was crowded in here, and I couldn't see clearly through the smoke and the heads of all the customers. Couldn't hear a thing, either. But he did speak to someone, there, in the doorway. I do remember that."

The owner could offer no further insights. Li Du placed an order for a modest meal and joined Hamza at the courtyard table. The food arrived quickly—simple, hearty fare that revived them both. When they had finished, Li Du, who had been watching the alley through the open door, told Hamza he had an idea.

"Before we crossed the alley," he said, "I noticed a woman standing in a doorway just behind us. The crowds are thinner now, and I think I can still see her. She hasn't moved from that doorway the whole time we have been here."

"Ah," said Hamza, understanding. "You are hoping she may be able to tell us more about this mysterious young man."

Li Du nodded and stood up. "If we are lucky." They left The Green Door and crossed the alley. The woman standing in the door was holding a lantern, which she lifted as they approached. She wore a robe of pink silk with an embroidered collar. Her face was powdered. Three silver butterflies were nestled in her hair, which was piled in intricate loops on top of her head.

She raised a hand coquettishly, as if to bar the entrance. "I am the guard of this gate," she said. "But I am not so stern as most soldiers. You could convince me to let you go inside." From over her shoulder, through the slightly open door, drifted the sound of feminine laughter. The air was redolent with rose incense.

"My hope," said Li Du, a little shyly, "was to speak with you. Do you often stand here in the evenings?"

She lowered her hand, and looked from Li Du to Hamza with a hint of uncertainty. "Most evenings," she answered.

Li Du indicated the restaurant. "This alley is so narrow that you must be able to see clearly the customers that go into The Green Door. I am hoping you recall a man who went there often, an official of the third rank." Li Du tried to picture Pan's face as it would have looked in life. "He was perhaps thirty-five years old, tall, and he had strong eyebrows—"

"Like willow leaves," she said quickly. "I know the man you mean. From Anhui?"

"Yes."

She gave a little sigh. "We all like to watch him, though he never comes here."

Li Du didn't ask her how she knew Pan came from Anhui. It was one of the most remarked-upon characteristics of the capital that a man could never hide his place of origin. The accents of the provinces were easily identified. But his hopes rose.

"You say he never came here," Li Du said. "Still, you know his voice. Seven days ago, he stood outside that door and spoke to a young man. Is it possible that you witnessed that conversation?"

Her brow creased. "I might have been here, but how can I separate one day from another? I don't think I can help you."

"Are you certain you cannot remember? The conversation took place the last time he was here."

She was silent for a long moment. Li Du saw her turn her focus inward as she moved through her memories. The lantern, now lowered, left her face in shadow. It cast a pool of light on the ground, which was sprinkled with feathers that had blown across the alley. "I do remember," she said finally. Her forehead relaxed, leaving faint lines in the powder.

"There was a young man, not much older than a boy. He was

pacing outside the restaurant, back and forth and back and forth, the whole time the man from Anhui was inside. I remember thinking he was like an anxious little pigeon, going back and forth like that. When the man from Anhui came outside, I don't think he recognized the youth. He would have walked past him, but the youth grabbed his sleeve, like this." She clutched the silk of her own sleeve, so voluminous that it touched the stone threshold of the door, and pulled at it.

"Then you don't think they knew each other."

"They *did* know each other," she said. "The man from Anhui recognized him. I am certain of it."

"Did he say his name?"

She shook her head. "Not his name, but he said something else. I remember it because he smiled. Whenever he smiles, my whole heart turns to butterflies. He smiled, and he said to the young man, *What would the kiln master say if he knew his son was here?*"

Li Du blinked. *The kiln master's son.* "Did you hear anything else they said?"

She gave a little shrug. "Nothing more. They walked away together. A troupe of acrobats began to perform, breathing fire and making their false swords into glittering mountains. Everyone stopped to watch and it was so crowded, I had to step backward out of the street so that I would not be crushed." She glanced behind her to the doorway.

Hamza followed her look. "My friend and I are in need of a place to stay tonight," he said in a tone of courtly respect. "If you have room within your fragrant establishment to house two tired guests who have stayed too late from their homes, we would be most grateful."

After a short consultation with the manager of the establishment, a woman who went by the name of Big Sister Wu, it was determined that space could be made for a reasonable price. Li Du and Hamza were ushered into a spacious dining room, where two pallets were assembled for them on the floor. Hamza accepted a cup of warm wine and an invitation to tour the courtyard gardens, which were more extensive than they could have guessed from outside the high wall.

Li Du stretched out on his pallet with relief, but it was some time before he slept. His thoughts hovered around the anxious youth he had met in the offices of the South Church. To his knowledge, there was only one kiln master within the city walls who had forbidden his son from speaking to Pan. If he was right, the young man who had met Pan that evening, and who almost certainly had been among the last to see him alive, was the young secretary to the Jesuits, Hu Erchen.

Chapter 31

Li Du woke early to the sound of clinking dishes and water splashing on stone. He rose quickly from the pallet that had been laid out for him in the corner of the dining room and went outside to find the cook washing dishes in a bucket. A sturdy woman with reddened hands and an authoritative voice, she insisted on stopping her work to serve him tea and steamed rolls. While he ate, she informed him that his friend had been up all night telling stories to the women who had found no employment that evening, and had only gone to sleep himself when the sky began to lighten.

Leaving Hamza to his slumber, Li Du left the courtyard to find the neighborhood transformed, the shops open and the strings of unlit lanterns pale and unobtrusive against the wan morning sky. Yawning soldiers at an open alley gate made no comment as he passed through to the adjoining neighborhood. He was pleased to find Wu's bookstore also open. The bookseller was sitting on his front step, finishing a bowl of noodles, a book open across his knees.

"You're too early to have come from Water Moon Temple," said Wu. With raised eyebrows, he looked over Li Du's shoulder as if the night's activities were visible behind him. "I never took you for a theatergoer." A subtle emphasis on the word *theater* suggested that Wu knew well that the most popular activity within the opera district was not attending operas.

Li Du explained that he had been returning home from the Inner City, and had misjudged the hour. "I was fortunate to find a room," he said, "given the demand for them."

Wu cocked his head to indicate the shop interior. "You don't have to tell me," he said. "You'll find my shelves bare as a larder after a hard winter. The candidates this year are a particularly voracious group."

Li Du smiled. "I see they have left you at least one book to accompany your breakfast."

Wu set his bowl down beside him on the step. "It is the latest from the Master of Fox Tales. You must delay your errand long enough to hear one passage. Am I wrong to rejoice that the poor man has not been able to pass the examinations? If he ever does, we will be denied his bitter parodies."

The man to whom Wu referred was a well-known scholar who had failed the examinations a humiliating seven times. Most recently, he had been automatically disqualified for skipping a page in his answer book. It was, the examiners argued, a suspicious discrepancy. What if the blank page had been a predetermined signal to a corrupt clerk or examiner who had been paid to give a passing grade?

"Sit!" Wu patted the stone beside him. As Li Du took a seat on the cool stair, Wu flipped through pages, humming with indecision over which passage to read. "This one," he said finally. "The seven forms of the examination candidate."

Li Du had to restrain himself from directing an anxious glance into the store. He enjoyed his visits with Wu, but the bookseller's words, especially when he was inspired to read passages aloud, could have an ensnaring effect.

"'First, the examination candidate is a beggar,'" Wu began, seemingly oblivious to Li Du's impatience as he concentrated on the text before him. "'He enters the examination hall with only a single forlorn basket to hold all his possessions. Second, he is a prisoner who cannot leave his cell. Third, he is a cold bee, sitting at his desk with stiff legs and arms stuck out in front of him. Fourth, he is a sick bird, released from the examination yard, fluttering and dragging his plumage. Fifth, he is a captive monkey, one moment mad with dreams of success, the next plunged into despair, sullen as a corpse. Sixth, he is a fly who has been poisoned. The list of successful candidates is posted, and his name is not there. He throws his notes into the fire, and says he will never study again. Then, after a month has passed, he adopts his seventh form. He is a turtledove, just hatched. He begins to study for next year.'"

"By lining his nest with books from your shop," said Li Du. "But the volume I have come to find would not interest students of philosophy. Do you have the *Compendium of Named Temples* somewhere on your shelves?"

Wu scrunched his features thoughtfully. "Are you looking for the edition published in the twentieth reigning year, or the forty-second?"

"Either, or both. I have come merely to consult the text, if you will permit it."

Twisting to look over his shoulder into the shop, Wu clicked his tongue against his teeth. "At another time of year, I would be tempted to remind you of the difference between booksellers and librarians. But with my shelves almost empty, and my purse filled with coins, I am disposed to be generous. You will find the earlier edition in the back. It's to the left, in the cabinet labeled *Books of Miscellaneous Records.*"

Li Du thanked him, rose, and made his way into the depths of the shop, where a trace of night lingered, evident in the cooler air and a sense of slumber to the books. He located the compendium easily. There were a few smudged fingerprints on its white silk cover, left by customers who had started to pull the book from the shelf, realized it held no key to examination success, and slid it back into place.

It was a simple list of the temples of Beijing. Most entries consisted merely of a name and a location. A few offered additional information, such as descriptions of curiosities displayed at the temples, including such objects as a meteor fragment, an iron ship's anchor, and a carved stone taken from a famous ruin. Li Du found the name he was looking for, repeated its location to himself until he had memorized it, and closed the book.

"I did not know you were visiting temples," said Wu, when Li Du emerged from the shop. "Are you compiling a guidebook? Surely your visit can have nothing to do with the terrible crime at the factory. I heard that matter was resolved, however unhappy its conclusion."

Li Du hesitated. "Come," said Wu. "This is my price for your consultation of my shelves."

The bookseller's shrewd gaze warned against unnecessary dishonesty. Li Du stayed as close to the truth as possible. "It is the factory case that brings me here," he admitted. "But you are correct when you say the matter is closed. I am only writing a report, which demands the clarification of certain details connected to the events."

"Of course," said Wu. He stood up, shook the dust from his robes, and picked up his bowl. "It is best to be thorough."

Before Wu could renew his questioning, Li Du thanked him and gave the excuse that he had a pressing appointment. Then he hurried to retrace his steps and retrieve Hamza, whom he found miraculously fresh and bright in appearance, and ready to depart. The cook gave them an additional helping of steamed rolls to take with them, and they left the neighborhood, walking east, Hamza holding a roll in each hand.

"Did you know," he said, "that there are examination candidates who pay the women who hosted us last night to assume the roles of examiners? I will be clear. I do not have the impression that they stay up all night practicing answers to essay questions."

Li Du cleared his throat. "I am aware," he said. "Though that was not my own strategy for relieving stress before the exams began." He thought back to those exhausting evenings, when the pieces of knowledge he had arranged so carefully in his mind had turned to leaves caught in a tempest. What was the point, he remembered having thought at the time, of memorizing so much when, now that the exams had arrived, it had all turned to a jumble? But he had been one of the privileged few who lived in the capital, and could seek calm within the familiar setting of his own home.

He had not been forced to participate in the poisonous solidarity of the overcrowded inns.

"Speaking of examination candidates," said Hamza, "I assume we are going to speak to the youth who failed to mention his conversation with a murdered man hours before the murder."

"We are."

"Where does he live?"

"When he is not providing his secretarial services to the Jesuits, he lives in his father's house. It is near the Black Tile Factory. So near, in fact, that a person could, with no trouble, move from one place to the other, even in the dead of night."

Chapter 32

Hu Gongshan owned a modest home with a single large courtyard. The space was crossed by laundry lines, from which unadorned clothing swung in cloudy shades of gray and white. The servant who answered the door told them that Erchen was in his study, but the room to which he led them had nothing in common with the scholar Bai's airy haven for contemplation and composition. On one side of the room, two small children were playing with a kitten. At its center, an older boy and girl sat beside each other at a table, practicing calligraphy. The remaining side of the room was divided from the rest of the space by hanging blankets. Pinned to these partitions were numerous charms and bouquets of herbs. Dried leaves and fallen petals littered the floor.

The servant addressed the curtain, and received from behind it a request to wait. The servant, embarrassed, explained that there were two men from the North Borough Office who had come on urgent business. At this, the curtain was jerked back. Erchen emerged, half tripping. Seeing Li Du, he dropped into a formal bow and began to apologize profusely.

"I should not have spoken so rudely," he said. "Even if I did think one of my brothers or sisters wanted to interrupt me again. I beg you to forgive my behavior, and allow us to serve you tea. My father is at the factory, and my mother and grandparents have gone to visit our uncle outside the city."

A small voice piped up from the corner. The speaker was the smallest child, a girl who was gently dangling a string over the kitten. "We want to play that the bushes are kilns, and when we go inside them we turn into animals."

"Fire is dangerous," said Erchen. "You should never go into a kiln, not even when you are pretending." Erchen's face was thinner and sharper than his father's, but his expression as he spoke these words made the resemblance obvious. His look was stern, but the sternness was all in the brow. His eyes remained gentle, his mouth soft. The girl looked ready to argue, but was prevented by her elder sister, who picked her up and carried her into the courtyard.

"We came from the North Borough Office to speak to you," Li Du said, responding to the look of anxious inquiry from Erchen. "As the matter pertains to the crime at the Black Tile Factory, perhaps there is a more private place—?" He glanced meaningfully at the children who remained in the room.

"Of course. Yes." Erchen bobbed his head. "We'll sit in the courtyard." After asking the servant to bring tea, he led Li Du and Hamza through the curtains of laundry to the narrow outdoor space between the home's outer and inner walls. Nestled among tangled vines was a low stone table with three stone stools. With a look of embarrassment, Erchen removed a wooden toy from where it rested in the center of the table, and brushed dry leaves from the seats with his sleeve as he invited them to sit.

Li Du introduced Hamza, implying vaguely that he was an assistant. Erchen seemed barely to be listening. His cheeks were flushed. "When I spoke to you at the South Church," Li Du began, "you told me that, on the night Madam Hong and Pan Yongfa were killed, you were here at home."

Erchen nodded. "I was."

"Studying."

Erchen nodded again, but said nothing.

"You also said that you knew Pan Yongfa only slightly."

"That's the truth. I saw him at the factory sometimes, but I—I didn't know anything about him."

"Apparently, you knew that he would be eating dinner at The Green Door on the night he was murdered."

The color drained from Erchen's face. "I don't know what you mean," he whispered.

"You were seen," said Li Du. "You were seen speaking with Pan only a few hours before he died. I am sure you understand that by withholding this information, you have given me good reason not to trust you. I should bring you into the North Borough Office to be questioned by Chief Inspector Sun."

"Please don't," Erchen pleaded with a look of broken, exhausted desperation. "Please don't take me away from my books. I have only three days left. There is so much still to review. I promise I had no idea that Pan was going to meet Madam Hong. It was only a terrible coincidence that I spoke to him that night. When I heard that he was dead, I was frightened. I didn't want to be accused of having something to do with it. I had *nothing* to do with it."

"Then tell me why you met him that evening, and what passed between you."

"I can't tell you."

Hamza spoke gravely. "I have heard accounts of spirits that haunt the examination yard, reminding candidates of their past crimes."

Erchen's eyes widened. "I know," he said. "They say that inside, the examiners unfurl black banners with words painted on them in red. *Wrongs will be righted,* they say. *Those aggrieved will take revenge.* And they say there is a demon who pretends to be the god of literature, and tricks candidates into spilling ink on their papers."

Hamza leaned forward, his eyes alight with interest. "What else do they say?"

Erchen hesitated, then turned confused eyes to Li Du. "I haven't committed any crime."

"Then tell me what happened." Erchen was silent. Li Du started to stand up. "If you will not, I have no choice but to summon—"

"Wait." Erchen stopped him. "Wait."

"A wise decision," said Hamza, as Li Du returned to his seat. "You will not find a fairer questioner than the one who now sits across from you."

Li Du was relieved. He strongly suspected that whatever Erchen was hiding did not merit martial intervention. "I know that Pan once offered to help you cheat on the examinations," he said. "And I know that when your father found out, he forbade you from speaking to Pan again. Was it your purpose, when you met him that evening, to take him up on his offer?"

As Erchen began a stammering denial, Li Du interrupted him gently, but firmly. "I am not here to trap you, or to enforce the rules of the examinations. It is my opinion that, because they have not yet been administered, you have not yet committed an infraction. Trust me, please, and tell me the truth."

Erchen let out a shuddering sigh. "I did talk to Pan," he said. He glanced furtively toward the door into the main courtyard, as if he was afraid someone was listening. Then he leaned forward, so close that Li Du could see tears gathering in his eyes. "I just wanted to ask him for help. *Please* don't tell my father."

The same servant who had greeted them at the door arrived with tea. They waited silently until he had gone, at which point Erchen began, meekly, to tell his story. "I obeyed my father. I never spoke to Pan again, after the night he made the offer. But when I saw him at Hong's gathering, I—The exams seemed so close, and my father, well, my father doesn't speak like any of the men who hold degrees. I thought he might have been wrong. I thought—I couldn't stop thinking—that someone like Pan could help me. I know that many candidates have advantages. My father doesn't believe it. He thinks that because I have studied hard, I will pass the test. But he doesn't understand that there are so few places and that, well, I don't know for certain, but that—"

"Corruption exists," said Li Du.

Erchen nodded miserably. "I just thought that Pan might be able to tell me if my father was being naïve."

"So you went to The Green Door in search of him?"

Erchen bit his lip. "No. I went to the Ministry of Rites. I waited outside the gate. When I saw him come out, I followed. There were so many ministry and palace officials around us that I was afraid to speak to him. I just—followed a little way behind. It was stupid. I see now how stupid it was."

"And you followed him all the way to the restaurant?"

"Yes."

"Did he go directly there?"

"No. He stopped to speak with someone. Well, not to speak. To deliver a letter, I think."

"Where did this happen?"

"In an alley market not far from the palace—just southeast of Rainbow Bridge."

"And did you recognize the person to whom he delivered this letter?"

Erchen seemed to concentrate on the memory. "It didn't really look like a letter. The shape of the paper—it was more like an official document. It looked white, but it might have been pale blue. The ink was dark, not red or green. And yes, I did recognize the man he gave it to, because I'd just been told who he was the day before, at Hong Wenbin's home. He was there, you see. His name is Kirsa."

The Manchu name was familiar to Li Du from the list of guests who had attended Hong's party, but it was the first time he had heard it mentioned in connection with Pan Yongfa. "What were you told about him?"

"Not very much. Only that he is a very high official in the Imperial Household Agency, and has been for many years. They say he's very influential, and that he knows all the most important people in the palace *and* the ministries."

"So Pan met Kirsa, and gave him a document. Did they converse?"

"I couldn't hear them, but they cannot have spoken more than ten words. Kirsa seemed as if he was in a hurry. They parted as soon as Pan had given him the document."

"Other than Kirsa being in a hurry, what was the tenor of their interaction? Did they seem friendly with each other?"

Erchen hesitated. "If you speak to Kirsa, you will see that he does not—That is, I'm not certain I can imagine him appearing friendly. He has a—a stern aspect. I think it would be intimidating to speak to him."

"I see. What happened after they parted?"

"Kirsa went in the direction of the palace, and Pan Yongfa went to Zhengyang Gate. I followed him through it, and that's how we came to the restaurant."

"Where you paced outside, waiting for Pan to emerge."

"Yes." Erchen's head sank a little in shame. "I couldn't find the courage to go in and speak to him. I kept telling myself to walk away, only to think, *What if he is my only chance.* I hardly noticed the time passing, I was so caught up in trying to decide what to do. Then suddenly he was at the door, and starting to walk away. I reached out and found myself clutching his sleeve. I think he would have struck me, thinking me a thief, but then he recognized me. He asked me what I wanted, but I think he guessed right away why I was there. He was smiling."

"He was amused?"

Erchen struggled for words. "No. It was more as if—as if I'd proven him correct about something. But it was that smile that made me see clearly what a mistake I'd made. We walked together to a quieter alley to talk, but by the time we got there I was certain that I was not going to ask him for anything, that I wanted nothing from him. It is less disgraceful to fail than to cheat."

"Is that what you told him?"

"I told him I'd made a mistake. That I hadn't come to speak to him at all."

"What was his reply?"

"He told me that he had somewhere to be, and to enjoy my evening."

"And that was the last you saw of him."

"Yes."

"Did you return home after that?"

Erchen blinked. "I couldn't. By the time I parted from Pan, the gates were closed. I had no money, so I—I found a place on the street and slept there. I told my father I'd stayed late at the South Church. I know I am not in a position to ask for anything. I know that you could send me to the examination officials for judgment. But please, *please* don't tell my father."

Li Du sighed. "I remember being a candidate," he said. "There were always whispers from the alley shadows, offers of connections, of the names of officials who could be bribed, of advance knowledge of the questions, of hidden places within the examination yard. You are fortunate you did not follow temptation any further. Not only would you be wrong to have done so, but many of these offers are traps."

Erchen waited, hope shining in his frightened, gentle eyes. Li Du stood up. "My advice to you is that joining your little brothers and sisters in their games of pretend will serve you much better than joining your fellow candidates in schemes and shortcuts, and indeed may serve you very well. Close your books, and rest your mind. When the time comes to enter the examination yard, don't be afraid of spirits. Remember to bring enough food, and keep your hand steady as you write."

They left Erchen standing in the doorway of his home, watching them go with a look of puzzled gratitude, and renewed determination in the set of his narrow shoulders.

Chapter 33

This must be Narcissus Temple. It's where Wu's compendium said it would be." Li Du studied the dilapidated plaque above the entrance. Whatever words had once been painted onto it were gone. The wood was rotten, swollen from moisture and chewed by insects. The door below it was closed, wedged crookedly into its warped frame. Dry leaves covered the threshold.

"A ruined temple," said Hamza, "is an ideal place to hide a secret."

"I hope it is not too well hidden," replied Li Du, looking at traces of paste on the door where a paper god, long since disintegrated, had been affixed. "I don't think we're going to find any helpful clerics here, ready with answers to our questions."

They were in a corner of the West Borough. Similar to its corresponding corner in the East, it was sparsely populated. Temples and homes were separated not by alleys, but by marshes and fields, through which ran faint dirt paths. It was on one of these paths that they now stood, their backs to a marsh that exuded drifting odors of waste.

The door required a hard shove from Hamza's shoulder before it gave way, allowing them to enter a small, dingy courtyard with a single building at its center. Dense weeds obscured the pattern of colored cobblestones on the ground. After taking in his surroundings, Hamza crossed to a section of wall and pointed to the flower painted on it. "Narcissus," he said. "There are stories about this blossom."

They decided that Hamza would explore the courtyard while

Li Du searched the central shrine. As Hamza began to pace the perimeter, studying the crumbling wall and looking for objects hidden in the tall weeds at its base, Li Du climbed the stairs to the veranda and opened the doors of the shrine wide to let in the light. There was an altar toward the back of the room, in the center of which was a bronze statue of a man in scholar's robes, one of a multitude of virtuous men rewarded, over the course of the empire's history, with deification. Cobwebs seemed to bind him where he stood. Old incense sticks littered the floor in front of the altar like a crooked line from a child's calligraphy exercise.

Li Du's careful examination uncovered nothing beyond more signs of neglect and abandonment. He exited to find Hamza crouched over a pile of leaves and fluff in a sun-soaked corner of the courtyard. The storyteller looked up at his approach. "I have found the goddess of the temple," he said. "She has been reduced to the humble form of a mouse." He opened the small purse at his belt and drew from it a tiny stone, which he placed in the center of the nest. "A gift, so that she knows she is not forgotten." He stood up, brushing the dirt from his knees. "Unfortunately, I found no secret passages leading to the impossible tunnels of Beijing, no coded messages concealed in pots, and no buried trove of agates. Was there anything inside?"

"No," said Li Du, turning to face the shrine. "It resembles every other small, forgotten temple in the city. There are dozens of them. The only detail that is unusual about this one is the roof."

"The roof?" Hamza looked at it. "The roof!" he repeated. "Of course. We must search the seams between the tiles. There could be numerous items hidden there."

"That is not exactly what I meant," said Li Du. "Look at the rest of the temple. The walls are crumbling, the wood is infested with insects, the incense is unlit, and the bowls for offerings are empty. It is clear that no one has cared for this property in years. Now look at the roof."

Hamza raised his eyes obediently. His eyebrows rose. "It's new," he said.

"So new," Li Du echoed, "that it looks as though its tiles could still be warm from the kiln. I see no cracks, no moss, not even a trace of debris."

"And they are black tiles," said Hamza.

Li Du nodded. "Exactly. It certainly would seem that these tiles were produced by the only kilns within the city that make them, those of the Black Tile Factory. This raises several questions. First, why repair the roof of a temple that is not in use? Second, who commissioned the repair? Third, why was Pan talking about it two days before he died?"

"And with whom?" asked Hamza. He resumed his amble around the inside of the wall, studying the ground as if for inspiration.

Li Du fell into step beside him. "Pan worked for the Ministry of Rites," he continued. "The Ministry of Rites is responsible for the upkeep of public temples. Perhaps the ministry wants this place restored, but has not yet completed the restoration. If Pan was involved, the conversation Bai overheard him having at Hong's party might have been entirely innocent." He rubbed his forehead, trying to think clearly. "What do we *know*?"

"We know," said Hamza, "that this Pan Yongfa was not an innocent sort of man."

Li Du considered this, then nodded agreement. According to Pan's coworkers at the ministry, Pan had been an intelligent and efficient civil servant, but most of what Li Du had learned over the course of the investigation had eroded the image of Pan as an upstanding citizen. Not only had Pan's charm failed to convince the scholar Bai, who despite his arrogant obsession with his own importance was a keen observer of human behavior, but Pan had also earned the enmity of Hu Gongshan by trying to set the kiln master's son on a potentially ruinous course of examination misconduct. And while the business Pan had intended to conduct on the night of the murder remained a mystery, there was now little question that it was of a criminal nature. "It would help," Li Du said, "to review the events leading up to the murders."

"Facts are more your area of expertise than mine," said Hamza. "I am listening."

Li Du collected his thoughts, his head bowed as he rested his eyes on the weeds, now trampled into a path by their boots. He began. "Pan attended the literary gathering at Hong's manor, where, according to Bai, he had a conversation with two men, a conversation that was not intended to be overheard. We don't know who these two men were, but we know that Pan spoke of tunnels, and of the temple in which we now stand."

Hamza gestured for Li Du to continue. "On the following day," Li Du went on, "Pan left his home in the morning with sixty taels of silver. He had it in his possession when he arrived at the Black Tile Factory that afternoon to review contracts in connection with a ministry audit. We know this from Zou Anlin, to whom he paid two taels in exchange for a promise to leave the factory door open that evening."

"And for all Pan's connections to the city's web of corruption," Hamza interjected, "it was that simple act of bribery that issued Death an invitation to seek him out. But I am pulling your account out of its proper order. Continue."

Li Du drew in a breath. "Pan returned to the Ministry of Rites, where he appeared to go about his work as usual. When he left at the end of the day, he failed to notice that he was being followed—"

"By our anxious student, Hu Erchen," finished Hamza.

"According to whom," Li Du went on, "Pan met with a high official named Kirsa outside the palace walls, and delivered a document to him. Erchen followed Pan to the opera district, where they eventually spoke."

"Which brings us," said Hamza, his brow tensed in determined concentration, "to the fatal events at the Black Tile Factory."

"Almost," Li Du corrected him. "But I have a question. Erchen told us he could not return to his home that night because, by the time he parted from Pan, the gates were closed and the watch was set."

"I remember. Do you suspect him of lying?"

"Not necessarily. My question is this. If the gates were closed and guarded, how did Pan get from the opera district, which adjoins the Inner City wall, all the way to the Black Tile Factory?"

Hamza blinked. "Are you asking whether he walked?"

"Whether he walked, rode, or hired a sedan chair, there is no way Pan could have journeyed from one place to the other without passing through multiple city gates *after* they had closed for the night. If he had been able to convince the soldiers guarding them to let him through, the chief inspector would have heard of it when he interviewed the soldiers stationed at the North Borough sentry points. It's almost as if Pan disappeared from the opera district, and reappeared in the factory."

"Or became invisible," said Hamza, his eyes aglow with possibilities.

"Somehow, Pan *did* reach the factory," said Li Du. "As did Madam Hong, though her residence was so near to it that she had no gates or soldiers to impede her. But why were they there? Who was blackmailing whom?"

"It was Pan who brought the silver," said Hamza. "Which suggests that it was he who intended to make a payment."

"Yes, but to Madam Hong? How could a woman whose interests and activities were confined to her home and her collections have attained the power to blackmail Pan?"

"Or," Hamza offered, "was the blackmailer the one who joined them there in the middle of the night, cut the throat of a man who was already dead, and pierced a woman's heart?"

They had reached the section of wall that contained the painted narcissus. Hamza began to trace the ghostly outlines of its petals as if he was moving his finger along the paths of a map. "What is our next destination?"

"The Ministry of Rites," declared Li Du, after a moment's thought. "I think it is time to see where Pan Yongfa was officially employed."

Hamza dropped his arm. "I hope you will allow me to accompany you. I have never seen the inside of a ministry."

Li Du nodded. "But we will make a stop on the way. I would like to speak to Kirsa, the palace official to whom Pan delivered a document only hours before his death."

"Does that mean we are going to the palace?" asked Hamza, with a look of anticipation.

"I am sorry to disappoint you," Li Du replied. "I doubt even Magistrate Yin could secure a meeting with a palace official on such short notice. For a secretary, it would be impossible."

"Then how do you plan to speak to him?"

Li Du adjusted his hat and started through the dry leaves to the temple entrance. "This is a city that operates on schedules, and I know that every month, on this day, the palace holds a market outside its gates, allowing the public a chance to purchase items discarded from the Emperor's own household."

"I see," said Hamza, looking puzzled.

"The market is operated by the Imperial Household Agency," Li Du explained. "If that is indeed the institution that employs Kirsa, he will almost certainly be there." As he spoke, Li Du felt for an instant a sense of foreboding, like the hum of a wasp passing close to his ear. He thought of Sun. If the assistant to a chief inspector intended to approach a palace official, surely the chief inspector would want to know about it in advance.

"Then our destination awaits," said Hamza, unaware of Li Du's sudden hesitation.

Shaking off his misgivings, Li Du nodded. *After all*, he thought, as they headed north, *the surest way to be prevented from doing something is to ask permission before doing it.*

Chapter 34

The palace market bustled with the city's elite shoppers. Connoisseurs held porcelain bowls up to the light, evaluating the tints and textures of the glazes. Servants haggled on behalf of their mistresses for furs and jewels rejected by imperial consorts. Collectors hunted for pieces to add to their collections of bronze mirrors, miniature vessels, and jade carvings. The air hummed with the energy of choice and acquisition, but the voices were muted and movements careful. Guards and officials patrolled the narrow corridors between stalls. Behind the market, the palace wall loomed like a red cliff topped with a mantle of golden scales.

As Hamza and Li Du were navigating the crowded interior, they almost collided with a painting being unrolled for a potential buyer to assess. "*Heavy Snow on Mountain Passes*," proclaimed the palace official who was in charge of its sale. "A fine example of the painter's work, and an excellent aid to self-cultivation."

Obliged to walk the length of the painting in order to go around it, Li Du allowed his eye to wander the winter landscape. Triangular mountain peaks, some encrusted with frozen trees, filled the scroll from one end to the other. Tiny travelers, overwhelmed by their surroundings, appeared lost in a world enshrouded in snow. As he reached the end of it, which was misted by faint red seals and cascading lines of poetry, he heard the official continuing his efforts to make the sale. ". . . depicting noble loneliness and isolation," he was saying to the interested customer, who was leaning forward as if he were about to step onto the snowy path himself.

They passed incense burners, golden Buddhas, snuffboxes, and carpets until they came to the section of the market where rare and valuable books were sold. Waxed awnings, a precaution against sudden rain, flapped in the breeze over volumes spread across low tables. Old editions alternated with new ones designed and printed on expensive paper by the imperial workshops.

Behind one of the tables, a man fanned himself with an old copy of the *City Gazette*. Li Du recognized him, though nine years had whitened his hair. As an employee of the imperial printing workshops, Qiu had often come to the library to deliver volumes or consult the librarians on a replacement binding.

Qiu evidently recognized him, too. "Li Du!" he exclaimed. "But it's been years since I've seen you! I cannot tell you how pleased I was when I learned your sentence had been repealed. Are you collecting? I have a palace edition of *Illustrations for Cultivating the Correct* here. You won't find that in a city bookshop!"

"Thank you," said Li Du. "But I fear I have no cabinets worthy of it. I would not like to be responsible for such a volume being damaged from living on a damp shelf. I'm sure I would derive much pleasure from perusing every book on this table, but I have come today on a particular errand. I am looking for a man called Kirsa."

"You want to speak to Kirsa?" asked Qiu. His eyes flickered, with slight apprehension, over Li Du's attire.

"I would not presume to approach a man of his standing for any personal reason," said Li Du. "I have only come to deliver a message from my superior. If necessary, I will of course leave it in the keeping of a guard or secretary." Qiu looked relieved. "I take it," said Li Du lightly, "that he is not a man one wants to offend."

"He is not," said Qiu. He lowered his voice. "I hear it does not go well for those who do." A light breeze made the book covers flutter. Qiu produced several paperweights from a box and began to arrange them on top of the display. "He usually occupies a chair near the furs."

Li Du glanced in the direction Qiu indicated. "How will I recognize him?"

"He'll be the thin one to whom everyone is bowing," said Qiu.

Li Du thanked him, and he and Hamza wound their way to another section of the market. Qiu's description, however sparing, proved entirely sufficient. A tall, compact man stood beside an array of ermine pelts. His shoulders were broad, but his frame was so thin that his robes of sumptuous blood-red silk draped in a straight line down to the tops of his black satin boots. Not one, but two men were bowing to him, offering thanks and apologies, and they retreated slowly from his stern regard.

When they had gone, Li Du approached and bowed low. "If you are Kirsa, I am hoping to speak to you, briefly, on an urgent matter."

"I am he," said the man, looking down from his superior height. He had sharp cheekbones and tense, compressed lips. His eyes looked as if they were accustomed to assessing value. "But I don't know you." One of his fingers twitched as he prepared to raise his arm and summon the nearest guard.

"My name is Li Du. I am a secretary at—"

"I do not speak to secretaries who are not my own." Kirsa's hand continued its upward trajectory. "Submit your request to my office."

"I want to ask you about Pan Yongfa."

A guard was approaching. Kirsa motioned for the guard to stop, then dropped his hand to his side and examined Li Du's face. Nearby, Hamza pretended to browse a display of ink stones.

Kirsa's pale lips pressed together tightly as he considered his next words. "On whose authority do you come to me with questions?"

"On the authority of the North Borough Office."

The answer seemed genuinely to surprise Kirsa, but he recovered quickly. "The North Borough Office has no jurisdiction in the Inner City," he said. "What do you mean by this insolence?"

"I intend no insolence. I am writing the report of the murders at the Black Tile Factory, and have only a very limited amount of time in which to obtain all the facts. In the interest of finding the truth, I have come to ask for your help."

"Help? I know nothing of the murders."

"But you did accept a document from Pan Yongfa hours before he died."

"I accepted no document. That's a lie."

"I apologize," said Li Du. "You were right. I have no authority here, and should not have approached you so informally. I will have my superior submit a request to the Imperial Household Agency, seeking permission to interview you. I will, of course, explain why speaking with you is essential to the investigation." He paused. "Unless, upon consideration, you feel it might be easier and more convenient for you to answer my questions now."

Kirsa glared at him, but Li Du saw the calculation behind the look. He began to speak in a tense, clipped voice. "If you are suggesting I have some information relevant to the incident at the Black Tile Factory, and that I have not shared it with the proper authorities, you are mistaken. I do recall that I saw Pan Yongfa recently, but I had not made the connection until now that it was the same day he died. He delivered a message to me from the ministry. I don't recall what it was. I receive dozens of small notifications every day. If it had been connected in any way to that man's unfortunate and shocking demise, I would have volunteered the information immediately."

Li Du hesitated, and decided to risk a guess. "What about your conversation in the pavilion at Hong Wenbin's party the day before?"

Kirsa's nostrils flared. "What conversation?"

"Just as the rain began," Li Du replied. "You were speaking of Narcissus—"

"I will no longer permit this intrusion," Kirsa snapped. "This interrogation is at an end, and I intend to report this harassment to your superior."

He lifted his hand again, this time with the clear purpose of calling the guards. Li Du bowed low and retreated, as quickly as he could, into the forest of hanging pelts. Hamza followed close behind. As they weaved their way through stalls and between blankets cluttered with jade and pearls, Li Du felt his heart race, not from exertion, but from the anticipation of hearing, at any moment, the soft but inexorable pounding of soldiers' boots, and the metallic whisper of swords. It never came. They reached the edge of the market, continued into the nearest alley, and were soon subsumed by within the fast-moving current of Bannermen and officials flowing toward the ministries.

Chapter 35

Li Du presented his own credentials at the Ministry of Rites, and told the soldiers at the gate that Hamza was a visiting translator. Once inside, they enjoyed a considerable degree of anonymity. Li Du, who had spent two years stealing extra moments in various archives within the six ministries, had become adept at moving through them with the purposeful stride of a clerk performing an errand for someone important. The trick was to maintain a fast pace and an expression of faint anxiety, which communicated to milling clerks and officials that his business was too urgent to be interrupted, but not so urgent as to merit attention.

It was late afternoon. Within the halls and offices of the city's government sector, this was a time of rising tension, when tasks that were meant to have been completed by the end of the day were beginning to weigh on those responsible. Doors were flung open and slammed closed. Clerks hurried by without acknowledging each other. Li Du and Hamza were stopped only once, and that was by a thin young man who wanted to know where the examination copyist orientation was being held.

"Examination copyist orientation?" asked Hamza, after the man had rushed away to ask someone else for directions. Li Du, who was reading the signs painted above the office doors, did not answer immediately. "What manner of being," Hamza persevered, "is an examination copyist?"

"The examiners can't grade the candidates' essays in their original drafts," Li Du explained, once he had oriented himself and led them into a series of side courtyards. "To prevent them from seeing the names of the candidates, the essays are recopied in red ink, the names replaced with assigned codes. Examiners only receive them after they've been inspected for irregularities, copied, and proofread against the originals." He indicated a crowd of men similar in appearance to the one who had stopped them filing into a nearby hall. "The copyists," he said.

"But there is an army of them!" exclaimed Hamza.

"May I suggest a quieter voice when employing martial vocabulary within these walls?" said Li Du. "As for your observation, have you not yet noticed that the examinations have taken hold of the entire city? Six thousand candidates will enter the examination yard, and write as much as they possibly can in the time allotted. If the ministry didn't employ hundreds of copyists, these exams would remain unmarked through spring."

"But didn't you say the job of the Ministry of Rites is to maintain temples?"

"That is only one of its responsibilities," said Li Du. They were in front of a small keyhole door leading to a spare, well-tended courtyard. A painted sign read *Offices of Temple Construction* in Chinese and Manchu. Upon entering, they were met by a minor official who led them to one of the rooms bordering the courtyard, where an official one rank higher sat frowning in concentration over a set of documents spread over the desk in front of him.

"Good," he said, after Li Du had introduced himself. "I was hoping the North Borough Office would send someone." He gathered up several pages and thrust them in the direction of the official who had escorted them. "Review these numbers," he said. "I need more detail in the categories of incense expenditures, specifically vendors and suppliers. By the end of the day."

When the newly burdened official had gone, the man turned his attention to his visitors. "My name is Shen. Pan Yongfa left several of his personal possessions here at the ministry. Do you wish to make an inventory of them?"

"That would be helpful," said Li Du.

Shen gave a curt nod. "Most of the supplies he kept at his desk were ministry issued, and have been returned to our supply rooms. You will find the remaining items in the room two doors down from this one, on the left. Anything your office does not require, you may leave behind. We will ensure that it is conveyed to the family."

Li Du started to turn, then stopped. "There must be a great deal of discussion on the subject of Pan's death here at the office that employed him."

Shen, who had already returned to his work, looked up with a blank expression that implied he had not been expecting further conversation. "Not a great deal," he said. "Gossip is strongly discouraged. What happened was shocking, of course."

"He never mentioned trouble at the Black Tile Factory?" asked Li Du.

"Trouble? If I understand correctly what happened to him, his *trouble* was of a private nature."

"But he did visit the factory often in connection with his work," Li Du pressed, "especially on the recent audit?"

"The audit, yes." Shen's eyes dropped to the papers on his desk as if they were guests being kept waiting. "It has been our primary concern this month."

"Pan was reviewing contracts for temple roof repairs," said Li Du.

Shen's reply was clipped. "That was one of his assignments."

"We saw one of the repaired roofs recently," Li Du continued, pretending not to notice the other man's impatience. "At Narcissus Temple."

"Narcissus?" Shen looked blank. "I don't recall the name." He returned his attention to his papers. Then he paused. Li Du read in his expression the perfectionism common among officials. Shen stood up and drew a thick volume from a shelf behind his desk. "Narcissus," he muttered, scanning the text. After a little while, he touched his finger to a page. "Small temple in the West

Borough," he read. "Roof repair requested by neighborhood four months ago." He closed the book. "Now, if you have no more questions . . ."

Li Du accepted the dismissal. The room to which Shen directed them was a small reception room decorated with stately red vases arranged on irregular shelves built to match their sizes and shapes. In one corner was a round table, on which rested a bag made from rough silk. Next to the bag was an inventory of what it contained. Li Du read the descriptions out loud as Hamza pulled the objects one by one from the bag and set them on the table. There was a square, unornamented ink stone, a brush with an ivory and bamboo handle painted black and gold, a brush container of pale blue porcelain, two earthenware bowls, a white porcelain tea caddy with a decoration of bamboo leaves in blue, and a set of chess pieces in a latched wooden box.

Hamza lifted the lid from the tea caddy and sniffed the dry leaves inside. "Fine quality," he murmured. Then he picked up the slim wooden box. It was rectangular, rounded at the edges, and covered in black lacquer inlaid with fragments of iridescent shell arranged in a geometric pattern. He lifted the latch and opened the box. It had obviously been made to accommodate the chess pieces, which, arranged in two layers, fit tightly into the space. The pieces themselves were made of polished wood, each disk incised and painted on the top with the character assigned to it: *pawn, rook, knight, elephant, cannon, adviser, general.*

Li Du studied the modest collection that was spread out across the table. *For so few items,* he thought, *they present a clear portrait.* The ink stone, brush, bowls, and tea were the tasteful, anonymous tools of a dedicated bureaucrat. Clean and impersonal, there was nothing about them to suggest that they had belonged to a man of unique passions. This was the face Pan had presented to the ministry, but the chess pieces spoke of the face he had kept hidden, the one that saw the city as a game to be mastered. *What self-assurance it must have required to behave as Pan had.* Li Du felt a twinge of envy. While he had spent the past two years inhibited by the maddening limitations of the city's rules, Pan had been confidently flaunting them.

He was pulled from his reflections by Hamza, who was examining the chess pieces. "I prefer the design favored by the western kingdoms of the world, who have their own version of this game. These neat disks do not evoke war. I would rather see a tiny queen in a gown of ivory, her pale eyes fixed on her quarry, a row of soldiers advancing, ready to be sacrificed, their shields etched with runes, and horses with sculpted manes that ripple when they are touched by firelight."

He was turning one of the pieces over in the palm of his hand when suddenly he gave a low exclamation and lifted the piece toward his face to examine it more closely. "Blood," he said, and handed the piece to Li Du. "There's blood."

Too surprised to remember his spectacles, Li Du took the piece from Hamza and held it where he could see it clearly, searching until he found what Hamza had seen. On the curving edge of the piece was a trace of a red, sticky substance. Li Du frowned. "This isn't blood," he said. "It's red ink."

"Ink," Hamza echoed. "I thought for a moment that the piece, like a true warrior, was bleeding from a wound, and would have retracted all my criticisms of your craftsmen. But ink is not so shocking. There must be enough red ink in the cabinets of these halls to drown a person."

"Certainly," said Li Du. "And yet I don't know how it came to be on a chess piece." He examined it again. The ink indeed appeared to have come from within the disk, seeping from a thin, straight cut. But that didn't make sense. He ran his thumb lightly around the edge and felt a seam as fine as a strand of hair. As Hamza watched, he gripped the top and bottom of the piece as tightly as he could with both hands, and twisted. At first, nothing happened. His fingers slipped on the smooth wood. He covered them with cloth from his sleeves and tried again. The wood squeaked as the

two halves slid against each other. After three full turns, they separated.

Hamza drew in a breath and leaned forward across the table
to see. One half of the piece was slightly hollowed to accommodate the relief on the other half, which was coated in a thick, oily
residue of red paste. "It looks like a—"

"A seal," Li Du finished. He put down both halves and picked
up another piece from the open box. Hamza did the same. Among
the pieces, they found four that opened. Li Du reached into his bag
and drew from it his notebook, as well as a small box of black seal
paste. He opened the notebook to a blank page. One by one, he
touched the hidden seals to the paste and pressed them to the paper. Then he put on his spectacles to view the result, a set of four
circular impressions, black with a blur of red at the edges.

Hamza stared at them. "Each one is different," he remarked.
"To whom do they belong?"

"They aren't personal seals," Li Du said. "They belong to offices."

Hamza lifted his eyes to look at Li Du's expression. "You recognize that one," he said, tapping his finger to the page.

Li Du nodded slowly. "I do. It is a key that allows its bearer to
leave the city." He fell silent, lost in thought.

"I don't understand," said Hamza, his eloquent brows drawing
together.

Li Du spoke slowly. "A key," he repeated. "But not a key for
people. It's a key for paper. And I know where we must go next."

Chapter 36

Father Calmette was sitting on the steps of the South Church, an open book resting on his knees. He appeared deep in concentration. His shoulders were rounded forward. His left hand was pressed against his chest, pinning his long white beard to keep it from obscuring the text in front of him. In his right hand, he held a stylus worn down almost to the nub, and was tapping it thoughtfully on the corner of a page. It was not until Li Du and Hamza had crossed the courtyard, and were standing before him at the base, that he looked up.

"How wonderful to see you again, and so soon!" he exclaimed to Li Du. He struggled to his feet and accepted Li Du's assistance in navigating the stone steps down to the courtyard. Hamza quietly retrieved the cane he had left behind.

Holding Li Du's arm for balance, Father Calmette gestured with the hand that still held the book. "The other day," he said happily, "I was honored with an opportunity to peruse the paintings in one of the palace workshops. There was one I particularly enjoyed. It depicts two pines and a cypress in close proximity to the viewer, and a ridgeline of boulders beyond. I marveled at the artist's ability to show so little, and yet to imply a vast forest and towering mountain beyond the painting's edge. The effect was at once intimate and overwhelming. You know, Li Du, when I first came to this city, I thought our painters had a great deal to teach yours. What arrogance, when now I see it is the other way around. And what variety of texture this artist produced with his brush! Truly an example of *the hand moving at the heart's desire.*" Father Calmette paused, a trace of worry on his brow. "Or do I misapply the quotation?"

"Not at all," said Li Du. "Sun Guoting's essay on calligraphy is perfectly relevant."

Father Calmette looked pleased. "Good, good. And indeed, it is with writing that I need your help. I would not presume to attempt a copy of the painting itself, but I did take down the poem written on it." He held up his book. "I am endeavoring to produce a translation, but there is a line that is giving me trouble. The artist writes that the evening wind on Lake Dongting stirs a—and there I am not sure if the character refers to a boat that looks like a leaf, or a leaf that looks like a boat." He looked at Li Du inquiringly.

"I would take great pleasure in working with you on a translation of 'The Fisherman's Ode,'" said Li Du. "But I am afraid there is not time today—"

"Time," said Father Calmette with a sigh. "I myself have much I should be doing, and here I am idling with my poetry." He released Li Du's arm, and looked around in search of his cane. When Hamza presented it to him with a bow, Father Calmette smiled, his disappointment at once forgotten. "But who is your friend who so kindly carries my cane for me?"

Li Du hesitated. "Hamza and I traveled together in the southwest. He is visiting from—"

"Shaanxi," said Hamza easily, with another bow.

"Ah," said Father Calmette. "But I know the road to Shaanxi! I traveled it once, when I was a much younger man. I recall the marble bridges carved with lions at—" He paused, then pronounced carefully, "Loo koh kiao."

"I know those lions well," said Hamza. "It was my own grandfather who carved them. He told me that he received a letter from an imperial consort, accompanied by a purse filled with golden coins. She wanted lions for her bridge. Each lion was to be unique, sculpted according to her specifications, which were the most precise my grandfather had ever seen. He completed the work, and wrote to the palace saying the sculptures were ready to be inspected and approved. Only then was it discovered that the consort who had written to my grandfather, and to the bridge-builder, did not exist. The bridge and the lions became a great attraction, but the identity of their exacting patron has never been ascertained."

Father Calmette listened, captivated. "But that is a strange tale, indeed," he said. "I will certainly include it in my next letter to Rome."

Li Du's attention moved to the open door into the offices. He thought he saw a figure start to step into the courtyard, then retreat into the shadows. "I hoped to speak to Father Aveneau," he said. "Is he here today?"

Father Calmette was enthusiastic. "Of course you may speak to Father Aveneau. I would have made the suggestion myself, if you had not. He has been afflicted with a morose humor ever since he returned from the Black Tile Factory. Conversation is just what he needs. We will go to him at once."

They found Father Aveneau seated at a desk in one of the common rooms, staring unseeingly at an open book before him. Despite the warm glow of rosewood in the room, he appeared cold. Hearing them come in, he looked up from beneath swollen eyelids. His face was haggard. Recognition flared as his gaze settled on Li Du. He rose slowly to his feet.

Father Calmette, who seemed to be the only person unaware of the tension in the room, made the suggestion that they adjourn to his study, where they could speak without interruption. He led them to a small room furnished with a desk, a couch, a cushioned armchair, and a mismatched assortment of small tables and stools. The space was cheerfully untidy. Drops of candlewax studded the tabletops beside piles of books and pencil shavings. Geometrical instruments had been used as paperweights at the corners of open scrolls. Father Calmette lowered himself into the embrace of a cushioned armchair, leaned his cane against the wall, and waited expectantly for his guests to sit down. Father Aveneau took the desk chair, while Hamza and Li Du drew up two stools.

"Is there—" Father Aveneau's voice caught. "Has something happened?"

"Hamza and I have just come from visiting the Ministry of Rites," said Li Du. He indicated Hamza. "My friend was surprised to learn that the ministry administers the examinations. As I was explaining to him that the ministry has many responsibilities other than the maintenance of public temples, I remembered another one of its duties. The Ministry of Rites is responsible for welcoming foreign tributaries, a group that includes the Jesuits. When priests of your order come to this city, it is the Ministry of Rites that arranges their first audiences with the Emperor."

Father Calmette spoke from the corner. "I will never forget the day *I* arrived. Twenty years, it has been. *More* than twenty years. It was the day of Father Verbiest's funeral. Within an hour of entering your city for the first time, I was walking in a funeral procession. I remember the white silk covering the coffin, and the red tapestry bearing Father Verbiest's name in brilliant gold. I was terrified lest I commit some unintended offense. I found myself standing before the tombs of Father Ricci and Father Adam Schall, and was so overcome with emotion, I feared I would faint in the presence of the Emperor. How I shook as I knelt before him!"

As Father Calmette lapsed into silent recollections, Li Du turned to Father Aveneau. "You have not been here very long," he said. "When was your first audience with the Emperor?"

"I met him last year," said Father Aveneau stiffly.

"And you were prepared for that meeting by officials from the Ministry of Rites?"

"Yes."

"I am wondering," said Li Du, "whether Pan Yongfa was one of them?"

There was a silence. "Yes," said Father Aveneau finally. "He was."

Father Calmette turned to the other priest with a look of surprise. "Pan Yongfa?" he asked. "The man who was killed? But I thought you didn't know him."

"That is what he claimed," said Li Du. He glanced at his old acquaintance. Father Calmette's expression of bewildered curiosity, framed by wispy white hair, reminded him of a young bird, its downy feathers disarranged by a gust of wind. "I am sorry to bring distress to your house," he continued. "But I must ask you and Father Aveneau some questions."

"Of course you must ask them, if they pertain to your investigation," said Father Calmette.

After a glance at Aveneau, whose expression was stony, Li Du continued to address Calmette. "The letters you write to Rome are not permitted to leave the city until they have been reviewed and approved by the Censor's Office. Is that correct?"

"But of course," said Father Calmette. "It is the Emperor's rule."

"And the Censor's Office often requires you to make many changes to your letters."

"It does," replied Calmette.

"How does the Censor's Office indicate that a draft has been approved, and requires no further emendations?"

Calmette looked mystified. "It applies the seal of the office," he said.

"And only once the letter has received this seal can it pass out of the city and begin its journey west," said Li Du. He glanced at Hamza. "The seal is, in effect, a kind of key?"

"Yes," said Father Calmette. "But I don't understand. What do our letters have to do with Father Aveneau's audience with the Emperor, or with the man who died?"

Li Du turned his attention to Father Aveneau. "We have just discovered that Pan Yongfa had a counterfeit seal of the Censor's Office hidden among his possessions, the same Pan Yongfa who met with you on behalf of the Ministry of Rites a year ago, the same Pan Yongfa who was lying dead in the Black Tile Factory on the very morning you chose to visit it."

Father Aveneau raked thin fingers through his hair. "If you are accusing me of having something to do with his death, I didn't."

"But you were paying him, weren't you, to apply the seal of the Censor's Office to letters that never passed across a censor's desk?"

"You cannot know—"

Li Du cut him off, quietly but firmly. "It is easy to verify that he was the official the Ministry of Rites sent to prepare you for your meeting with the Emperor. I expect it would be easy to verify that you have met with him several times since then. Given this, the fact that you denied recognizing him when you saw his body would be enough to convince any magistrate to conduct a strenuous interrogation. I advise you that whatever secrets you are hiding are better shared with me, here, than under such circumstances."

After considering these words for a while in silence, Father Aveneau appeared to come to a decision. "I never had any ill intent," he said. "I would never have imagined it, had not Pan Yongfa himself made the suggestion."

"Ah," said Hamza. "This is not the first time in recent days that we have heard of Pan Yongfa leading others toward trouble. This is when my friend will suggest that you tell us everything."

Three pairs of eyes turned to Father Aveneau. Despite the resigned expression on his face, there was a hint of defensive pride in his tone. "You were correct," he said to Li Du. "I met Pan Yongfa when he came to instruct me on how to behave at my audience with the Emperor. I saw him again several weeks later, when he came to return one of my letters from the Censor's Office. Perhaps it was because we had met before, and because his demeanor invited confidence, that I did not conceal my frustration when I saw that more than half my words had been struck through by the censor's brush. Pan perceived the reason for my ire. He told me, then, that if I ever wished to compose a letter without deference to the Censor's Office, he—he could arrange it." He lifted his eyes to meet Li Du's. "I will not lie to you now. I did take him up on his offer."

"By doing so," said Li Du, "you were giving a great deal of power to a man who might at any moment have decided to betray you. Why did you trust him?"

Father Aveneau flinched. "I realize now that it was unwise. More than anything else, it was something in his manner. He expressed himself with such easy confidence. He told me that every city has its official systems, and its unofficial ones. He made it all seem so normal, so expected. I reasoned—"

"How could you?" The question burst from Father Calmette. Distress had turned his cheeks a bright, uneven pink. "How could you risk so much? My soul glorifies the Lord, and we are His servants, but we are *subjects* of the Chinese Emperor. We are in this place only because he permits us to be. We are *alive* because he permits us to remain so! Did you not consider what would happen to our community, should you be caught in such a transgression?"

Father Aveneau's pale green eyes sparked. "I intend no disrespect, but you have been away from Rome for many years. You do not know how perilous our situation is within the church. Do you know what they think of us? They think we have set aside our mission in favor of learning the customs of this country. They think we wear silk because we have been seduced by luxury. They think we have made no progress. And how can they think otherwise, when the Censor's Office prohibits us from writing anything other than pleasantries and obsequies? If we do not make some effort to show our supporters in Rome that we *are* succeeding, then we may face as grave a fate at home as we do here."

Father Calmette dropped his face into his hands. Muffled words emerged through his fingers. "What was the content of these letters you sent?"

Father Aveneau spoke quickly. "I assure you, they contained no threat, no conspiracy against our hosts. In my first letter, I wrote only of the continued imprisonment of Father Appiani, about whom I know there has been much concern in Rome. In my second, I offered some small insight into the complex nature of the rites controversy. I am confident our detractors in Rome will be more sympathetic to us now that they are apprised of circumstances that had not been clear to them before."

In the middle of this speech, Father Calmette lifted his face from his hands. His expression conveyed new worry. "You didn't . . ." he said quietly, and stopped. He turned to look at Li Du. "He wasn't involved in the crime, was he? Is that why you are here?"

"I am here only to ask for an explanation," Li Du replied.

"I had nothing to do with Pan's death," said Father Aveneau. "All that you say is true, but I beg you to believe me when I tell you that my reason for going to the Black Tile Factory that morning was exactly what I told you it was. You see yourself the damage to the roof. Father Calmette knows I went with the intention of commissioning a repair. That's all. I never expected to see Pan Yongfa there, alive or dead. My shock, when I saw the bodies, was not feigned."

"You maintained your composure enough to withhold the fact that you recognized one of the victims."

Aveneau swallowed. "When I saw who it was, I was struck by fear. You see, he had one of my letters in his possession. I had given it to him only days earlier, and was awaiting its return. *What if he has it with him?* I thought. *What if it is found?*" He looked urgently at Li Du. "That is why I returned later to the office. I had noticed, that morning, that the desk there was covered in papers. I hoped against hope that they had not yet been searched, and that the letter might be among them."

"But it wasn't."

Aveneau shook his head. "The letter is still missing."

"What did it say?"

"It was about the succession," said Father Aveneau quietly. "It was about the rumor that Prince Yinzao, the one who is returning to the capital, may be named the Emperor's heir, now that he is once more in favor." He hesitated. "The letter discusses the possibility that he will be more receptive to our teachings than his father has been."

Father Calmette raised a trembling hand wearily. "I cannot listen to more. You have quelled any hope I had that the contents of the letter might be too benign to attract attention. The topic of the succession is the most sensitive one in the city, save, perhaps, for the topic of the previous dynasty. The penalty, should your letter be found . . ."

There was a long silence. Then Father Calmette lifted himself from his chair, pulled his shoulders back as straight as he was able, and addressed Li Du. "I must beg you to help us," he said. "If I had known, I would never have permitted Father Aveneau to act as he did. I trust you not to send us to our doom without consideration. I am asking you, please, to help us find this letter. I cannot tell you what to do when you have found it, but I can say that if I could choose one person to pass fair judgment under the circumstances, it would be you."

Chapter 37

The evening closed in quickly, dense gray clouds turning violet for only a few moments before darkness fell. To Li Du's relief, he and Hamza were back at Water Moon Temple by that time, eating a simple meal of rice and bony carp. They sat on the steps outside the kitchen, not wanting to disturb the clerics, who usually adhered to a rule of silence during meals.

A clink of earthenware dishes, followed by the sound of wooden stools being drawn back from a table, announced that the clerics had finished eating. The head cleric, in robes of deep crimson, emerged from the kitchen holding a letter. After he had expressed his relief that his tenants had not come to harm during their night away from the temple, he handed Li Du the letter, and told him it had been delivered by a messenger earlier that day.

The cleric turned to Hamza. "A message came for you, also," he said. "I believe Chan has already taken it to your room."

Li Du waited until he was in his room before he opened the letter. He lit a candle and examined it. Though the paper and ink were of the fine quality used by the palace, it was written in the rushed scrawl of an overworked scholar completing one task while his mind moved on to the next one.

He was rummaging through his satchel in search of his spectacles when Hamza appeared at the door, holding aloft a sheet of red paper. "An invitation," he announced. "To perform, the day after tomorrow, at a party to be held at the mansion of one Baldan." He presented the invitation to Li Du. The message, written in a dignified script, cascaded down the page, enclosed by a gilded design. It was addressed simply to *The Storyteller.*

"The address is in the district of the White Bordered Banner," said Li Du. "And Baldan is a Manchu name. I wonder how he came to hear of you."

Hamza lifted his chin. "I have earned a certain renown in my profession."

Li Du smiled faintly. "I am not challenging the strength of your reputation." He looked down at the invitation. Reflected candlelight flickered along the golden frame that curved around the text.

Hamza filled two cups of wine by the light of the guttering candle. "And what have you received?"

"It's a reply to my message," said Li Du.

"What message?"

"I'd almost forgotten that I'd sent it. I wrote to an old acquaintance from the palace, asking him if the records of temples funded by the imperial family contained any mention of Narcissus Temple." He found his spectacles, put them on, and sat down at his small desk. "But now that we know the temple falls under the auspices of the Ministry of Rites, I doubt the palace records will have much to tell us."

Li Du accepted the cup Hamza offered and took a sip from it without looking up from the letter. "No wonder your eyes have become tired," Hamza said. "You remind me of the peddlers and merchants who begin to resemble what they are selling. The brick seller is covered in brick dust. The ribbon seller is draped in ribbons. The blacksmith's arms are as strong as if they themselves were made in the forge."

"Hm?" Li Du pulled himself away from the text and looked quizzically at his friend.

"Eyes like ink pots, cheeks like parchment," said the storyteller, shaking his head. "You spend so much time with your letters and records and reports that I fear you will turn into one. You can't find all the answers in paper."

Li Du nodded, only half listening, and began to read again. "Consider the Jesuits," Hamza went on, oblivious to Li Du's distraction. "If they had chosen to keep more of their secrets in their heads, and commit fewer of them to writing, they wouldn't be in the predicament they are now. And—"

"I was wrong," Li Du interrupted. "There *is* information here." He took another sip of wine and read the letter out loud, starting again from the beginning.

"'Your request was not a simple one,'" he read.

I was obliged to search numerous cabinets before I found any mention of Narcissus Temple, the documents relating to it having been grossly misfiled. Little wonder, for the temple has been known by several different names, rendering its history unclear at best.

Are you certain it is Narcissus Temple that interests you? It appears to be a place of little consequence to the past, or to the present. It seems that it was built during the reign of Wanli, at the request of the third consort of the fifth prince. A woman of exceptional talent as a poet and painter, she unfortunately succumbed to illness a year after the temple was completed.

After the loss of its patron, Narcissus Temple disappears from the records, with one exception. You will recall from our student days that I always took pride in thorough research. I may have clerks to do my work for me now, but let it not be said that I have forgotten how to do it myself! It was not easily done, but I unearthed from the records a contract, dated not three months ago, for the replacement of the roof of Narcissus. The contract authorizes payment from the Imperial Household Agency to the Black Tile Factory for the completion of this project.

I cannot imagine what use this information may be to you. If you are searching for old temples to inspire a collection of poetry, my recommendation is that you research the temples of the Western Hills. In my humble opinion, they outdo the temples of the capital both in beauty and literary significance.

Hamza had been leaning with his back against the rough wooden wall. Now he pulled a small chair from its place in the corner, set it by the desk, and sat. While Li Du closed his eyes in silent contemplation, Hamza read the letter again. "I confess I am confused," he said, when he had finished. "I thought it was the Ministry of Rites that replaced the temple roof."

"It was," Li Du replied, opening his eyes. "And I believe we have found our way to another of Pan Yongfa's schemes."

"Another?" Hamza's expression was a combination of incredulity and respect. "I have never heard of such an overachieving criminal. What other scheme?"

Li Du took a long sip of wine. The dancing light from the candle was casting confused shadows across the letter. He trimmed the wick, and the light steadied, along with his tumbling thoughts. "There are hundreds of shrines and temples within the walls of this city," he said. "And hundreds more in the villages and parks outside it. Since the fall of the previous dynasty, many of these temples have, like Narcissus, fallen into decay and disrepair."

Hamza drank, and refilled their cups. "I have noticed. Leaking roofs, crumbling walls, worn and uneven cobblestones covered with weeds. Most gods and goddesses do not have the power to restore their houses without the assistance of the devoted."

Li Du nodded. "Assistance that requires silver. Of these temples, some receive help from private patrons, neighborhoods, or guilds. Others are maintained by the Ministry of Rites on behalf of the citizenry. Still others are fortunate enough to be patronized by members of the imperial family, whose donations are administered by the Imperial Household Agency. It is important to understand that the ministry and the palace do not collaborate in this area. A temple may be supported by one entity or the other, but not by both."

"I understand," said Hamza, his features set in a look of determined concentration. "So was it the Ministry of Rites that paid for the new roof on Narcissus Temple, or the Agency of Imperial— the Imperial Agency of—I cannot remember."

"The Imperial Household Agency," Li Du supplied. "I believe the answer to the question is that *both* of them paid for it."

Hamza looked slightly betrayed. "But I have been paying attention! You just said that a temple cannot be supported by both."

"They both *paid*," Li Du said. "But each one believed itself to be the only patron."

"Continue," said Hamza, lifting his cup again. "I know you to be not only a scholar, but a sensible man. I trust you will soon begin to make sense. If it is possible, may I request that you populate your explanations with people, rather than institutions. It will make it easier to comprehend."

"Consider, then, two men," said Li Du, acquiescing. "They are both men of high official rank and low moral character. One is employed by the Ministry of Rites. He is new to the city, arrogant, eager to prove himself cleverer than the rules that constrain him. The other is employed by the Imperial Household Agency. He is older, more settled in his corruption. He has spent many years taking lucrative advantage of the little opportunities that present themselves within the vast system of imperial finance."

"I can see them," said Hamza. "And I have a guess as to who they are. The first is Pan Yongfa. The second is the man who almost had us arrested at the market—the palace official, Kirsa."

Li Du nodded. "Both of these men know that, like so many institutions within the capital—the Banners, the Gendarmerie, the Magistracy—the Ministry of Rites and the Imperial Household Agency rarely communicate. They also know that both their departments are overwhelmed with paperwork. No matter how many clerks are employed, it is impossible to prevent duplicated documents, lost documents, misfiled documents, outdated documents."

"In other words, opportunities," said Hamza.

"Exactly." Li Du went on, "Kirsa cut off our conversation as soon as I mentioned Narcissus Temple, and the meeting Bai overheard in the pavilion of Hong's manor. I suggest that this scheme was the subject of that meeting."

Hamza raised a hand to request more time to think. "You are

saying," he said finally, "that Pan and Kirsa were working together to profit from the repair of temples."

"Old, forgotten temples," said Li Du. "Yes."

Hamza leaned forward. "But how?"

Li Du drummed his fingers absently on the table, thinking. "We've been told they were both frequent guests at elite gatherings. It's only speculation, but I imagine they met at one of them, shortly after Pan's arrival in Beijing."

"And criminals have a way of recognizing each other," said Hamza.

"My thought precisely," said Li Du. "Pan had the authority to allocate ministry funding to temple repairs. Kirsa had the same authority at the Imperial Household Agency. Once they realized this, they began to build a system to profit from it. I suspect they identified temples that were small and unsupported, and obtained funds for repairs from *both* the ministry and the palace. They used one institution's money to complete the repair, and the other's to enrich themselves."

"But how was it kept secret?" asked Hamza. "Even if the ministry and the palace didn't know about the double payment, surely the Black Tile Factory would notice when it received two contracts for the same projects."

Li Du considered this. "Pan was the ministry's connection to the Black Tile Factory," he said. "Which gave him the opportunity to duplicate, delay, or destroy paperwork connected to the commissions. He must have been the one making sure Hong remained ignorant, no doubt making use of the well-known fact that Hong was a disorganized record keeper. Unless, of course, Hong was involved."

Hamza sighed. "And it is too late to interview Hong." He sighed again. "So Narcissus Temple has no patron after all. What a mournful end for a place that once was loved."

"What we still don't know," said Li Du, "is what connection any of Pan's schemes had to the murders."

"And the tunnels," said Hamza. "Do not forget the tunnels."

"The tunnels were part of the same conversation in the pavilion," Li Du mused. "Which means Kirsa must know about them."

"Perhaps," said Hamza. "But I doubt Kirsa will speak to you again."

"He certainly will not," Li Du agreed, wishing he had been able to glean more information from the interaction. "But according to Bai, there was a third man in the pavilion. I begin to think that any hope of discovering the truth lies with him."

That night, Li Du listened to rain drumming on the roof and plinking into the bucket he had placed beneath the leak. An occasional distant rumble of thunder entered his tired mind like the memory of a past argument. He was aware that his investigation of the murders at the Black Tile Factory had preoccupied him over the past several days. He suspected that, since his return, it was the longest stretch of time he had spent not thinking of his purpose for being back in Beijing.

Now his thoughts took him back in time nine years, through the palace walls, to the library. He conjured, as he had so often done, the final meeting of the traitors. Over the years, as he pieced together the events leading up to the attempted assassination, the meeting in the library had gained definition and detail, until it had begun to feel more like memory than conjecture. He observed the room as if he were standing in it. He could smell the books, the faint fragrance of scented ink, the warm resin of cabinets, and the barely perceptible sting of poisoned paste used to deter hungry moths.

From his ghostly vantage point, he saw Shu, concealed in the shadows on the far side of the table, watching and listening, as Li Du was now. And seated at the table, he saw the conspirators, only now his tired mind gave them new faces. He saw Hong, angry and frightened, and Father Calmette, determinedly optimistic. He saw

Hu and Erchen, proud father and anxious student. His tired imagination moved to the fixed, bloodied face of Madam Hong, then to that of Pan Yongfa, where it hovered.

How different Pan had been from the Ming loyalists who had conspired around that table in the library. They had been devoted to a cause they must have known would almost certainly fail, acting out of loyalty to a dead dynasty, plotting an assassination they hoped would alter history. Pan's crimes, motivated by boredom and greed, had been designed to go unnoticed, flowing through the daily movements of the city like dead leaves carried along by a rushing stream. As Li Du finally succumbed to sleep, the faces around the table disappeared, transforming into fluttering clouds of paper and spinning pieces of silver.

Chapter 38

Li Du awoke suddenly to a tapping sound. Though his room was dark, the pale seams between the window shutters told him that it was dawn. The tapping stopped, but before he could close his eyes and try to sleep a little longer, it began again, louder than before. Someone was knocking on his door. He had a vision of soldiers, which faded as the knocking continued. Soldiers would not remain outside, waiting politely for him to answer. He rose. Holding his coverlet around his shoulders, he crossed the room.

"Who is there?" He sounded hoarse and confused to his own ears.

Chan's familiar voice replied. "I know it's early, but there's a man here who wants to see you."

Li Du opened the door. Chan, an inveterate early riser, regarded him with eyes as bright as if he'd been drinking tea and enjoying the sunshine for hours. His robes smelled of incense and kitchen smoke.

"It's barely dawn," Li Du said.

Chan nodded. "I told him you'd still be asleep. He said to wake you, and tell you that Bai Chengde has come on an urgent matter."

"Bai Chengde?" Blinking in an effort to focus, Li Du peered over Chan's shoulder at the quiet, misty courtyard. "Where is he?"

"In the temple," said Chan, gesturing to it. "Lighting incense and making an offering of fruit with the fervor of someone hoping to turn a bad day into a good one. A man burdened by troubles, I'd say. Is he a friend of yours?"

"An acquaintance," said Li Du. He rubbed his eyes. "Will you be so kind as to tell him I will be with him shortly?"

"I will take him to the office and serve him tea," declared Chan. He turned and padded lightly across the courtyard, his red robes dark in the muted blue light that preceded dawn. Li Du retreated into his room, where he hurriedly rinsed his face and mouth and donned a clean robe, all the while trying to guess what could have brought Bai to see him.

As soon as he was ready, he went to the small office that was used by the clerics to host visiting benefactors and manage the temple accounts. Inside, he found Bai sitting on a bench padded with rugs, and Chan hovering attentively nearby. At Li Du's entrance, the scholar looked up, revealing a countenance that had undergone a subtle change since their last conversation. Bai's face was drawn, as if he had not been sleeping well, and there was a rigidity in his shoulders that had not been there before.

Bai looked at Chan, who had moved to the corner of the room with the obvious intention of staying to listen. "Thank you for your solicitude," said the scholar stiffly. "I'm afraid I must trespass a little further on your hospitality. The matter that brings me here is of a confidential nature."

The dismissal did not appear to dampen Chan's spirits, though the look he gave Li Du as he left was alight with curiosity. When the door was shut behind him, Li Du waited for Bai to speak. He noted that the scholar's fatigue had not diminished his capacity for fastidiousness. Bai's gaze lingered on the worn, unmatched furnishings with evident displeasure.

"I admire your forbearance," said Bai, "to be able to live in such conditions."

"I am very comfortable here," Li Du replied, trying to repress his annoyance. If he was going to start the day so early, he had many more important things to do than listen to Bai criticize his lodgings.

"That cannot be true, but I understand it was necessary in order not to draw attention to yourself. You are employed as an office assistant. You must live within the means of an office assistant. It must be convincing, and it is."

Li Du was instantly, completely awake. "Convincing? I'm afraid I don't take your meaning."

Bai nodded. "Of course that is what you must say. But you see, *I know.*"

Trying to ignore the tension that gripped his throat, Li Du did his best to look merely puzzled. "I think you have made a mistake."

"I thought so, too, at first. I wasn't sure. But now that I have considered everything, what I know of your past—" Bai made a small gesture, indicating the room around them. "—what I know of your present circumstances, and perhaps most important, what my instincts have told me from the moment we became reacquainted, I am certain. You are not what you claim to be."

Li Du spoke carefully. "My past has, without a doubt, required me to adapt to diverse occupations and living situations, but that is no secret."

"Let us not circle around each other," said Bai. "I know about your visit to Feng Liang."

The name remained suspended between them. With an effort, Li Du kept his voice steady. "I don't know anyone of that name."

The scholar exhaled slowly. "Then it is I who must leap. So be it." He stood up, lifted his chin, and met Li Du's eyes with his reddened ones. And, for the first time, Li Du saw that the arrogant scholar was afraid. "Have—" Bai swallowed. "Have you reported the document you saw on my desk to your superior?"

This was not what Li Du had expected, but even in his surprise, he perceived that the revelations were more likely to continue if he concealed his mystification. Still, his next words were not as deliberate as he would have liked. "My superior?"

Bai paled. "Yes, whoever he is, unless, you cannot—surely you cannot report directly to the Emperor himself?"

Li Du's expression remained carefully blank. "I have made no report."

The scholar sagged, sinking back down to the cushion of faded rugs. "I am greatly relieved to hear it." His voice was slightly hoarse, and he cleared his throat. "I fear you have fallen into a misapprehension about me, a misapprehension for which I know I am, myself, responsible. I have come to tell you everything." Hoping that Bai would continue unprompted, Li Du remained silent.

"I give you my word," Bai went on, "that I have played no part in the corruption that has infiltrated our ancient sanctum of knowledge and achievement. You must believe that I would never compromise the integrity of the examinations. They are *my life*. Which is why I have been trying to discover the means by which they *have* been compromised. You and I share an objective. The only difference between us is that your authority was given to you by the Emperor, while mine comes only from my own—" Bai hesitated. "From my own commitment to what is right," he finished.

Understanding arrived, and spread in waves of relief through Li Du's mind. If the situation were not so precarious, he might almost have laughed. "You believe me to be a spy for the Emperor," he said. "One of his agents, disguised as a citizen."

"I understand you cannot admit it to me officially," said Bai. It was the first time Li Du had ever detected humility in the scholar's voice.

Aware that if he hesitated he would risk ending the charade before he had the chance to see how far it would lead, Li Du made his choice in an instant. "What, may I ask, gave me away?"

A hint of Bai's natural arrogance returned. "As I told you in my studio, I am a perceptive judge of character. When I said you did not belong in these reduced circumstances, I meant it more than I myself knew at the time. You cannot hide your intelligence from the man who graded your examinations. I never forget the minds that write the essays worth remembering. In the days since I saw you at the North Borough Office, I have become more and more convinced that you could not possibly be merely an assistant spending his days answering invitations and making copies."

"I am certainly flattered by your reasoning," said Li Du. He tried to think what a spy for the Emperor would sound like in conversation. "You must understand that I cannot speak to you about current investigations. If, as you say, you feel I am under some misapprehension, you have my attention."

Bai regarded this new Li Du as if he wasn't sure whether to be relieved or wary. "When you came to interview me about the murders at the Black Tile Factory," he said, after a pause, "I wondered why you were devoting yourself so assiduously to an unremarkable crime of passion. I also wondered why you chose to speak to me about it, when I have so little connection to the events. With these questions in mind, I noticed that when you left, you stopped to examine the papers on my desk."

Li Du thought back to the morning in Bai's studio. He hadn't been looking at the papers at all. He'd simply been staring at the ink stone, lost in memories. "I see," he said.

"Even then," Bai went on, "I would not have been concerned, had my servant not informed me that he recognized you."

Now Li Du remembered the wide, penetrating eyes that had stared at him so intently. With a sudden jolt, he knew where he had seen the man before. "Your servant," he said. "He was watching Feng Liang's door from the temple across the lane."

Bai nodded vehemently. "He was there on my orders. I had received information that Feng Liang has been using his seat on the Examiner Selection Committee to pressure examiners into agreeing to pass certain candidates. No doubt the families of the candidates are paying him a generous sum. I sent my servant to watch his door, in the hope of gaining entrance to Feng's home, and obtaining some proof of his guilt. In this, my servant was unsuccessful, but he did see you." Bai took a deep breath. "At first, I thought you might be complicit, but I dismissed the idea almost at once. I can identify corruption in a man's face as easily as I can identify the soot that stains our walls. I do not see it in yours. So, having dismissed the idea that you were working with Feng, I began to wonder if you, too, were there to investigate. In the days since you visited me, I have looked more closely at what is known of your past, specifically the pardon that ended your exile. *In gratitude for performing a great service to the Emperor,* they say. From there, the pieces fell into place. Whatever you did earned you the Emperor's trust. He brought you back to be one of his agents in the capital, and you have been investigating examination fraud, just as I have."

"You have been acting alone?" asked Li Du.

Bai nodded. He withdrew a piece of paper from a purse at his belt. "I became suspicious of one of my fellow examiners. With some effort, I was able to persuade him to confide in me that he had accepted a bribe. With still more effort, I convinced him to give me the name of the person who had paid him—Feng Liang— and the list of candidates he had agreed to pass. This is that list, which I know you saw on my desk. If I am right, and you did come to my home that day because you suspected me of involvement in this crime, I hope I have convinced you of my innocence."

Bai extended the paper to Li Du. "I leave this in your charge. I don't know who among the thousands they are, or how it was arranged, or how much they paid, but I know you must have the resources to discover the answers to those questions more quickly than I can."

Li Du took the list. As he scanned the names, the sense of calm he had just been starting to regain deserted him. He pretended to continue his perusal, making use of the time to think. When he knew he could not wait any longer, he forced himself to commit to a strategy he could only hope would succeed. "Why didn't you report any of this earlier?" he asked as sternly as he could.

Bai looked as if he'd swallowed something bitter. "I was so close to finding all the answers," he said. "I thought—"

"You thought you could conduct the investigation yourself," said Li Du, cutting him off. "And in doing so, you lied to the Emperor."

"I would never," said Bai, looking horrified.

"You withheld vital information." Li Du kept his expression stony. "The examinations are of paramount importance to the stability of the empire."

"I know," Bai burst out. "Imagine what could happen if the public begins to question the integrity of the examiners. I wanted to prevent that. I acted as I did in order to preserve the reputation—"

"The reputation of the exams, or your own reputation?" asked Li Du. Two spots of color appeared on the scholar's pale cheeks, and he dropped his gaze. "You have acted wrongly," Li Du continued. Then he allowed his voice to soften. "But I believe that you were not involved in any criminal behavior. I will not speak against you to the Emperor. I will even praise your initiative. *If* I may tell him that you do not intend to interfere, ever again, in his policing of the capital, unless he personally asks you to do so."

"Yes," Bai said, almost before Li Du had finished speaking. "I give you my promise. Please understand—I was only trying to do what was best for the city."

"I do understand. Now, I must kindly ask you to leave me to my work. There is a great deal to accomplish."

When Bai had gone, Li Du, who had remained standing throughout their conversation, sat down in a wooden chair beside a wobbly table. He took a long, exhausted breath. He needed a strong cup of tea.

Hamza was disbelieving. "Feng Liang, *our* Feng Liang, is taking money from rich families who want their sons to pass the examinations? But I cannot picture that at all. The man we met is a recluse, an eccentric, a collector of books. Such a man does not decide, in the twilight years of his life, to become involved in examination fraud."

"According to Bai Chengde, that is exactly what he is doing." replied Li Du. They were sitting on the veranda outside their rooms, drinking tea and watching the sunlight advance toward them across the courtyard.

Hamza shrugged. "I will say that I like this arrogant examiner, Bai Chengde, much better now that I know he has aspirations to be a detective. And it pleases me that, upon seeing through your secretarial affectations, he came to the conclusion that you are an elite agent of imperial power in disguise." An idea occurred to Hamza, and he grinned. "I'll wager that behind the ponderous tomes on his bookshelves, he hides numerous collected tales of mystery and adventure."

"I am just relieved that his conclusions about me were incorrect," murmured Li Du.

Seeing that his friend was not deriving as much amusement from the morning's revelation as he was, Hamza became more serious. "Perhaps Feng Liang needs silver in order to acquire the books he covets. What will you do? Will you go to Chief Inspector Sun, or directly to the magistrate?"

"Neither," said Li Du. "Not yet, at least."

Hamza's look turned to one of puzzled concern. "It is not like you to ignore a crime. And, if you do not intend to act, why discourage the scholar from doing so?"

"Because," said Li Du, "if the names on the list Bai gave me are brought to the Emperor, the candidates and their families will face grave consequences. The candidates will never be permitted to take the examinations. They may face exile, or worse. If the currents of power dictate that an example must be made, they could face execution."

He stood up and went into his room, still holding the list. "Where are we going?" Hamza asked, following after him.

Li Du handed him the list, and began to search for his hat. "Look at the sixth name," he said.

Hamza looked. "Li Yujin," he said. "And there's a number beside it."

"The number is the code assigned to the candidate," said Li Du as he put his notebook into his satchel. "Intended to keep the grading anonymous."

"Li Yujin," Hamza said again. "Li—" He stopped. "But he cannot be a relative of yours?"

Shouldering his bag, Li Du started toward the door. "We have to see Lady Chen," he said. "Li Yujin is Tulishen's son."

Chapter 39

Tulishen's mother was receiving visitors that morning, which meant that before they could speak to Lady Chen, Li Du was obliged to pay his respects to his aunt. Leaving Hamza in a courtyard garden, he entered an ornate sitting room and bowed to the woman seated on a low couch. Lady Li, a venerable matron with a lifelong passion for sumptuous fabrics, was resplendent in layers of silk and velvet that most would have considered too heavy for the warm weather. Her snowy hair was sculpted into elaborate loops atop her head, secured by jade pins and thick pomade.

"It occurs to me," she said, after they had exchanged pleasantries, "that you should apply to one of the ministries. After all, it is not *impossible* for you to advance, even now. Others have recovered from situations worse than yours. We must keep in mind that you were invited back from exile. This should motivate you to demonstrate your worth, and show your gratitude for the opportunity you have been given to regain your status in society. Now is not the time for lassitude and lack of ambition. Once you have found a more respectable occupation, you must find a better place to live. When you have done that, you *must* remarry. Look to my son as an example. You will never approach his level of success, but you *could* improve your current circumstances."

It was a speech Lady Li had made to him before. Li Du knew it well, and had to prevent himself from completing her sentences when she paused. Of all his living family members, his aunt was perhaps the only one who had shown him more warmth after his exile than she had before it. While he believed that she genuinely wanted to help him, he also knew that her willingness to do so was dependent on his failure to outshine her son, upon whom she doted.

"Your cousin has offered to assist you," she was saying. "You must take him up on his generosity. At present, of course, his time is consumed with preparations for the return of Prince Yinzao. You know that the prince is to compose an inscription for our temple. What an honor. They say the Emperor will favor Prince Yinzao, now that he is home, and no longer out of the Emperor's good graces. And he will be *our friend*. It is difficult to speak of it, I am so overwhelmed."

Not too difficult, thought Li Du uncharitably. Like her son, Lady Li had spoken of little else since the arrival of the prince's letter of intended support.

"And yet you may not know," continued Lady Li, "that Tulishen has been invited to attend the welcome banquet? It is a fortunate mother who has such impressive children."

A servant appeared with a question about the evening's menu, and Li Du took the opportunity to extricate himself. Before Lady Li could resume her lecture, he thanked her graciously, promised to devote himself to the reinvigoration of his career, and left to re-join Hamza. Together, they went in search of Lady Chen. They found her in a garden, seated before an embroidery frame. To Li Du's disappointment, she was surrounded by a small company of household women, each focused on their own frames.

At the sound of their approach, Lady Chen was the first to look up. She had disclosed to Li Du in the past that she disliked embroidery, and used the time she was required to devote to it to re-view memorized poems. In the glimpse he had of her expression before she recognized him, he tried to guess what poem she had been silently reciting to the gleaming, colorful thread. An image of moonlit water and mountain stone appeared briefly before him as his gaze rested on her face.

She stopped her work and rose to greet them, the ornaments in her hair catching and scattering light. "You find your cousin absent once more," she said, in a slightly louder voice than usual. She stepped through the keyhole door out of the garden, implying that they should follow.

"I must speak to you privately," said Li Du.

She gave a small shake of her head. "Today, it is impossible. Lady Hua thinks she has not been getting enough attention, and is searching for excuses to do battle. My conversations are more circumscribed by propriety than usual. I must go back."

"The matter is an urgent one," said Li Du.

Lady Chen smiled dispassionately. "Men forget how high the stakes can be in the play of power within a house. I would make an exception if I could."

Li Du was prepared to accept her refusal without further argument, but as Lady Chen began to turn away, she suddenly stopped. "Perhaps," she said, "if there were some distraction?" She looked inquiringly at Hamza. As understanding dawned, his face was illuminated by a wide smile. He bowed. "It would be my pleasure."

Together, the three of them reentered the courtyard. Lady Chen wore on her face an expression of girlish delight. "Look who our cousin Li Du has brought," she said. "This man is an acclaimed storyteller and a traveler. He will not bore us with the same stories that are told and retold in our markets or at our banquets. He can tell us tales that have never been heard anywhere in the empire. Shall we allow ourselves a moment's respite from work, and listen?"

The other women exchanged nervous, excited glances. Hamza stepped forward. "I do perhaps have a tale that I humbly suggest will amuse you."

Lady Chen spoke again. "The breeze moves through this garden with too much strength. I am afraid it will carry away your words. I suggest we adjourn to a more sheltered place. I will arrange for refreshments to be brought to us there."

There followed a period of careful manipulation that resulted in the women who had been sitting at their embroidery finding themselves in a shady pavilion, captivated first by Hamza's velvety eyes and warm smile, then by his words.

"What is so secret and so urgent?" asked Lady Chen. Having

issued orders for the preparation of snacks, she guided Li Du to a bamboo grove a short distance from the pavilion. They stood facing each other amid dense bars of shadow.

"Something has come up in my investigation that concerns this house," said Li Du. "Lady Chen, did you know that Li Yujin paid a substantial bribe to ensure that his name will appear on the list of passing examination candidates?"

Her expression took on a crystalline quality as she absorbed what he had said. "Who told you this?"

As briefly as he could, Li Du explained how Bai Chengde's independent investigation had led him to share what he knew with Li Du. He left out the visit to Feng, and emphasized Bai's promise not to pursue the matter further.

Lady Chen looked relieved. "Then we have some time." She retreated into her own thoughts for a short while. "Not only was I unaware of it," she said finally, "but I don't believe it. This is either a mistake, or deliberate, false incrimination."

"How can you be sure?" asked Li Du, taken aback by her certainty.

"Because I would have known he was going to do it before he did it, and I would have put a stop to such nonsense. Yujin may possess a cheater's combination of stupidity and intelligence, but he is not clever enough to conceal an actual attempt at it from me. I keep a close watch on what happens within these walls, and regularly detect far more subtle intrigues."

"I have every confidence in your perceptiveness," said Li Du. "But the evidence against him is strong. His name is written on a list of candidates given to a bribed examiner with the instruction to award them passing grades. Is Yujin here?"

"No," said Lady Chen. "He has been spending his afternoons enjoying the pleasures and temptations surrounding the examination yard." Despite her self-possession, Li Du observed the tension in her lips and read the growing concern in her eyes. He did not have to ask if she knew the consequences for the candidate, and for his family, of being caught cheating on the examinations.

"I will speak to Yujin as soon as possible," she said finally. "Though my initial opinion has not changed. He wouldn't have done it." They heard a sound behind them, and turned to see four servants advancing toward the pavilion, carrying trays of food. "I must go back," said Lady Chen. "Or my absence will be noticed. What action do you intend to take?"

"None, at present," said Li Du.

She nodded. "Good. Leave it to me to make discreet inquiries."

Li Du opened his mouth to protest, but she stopped him. "I can obtain the truth from Yujin, as much of it as he knows. I can use what he tells me to come up with a strategy to contain this secret. I have prevented scandals before."

"What scandals?" asked Li Du.

She smiled. "This is a large family, and now that I am here, it is *my* family to protect. Do you think I do nothing with my time? Now, is there anything else you can tell me, or anything else I can use?"

After a moment's hesitation, Li Du pulled a piece of paper from his satchel and handed it to Lady Chen. "This is the list of candidates," he said. "If you think it could help you, I will entrust it to you."

"I did not know my trustworthiness was in question."

"That is not what I meant. Having it in your possession puts you in danger."

"It is often necessary to take risks," said Lady Chen. "You may be sure I will act in everyone's best interests, including my own."

Li Du glanced toward the pavilion, where Hamza sat, straight-backed, tracing his hands through the air, building palaces and oceans. "Tell Hamza that I will see him at Water Moon Temple."

She nodded, and hurried to join the servants. He watched her blend into the group so smoothly and quietly that she might never have been standing beside him. With a determined set to his shoulders, he turned away.

Chapter 40

Before returning to the North Borough Office, Li Du decided he would go once more to the home of Pan Yongfa. He knew Sun would note his prolonged absence, but fresh in his mind was the desperate, helpless look on Father Calmette's face as he had comprehended the incriminatory power of Father Aveneau's lost letter.

Though it could not be publicly discussed, it was known that the succession weighed heavily on the Emperor's mind. Preparations for his sixtieth birthday had already begun. Letters had reportedly been sent to some four thousand aged but healthy men throughout the provinces, inviting them to the celebration, where they would be presented with gifts and allowed to sit at the Emperor's own table. Officially, this was to congratulate them for living so long. Unofficially, it was to surround the Emperor with guests who made him appear young. Darker, quieter rumors spoke of Kangxi's disappointment in his sons. It was said that every time he had chosen a successor, he had subsequently been given a reason to change his mind.

Of the twenty-two princes, Yinzao had been the favorite before he evidently had displeased his father. He had been gone for nine years, during which time he had campaigned successfully against the Mongols on the western frontiers. Now he was returning, and the lavish parades set to welcome him suggested that he had re-entered the Emperor's good graces. Li Du thought of the glow in his aunt's eyes as she had discussed Prince Yinzao's intention to patronize their temple. Even before his arrival in the capital, the prince had obviously been preparing his path into the hearts of the citizens who would welcome him.

The safest place to deliberate on the subject of the succession was in the silence of one's own mind. The least safe place to do it was in a letter. Should Father Aveneau's missive be discovered, the Jesuits could be accused not only of anticipating the Emperor's death, but of making plans to manipulate his heir. And, Li Du reminded himself, the foreign priests were not considered guests of the Emperor, but subjects, as vulnerable to accusations of treachery as any other resident of the capital. Their punishment would not entail safe passage back to Rome.

Once he had passed through Xuanwu Gate into the Outer City, Li Du searched for a sedan chair to convey him as quickly as possible to his destination. For all he knew, the Jesuit letter could be sitting on Pan's desk for anyone to find. He hailed a chair, paid the bearers extra coins, and told them to hurry. In good time, he arrived at the door of Pan Yongfa's residence somewhat sore and jostled, but relieved to have avoided the blocked alleys and avenues reserved for examinations events or festivities related to the prince's return.

The door had been opened to admit a peddler, who now stood in the outer courtyard surrounded by five maids perusing the wares displayed in his wooden cart. Separated into different baskets were nests of hair pins, combs, and silk sashes like tangled snakes. One maid examined a pin and grimaced. "This is a cheap thing," she said. "If you don't offer a lower price, then you're a swindler, and we'll go to the market instead."

"Those are quality pins," insisted the peddler, a stout man with ruddy checks. He had an assortment of hairpins arranged on his dirty collar. "I'm on the way to the market to sell them now, and I'll charge more for them there. They are made in my own village, and don't tell me they're cheap, because I can tell you for a fact that they are favored by several imperial consorts."

One of the other maids held a pin up to the light. Li Du recognized the girl who had told him about Pan's silver. "Oh, sir," she said, noticing him. "I didn't see you there." She returned the pin to the cart. "We are looking for an ornament to cheer our mistress."

"A hairpin seems a small thing to counter grief," said Li Du.

She nodded. "We know, but we have tried something new every day, and nothing has helped. We've purchased ginger and cinnamon for infusions—they are prescribed for sadness—and rosehip, and all the foods she likes best. Nothing will bring the light back to her eyes."

The elder maid to whom he had spoken before was there also. Now she came around the cart to join them. "We have been told that Hong Wenbin took his own life, sir."

Li Du hesitated. "It appears so," he said.

"He punished himself when the law would not punish him," said the maid, making no attempt to conceal her approval.

"You held your master in great affection," said Li Du.

"Oh, we all did," broke in the younger maid, her eyes sparkling with tears. "Whenever he smiled, it was as if a god had stepped right out of a painting. And he was so clever. I think he knew everything. He would say to me in the morning, *Hurry to the door or you will miss the dumpling seller.* He always knew which day each peddler would come, and at what hour, and he was never too proud to remind us." Observing the open, worshipful face of the girl, and the nods of the other maids behind her, it was obvious to Li Du that they had known nothing of Pan's criminal activities.

"And your mistress?" he asked. "Did it comfort her to know that Hong Wenbin is dead?"

The elder maid answered. "When we told her, she didn't even seem to hear us. She remains in her room. I hope you have not come to disturb her, sir." She spoke with polite deference, but Li Du perceived the sharp edge in her tone. He suspected it was unpleasant to be one of the younger maids facing her displeasure.

"I did not come to interrupt Lady Ai's solitude," he said, and explained that he hoped to conduct a brief search of Pan's study, if Pan had kept such a room. The elder maid said that he had. She told Li Du to follow her, and led him through the keyhole door to the inner courtyard. It was quieter than any place he had visited recently within the city walls. Dry, curling leaves were harbingers of cold autumn days to come, and there was a premonition of winter's light on the stone faces of lions.

Li Du was left alone in Pan's study. A desk, heavy and ornately carved, centered the room. Against the walls were a low couch covered in a single flat cushion, two tall tables with drawers, a clean, unlit brazier, and a chess table on which the pieces were arranged in an unfinished game. Li Du's first action was to pick up one of the pieces and run his fingers carefully around it, but he found no seam or suspicious flaw in its construction. He returned it to its place on the board, his gaze lingering for a moment on the game that would remain unfinished. The opponents were evenly matched, and Li Du could not tell who would have won.

Moving to the desk, he opened its drawers one by one. In addition to brushes and ink, they contained neat stacks of documents. He glanced at each one, but found nothing relevant. Pan had kept bills, invitations, and letters arranged separately. Li Du removed each drawer and felt inside the desk for hidden compartments. There were none. He replaced them and moved to the shelves. The books he found there were standard, respectable volumes for a gentleman's study, consisting mostly of tasteful but unremarkable editions of classics. Father Aveneau's letter was not tucked into the pages of any of them. He looked inside vases and porcelain boxes, beneath the cushions, and in the drawers of the tall ornamental tables, which were empty.

It was not long before he acknowledged that his decision to come had yielded no helpful information. He could at least be certain that if Father Aveneau's letter was there, it was well hidden, and would, he hoped, stay that way forever.

Sun put up his hand as if he could physically prevent Li Du's words from reaching him. "The investigation is over," he said.

When Li Du had entered the chief inspector's office, Sun had taken a seat, placing the solid expanse of his desk between them. Li Du had remained standing, oblivious to the mud that spattered his robes from the hem to the knee, and the faded hat that rested askew on his head. "I mean no disrespect, but I am not certain you understand what I have been telling you. I spoke to Kirsa myself. His involvement in the crime is undeniable. If he didn't commit the murder, I am convinced he knows who did."

"You think *I* am the one who doesn't understand?" asked Sun, staring at Li Du, his face slack with incredulity. "Listen to what you are saying. You spoke to Kirsa."

"Yes," Li Du said. "And if we could just arrange to speak to him again—"

Sun slapped both his hands down onto the desk. He leaned forward. "Did you realize, when you *spoke* to Kirsa, that you were accosting a powerful Manchu whose contacts in the ministries, not to mention the palace, are sufficient to end both our careers?"

Li Du was startled. "I didn't accost him."

"He says you did."

"But the investigation led me directly to him," said Li Du, too caught up in his own thoughts to catch the implication of Sun's words.

"I am not questioning the direction of the path," snapped Sun. "I am questioning your decision to follow it."

Li Du was silent for a moment. "If we cannot interview Kirsa," he said, "I will find another approach. Perhaps a closer examination of the guest list from Hong's party would yield—"

"You still don't understand," Sun broke in. "I told you Kirsa is a man with numerous contacts. One of them is our own Magistrate Yin. When Kirsa found out who you were, he issued a complaint against you to Yin's office. Naturally, the magistrate was mortified to learn that one of his most powerful friends was accosted, in gross violation of etiquette and official procedure—"

"But I didn't—"

"Was *accosted* by a secretary of the North Borough Office while he was engaged in performing his duties in service of the imperial family."

Li Du seized upon this. "But don't you see? Kirsa's behavior supports everything I have said. By trying to silence me, he is only providing more evidence of his guilt. If it's true that Kirsa has been stealing from the imperial coffers, the thought of being questioned further must terrify him."

Sun raised both hands in a gesture of exasperation, exposing damp imprints on the surface of the desk. "Kirsa isn't afraid of this office. If Kirsa is willing to call attention to you with his complaint, it is only because he knows we have no power over him."

"Or he is bluffing."

As if he could no longer sustain the heightened emotion, Sun gave up and sagged back in his chair. "Please sit down," he said. "I can see that you are tired."

Li Du was about to refuse, but realized that his legs were shaking. He drew a chair to the desk, and sat down facing Sun.

"I blame myself," said the chief inspector. "I should not have given you so much encouragement. But if you had only come to me and declared your intention to approach Kirsa, I would have prevented you."

Li Du read genuine apology in Sun's broad features. "I should have come to you," he said. "But securing an appointment to speak with him would have taken weeks, even if he had agreed to see us at all. Now we have confirmation that he is hiding something. We can look for discrepancies in the contracts at the Black Tile Factory, find evidence against him—"

"No," Sun interrupted. "We can't. I'm sorry, but there's nothing I can do. Our involvement in this matter has run its course."

"Perhaps you could speak to Magistrate Yin," Li Du said.

"Magistrate Yin has given me his orders, and I cannot disobey." Sun heaved a sigh. "I have a family. I am my father's only son. I have daughters who must be married, and a wife who must have the means to manage our household. My duty is to them. It is a form of duty you have perhaps allowed yourself to forget."

Li Du was barely listening. "What about the report?"

Sun rested one hand on a document in front of him. "I had Ding draft the report this morning."

"What does it say?"

To his credit, Sun did not avert his eyes as he gave his answer. "It says that Pan and Madam Hong were lovers. They planned to meet that night in the Black Tile Factory. Zou Anlin, as you did us the service of discovering, poisoned Pan in order to steal his silver—"

"Silver Pan brought to pay a blackmailer," said Li Du.

"That was only speculation," said Sun. "Wealthy, urban men sometimes carry large amounts of silver with them. It is not so unusual. The report says that Madam Hong arrived to meet her lover, and found him prone on the bed. She did not know that she was seen entering the factory by her husband, Hong, who was on his way home. He followed her inside, where he found her tenderly looking down at her sleeping love. In his rage and inebriation, he attacked them both, never realizing that Pan was already dead. Later, overcome with remorse at what he had done, he ended his own life."

Sun looked down at the report. "It is neatly crafted. It gives a plausible explanation of what happened. It might even be true. Should the Emperor choose to review it personally, he will find no fault with it."

"I understand that this is the report you will submit," said Li Du. "But perhaps I could continue my inquiries. There is no reason not to conclude what we started."

Now Sun did look away. "That will not be possible. I'm sorry, but it has fallen to me to tell you that you no longer have a place in this office."

Li Du stared. "What do you mean?"

"I mean that there are consequences for disobeying orders, and for attracting the ire of a palace official. This wasn't my decision, but it is one I cannot challenge."

When Li Du did not answer, Sun began to search through the

papers on his desk. He produced a document, and handed it to Li Du. "You are not to be unemployed. You are being reassigned to Tongzhou."

"Tongzhou?" Li Du was stunned. Tongzhou was a day's hard journey north of the city.

Sun nodded. "The governor has found himself embroiled in a controversy over grain shipments. He requires additional clerks to help untangle the problem. You are to be one of them."

"But—when am I to go?"

"The sub-prefect expects you by the end of the day tomorrow. If you do not report to him by then, you will be in violation of these orders, and I will not be able to protect you."

Li Du took the paper, noting the dense layer of official seals appended to the text. Sun watched him read it. "You are an intelligent man," he said, once Li Du had slipped the paper into his bag. "More intelligent than I am. I've never understood why you wanted to work here, notwithstanding our family connection. I am not ashamed to admit that I preside over an office of little significance to the city. But you—you could be a man of influence. This assignment may be Kirsa's vengeance, an attempt to disgrace you, but perhaps it will be an opportunity. Perhaps, one day, you will have the authority to prevent men like Kirsa from getting what they want."

There was little more to say. Li Du rose, bid Sun farewell, and went to his office, where he packed away the objects that were his, left those that were not, and departed. Through the open windows of their offices, the clerks, feigning absorption in their tasks, watched him go.

Chapter 41

Chaoyang Gate was routinely crowded with merchants and tax officials coming and going from Tongzhou, the northern shipping terminus of the Grand Canal. This afternoon was no exception. Mules waited passively as laden baskets were adjusted on their backs, their sides twitching in response to biting flies. Horses stood proudly beside armed Bannermen radiating confidence in their sturdy travel attire. Vendors with streaks of charcoal on their cheeks stoked fires while customers shouted orders. The muddy ground was sprinkled with spilled grain and imprinted by boots, hooves, and cart wheels. Barrels and boxes teetered in crooked stacks, through which inspectors slowly circulated, paper and stylus in hand, making notes and issuing receipts. As the sun sank and the hour of the dog approached, guards prepared to close the gates and set the watch.

On the opposite side of the Outer City from Chaoyang, Li Du and Hamza sat at a stone chess table in the tall grass of a neglected park. In place of chess pieces, an earthenware bottle and two cups rested on the outlines of the game board, faintly incised in the stone, worn down by years of rain and snow and city grit.

"I have been wondering what stories I will tell to entertain my audience at the mansion of Baldan tomorrow night," said Hamza. "I am inspired by secret tunnels. Perhaps I will invent some. I am considering a kingdom inside a mountain, vast caverns lit by rocks charmed to believe themselves stars. I was told, once, of a piper who entered a cave on the coast of a small island and was never heard from again. Perhaps I will cast him as the adventurer in my story, and say that he found his way to that stone city."

After several cups of wine, it was easy for Li Du to envision the subterranean world. He saw the stones glowing blue and violet and white, and the tunnels leading from rocky chambers like spokes from a wheel. But as the song of a myna reached him from somewhere in the tangled branches overhead, he felt grateful to be above ground.

"What is in Tongzhou?" asked Hamza. He had found a lost chess piece in the grass, a pawn, and was flicking it so that it spun over the stone surface of the table.

"Granaries," replied Li Du, picturing the immense repositories of the capital's grain supply, delivered from the central provinces along the Grand Canal. Complex and ever-shifting policies of grain distribution made it a haven for officials who enjoyed bureaucratic puzzles, and a nightmare for those who didn't.

Hamza refilled their cups. "And what will happen tomorrow evening when the sub-prefect who is expecting you realizes you have not arrived?"

Li Du looked up. The sky was a churning, unsettled gray. "I suppose he'll write to Chief Inspector Sun. Or to Magistrate Yin."

"And?"

"And someone will come looking for me."

The chess piece had stopped spinning. Hamza placed a finger on it, and began absently to move the disk along the lines of the game. "I would like to know which puzzle you are staying to solve. Are you disobeying the command to leave in order to find the Black Tile Factory murderer? Or are you remaining for the same reason you came back to Beijing two years ago? Are you still determined to uncover the truth about Shu?"

Li Du picked up his full cup and drank half of it. "I don't know. Ever since we went to the home of Feng Liang, I have felt—" He hesitated.

"Discouraged," Hamza said. "It has not escaped my notice."

"It's more than that," said Li Du. "After two years of letters and reports and records leading only to more letters and reports and records, I'd finally found someone who was alive, someone who could speak to me."

Hamza was studying the solitary disk now resting at the center of the table. "But Feng Liang had no answers, which means you face once more the dim ministry corridors and their silent shelves."

"If there is no one living who can tell me what happened," said Li Du, "then those corridors are all that remain before me. And I begin to think you were right. I begin to think I have been losing my way in documents so filled with lies that there is not enough truth among them ever to tell the whole story. I begin to feel that all the words I've read, all the papers connected to that day in the library nine years ago, are starting to char in the back of my mind, turn to ash, and disappear."

"And what is left?" asked Hamza.

As the question hovered between them, Li Du perceived that there was more color in the gray sky than he had initially noticed. The tall grass whispered around him, but instead of conjuring the dry hiss of unsettled ghosts, it reminded Li Du of children playing. He thought of Shu watching his grandchildren make boats of leaves beside the pond at sunset, of the smile on his face when he chose books to give as gifts, and of his impassioned diatribes against sunning books too early in the spring. "What is left are memories," he said slowly. "And I realize now that I am ready to leave the maze, and keep that which has always belonged to me—the memory of a friendship."

They sat in silence. The light started to fade. Finally, Hamza spoke. "What you have said sounds more like a reason to leave the city than to stay."

"And I expect, whether by choice or by force, I *will* leave," Li Du replied. "But not yet. I came back too late to discover why Shu died. Too much had been buried in my absence."

"But you are not too late to solve the murders at the Black Tile Factory," said Hamza. "I see."

Li Du lifted his cup again. "The killer hasn't had time to hide."

"On the subject of time," said Hamza, "we will have to work quickly, if we are to succeed before it's discovered that you have not gone to Tongzhou. What will we do?"

Li Du was silent. He allowed his gaze to wander the hillside, picking out the other stone tables almost lost amid the tall grass and trees. As a child, he had come to play in this park. He remembered populating it with the conjurations of his mind. The stone tables and benches had become the scattered bones of monsters. The chess pieces hidden in the grass had become tokens to present to gods in exchange for information. *Children's games*, he thought. *Tunnels*. "Where did we hear of tunnels recently?" he asked.

Hamza's brows lifted, and he glanced at Li Du's empty wine cup. "Have you forgotten?"

"No," said Li Du. "I don't mean what Bai overheard in the pavilion." He closed his eyes, saw a maze of hedges lit emerald green in sunset light, and heard the patter of running steps, light as raindrops on courtyard stone. He was thinking, he realized, of Mentougou. "Mei's children," he whispered.

Hamza was staring at him. "What about them?"

Li Du spoke with his eyes still closed. "Do you remember the evening we went to Mentougou? The children were playing a game when we arrived."

"I remember," said Hamza. "They had turned the boxwoods into the walls of a labyrinth."

Li Du nodded. "And they said they were playing *tunnels*. Why were they playing tunnels?"

"Because children cannot study calligraphy all the time," said Hamza reasonably.

"I wasn't talking about playing in general," said Li Du. "I was talking specifically about tunnels. Mei spoke to us about the children's recent exploits. She said they had been regularly sneaking into the Glazed Tile Factory to collect broken shards of colored tile."

"Yes."

"A child's imagination turns whatever enters her game into a part of the game. What if the children overheard something in the Glazed Tile Factory that inspired them?"

"You think they heard something about tunnels," said Hamza, beginning to understand.

Li Du tried to focus. "At Hong's party, Pan discussed the tunnels with Kirsa and another man. What if it was Ji Daolong?"

"The owner of the Glazed Tile Factory," said Hamza. "The man who claimed to know so little about his old family friend. You are suggesting that he lied to us?"

"I am. Consider the old temples Pan and Kirsa used in their scheme. The roofs might have required glazed tiles as well as black ones. Pan could manipulate the paperwork at the Black Tile Factory, but who would manipulate it at the Glazed Tile Factory?"

"So you think that Ji was working with them all along," mused Hamza. "And that the children might have overheard Pan and Ji talking about the tunnels at the Glazed Tile Factory, the same tunnels they were discussing in the pavilion."

"I think it's possible," said Li Du. "We will have to ask Ji himself."

"Then we are to return to Mentougou?"

"That won't be necessary. Ji told us he would be at the examination yard the day before the exams begin." Li Du looked at the darkening sky. "Which means we'll find him there tomorrow."

Chapter 42

Overcrowding was beginning to take a toll on the area surrounding the examination yard. Intermittent odors of sewage fouled the air. Efforts to sweep litter into shadowed alcoves had been undone during the night by dogs and rats. A small army of laborers toiled with brooms and buckets, preparing the space for the day of pomp and ceremony to follow, while soldiers patrolled the vast examination yard.

Li Du, recognizing that an appearance of authority was the only authority left to him, had taken some pains with his dress that morning. He had shaved carefully, washed his boots, brushed the dust and grit from his hat, and donned his newest robes. While not drawing attention to himself, he wanted to appear capable of commanding obedience from any nearby soldier simply by stating his own name and rank.

Ji Daolong was standing among several stacks of green glazed tiles that gleamed in the morning light. He was pointing up at the roof, at the corner of which temporary scaffolding had been erected. As Li Du and Hamza approached, they heard Ji speaking to a laborer who stood beside him. "The black tiles are well laid. We'll have no trouble mounting ours to the ridge." He bent to pick up one of the tiles. Then, noticing Li Du and Hamza, he set it back down. When they reached him, he bowed.

"We spoke at Mentougou," said Li Du.

"Of course," Ji replied. "I have since learned of the death of Hong Wenbin." He raised a muscular arm to indicate the roof behind him. "It cannot have been easy for Hu Gongshan to assume responsibility for replacing the black tiles, given all that has happened. If the Hong family chooses to close the factory, and Hu is in need of employment, I will encourage him to come work for me."

"From what I know of Hu," said Li Du, "he is averse to illegal activities."

Ji regarded Li Du quizzically. "My apologies, sir, but either I misheard you, or you have made a mistake. I meant I would hire Hu to assist me at the Glazed Tile Factory. I am not involved in anything illegal."

"You did not mishear, and I did not make a mistake." Li Du spoke in a calm, direct tone. "I know about Narcissus Temple."

"Narcissus Temple?" Ji glanced away as if to check the progress of the laborers, who were passing the green tiles up the scaffolding. "I don't know what you mean."

"You were commissioned to replace the glazed ornaments on the roof of Narcissus Temple," said Li Du. "You installed a row of small black dragons along its ridge."

"Ah, I remember now," said Ji. "It was a modest commission. I only had to produce a few pieces to complete it. But there was nothing illegal about the work."

"Who commissioned it?" asked Li Du.

Ji hesitated. "There have been so many projects this summer. Forgive me, but I cannot be certain. If this matter is not urgent, may I beg you to allow me to continue my work? With the examinations set to begin tomorrow, there is little time for error."

"We, too, have little time for error," said Hamza. "Therefore, may I suggest that we put an end to prevarication. Here is what I will do. I will tell you what we already know. When I am finished, you may decide whether you wish to continue your denials." Without waiting for a response, he began. "We have already mentioned Narcissus Temple to you. Now I will add two names. The first is Pan Yongfa, your friend who is now dead. The second is Kirsa, a man in the employ of the palace." Ji's flinch at the sound of Kirsa's name was unmistakable. "We know about the Ministry of Rites," continued Hamza. "And we know about the Imperial Agency of—the Agency—"

"The Imperial Household Agency," Li Du said quickly.

"I conclude my list," continued Hamza, "with duplicated contracts, a secret meeting in a garden pavilion at the home of the deceased Hong Wenbin, and finally, *tunnels*. Now, may I suggest that you cooperate with my friend?"

Ji's jaw was so tense that a twitching muscle was visible below his right ear. "H-have you come to arrest me?"

"At present, we are here to speak with you," said Li Du. "You are being given the opportunity to answer my questions in a context other than an official interrogation. I strongly suggest you take advantage of it."

After a tense silence, Ji nodded slowly. "I accept with gratitude. I will tell you what I know."

Masking his relief, Li Du indicated an unguarded booth not far from where they stood, and suggested it as a place to speak more privately. They entered, and found it full of garlands, pennants, and painted signs being stored for the following day. Ji cast an assessing eye over the ornaments, as if, despite the gravity of the situation, his fascination with color compelled him to evaluate their brightness and saturation.

"We know that Pan and Kirsa were defrauding the Ministry of Rites and the Imperial Household Agency. We know you were involved because your conversation in the garden pavilion at Hong's manor was overheard."

"I thought I saw someone that day," murmured Ji. "A gleam of silk through the rain and leaves. *How beautiful*, I thought at the time, *the red amid the green*." He turned away from the ornaments and looked at Li Du. "Yes, I was involved. They approached me over a year ago with the idea."

"Pan and Kirsa approached you? How did that happen?"

Ji crossed one arm over his body and rubbed his shoulder, as if he was trying to ease the tension from it. "How did it happen? That question has been in my mind ever since I learned of Pan's death.

How did any of it happen?" He drew in a breath, and exhaled with weary resignation. "When you spoke to me at Mentougou, I told you I hadn't known Pan Yongfa well. That was not true. Back home, I was as close to him as an older brother. I watched him grow up. When he came to Beijing, it was like welcoming a member of my family. But—" Ji paused.

"But he had changed since he was a child?" asked Li Du.

Ji smiled sadly. "No," he said. "Pan hadn't changed at all. As a child, he was the cleverest boy in our village, and the most mischievous. Adulthood had only enhanced both qualities. Soon after he arrived in Beijing, he came to visit me at Mentougou. He was so sophisticated, so handsome in his official robes, but I recognized at once the boy who had stolen his sister's jewels, hidden them in the forest, and made up a game of riddles to lead his friends to their locations, the boy who had learned to bribe officials by the time he was seven, the boy so adept at deception that it seemed he could turn a lie into truth. Pan was still that boy, and I was still the boy who was grateful for an invitation to play his games. When he asked me if I knew anyone in the city who could make his life here more—" Ji searched for a word. "—more stimulating, I wanted to impress him. So I introduced him to Kirsa."

"How did you know Kirsa?"

"I had met him some years ago at the Imperial Market, when I went in search of rare agates for my glazes. I was told that the stones I wanted were reserved for use only at the imperial kilns. But before I left the market, Kirsa approached me and said he could make arrangements for me to acquire what I sought. We made a deal, and until Pan's arrival in Beijing, that was the full extent of my transgressions. But I wanted to impress Pan, and Kirsa was the only man I knew who seemed dangerous. So I introduced them. They must have discovered common interests quickly, because only a month later, Pan came to me with an idea to make some extra money."

"The temple scheme."

"Yes."

"And you agreed to participate."

"Yes. Pan explained that he had been put in charge of temple construction contracts for the Ministry of Rites. He and Kirsa had a plan to charge both the ministry and the imperial household for the same roofs."

"You found small, neglected temples," said Li Du. "With ambiguous histories of patronage."

Ji nodded. "Pan would submit an order for temple maintenance to the Ministry of Rites, and Kirsa would do the same at the Imperial Household Agency. Once each request was accepted, and money allotted for the repair, Pan sent work orders for glazed tiles to me, and for black tiles to the Black Tile Factory. When the job was complete, I sent a bill to the Ministry of Rites, as did the Black Tile Factory. We received our first payment from the Ministry of Rites. Then all Kirsa had to do was take the same amount of money from the Imperial Household Agency, and submit duplicate bills for the imperial household records. As long as the ministry and the agency never communicated, we could continue."

"With or without Hong Wenbin's knowledge?" asked Li Du.

"Without," Ji replied. "Hong was an inattentive owner, disorganized, and often drunk. Pan was able to manipulate the paperwork at the Black Tile Factory easily. We divided the extra payment between us. Kirsa took most of it, claiming the risk was highest for him."

"And Pan accepted this?"

"Pan enjoyed what he was doing. I don't think he ever cared very much about profit."

"Why did the three of you meet in Hong's garden on the day of the party?"

Ji took a deep breath. "We had learned that the ministry and the imperial household were going to audit their temple construction contracts. Pan and Kirsa had reviewed the paperwork and discovered that they were missing the invoice from the Black Tile Factory for the Narcissus Temple roof. Hong must have forgotten to send one. But we had already taken the money. The audits were beginning. If the discrepancy was noticed, it could initiate an investigation. Pan said he would find the invoice details in the Black Tile Factory records, create the document, and deliver a copy of it to Kirsa."

Li Du and Hamza exchanged glances. That must have been the paper Pan had given Kirsa on the afternoon before Pan died, when Erchen had witnessed their meeting. "When was the last time you saw Pan?" asked Li Du.

"When we spoke together in Hong's garden. I had nothing to do with the murders. What I told you about that night was true. I was in Mentougou."

"But Pan must have said something to you about Madam Hong. You were his friend."

Ji shook his head. "He never mentioned her."

"When you learned that he was dead, what did you think?"

"I didn't know what to think. Kirsa summoned me to meet him. He asked me the same questions you are asking me now, whether I knew anything, what I thought. I told him what I've told you. I don't know anything."

"And Kirsa? What did he know?"

"He seemed as confounded as I, though less anguished. Pan was my friend, but Kirsa's only concern was that the investigation of Pan's death might expose Kirsa's own crimes. Kirsa knew Hong was in prison, that he claimed to have no memory of what happened that night, and that circumstances strongly suggested his guilt. Kirsa told me he would make the investigation stop before anyone began looking too closely at Pan's activities." Ji paused.

"Did he say he intended to have Hong killed?"

"No, but I should have known."

"And yet, when you heard Hong *was* dead, you chose to say nothing."

Ji made no attempt to defend himself. Li Du read contrition in his eyes. "Are you going to arrest me now?"

"No," said Li Du. "But I do have one final question. When you were overheard speaking in Hong's garden, Pan said that, if it became necessary, he could use tunnels to deliver the copied bill to Kirsa. What did he mean by that?"

To Li Du's surprise, a faint smile rearranged the clay-dusted wrinkles of Ji's face. "Pan was always boasting about his tunnels."

"*His* tunnels?" asked Hamza. "But where are they?"

"They are gone, now," said Ji. He looked from Hamza's face to Li Du's, and his mouth twisted into a bitter smile. "I see you don't understand. For a long time, I didn't either. Pan's tunnels were not dug beneath the city or hidden in manor walls. They weren't really tunnels at all." Ji paused. "You know, I never saw Pan lose a game of chess. It was his unique skill to hold in his mind the movements of many individuals at once. That's how he built his tunnels."

"I don't understand," said Hamza. "What authority did he have to move the people of this city like pieces on a board?"

"It wasn't authority," said Li Du, beginning to understand. "It was observation."

Ji nodded. "The carpenter neglects to fix the lock on an un-guarded alley door, so that it can be opened if it is lifted slightly on its hinges. The guards at another gate reliably begin to gamble every night at the hour of the goat, and from then on, ignore their posts. There was some manipulation, of course. Pan was adept at forging seals that could be applied to letters authorizing passage through the city after dark. He also had a supply of tidbits of information he could use as leverage. Tell a soldier to open a gate if he doesn't want news of his father's illegal salt speculations to reach the salt merchant's guild, and the gate will almost always open."

So that was how Pan managed to get from the Opera District to the Black Tile Factory, when Erchen could not, thought Li Du. "The tunnels let him move through the city at night," he said.

"Just so," said Ji. "Pan was not a man who accepted barriers between himself and what he wanted."

"Did Kirsa have access to these tunnels as well?"

"No. As I said, Pan liked to boast about the tunnels, but that didn't mean he was willing to share them with us. He guarded his secrets as any player of games guards his strategies."

They were interrupted by the musical sound of something shattering. Upon leaving the booth, they saw that one of the tiles had fallen from the scaffolding. Ji squinted up at the roof. "The laborers are in need of supervision. If you intend to take me to prison, I suggest you summon Hu to oversee the final stages of the project."

"That will not be necessary," said Li Du. "I have no more questions for you at present. As I am investigating murder, not theft, I will allow you to return to your work."

They left Ji staring after them, his expression one of incredulous relief. As Li Du left the examination yard behind, he found himself looking at every gate they passed. He tried to see them as Pan had seen them, not as barriers made of boards and hinges, but as sets of circumstances that could be altered. Pan had built a dark, crooked path through a city that prided itself on limiting the movements of the people within it. Ji's words echoed in his mind. *They are gone, now.* With Pan's death, the tunnels had collapsed, never to be walked again.

Chapter 43

"You know the way to the district of the White Banner?" asked Li Du.

Hamza oriented himself so that he was facing the city's northeast corner. He was resplendent in a tunic and pantaloons of ocean blue silk embroidered with tiny silver crescent moons. Li Du had no idea where Hamza had come by the outfit, which called to mind a child's description of an adventuring deity. "Through Chongwen Gate," said Hamza, concentrating, "past the Observatory and the examination yard. To reach the mansion, I turn left at Dongzhi."

Li Du nodded. "If you see the Russian church, you have gone too far north." It was late in the afternoon. They had left Water Moon Temple together, and now stood a little removed from the bustle and clutter of antique shops selling bronzes and porcelain vases.

"When we meet in the light of morning," said Hamza, "I will have sampled the finest delicacies of the capital, and guided its most glittering citizens—excepting the princes and consorts within the palace, of course—to vast kingdoms that lie far beyond these city walls." His expression turned grave. "And yet I am still not sure if it is correct for me to leave you, when time is short and our answers remain distant."

Li Du reassured him. "At present, I am convinced that the best use of my time is simply to think. No one is searching for me yet. As I am officially neither in Beijing, nor in Tongzhou, I can enjoy some quiet."

"Perhaps," said Hamza. He directed a skeptical look over Li

Du's shoulder in the direction of the temple. "If you can think through the sound of statues toppling from their altars and crockery smashing against the floor." He was referring to Chan's most recent efforts to rid the temple of rodents by introducing a lithe, glittering-eyed ferret to the temple's small community. The creature had fascinated Hamza until it had earned his ire by ripping one of his hats to pieces.

They parted, and Li Du returned to Water Moon Temple to find Chan in transports because the ferret had succeeded in catching a rat, which it had left unconsumed under the golden knee of a goddess.

It was late afternoon when, tired of being trapped in his room with his ruminations, Li Du ventured out of the temple with the goal of purchasing a bowl of noodle soup in a nearby establishment. He ate quickly, listening to the chatter at the tables around him. There were only two subjects under discussion. Anyone who wasn't talking about the return of the prince was talking about the examinations.

He was about to tip the bowl to his lips and drink the remaining broth when he noticed a man standing in the doorway on the other side of the alley. Li Du knew with instant certainty that the man was waiting for him. It had started to drizzle. They watched each other, Li Du surrounded by oblivious chatter and steam from the boiling pot, the stranger standing alone in the rain. Li Du was the first to move. He stepped out onto the cobblestones and crossed the alley. Cold drops pricked the back of his neck and left dark patches on the shoulders of his robe. "You're here for me," he said. "Who are you?"

The man, of middle age and dressed as a servant, nodded his head in an approximation of a bow. "I have a message for you," he said. He took Li Du's hand, and pressed something into his palm. By the time Li Du had realized that it was a folded note, the man was hurrying away, his shoulders hunched against the rain. He reached an alley, turned, and was gone.

The note was damp from the rain and from the sweat of the messenger's palm, but the words on it were clear. *I have information you want. Come as soon as you can to the Temple of the Fire God in the district of the Red Banner. Come alone, or I will not speak.*

There was no signature, no clue as to who had sent it, or why. Li Du did not hesitate long. He tucked the letter into the purse at his belt and set out, making his way north on foot. Heavy gray clouds muted the sky. The cracked walls and stagnant pits of the Outer City gave way to the bone-white balustrades and painted pavilions of the Banner districts. Raindrops fell intermittently, mottling the pale manes of stone lions that snarled at Li Du from outside closed doors.

The streets were sparsely populated, pedestrians having been drawn toward the parade for the return of Prince Yinzao. He narrowly avoided being struck by a carriage as it hurtled down an alley toward the celebrations. Backed into a door alcove, he watched it pass in a blur of horse hooves, purple reins, and bright red wheels, on the way to the celebration. Purple and red were imperial privileges. He could almost see the glittering, gem-studded hats of its occupants.

As he was nearing his destination, the air around him was suddenly filled with a long, desolate moan. It flowed overhead then seemed to descend, enfolding him like the arms of a pleading ghost. He lifted his gaze and saw the bell tower rising above the rooftops to the northeast, massive and solemn. The green glazed tiles of its vast roof rendered it a stately, moss-covered denizen of a vanished city. He heard the moan again, and remembered how afraid he had been when, as a child, he had first heard its sigh through the window of his nursery. His mother had comforted him, saying that it was only the goddess of the bell, who had lost her slipper and was searching for it.

The Temple of the Fire God was unguarded, the nearest sentry post unmanned. Li Du pushed open a heavy wooden door and entered. A solitary, raised building stood in the center of the courtyard, its open doors exhaling hot golden warmth onto the gray stone that surrounded it. At the base of the stairs leading to it were two stone slabs bearing sutras. Li Du passed between them, automatically recognizing the script as that of a renowned Ming calligrapher, reproduced by the sculptor's chisel.

The hall was not empty. Two worshippers were prostrated in prayer on opposite sides of the space in front of the altar. One wore a soldier's leather jacket, the metal studs shining on the rounded curve of his back and shoulders. The other was an old man, so thin that the ridge of his spine was visible through his robe. Li Du looked from one to the other. Their faces were hidden. Neither of them moved.

Li Du walked down the center of the room, allowing his feet to scrape lightly across the floor to announce his presence, until he reached the altar. He stood before a row of candles. Their wicks had burned low, causing the flames to reel drunkenly against the edges of the brass holders. Li Du watched them uneasily. He hadn't expected to wait. He drew in a long, slow breath. An unanticipated odor overwhelmed him, pungent, stinging, and familiar. It smelled of earth, and the energy of decay. He coughed as it burned his throat.

The source of the caustic smell was a bowl at the altar's edge. The powdered crystals were familiar to him. *Dragonbrain camphor,* he thought, recalling Chan's enthusiasm for the rare resin. Beside it were several other bowls filled with less potent powders. They were arranged with a collection of small tools beside a stand topped with a round, flat face, from which a single line of smoke snaked upward from a tiny, dying ember.

"I haven't seen you here before."

Li Du started and turned. The speaker was the old man, who now regarded him with aged eyes draped in papery lids. "I am not often in this neighborhood," said Li Du warily.

"You must be here for the examinations," said the man. Li Du didn't correct him. "The temple is too small to have a cleric," the man went on. "But I keep it the best I can." He turned his attention to the altar. "The clock has burned to the end," he murmured. "How long?"

"It only just went out."

"Good, good." The old man picked up a spoon from among the tools set out beside the bowls. Li Du watched in silence as he scooped powders into an empty bowl, first the camphor, followed by sandalwood, agarwood, and cloves. When these were mixed, the old man set the bowl aside and spread a layer of damp ash over the surface of the plate. He searched the objects on the table until he located a pale metal disk incised with the shape of a maze. He fitted this stencil to the stand, spread the blended incense over the pattern, and tamped it firmly into the grooves. When he lifted the plate, the path of incense remained. Carefully, he lit one end, and blew out the flame. From a glowing speck, a new line of smoke climbed a winding journey up to the temple rafters.

"It will take two hours to burn," said the man.

Two hours, thought Li Du. *How long am I expected to wait?*

Moving a little closer to Li Du, the old man rolled his eyes backward and spoke in a whisper. "Soldier or no, I don't think it's right to bring weapons into the temple."

Li Du turned and saw the scabbard resting on the floor beside the prostrated soldier, almost hidden in the folds of his robe. He said nothing. The old man rearranged the bowls and tools neatly, checked that the incense was burning properly, and prepared to leave. His chest suddenly heavy, Li Du watched the man shuffle through the door. Long moments passed, and he pictured the old man crossing the empty courtyard, entering the empty alley, and passing the empty sentry post. No one would see him leave. Why had the sentry post been empty?

The remaining figure still hadn't moved. Li Du saw that the queue on his back was thick and untouched by gray. The line of neck and jaw were hard and youthful. With the departure of the old man, the hall was silent, except for the soft flap of a hanging scroll caught by a breeze through the door.

Suddenly convinced that he should go, Li Du took two steps in the direction of the door, then stopped. He had seen the soldier's shoulders tense, preparing for movement. He knew suddenly, and with certainty, that he would not be allowed to pass. His heart hammered in his chest. He turned to face the altar again, searching the offerings spread across it for some object with which he could defend himself. But there was no ceremonial blade, no heavy statuette within reach. His eyes fell on the bowls of incense powders.

Sensing movement, his eyes flickered to the statue before him. Reflected in its golden robes, he saw that the man who had been kneeling was slowly, silently rising to his feet. Li Du remained transfixed, watching the figure grow to an unnatural, stretched shape as it came closer. He reached for the bowl of camphor and plunged his hand into it, almost recoiling from the sensation of frost that laced up his wrist. As he turned, he heard a blade sing from its scabbard, saw a gleam of steel, and flung the handful of opalescent powder directly into the face before him. The sword fell with a clatter as the soldier's hands came up to his eyes. He stumbled backward from the altar. Li Du ran.

Above his pounding heart he heard only the crunch of the fallen leaves beneath his feet as he hurled himself through the courtyard. When he was through the gate, he bore right and ran toward the nearest intersection. He thought he heard footsteps behind him, but he didn't turn to look. His legs felt as if they were bound by weights. Rain and mist surrounded him, confusing his sense of time and direction. Desperately, he made another turn. After two years of wanting to avoid notice, now he desired nothing more than a vigilant group of guards. He bore left, and found himself in a narrow alley. At its far end was a gate, half open. He chanced a look behind him. The soldier from the temple filled the alley's entrance. His hand was on the hilt of his sword, but he was looking past Li Du.

"Who is running?" The shout ricocheted down the alley toward him. Li Du turned again to the gate, and now saw two guards there, looming out of the mist.

"Come forward and announce your identities," came the voice again.

There was silence. Li Du turned. His pursuer was gone.

He assured the guards that there was no trouble. He was a scholar, he explained, in a great hurry to return home and set an idea to paper. Could a sedan chair be summoned to convey him to his destination? The soldiers, used to shabby scholars with an air of privilege, assumed he must be an influential man to make the eccentric request with such confidence. A sedan chair was procured. Li Du climbed inside and pulled the curtains closed over the latticed windows.

The journey back to Water Moon Temple seemed to stretch on for hours, but it was not yet twilight when the sedan chair was lowered to the ground. Li Du paid the bearers with shaking hands, and hurried into the courtyard. Before he could reach his room, he was stopped by the head cleric, who called to him from the kitchen door.

"Ah, Li Du. You have missed your friend, I'm afraid."

Li Du tried to clear his head. He glanced in the direction of Hamza's room. "My friend?"

"Oh, no, not your friend from outside the city," explained the head cleric. "No, this was someone else. He was sorry not to see you. He asked if he could leave a note for you in your room. Of course I said he could. You don't mind?"

"Of course not," said Li Du. "Thank you." He turned away before he could be asked another question. When he opened the door of his room, he saw no note. He looked on the desk and on the chair. Then he lowered himself to his knees and scanned the floor, in case the letter had fallen. There was nothing there. He stood up. Slowly, his eyes moved over his meager furnishings until they fell on the single cabinet against the wall. It was an old item, with scrapes through its lacquer like cracks in ice. He pulled it open. Everything seemed to be as he had left it.

Then his gaze shifted to the cabinet's small inner compartment. It was the only door in his room that could be locked, and the wood around the fragile lock was splintered. Li Du allowed it to swing open. The single object he had kept inside it was gone. He stood looking at the empty space. A strange calm settled over him as he thought back to words that had been uttered, and expressions that had flitted across a face, only to disappear before he understood them. The calm lasted only a few moments before a new thought occurred to him. He looked outside. In less than an hour, it would be dark, which meant he had less than an hour to reach the White Banner District.

He hired a mule at the nearby stables and rode with as much speed as was possible to achieve without attracting the attention of soldiers. He kept to streets that were just populated enough that he could travel under the cover of crowds, but not so busy as to slow his passage.

Upon reaching the White Banner District, he slowed the mule to a walk as he tried to remember the name and address that had been written on Hamza's invitation. He received a curious glance from a refined-looking gentleman passing by on a refined-looking horse, and asked him where he could find the home of Baldan. The man gave him directions and continued on, glancing back at him over his shoulder.

The district was quiet. Music drifted up and over the walls, and a shimmer of lantern light was beginning to be perceptible against the dimming sky. But when Li Du reached the place to which the rider had directed him, he found the door was closed tight. No light or sound emanated from within. The manor was obviously luxurious and well maintained, but it had the sleeping air of an empty garden. Li Du dismounted and knocked on the door, only half expecting an answer. There was silence.

He walked until he came to the nearest alley gate, an intricate latticework door that was still open. Two soldiers sat on stools to one side of it. One was polishing his sword, the other staring ahead with a bored expression. "I'm looking for the home of Baldan," Li Du said. "There is supposed to be a party there tonight."

The two soldiers exchanged glances. "You're the second person to ask about a party at Baldan's," said the one polishing his sword. "Is this some kind of prank?"

Li Du shook his head. "I don't understand. I saw the invitation to the party myself."

"Baldan's mansion is there," said the soldier, pointing over Li Du's shoulder, indicating clearly the door on which Li Du had knocked. "But there's no party there tonight. Baldan has been on a hunting trip for weeks, and his household is at their villa west of the city."

With an effort, Li Du kept his tone light, almost curious. "How strange," he said. "I must have mistook the date. At least I was not alone. You said someone else was here? I wonder if he was someone I knew."

"I doubt it," said the soldier. "He looked foreign to me. Tall, with a short beard like this—" The soldier drew his fingers in a point from his chin. "—and he wore strange clothes."

"Where did he go, when he discovered the event was not tonight?"

The soldier's eyes narrowed in gathering suspicion. "The man was wandering the streets at twilight in a neighborhood that isn't his, trying to enter a house that is locked. We had him taken into custody. He's at the Gendarmerie prison by now. And if you don't want to end up there tonight, I suggest you find a place where you are welcome. The gates are closing soon."

Chapter 44

It was too late to return to Water Moon Temple. The South Church, situated in the opposite corner of the Inner City from his present location, was also too far. Li Du could think of only one place to go. The district of the Yellow Banner was a short distance away, separated from him by, he guessed, no more than two gates. If he hurried, he could cross the boundary into Tulishen's neighborhood before they closed. At the mansion, he would have a chance to rest and think until dawn. Then he could go to the Gendarmerie headquarters and attempt to negotiate Hamza's release.

The servant who answered his knock invited him inside with the same efficient courtesy that had been instilled in each member of Tulishen's household staff. The mule was led to the stables. Li Du was escorted to a comfortable room, already lit by candles by the time he arrived, and presented with a cup of wine and assorted refreshments. Informed that the family had retired, he assured the servants that there was no need to rouse them. He had attended a party, he explained, and missed his opportunity to return home before dark. He would not intrude long on their hospitality, as urgent business required him to depart at dawn.

A guest room was soon prepared. As soon as he was alone, Li Du sank gratefully onto the bed. Lying on his back, he stared up into the cavernous wooden canopy, listening to the flutter of wings from the birdcages hanging on branches in the garden outside his window. He thought of Hamza, hoping that, tonight, the storyteller was safer in his cell than he would be outside of it. He tried

not to think about Hong's death, which had served as a grim reminder that prisons were not safe places.

Time passed. Though his thoughts became less coherent in the
drifting darkness, sleep eluded him. After a while, he sat up. For
a moment he remained seated on the edge of the bed, trying to fur-
nish the room from memory. He had stayed in it several times
before, during family celebrations. There had been books on the
shelf, volumes of poetry neatly grouped by author. If he couldn't
think, and couldn't sleep, he could at least read. He rose and felt
along the surfaces of the desk and table in search of a candle or a
lantern. To his surprise, there were none.

Now fully awake, he found the prospect of returning to bed to
endure long hours of anxious speculation in the dark unacceptable.
Quietly, he opened the door and went outside. The air was cool,
and there was just enough moonlight to fill the garden with blurred
shadows. His room was not far from Tulishen's library. With soft
steps, he followed the path that led to the adjacent courtyard. Removed from the family's residential halls, the library was solemn
and quiet, its ornate columns and intricate latticework softened by
night. He went inside. Carefully, he made his way to a desk he knew
to be in a corner alcove, where he found a candle in a bronze holder,
and a box of sulfur matches. He lit one. With a hiss, it ignited,
sending a flood of warm light over his hands, the surface of the
desk, and the laden bookshelves closest to it.

As he lit the candle, he felt more than heard the door of the library open again. It was almost silent on its oiled hinges, but a
whisper of cool air touched his cheek, and made the flame dance.
He turned around. "Lady Chen. I'm sorry. I didn't know you would
be here."

"But I hoped you would come to the library," she said as she
crossed the space to join him. "Knowing you like to read at night,
I neglected to put a candle in your room."

"How did you know I like to read at night?"

"Because when you stay here on holidays, the candles in your
room are burned down each morning. I am not so brazen as to

knock on your door when the household is sleeping, but there are many ways to justify our mutual presence here, should we be interrupted. Now, I cannot be kept in ignorance. What happened to bring you to our door so late?"

Li Du hesitated. She waited, watching him with an expression of calm concern. "To explain what happened tonight," he said finally, "it will be necessary to tell you why I came back to Beijing, and what I have been doing since I returned."

"I thought it might be," she said. She picked up the candle and led him to a small study, where she set it down on a low table between two chairs. They sat, facing each other. In the warm, unsteady light, Lady Chen's simple robe of pale gray silk would have made her appear carved from marble, were it not for her keen eyes and flushed cheeks, enlivened by anticipation.

"You know I was exiled for my close friendship with a traitor," Li Du began.

"I do," she replied. "Your mentor was accused of leading eight Ming loyalists in a plot to assassinate the Emperor."

"He was. Now I will tell you what you do not know." Li Du drew in a deep breath, and began. He revealed to Lady Chen the devastation he had felt upon learning that Shu had confessed, and the guilt that had followed him through the lonely mountains of his exile. He told her of the spy on the snowy pass beyond Gyalthang, who had whispered to him of Shu's innocence. He explained to her his decision to seek employment in the North Borough Office, and recounted his prolonged efforts to study the records of the assassination plot, and the case against Shu. Finally, he told her of Hamza's journey with the book, of their meeting with Feng Liang, and of the events that had transpired in the hours leading up to his arrival at the mansion.

She listened, rapt, interrupting only to ask for clarification. "But why are you so sure it was Feng Liang who arranged this attempt on your life?" she said, as soon as he had concluded the account. "Have you not considered the possibility that the attack was connected to your investigation of the murders at the Black Tile Factory?"

Li Du studied the surface of the table between them. "That's what I assumed when I received the note this afternoon. It was only after I returned to Water Moon Temple that I knew it was Feng."

"How did you know?"

"Because there was something missing from my room, a single item. A man had been sent to procure it during the very same hour I was supposed to die. The item is a Song edition of *The Commentary on the Book of Rites*."

Lady Chen's eyes widened. "But that would be a very valuable book indeed."

"Yes, and there are only two people who knew I had it in my possession: Hamza and Feng Liang."

"Then—Feng Liang sent the man to steal it?"

Li Du nodded. "However many lies he must have told me, he did not lie about his passion for books. His collection is his obsession."

"But you don't think he tried to kill you just to get the book."

"No. I think it is more likely that when he made his arrangements, he realized the book could be his. He only needed to make sure he obtained it after I was gone, and before it was pulled from his reach."

"Did he also arrange for Hamza to be lured away so that you would be alone?"

"I am almost certain he did. Lady Chen, I assume you have not told anyone of Hamza's profession?"

She thought. "No," she said. "It was obvious that his decision to visit our city was not merely the whim of a traveler. I could see neither of you wanted to draw undue attention to his presence."

Recalling the alluring red letter with its gilded border, Li Du berated himself for not having guessed its real purpose. "I was surprised when Hamza received an invitation to perform," he explained. "I should have known. Hamza *told* Feng he was a storyteller. As far as I know, he told no one else."

Lady Chen's expression was grave. "Feng must have begun planning this within hours of your conversation with him."

Li Du nodded. "What I cannot understand is *why*."

"But it seems obvious to me," said Lady Chen, with a slight arch to her dark brows. "Feng Liang lied when you confronted him. He *was* one of the conspirators. He must be the one you have been looking for all along, the one whose place Shu took. He wants you dead so that you cannot expose him."

Li Du rubbed his forehead. "It's difficult to explain, but even if that is true, I cannot help but feel that Feng is protecting a *different* secret. When Hamza and I entered Feng's library, he seemed afraid of what I was going to ask him. But when I told him I wanted to know about the Ming conspiracy, and Shu, he seemed almost *relieved*. It was as if he had expected me to ask him about *something else*."

Lady Chen looked doubtful. "What else could rouse him to such an act of violence?"

"When I gave you the list of students," said Li Du, trying to gather his thoughts, "I didn't explain everything to you." Quickly, he told her how Bai Chengde had drawn his erroneous conclusions about Li Du after learning that Li Du had visited Feng's residence. "But Bai Chengde seems firmly convinced that Feng Liang is behind this examination fraud."

"Even if he was, you weren't investigating examination fraud," said Lady Chen. "Why would he risk attempting your life when you were obviously in complete ignorance?"

Li Du didn't know. "Perhaps he is so afraid of being discovered that he perceived within my question—" He stopped. "No, it doesn't make sense."

"I have been thinking about that list," said Lady Chen.

"Of course," Li Du replied. "You must have spoken to Li Yujin by now."

"I have. As I suspected, he insists he knows nothing about it."

"It makes sense that he would deny it," said Li Du.

"Even so," said Lady Chen, "I maintain that he is telling the truth."

Knowing better than to challenge her when she spoke with

certainty, Li Du chose not to comment. He waited for her to continue. "If he didn't put his name on that list," she said, "then someone else arranged for him to pass the examinations without his knowledge."

"Could Tulishen himself have done it?"

Lady Chen rejected the idea at once. "Your cousin may be ambitious, but he would never put his child in such danger." A small purse was tied to the sash of her robe with a length of braided red silk. She drew from it the crumpled paper Li Du had given her on his last visit, and set it on the table between them. "I've been looking at the names in search of something they have in common. These are all families who enjoy the envy of others. Successful families, secure in their wealth and status."

She pointed to the first name. "This man's father, like your cousin, was given a Banner title. The family lives in the district of the Bordered Yellow Banner. They have a son already in the Hanlin Academy, and have instructed several princes in calligraphy and mathematics." Tracing her fingertip to the next name, she continued. "This is another family of high status, Manchu. His father fought in the Dzungar campaigns in the thirty-sixth reign year, returned with honors, and now occupies a high position in the Ministry of Military Affairs."

Li Du recognized the third name. "I used to know this candidate's father," he said. "Before he was promoted."

"To the president of the Ministry of Revenue," said Lady Chen. "One of his daughters was chosen to be an imperial consort. The family boasts endlessly of the fine gifts she sends them." Lady Chen passed a hand vaguely over the remainder of the names. "One made wealthy through a monopoly of the salt trade, one just returned from campaigns in Longfan—"

"Longfan?" Li Du repeated the word. A connection, thin and fragile, like a film of ice on water before the sun touches it, was forming in his mind.

Lady Chen was still thinking out loud. "If these men pass the examinations, their families gain more wealth, more honor, more influence, but if they are caught cheating, they are disgraced. Who-ever paid the bribe on their behalf can elevate them or ruin them. In short, control them." She stopped, noticing Li Du's distraction. "Something has occurred to you."

Li Du spoke slowly. "This family," he said, pointing to the list. "You mentioned they have a daughter in the imperial household. Do you know whose consort she is?"

"Of course. She is the consort of Prince Yinzao."

"The same prince," said Li Du, "who returned only today from Longfan, where he has spent most of the last—" He paused. "The last nine years." He looked at the list again. "You said this family tutored princes. Do you know which princes?"

"I know one of them was Prince Yinzao," murmured Lady Chen. She lifted worried eyes to Li Du's face, her composure shaken. "You must realize these are very dangerous speculations."

Li Du tapped the list once more. "This one," he said, "whose father served in the campaign against the Dzungars. That was Prince Yinzao's first campaign."

"But you forget that our own family is also on the list," said Lady Chen. "We have no connection with—" Realizing her error, she went silent. "The temple," she whispered, after a moment. "Prince Yinzao is a patron of your cousin's temple."

Li Du nodded. "Of the seven names on this list, we know five have a personal connection to Prince Yinzao. I think it very likely that the other two do, also." He stared unseeingly at the paper as his thoughts tumbled over each other, falling into patterns only to break apart. "I must think," he said finally.

Lady Chen stood up. "And rest," she said firmly. "And I must return to my chamber. If there is trouble coming to this house, there is no room for errors or misunderstandings." She picked up the list and handed it to Li Du. "This should not remain here."

He took it, and thanked her. He wanted to tell her that there was no danger, but he could see by the set of her expression that she understood the situation too well to expect or want false reassurances. They both knew that, in matters of palace intrigue, there was no certain outcome, and innocence was no guarantee of safety.

At the door of the library, Lady Chen blew out the candle. They stood in the dark, entwined in pale smoke. "Will what you know help you to free Hamza?" she asked.

"I hope so, but before I try to liberate our friend, there is another errand I must perform."

"What is that?"

"As soon as the gates open, I need to visit a bookstore."

Chapter 45

The examination yard opened at dawn. Shopkeepers with sleepy eyes waved signs in front of their stalls in a final effort to sell brushes and blankets. Friends and relatives pressed small gifts of food into the hands of candidates, adding to the odor of perspiration and incense a sweet note of pears. From a platform outside the entrance, an examination official shouted instructions, issuing dire warnings about carelessness with candles, and reminding everyone of the year a thousand candidates perished in smoke and flame within those very walls. The candidates listened as their baskets and bodies were subjected to rough inspections by clerks searching for hidden copies of the classics.

Within the yard, candidates shuffled along the narrow alleys that divided the rows of wooden cells, searching for their assigned places, trying not to trip over jugs of water spaced at regular intervals along the ground. Once inside their cells, they arranged their meager belongings as best they could on the two moveable planks provided for use as a desk, a seat, and a bed. Nervous stomachs put the latrines to immediate use, and those unfortunates in the cells closest to them prepared to endure the stench that would only intensify over the next three days.

Once the thousands were searched and seated, the examiners would arrive with their clerks and cooks, and proceed either to the comfortable offices built for them, or the high, covered platform that allowed them a view of every candidate. The open cells exposed the test-takers not only to the watchful scrutiny of the examiners and guards, but also to the sky. If it rained, six thousand oilcloth sheets would be seized and thrown over pages before the words written on them could blur. If the weather remained clear, the night would turn the yard into a reflection of the starry sky, as thousands of students determined not to stop working lit their single candles.

While the candidates were filing into the examination yard, Li Du was making his way back to the Outer City, eerily empty after weeks of being overcrowded. Newly washed blankets hung from sagging clotheslines in the courtyards of inns, whose proprietors at last had time to clean. Passing one of these inns, Li Du heard the slap of running footsteps. A moment later, he was almost knocked over by a man who came hurtling through the open door into the alley. His feet were bare, his robes hung open, and his hair was unbraided. He skidded to a halt, looked wildly to the left and right, then fixed red-rimmed eyes on Li Du. "When do the exams begin?" His breath reeked of alcohol.

Before Li Du could answer, an older man in servant's attire rushed out, took the young man's arm, and begged him to be calm. The young man stared, then nodded obediently. "I have to find my ink stone," he said vaguely. "Do you have my brushes?" As the servant coaxed his charge back into the courtyard, Li Du caught a glimpse of his agonized expression. The young man freed himself and began tracing words in the air in front of him with his finger.

"It's too late," the old servant said to Li Du. "I shouldn't have let him near the common room last night. He's not used to wine. He'll never forgive me when he comes to his senses."

Li Du looked at him sympathetically. "Give your master a strong cup of bitter tea and get him to the examination yard. I can assure you of two things. He is not the only candidate taking the tests after a night of overindulgence, and some of history's best essays have been written by inebriated scholars." Hope kindled in the servant's eyes. After delivering a torrent of grateful words in a thick provincial accent, he spun around and threw himself into action. As Li Du walked down the alley, he could hear the old man issuing instructions with the confidence of a general entering battle.

He arrived at Wu's bookstore to find it empty of customers. Wu was at his desk. He looked up, recognized Li Du, and raised the paper he was holding, fluttering it beckoningly. "At last," he said. "The candidates are locked up, and the old men of the capital can read for a while in peace. I have the newest edition for you. Without giving away too much, I can promise you will be entertained. To give you just a taste, the Zhens have been accused of misallocating funds for flood relief, a merchant has been convicted of manslaughter for beating an innkeeper who, he says, served him spoiled wine, and the rumors that a Seventh Dalai Lama has been identified continue to gain strength. And that is only the first page."

Li Du accepted the gazette that was handed to him, but didn't look at it. "I have come to ask a favor."

Wu, who had taken another copy from the pile on his desk and resumed his perusal, looked up at Li Du from beneath his cloud-like eyebrows. "One of these days, you must start *buying* books, and not simply *looking* at them. Can I tempt you with a facsimile of a Song edition of *The Records of the Grand Historian?*"

"I *am* in search of a text," said Li Du. "But it is not one you keep on your shelves."

He saw an infinitesimal narrowing of Wu's eyes. "How intriguing. If you are looking for a rare title, I can make inquiries."

"I would like to examine the documents associated with a death that occurred under suspicious circumstances."

"You mean a case record?" Wu sounded mystified. "Of course you won't find such a record on my shelves. You'll have to go to the Ministry of Punishments and submit a request to search their archives. Surely that is common knowledge among secretaries?"

"It is, and I would go to the Ministry of Punishments if I wanted to see the official, final version of the record. But I am interested in an earlier draft. I'd like to see the case as it was originally presented to the Emperor, and I'd like to see the notes the Emperor made in the margins as he reviewed it."

The gazette scraped softly across the desk as Wu slowly pushed it aside. "The words the Emperor writes are an extension of the Emperor himself," he said. "They are neither sold in bookstores, nor stuffed in disorganized ministry record halls. They are kept within the walls of the palace. Of all people, you must know where." The bookseller was looking at Li Du very keenly now.

"I do," Li Du said. "They were kept in the imperial library, where I occasionally had the honor to see them myself. But as I have no access to the palace, and no knowledge of where to find them now that the library is not what it once was, I need your help."

Wu smiled, not unsympathetically, and tapped the side of his temple gently with the tip of his finger. "I have seen this before," he said. "The day of the examinations can set a former candidate's nerves on edge, even after many years. You look as if you didn't sleep well last night. May I guess your dreams? You dreamed you finished your essays, only to look at the pages and realize they were blank. You dreamed you could not pack your basket to take into the examination yard, because the objects you placed inside it kept flying out again. You dreamed you arrived too late, and the gates of the yard were closed. This is no cause for concern, but I advise you to get some rest. Once your mind is clear, you will wonder why you came to me so early in the morning, asking questions to which I cannot possibly know the answers. And I will reassure you that, among us old eccentrics, such wanderings of the mind are easily forgiven."

For a moment while Wu was speaking, Li Du almost believed he was right. "I *am* tired," he said, when Wu had finished. "But it is essential for me to examine that record."

"Essential or not, it's not possible."

Li Du pulled his shoulders back and regarded Wu with a level gaze. "I believe that, as the Emperor's spy in Liulichang, you have the power to make it possible."

"Spy?" Wu stared. "What strange fancy has overtaken you? I am no such thing."

Li Du's affect remained unchanged. "I turn to you because I have no other choice. If you assist me, I can offer you information vital to the Emperor."

Wu's countenance was undergoing a subtle alteration. He

looked the same, but younger, somehow, and straighter. There was a steely glint in his eye that suggested the discipline not of a bookseller, but of a soldier. "As a citizen of the capital," he said, "I strongly urge you to report whatever you know to the authorities at once."

"I am offering to report it, now, to *you*."

Wu glanced toward the door. "Please," Li Du said quickly. "Don't summon your soldiers. You have asked me many questions since my return to the capital, more questions than most booksellers ask their patrons, and of a different tenor. Do you think I am a criminal?"

"I do not," said Wu.

"Or a liar?"

"I think you have secrets."

"I would not do you the discourtesy of denying it, but I am not here to trick you. The information I am offering is worth the favor I ask."

Wu stood up, walked silently to the door of the shop, and closed it. "You don't have much time," he said. "I know that you were dismissed from the North Borough Office, and I know that you are not supposed to be in the city. The chief inspector and the magistrate are looking for you. What is it you have to tell me?"

"It concerns Prince Yinzao."

Li Du would have thought it impossible for Wu's attention to sharpen any further. Now it became like the point of a knife. "What about the prince?"

"Will you give me access to the records I need?" When Wu hesitated, Li Du continued. "They are not secret. If I were still a librarian, I would have been able to see them at any time."

Wu gave a stiff nod. "I will do what I can."

Li Du accepted this, knowing he had to. Then he drew in a breath. He had been given the whole night to think, and he had not wasted it. "Prince Yinzao," he began, "in collusion with a man called Feng, has been selecting certain candidates, and ensuring that they pass the examinations."

Wu's face was tense with concentration. "Why?"

"In order to place in positions of power individuals who will support him in the battle of succession."

"It is unlikely that a few high-ranking officials could influence the Emperor's choice of heir."

"Not a few, no. But I am not talking about this year's examinations alone. I believe Prince Yinzao has been elevating his supporters within the government for years, while gaining power over them by making them unwittingly complicit in examination misconduct. Ever since he was sent away, he has been preparing for his return."

"I trust," said Wu, "that you have not spoken of this to anyone else?"

"I have not."

"What else can you tell me?"

"Nothing at present."

Wu took a deep breath and sighed, which made him look more like the bookseller to whom Li Du was accustomed. He removed his hat and jacket from behind the desk. "Then I know the task that lies before me," he said. "And you seem to know the one that lies before you." Wu opened a drawer in his desk. Withdrew a sheet of thick, formal paper. "You cannot go directly to the palace," he said as he prepared ink. "Arrangements must be made." He glanced up, taking in Li Du's plain, wilted robes. "And you need to dress more formally."

"I still have the robes I used to wear," said Li Du.

Wu composed a brief message, sealed it, and handed it to Li Du. "At the hour of the goat," he said, "present this at the palace gate, and you will be taken where you need to go."

Li Du thanked him and turned to leave. As he pulled open the door, he heard Wu's voice again. "Tread softly, if you are walking toward the past," he said. "I offer you this advice as a friend."

Chapter 46

In the courtyard of Water Moon Temple, Li Du was intercepted by the head cleric, whose hurried passage past the incense cauldron spread tangled swirls through the cloud of smoke.

"You have returned," he said. "We have been worried, not for the first time in recent days, that you might have come to harm during the night. And are we to understand that you intend to leave our humble community?"

Li Du had continued walking, so that they now stood just outside his room. "Who told you I intend to leave?"

"A clerk from your office came here earlier this morning to ask whether you had departed the capital. I was surprised. I told him you didn't return to your room last night, but that you had not, to my knowledge, departed permanently. Can you explain?"

Li Du placed a hand on his door and pushed it open. "I'm sorry, but I can't. Not now."

The head cleric stepped forward, prepared to follow Li Du into his room. "But are we to begin searching for a new tenant? What about your friend? When can we expect answers, if not now?"

"Tomorrow," said Li Du. "I intend to resolve the situation by tomorrow." After murmuring an apology, he slipped inside and shut the door behind him. He went directly to a corner of the room, where he knelt in front of a heavy trunk difficult to distinguish from the dark wood of the walls and floor. There were travel supplies resting on its lid—blankets, satchels, pots, and a worn guidebook. He set them on the floor. Then he opened the trunk, releasing a faint fragrance of cedar and an incense of sandalwood that, in years past, had been popular at court. The smell of it surprised him, not only because it transported him to mornings in his study filled with books, when his court robes were presented to him, brushed and scented, but because he had forgotten that he had ever used it.

Gently, he withdrew the books that rested in a layer at the top of the trunk. Beneath them, carefully folded, were two robes. The first was of blue silk, a rich, deep blue that slid through his fingers like a piece cut from the night sky. The second was an undercoat with a wide, embroidered hem depicting two dragons stretching their claws toward a pearl suspended between them. Beneath the robes were a pair of black silk boots with white soles, and a hat of black and red, topped with a small golden sphere. He dressed quickly. After nine years, the robes hung a little looser on him than they had before, but the effect was not pronounced.

He left the temple through the side gate nearest to his room in order to avoid further questions from the clerics. During the short, uncomfortable journey by sedan chair to the headquarters of the Gendarmerie, he silently tested the strategies he had considered to effect Hamza's liberation. Names rattled in his mind with each jounce and dip of the sedan chair—connections he might use, and identities he might assume. He studied a mental map of the court-yards and offices within the complex, and reviewed what he under-stood of the Gendarmerie's unique administrative procedures.

Upon arriving, he set his face into what he hoped was its most authoritative expression and stepped down onto the cobbles, only to look up and discover that his preparations had been un-necessary. Hamza was sauntering toward him from within the Gendarmerie's outer courtyard. He was flanked by two soldiers, who, upon reaching the entrance, exchanged words with him and, Li Du thought, friendly gestures. As he watched, Hamza bowed, then strode into the sunlight.

He recognized Li Du and hurried forward, beaming, to greet him. Looking only slightly wilted from the night's adventures, he took in Li Du's appearance with a look of bemused appreciation.

"Yesterday you were a humble clerk with ink stains on your sleeves," he said. "Today I find you transformed. How did you come by this finery?" He studied with interest the embroidered badge affixed to Li Du's chest. "What frothing sea is this, with red and golden waves? And what bird? And why is he flying toward a sun?"

"It is only a symbol of rank," said Li Du self-consciously. He directed them down an alley toward a nearby market that promised enough noise to muffle their conversation. "What happened to you last night?"

Hamza exhaled through his nose in an affronted huff. "I found the street that was indicated on the invitation, but by some mocking magic of your city's shifting walls, the mansion had disappeared from it. I was determined not to deprive the guests, wherever they were, of the entertainment promised them, so I continued my search until I was accosted by two soldiers, who took it into their minds that I might be some variety of miscreant. As if a thief would dress in pale silk at night. I could have persuaded them not to take me into custody, but it occurred to me that, if I was not to enjoy the luxuries of Baldan's mansion, I was in need of a place to stay until morning."

"But how did you convince them to release you so amicably?"

Hamza bought a pear from a fruit seller and bit into it appreciatively. "Last night, when they asked me who I was, and why I had come to the capital, I told them the truth."

"The truth?"

"I told them that I am a storyteller, that I journeyed from the western deserts, beyond the empire's borders, and that my only intention is to entertain the good people of this city before I continue on my way. Then, as if to apologize for its temporary desertion, good fortune returned to me in the gloomy offices of the prison. The wardens asked me to prove my claim by entertaining them with a tale."

"I cannot imagine a challenge that would please you more."

"Indeed," said Hamza. "I had a better time than I would have had at any mansion. I do not presume to liken myself to the incomparable Scheherazade, who performed in circumstances far more dire than mine. Still, grave consequences are never distant for those in prison, and I admit with some pride that the *Tale of the Baker, The Goldfish, and the Seven Hundred Rubies* served me well. I might have obtained my freedom earlier, but the guards insisted I finish the story." He paused. For all the levity in his account, Hamza's expression remained serious, his eyes trained on Li Du's face. "Now you have heard of my adventure, and it is your turn to tell me of yours, for it is clear by your face that something has occurred."

"I must explain to you," said Li Du, "that Baldan's mansion did not disappear. It was my inattention that led you to an uninhabited home. The invitation that came to Water Moon Temple was a trap I should have seen."

"A trap?" Hamza's eyes narrowed. He listened while Li Du told him what had happened at the Temple of the Fire God. When Li Du came to Feng Liang's treachery, his eyes widened, but he remained silent until Li Du related his escape. "A handful of dragonbrain to sting the eyes," said the storyteller approvingly. His expression became grave. "I, too, should have recognized the peril. It chastens me to know how easily I was flattered by an invitation written on costly paper. And instead of realizing my error and remaining by your side, I spent a frivolous night in prison. You might have perished!"

"I was safe in my cousin's home."

"Your cousin's?" asked Hamza, the self-recrimination vanishing from his expression. "Did you see Lady Chen? Has she unraveled the schemes of the perfidious Feng Liang?"

"In a way, yes," Li Du replied. The bells were tolling the hour of the horse. They had come to the heart of the market. Near them, almost obscured by dangling copper pots, stacked saddles, and baskets of garlic, was a shop promising the finest fried bread outside of Yunnan. It was crowded, and filled with conversation. Li Du pointed to it. "There is much I have to explain," he said. "And we have little time."

To those customers who happened to spot, through the crowd, the two men seated in the corner of the restaurant, they presented an odd sight. One wore the illustrious robes of office, though they hung a little loosely on his frame, and their formidable embroidered insignia was at odds with his gentle face and earnest, forward-tilted posture. The other wore a costume of blue and silver that one might expect to see on an acrobat. But despite the ostentatious attire, it was his face that compelled attention. Those who saw it would think of it again, recalled to it by an expression in a painting, or the soft regard of a horse. The friendship between them was evident in the quiet intensity with which the man in official robes spoke, and the other man listened. After a while, they rose and re-entered the market bustle. The man in blue and silver issued parting words to the other, who, after a moment, turned and walked alone toward the palace.

Three white marble bridges sloped up and over a wide, deep moat. Of those approaching the vermillion walls of the Emperor's domain, Li Du was the only person on foot. On either side of him, the glistening shoulders of horses and embroidered hems of official robes proceeded as if he was not there. He would have felt invisible were it not for the six hundred soldiers guarding the wall, training their eyes on every man and animal seeking admittance.

The outer wall was so thick that its entrance was more a tunnel than a door, a cavern at once vast and enclosing. Inside it, individual voices blended into a single, watery babble. The air was still. Collars clung to damp napes. A hot, sticky odor of hair pomade mingled with the musky presence of horses. Li Du presented his letter three times, and three times it was whisked away to some inner office. The third waiting period was the longest. Just as he had convinced himself that he would be turned away, three soldiers appeared before him. He was told to follow them.

They walked in silence through the vast hidden city within the city. At first they stayed in the center, where bridges crossed inner moats and streams, their white balustrades doubled in blurred reflections on the water. As clouds altered the light striking them, the yellow rooftops of the great halls shifted from the color of coins to wheat to lion's fur. Below the tiles, painted latticework dripped like liquid gold through emerald and sapphire clouds.

Soon they turned away from the imposing halls and vast spaces into cooler courtyards shaded by trees and rocks. The path they followed was familiar to Li Du. He had taken it almost daily from the Meridian Gate to the library. He expected the soldiers to diverge from it, and lead him to whatever office now contained the records he had asked to see. They didn't. The courtyards grew smaller and more secluded. For Li Du, each step was like a candle held to an obscured memory. Were it not for the soldiers escorting him and the weight of robes to which he was no longer accustomed, he might have been carrying a handful of paper slips with the titles of volumes written on them. He would present them to Shu, and together they would locate the requested books, required for a prince's astronomy lesson, perhaps, or to answer a question of law posed by the Emperor to one of his advisors.

The reverie abruptly dissolved when he found himself looking across a bare courtyard at the library. It was unchanged. The roof gleamed the same obsidian black. The same line of animals paraded down its ridge, ending with the same dragons, crouched possessively over the corners. One of the soldiers spoke to him—he could enter alone, but was to remain within the library, and return within the hour—and he nodded, barely listening. No sooner had he walked away from them than he forgot they were there.

The interior was as it had ever been. There were no people, but he could almost see the ghostly shades of scholars absorbed in documents and books at the heavy desks. Familiar faces regarded him from the paintings hung on each wall. The sashes of gods and goddesses were fixed in the same loops and coils, caught in imagined breezes. The same books patterned the shelves in the same order. As he took in the rows of colored boxes and spines, he felt as if he were reading favorite lines from beloved poems. How many times had he dreamed himself back to this place? How like a dream this was, to be here with the books, and yet to be alone.

Realizing that he had been standing, unmoving, in the doorway, he drew in a deep breath and, with a small shake of his shoulders, stepped forward. Memories continued to whisper to him as he entered the maze of cabinets. He walked the most direct route to the room of records, a deep alcove lit by thin windows, and found the section he wanted. At first, he could not understand why the cabinet labels were blurred and indistinct. They were not so in his memory. It took him a moment to comprehend that, though the library appeared unchanged, time had not stopped since his last visit there. He searched his satchel for his spectacles and put them on.

It did not take him long to find what he wanted: *Reports to the Emperor, Forty-First Reigning Year*. The files were subdivided into provinces. Before he removed the records from Jiangsu from their place, Li Du lowered himself to his knees and bowed. The hand of the Emperor was to be treated as the Emperor himself. He remained for a moment, kneeling before the shelves, his forehead pressed to the cool floor.

He found the document he sought in the third slim box he opened. The report was written in black ink in the center of the page. Li Du pictured the southern magistrate who had composed it. The heavy, cramped calligraphy spoke of arrogance, insecurity, and fingers made heavier by rings. Two sections of the original judgment had been negated with broad vermillion slashes. The fiery ink spilled into the margin in a torrent of notes. Li Du read both the report and the commentary once, then again. Adrift in the dark ocean of his own thoughts, he stood, holding his answer.

"I am considering repopulating this place with scholars," came a voice behind him. He spun around. A figure stood in gleaming silk, as if the palace rooftops and the ink on the page had cohered into a vision of yellow silk and red dragons. The face above the robe was in shadow, but the voice and bearing were unmistakable. The Emperor had come to the library.

Chapter 47

Once more on his knees with his forehead pressed to the floor, Li Du waited for the Emperor to speak. He concentrated on the minute sounds and currents of air within the library. Nine years ago, he had been so attuned to them that he would have known the instant someone had entered the door. He could feel the weight of the imperial gaze on his shoulders. The report he had been holding rested on the floor in front of him. He heard a footstep, a rustle of heavy silk, and a soft crackle of paper as the report was picked up.

"It is not often that an Outer City secretary is granted the opportunity to walk through the gates of the palace into a room closed to all but the Emperor. I am curious to know what document is so important that you would trade Wu the information you had—I refer to the actions of the prince, my son—simply to examine it."

As he had not yet been invited to speak, Li Du remained silent. He heard the sound of pages slowly being turned. "And now," said the Emperor, "I understand." Forbidden from looking up until commanded to do so, Li Du could only wait, and wonder at the thoughts contained within the pensive silence that followed the Emperor's words. He felt oddly calm, despite being aware that a decision was being made about his fate by a man who could command his death with a nod.

"We will sit together and talk," announced the Emperor. "There will be no witnesses to our conversation other than the books on these shelves, and books cannot report anything beyond what they already contain. Stand up."

Keeping his gaze averted, Li Du rose to his feet. Following the Emperor's instruction, he pulled a chair from its place at a nearby desk and oriented it to face the one already in the alcove. A movement of the yellow silk sleeve indicated that he should sit. He obeyed. "This report," said the Emperor, taking a seat in the other chair, "was submitted to me nine years ago by a magistrate in Jiangsu Province. It recommends the execution of a woman found guilty of murdering her husband. Is this the document you came here to examine? Speak naturally. I give you permission to look at me."

Li Du removed his spectacles. Then he lifted his eyes and beheld the face of a man approaching sixty years of age. From small brows, the eyelids drooped expressively down to the outer corners of the eyes. Thin cheeks fell from high cheekbones in the same downward line, to a small mouth framed by a mustache and beard that were still dark. The outward signs of age and fatigue failed to dim the inner vigor expressed by the direct gaze and straight, slightly forward-tilted posture. The breadth of the Emperor's shoulders was only slightly augmented by his stiff, voluminous robes. He was still a man of considerable physical strength.

"Yes," said Li Du. "That is the document I came here to find."

The Emperor looked down at his own writing. "No matter how numerous the responsibilities of a ruler, he should not permit a sentence of death to be carried out within his realm unless he himself has approved it." The Emperor hesitated slightly. "As a father must bear the burden of punishing his children, so a ruler must bear the burden of punishing his subjects. With *this* report, I had a happier task. The magistrate had entirely misconstrued the evidence. It was clear to me that the woman was innocent."

"Which is why the final version of the report," said Li Du, "the one filed in the records room of the Ministry of Punishments, makes almost no mention of her. The case is listed as one of accidental death."

The Emperor nodded. "One might wonder why a secretary of the North Borough Office, with no connection to this province or to this case, would take an interest in it. But you are not simply a clerk of the North Borough Office, are you? And you do have a connection to it." Reading the answer in Li Du's expression, the Emperor continued.

"I have not forgotten you. Nine years ago, I sentenced you to exile. I took this action because of your close friendship with a man who, in this very room, plotted my death. Three years ago, I pardoned you. With your sentence lifted, you were freed from any association with the traitor, Shu." The Emperor lifted the paper so that it caught the light. "Why, then, have you come here to read a report concerning his daughter?"

Li Du looked at the ink that shone red as blood. "Because I wanted to find the truth."

"And did you find it?"

"Yes."

The Emperor lowered the report. Though his expression did not appear to change, his eyes now bored into Li Du. "What is it you think you now know?"

Li Du met the Emperor's gaze calmly. "Your son, the prince, has been manipulating the examinations, but that is only his most recent transgression against you. I know that, nine years ago, he was guilty of another treachery. I know that it was Prince Yinzao who plotted your death. He was the ninth conspirator. And I know that Shu had no part in it."

It seemed to Li Du that the books around them leaned closer, waiting in breathless silence for the dragon's jaws to snap closed around their old friend. The Emperor said nothing. He turned his face away from Li Du, and fixed his attention on the thin window closest to him. "It is the trouble with raising a son within walls," he said finally. His tone, thoughtful, betrayed no strong emotion. "Boys should grow up in open spaces. The sight of a bird should inspire him to urge his horse to a faster gallop, in imitation of that soaring freedom. It is unhealthy to be so confined."

If he agreed with the Emperor's words, Li Du would be acknowledging fault in the imperial family. If he disagreed, he would be disagreeing with the Emperor. He remained silent. The Emperor turned to face him again. "After I pardoned you, I invited you back to the capital. You refused my invitation. You were going to follow the path of a scholar recluse, and disappear into the mountains."

Li Du understood that a response was expected from him. He cast his mind back to the towering shoulders of the mountains, the forests of craggy oaks, and the silent, enclosing clouds. He had journeyed through that other world in order not to think of where he was now, not to think of the library. "I believed Shu was guilty," he said. "I thought the only way to escape my confusion, my disappointment, and my grief was to stay far away."

The Emperor was watching him closely. "What made you come back?"

"I no longer believed Shu was guilty."

A shadow appeared between the Emperor's brows. "You suspected I had made an error in condemning him?"

Li Du was careful. "I suspected that there was more to what happened."

"I was informed of your return," said the Emperor, relaxing. The trace of a smile touched his lips. "Exiles, even if they are pardoned, do not pass through the gates of this city unnoticed. At the time, I wondered what you would do here. When I heard you had accepted a humble position in the Outer City, I was disappointed, and did not think of you again. I see now that your choice was strategic. You wanted to remain inconspicuous. But from such a lowly vantage point, how did you arrive at this version of events you claim is the truth?"

The light in the room altered with a shifting cloud. It became difficult to see the Emperor's face above the golden silk that glowed so brightly. Li Du drew in a breath, and began. "I used my access to ministry files to learn everything I could about the conspirators, and about Shu's trial. My research led me to the conclusion that

Shu, for reasons I did not know, had assumed the blame that belonged to a conspirator whose identity had never been discovered."

"And so you began a search for the unnamed conspirator," said the Emperor.

"Yes. It led me to the man called Feng, a reclusive book collector who, like the other conspirators, had connections to Ming loyalists. Thinking I had found the man Shu had died to protect, I went to Feng, and demanded the truth."

"What was his reply?"

"He told me that while he had known the conspirators, he had never been one of them. He told me he didn't know anything."

"And you believed he spoke the truth."

"I did, until yesterday, when he sent a man to kill me."

At the Emperor's command, Li Du gave a full description of the attack in the Temple of the Fire God, and the theft of the book that had revealed Feng's hand. When he was finished, the Emperor was contemplative. "You escaped death," he said. "And you identified the man who orchestrated the attack. But how did you come to present yourself, not a day later, to my trusted employee Wu, and inform him that my own son was guilty of examination corruption?"

"I had the information I needed," said Li Du. "But I hadn't been looking at it correctly. I knew that Feng had a place on the Examiner Selection Committee. I had learned, in the course of my investigation, that he was using his position to ensure that certain candidates received passing scores. But I dismissed this as corruption, irrelevant to my questions."

"A mistake," said the Emperor.

"It was," Li Du agreed. "After the attempt on my life, it occurred to me that Feng's involvement in examination fraud was more significant than I had initially assumed."

"And that is how you discovered that the candidates he was assisting were all connected to my son."

"Yes."

"Which led you to the conclusion that my son has been surreptitiously filling ministry offices with compromised men who will support his eventual claim to the throne, an accusation I have spent the past several hours verifying."

So the plot has been toppled, thought Li Du. He tried not to let the anxiety that clutched his heart appear in his face. "I must tell you," he said, "that the families implicated in his scheme were ignorant of it. The candidates didn't know they were being given an advantage."

The Emperor's expression tightened. "Your concern is not surprising, given that a member of your own family is among them." Then a tired breath, almost a sigh, escaped his lips. "There will be no punishment where it is not deserved," he said. "I have no wish to inspire disloyalty where there was none before. Continue your account."

Li Du's shoulders sagged slightly in relief. His words came more easily. "Once I knew that the prince is scheming with Feng *now,* the possibility occurred to me that the two had also conspired in the past. From there, the pieces began to fall into place. You sent the prince away nine years ago, not long after the attempted assassination. I allowed myself to imagine that it was he who had orchestrated the attack, and the picture became clearer."

Li Du had been looking at the Emperor. Now his gaze shifted to another corner of the library. Rows of tall shelves separated them from the table around which the conspirators had gathered. An image rose unbidden before him of them seated there now, shades consigned to repeat their doomed preparations until they faded from memory. He turned back to the Emperor. "Shu was in the library when the prince met with his conspirators for the final time. Shu saw the meeting, but he didn't understand the significance of what he had seen until he learned that the men who had gathered there were all dead."

"All but one," murmured the Emperor.

The pain in the other man's expression caused Li Du to hesitate, but the Emperor made a small gesture, commanding him to continue. "Shu knew you would want to conceal your son's betrayal from your subjects. He offered to help you do it. Not only did Shu's arrest end the search for the rumored ninth conspirator, but his confession confirmed the story of the Ming conspiracy that was put in place to shield the prince."

For the first time in their conversation, Li Du's voice trembled. It did not escape the Emperor's notice. "This revelation upset you," he said.

Li Du steadied his breath. "I couldn't understand Shu's actions."

The Emperor's brows lifted slightly in challenge. "Why not? A loyal subject is willing to die for his Emperor."

"Yes," said Li Du. "And Shu *was* loyal. He would have given his life for you, but he would not have given it to protect the reputation of a son who had betrayed you. I knew there was something I had not yet uncovered."

"Which led you to this." The Emperor looked down at the report.

"I had seen the official report of the accidental death of Mei's husband," said Li Du. "It was included in the files associated with Shu, but it bore no trace of the changes you had made to it. I never considered its possible significance." He paused. "If Mei had been convicted of murdering her husband, you were the only person in the empire who could have saved her. Shu—"

The Emperor raised a hand, commanding silence. "The rest of the account is mine to tell. Shu came to me, as you said. He told me what he had seen in the library. Then he told me of his daughter, whom he loved. He had arranged a marriage for her, only to discover that he had given her to a monster, a man as cruel as he was brutal. In defense of her own life, she raised her hand against him, and by that action, caused his death. The magistrate had ordered her execution. His report would come before me within the month. Shu begged me to save her. In exchange, he offered me his help, and his life. This secret, that was mine alone to keep, is now yours, also."

For the entirety of their exchange, Li Du had heard only their voices, and the silence in the library. Now, small sounds returned.

He heard, faintly, a breeze rustle the dry stalks of lotuses in a nearby pond, a bird's trill, a distant bell.

The Emperor was thinking. A hint of a smile hovered around his lips. "What, now, is to be done with you?" he asked. "Among your other offenses, you have conducted a covert investigation intended to undermine a determination of the throne. Yet, in doing so, you have alerted me, for a second time, to danger. As I believe your unique talents would be put to better use elsewhere, you will not remain at the North Borough Office. But I perceive uncertainty in your expression. Surely you do not intend to refuse the command of your Emperor?"

"I will be honored to perform whatever service you ask of me," said Li Du. "It is only that, before I depart the North Borough Office, there is a certain matter I feel an obligation to resolve. I wondered if I might, most humbly, ask for your help."

Chapter 48

Three days later, the streets were once again populated with candidates. Allowed only a single day to recover before they reentered the yard for a second round of testing, they paced the inn courtyards, hollow-eyed and distracted. Some tried to rest, others to study. Once again, the purses of fortune-tellers were filled with coins, and temple caretakers rejoiced at the generous donations.

Chief Inspector Sun was in a relaxed mood. A good night's rest and a succession of positive developments had lifted his features. He had just returned from the offices of the magistrate, and was in his office, sharing a pot of tea with Li Du. "Kirsa has confessed to arranging Hong's death," he said. "It happened just the way you explained it to me. He feared the murder investigation would lead us to him, and hoped a quick confession from Hong would divert attention from Pan's schemes. When the confession did not come quickly enough, Kirsa had Hong killed, and the death was made to look like a suicide. I'm surprised he thought it was worth such a risk."

Li Du's expression was thoughtful. "The short exchange I had with him left me with the impression that he is not a patient man. I imagine he preferred to take control of the situation, rather than wait and watch. That also explains his insistence that I be sent away. I think he understood Magistrate Yin's disposition, and trusted him not to look too closely into the circumstances."

"If you ask me," said Sun darkly, "Magistrate Yin would not emerge unscathed from a corruption investigation." His expression cleared. "Fortunately, the question of whether Magistrate Yin was corrupt or merely incompetent is no longer of concern to my office. By all accounts, his replacement, Magistrate Po, is as fair and competent an administrator as I could hope to serve." He paused and looked at Li Du with a slight twinkle in his eye. "Though he will have to be exceptionally impressive if he is to compensate for the departure of a most valued assistant."

After delivering this compliment, Sun's expression became more serious. "We know that Kirsa is responsible for the death of Hong, and we know that Zou Anlin is responsible for the death of Pan. But I begin to think we will never know who entered the factory that night with a sharp blade, and murderous intent. It must have been someone connected to one of Pan's schemes, but how to begin, when he was involved in so many?"

Li Du set down his cup. Over the previous three days, numerous small plots, orchestrated by Pan, had been brought to light. Li Du had made several adjustments to the accounts he had given. Erchen's secret remained safe. Li Du himself had met briefly with the young candidate that morning, who, despite looking wan and exhausted, was tentatively optimistic about his essays. And, even though Aveneau's incriminating letter was still missing, Li Du had done his best to shield the Jesuits, including managing to misplace the chess piece containing the seal of the Censor's Office. The other forged seals, which Pan had used to facilitate his nocturnal wanderings, had been incorporated into evidence.

As for Li Du himself, despite having reassumed his secretarial robes, a change in his bearing must have been apparent. Since his return to the North Borough Office with an imperial letter canceling his assignment to Tongzhou, the clerks had begun to address him with increased deference. When he had informed Chief Inspector Sun of his intention to pursue other career opportunities, Sun had reacted with the affectionate pride of an older brother.

Now the chief inspector was looking curiously at his soon-to-be-former secretary. "I notice you are not trying as hard as you did in the past to hide your intelligence," he said. "Clearly, you have an idea. What is it?"

"I was thinking of Madam Hong," said Li Du.

"That unfortunate, beautiful woman," said Sun. "I do not expect we will ever know what purpose brought her to her fate that night."

Li Du refilled their cups, then leaned back in his chair. "Her purpose was blackmail. Madam Hong was the blackmailer."

Sun's eyebrows shot up. "But how do you know?"

"Because of a glimpse of red silk."

"Red silk?"

"On the afternoon of Hong's party, Pan, Kirsa, and Ji conducted what they thought was a secret conversation. They were, in fact, overheard."

"Yes," Sun said, a little impatiently. "By the scholar Bai." He motioned for Li Du to continue.

"When I confronted Ji with the subject of that conversation, he remembered that, at the time, he thought he'd seen someone. *Red silk among the green leaves* were his words. Ji is not a man to mistake color. It is his obsession."

"But what does this signify?"

Li Du thought back to his conversation that morning with the scholar Bai, who had been relieved to learn that his efforts had been appreciated, and that the matter was to be resolved quietly, so that the examinations would not be tainted by scandal. "Bai prefers the subtle shades of scholar's robes," he said, returning his attention to Sun. "I have since confirmed that Bai was not wearing red silk that day. According to her servants, Madam Hong was."

"But it was a gentlemen's party!"

"It was her home," said Li Du. "Whether Madam Hong intended to eavesdrop or not, what she heard gave her an idea. Her art collections had driven the household into debt, and she was badly in need of money. She recognized Pan, and knew that he came often to her husband's factory. It was Madam Hong who sent him the blackmail note, Madam Hong who quoted *The Bitter Plum* to communicate to him what she had overheard. *The moon shines on my beloved in the old pavilion, green with moss.*"

Sun nodded slowly. "If that is true, it explains why she was there that night, and it explains the silver. Pan was going to pay her."

"It also explains the motive for her murder," said Li Du.

"I don't understand. If she was blackmailing Pan, then *he* had a motive to kill her. But who else did?"

"Let us return to the blackmail note," said Li Du. "Madam Hong composed a message that, to anyone who had not read the novel, would appear to be merely a message of illicit love, and one not easily traced to her. She knew Pan *had* read the novel, and recently, because it had been selected for discussion at her husband's gathering. She didn't want to risk signing her name, so she relied on the content of the message to communicate to Pan that its sender had been at the party, and had overheard his conversation. Up to a point, her plan was successful. Pan received the letter—either in the evening after the party or early the next morning—understood its meaning, and came to the factory with the silver. I imagine he was even intrigued."

Li Du paused. "At the beginning of this case, when we stood in the dim room at the factory, you were certain of what you saw. You believed it was a crime of rage, a crime committed by a man who found his wife in the arms of her lover and exacted bloody revenge. I was the one who led us another way. As soon as I recognized the hidden meaning in the note, I dismissed the motive that had seemed so apparent to you. In doing so, I failed to consider that, despite the intent, the note could still be read as a love letter, and the scene still misinterpreted as infidelity."

Sun stopped him. "Are you saying that, all this time, it *was* Hong?"

"No," said Li Du. "But there was someone else who might have shared his motive."

"You cannot mean?" Sun stared at Li Du. "But that's impossible. You cannot be referring to Lady Ai? But she is a woman. And a woman wouldn't—" He paused, temporarily overwhelmed by his own incredulity. "A woman, especially a woman of such delicacy, would never have the strength to overcome two people."

"I believe that many women would," replied Li Du. "But recall that in this case, she would not have had to overcome two people. Pan was already dead."

"But she was in her home when the night watch began. I confirmed it myself. Even if she could have left the house unnoticed during the night, she couldn't have reached the factory without being stopped at walls and alley gates."

"No," said Li Du. "Not unless she knew how to avoid being stopped. Pan had a system of moving through the city at night, the system he referred to as tunnels. In the same way a map can be shared, the way through his tunnels could be taught."

Slowly, Sun rose to his feet and reached for his hat. "I hope you intend to come with me," he said.

When they arrived at Pan's home, they found both the inner and outer courtyards filled with people. Servants packed open crates, and hired laborers lashed the closed ones together in preparation for travel. A maid informed them of what had happened. A letter from the family had at last arrived. They requested Lady Ai to bring Pan's body home for burial. The Beijing residence had already been sold. Sun asked where they could find her mistress. The maid said she was in the former master's study.

Lady Ai was sitting at the desk, staring at its surface, now empty of papers or books. Her small hands rested on the lacquered wood. Her face was paler than it had been, her features sleepless and sunken. Her expression, upon recognizing Sun and Li Du, was unmistakable. She had been expecting them.

"Lady Ai," said Sun. "I have come—"

"Yes," she interrupted, in a tone more listless than impatient. "I know why you are here."

"Then you understand I must ask you to come with me now."

She didn't move. "May we stay a little longer? You must have questions. I would rather answer them here."

"It is not an unreasonable request," said Li Du.

Sun, looking slightly lost, did not protest. Lady Ai stood up, an action that seemed to require all her strength. Almost as if she had forgotten they were there, she went to one of the walls and began to touch the objects on the shelf, brushing her fingers gently over each one. "He brought me to the capital with him because he could not bear to leave me behind." Her voice was soft, but held an unexpected warmth that belied the brittle detachment of her bearing. "I knew everything about him. Everything. I knew that his mind insisted on finding every little path around what was required, around the rules. I knew he didn't care about what belonged to other people. I knew he thought he was superior to everyone else, superior even to the gods. I was the only one who knew, and I was the only one he loved. The *only one*." Her fingers reached a slim vase glazed the deep green of forest moss. "We were not a man and a woman. Ours was the love of moons and stars. We existed in the heavens together. These little cities and walls meant nothing to us."

Li Du spoke quietly. "But he didn't tell you everything. You found the letter when you mended his coat, didn't you? He had left it in his pocket."

Her hand dropped abruptly to her side, but she didn't turn around to face them. Words poured from her, conjuring dark heavens, unconfined and mad. "When I saw the letter, I could not bear it. I felt that something inside me had woken up, a black snake that coiled and spat and filled my veins with burning poison. He had never loved another. He *could not* love another."

Sun, looking as if he was caught in a storm, swallowed and spoke with an effort. "You used the paths he had taught you—the tunnels—to go to the Black Tile Factory."

The narrow shoulders relaxed, and Lady Ai resumed her inspection of the shelves. She reached her hand up again, and traced the maze pattern on a square porcelain box. "The tunnels, yes," she said. "They were our secret. We could make walls move. We could make the whole city open up for us. I took the knife from our kitchen. I knew the way to the factory, his *special* way, the way through the dark. I stood concealed, just across from the entrance. I almost didn't go inside. It was so quiet. I thought I must have been wrong. He couldn't be there. He was home, waiting for me. Then I saw *her*. She crept down the street in the shadows, and went inside. I waited. I thought my heart would burn me. Then I followed. I crossed the courtyard and slipped into the room after her. At first I couldn't see him. Then I realized he was on the bed, waiting for *her*. And she was bending over him, in gold like a beautiful bird, about to wake him with a kiss. I had the knife in my hand. It was so dark. All I could see was that great golden bird, that treacherous goddess. And I—I killed him. He didn't even wake up. He never woke."

Lady Ai turned around, her hand at her throat. Her breath came in short gasps, as if she was suffocating. "The woman was screaming, but I didn't hear her. I wanted her dead. And then she was. She was quiet. They were both quiet, and so was I. And it was so dark." She stopped abruptly. Her hand dropped to her side again.

Sun opened his mouth to speak, then closed it. He glanced imploringly at Li Du. "You left the factory," said Li Du calmly. "And you saw Hong, didn't you?"

Lady Ai stared at him for a moment, then nodded. "I wanted to die for what I had done. I wanted to be with him again. So I went toward the soldiers at the end of the alley. I believe I planned to show them my hands, covered in blood. But then, as I drew nearer, I heard—I heard singing and laughing. And I saw him, *Hong*, stumble out into the alley. He came toward me. He was singing, and swaying from side to side, and laughing. He didn't see me. I wanted to scream at him. *Do you know where your wife was tonight?* And as soon as I thought those words, I realized that, if he *had* known, he would have done as I had. He would have taken up a knife and plunged it into his wife and her lover."

"And the law would have protected him," said Li Du. "Though it would not protect you."

Slowly, she nodded. "And I thought to myself, why should I be executed before a crowd, when he would not? Why should *I* die? He *would* have done it, had he known. Why not suggest that he had?"

"So you followed him home and hid the knife outside his door. He was so drunk he could hardly stand. You thought there was a chance even he would believe he had done it."

"I didn't think he would kill himself. I didn't mean for that to happen. Maybe he did it because he loved her, and could not bear to live—" She paused and met Li Du's eyes. "What led you to me?"

He glanced at the table in the corner, where the chess game remained, unfinished. "I believe it was when I saw that board," he said. "Ji told me that no one could defeat Pan at chess. That game is as even a match as I have ever seen."

A small, strange smile curved her lips. "I am glad you have come."

Chapter 49

The sun through the leaves of the pear trees cast red-tinted shadows through the open window of Lady Chen's study. Li Du and Hamza sat opposite Lady Chen at the green marble table, on which rested three cups of plum wine. Seven days had passed since Li Du had entered the palace. During that time, Prince Yinzao and his retinue had left the city. The abrupt departure, so soon after his celebrated return, had been explained with a brief announcement that he had been honored, once more, with a posting to the frontier.

Hamza was looking thoughtfully out at the crimson leaves. "Had Lady Ai discovered that there was no affair between her husband and Madam Hong, and that Pan was already dead when she attacked him?"

"She seemed not to know," said Li Du. "But I expect she has since been told."

"The murder of Madam Hong remains her burden to bear," said Hamza. "But perhaps it will ease her mind to know she did not kill the man she loved."

Lady Chen refilled their cups from a black bottle decorated with white plum flowers. "I don't think new revelations will matter very much to Lady Ai. From what you have told me, all that matters to her is that Pan Yongfa is gone. She will not choose to believe what gives her ease. She will choose to believe whatever protects her pain. Her anguish at his loss is all she has left of him. She will keep it close until they are together again."

After a silence, Lady Chen lifted her gaze to the Latin books and astronomical instruments arranged on the shelf. "You said you found Father Aveneau's letter."

Li Du nodded. "I asked Lady Ai if Pan had a place in the home where he kept secret documents. She told me to look in a pocket on the back of a certain painting—one depicting a hundred birds filling the branches of a willow tree. I found the painting already packed away for the return to Anhui. The pocket was well concealed in the silk that framed the picture. The letter might never have been found."

"And now?"

"Now it has been destroyed." Li Du had taken the letter to the South Church. Father Calmette had read it gravely, then held it to a candle flame. Together, they had watched the red seal of the Censor's Office turn brown as the paper curled, smoked, and became ash. Li Du credited Father Calmette for the immediate sense of relief that had filled the room with the disappearance of the letter. The priest had used the same candle to light his favorite incense. Over cups of tea, he had nodded contentedly at the sounds of construction coming from the roof repair, discussed progress on the new city map with undiminished enthusiasm, and shared with pride his work on translating "The Fisherman's Ode."

"One detail that is not clear to me," said Lady Chen, recalling him to the present, "is why the men who tried to assassinate the Emperor for Prince Yinzao all had histories of Ming loyalty."

"They *were* Ming loyalists," said Li Du. "I expect they were told that if the plot was successful, Prince Yinzao would return the southern provinces to the Ming heirs. The prince used them, knowing that if the plot failed, their allegiance to the Ming would make it easier to divert attention from himself. And that is exactly what happened."

"With Shu's help," said Lady Chen.

"With Shu's help," Li Du echoed. He fell silent. He had spent the previous night in Mentougou, where he had given Mei's children their final lesson for the year. He had made a gift to them of a fine edition of the *Manual on Calligraphy*, purchased from Wu's bookstore, and warned them that, when he returned from his journey and evaluated their progress, he would know if they had not practiced. All three had nodded gravely. To their delight, he had read aloud to them the author's list of all that could be identified in a page of calligraphy, from a drop of dew, to a flock of geese, to a sky filled with stars.

In the evening, while the children played in paths of light that spilled across the garden from the windows, he had spoken to Mei. He had intended to tell her only that her father had never betrayed his Emperor. But his words had freed hers. Haltingly, at first, they had spoken of his teacher, and her father, until their stories mingled like two coiling trails of incense smoke turning into one. Mei had long ago concluded that there was no coincidence in the concurrence of her father's death and her salvation from the magistrate's justice. The burden had been difficult to bear, until her marriage, and her children, had eased it. Learning from Li Du that the Emperor honored her father, even in secret, lightened it further.

"Shu accepted his own death because he knew he had saved his daughter," said Li Du, returning from the memory of the twilit garden to Lady Chen's bright study and questioning eyes. He had entrusted her with the secrets she had helped him uncover. "I am not certain the Emperor will ever attain the same peace with his decision to sacrifice a loyal subject to protect a son who has now, once again, betrayed him."

Once more, Lady Chen's eyes lifted to the shelf on which a winged horse gleamed from the surface of a celestial globe. "And yet, through all our tragedies, the stars follow their same paths across the heavens." She regarded Li Du. "I anticipate with pleasure the day our paths cross again."

An autumn breeze sent a sparkling path along the surface of the moat as the librarian and the storyteller crossed. With their mules close beside them, they shuffled slowly over the bridge, finding a way through the crowd entering the city. Once they had left the bustle behind, Hamza bought a candied crab way apple from a passing peddler, and shared it with his mule. "Have you decided where we are going?" he asked, looking at the hills that rose, blurred and blue, on the horizon.

Li Du patted the satchel he carried, feeling the corner of a slim volume tucked inside. He recalled the room in a shaded palace courtyard where he had recently sat opposite one of the Emperor's advisors. The stern official had slid the volume across the table to Li Du, and explained that within it was a collection of reports received by the palace that year, each describing an unusual occurrence. The order in which Li Du chose to investigate them was up to him. The Emperor looked forward to hearing of his travels.

"Naturally," said Hamza, interrupting Li Du's thoughts, "I am drawn to the account of the island that has appeared without explanation off the coast of Formosa, though the gold-worm poisonings plaguing the hill towns of Sichuan are not without interest." He paused thoughtfully. "Although," he mused, "I would very much like to question one of those oracular ghosts that have been seen in the forests of the Evenki . . ."

As Hamza went on, Li Du turned and looked back at the city. The walls, for all their weight of earth, rock, and brick, were already becoming smaller, their shape more simple. On either side of the path, buckwheat and millet fields spread in oceans of gold and green. He adjusted the buckle on the saddlebag closest to him. The wool blankets on the mule's back smelled faintly of campfire smoke and juniper. He gave the mule's neck a gentle pat. Her mane was soft and sun-warmed, but as another breeze breathed softly over the fields, he felt the cool touch of a changing season. He adjusted his hat and set his gaze to the path ahead.

Acknowledgments

As I set Li Du free to continue his adventures in places and dimensions of his own choosing, it seems right to pause and acknowledge the help he has received, outside the confines of these pages, to reach this point in his story.

I first envisioned Li Du in the shifting mists on Jade Dragon Snow Mountain, where I would not have been were it not for my husband, Robbie, whose botanical research brought me to Southwest China and whose imagination has fired my own since the day we met.

I would also not have been there without the field station staff, who kept us safe and healthy on the mountain. It must have been inconvenient and stressful to host two foreigners who could barely communicate (and who seemed likely to fall into a gorge or enrage a yak at any moment), but we were always made to feel welcome. I credit Mr. Zhao's pumpkin stew for inspiring just about every scene of comfort and companionship I've written. I am also forever grateful to Song and Na, who were always ready to help us navigate life in Lijiang.

It can be hard to lose yourself in a book when you care about the writer, and I want my family to know how much I appreciate their eagerness to be simultaneously engaged readers and loving relatives. My grandparents Hugh and Marge, Dickinsons, McFarlings, McCormicks, Savages, Trimbles, Steve and Karen Hart—I am so lucky.

Both my parents have given me so much, including a childhood abroad from which I've drawn inspiration. My mother has worked with me at every stage of writing, from identifying themes to polishing sentences. My father has waited patiently to be the first reader of the nearly finished manuscripts. My brother, Hugh, has a keen eye for scene structure, and a unique ability to listen to my confused ramblings and explain me to myself.

A number of writers have taken time away from their own work to offer me help and encouragement: Fred Moody, Usha McFarling, Donna Leon, Matthew Pearl, Julia Keller, Weina Dai Randel, and Louise Penny, whose hug when I met her at the St. Louis County Library still makes me glow to remember.

Stephanie Cabot, my fantastic agent, connected with me on my writing from our first phone call, and shepherded my books to and through publication. Ellen and the Gernert Company have been wonderful. I'm deeply thankful for the team at Minotaur who have worked to bring these novels to readers, especially my editor, Kelley Ragland, who saw how to make each book stronger and gave me the guidance and support I needed throughout each round of revisions.

The librarians at the Richardson Memorial Library at the St. Louis Art Museum allowed me to pore over *Peking Temples and City Life* for hours in their reading room. Sitting at the great, gleaming desk surrounded by books made me feel even closer to the scholars that wander in and out of my stories.

Of the many professors at Swarthmore College to whom I am grateful, two should certainly be acknowledged here: Dr. Stephen Bensch, who gave me my first historical fiction writing assignment, and Dr. Craig Williamson, whose lectures on Old English riddles and elegies defined my understanding of imagination as an adult.

And finally, thanks to my friends. Kate and I fashioned our first fictional worlds together, and those snow castles and ceiling worms and bunk-bed boats are never far from my writing. Mary and the whole Hartnett-Norland family have been so unhesitatingly kind always. Tyler and Katina, Dylan and Claire, companions in adventure, conversation, and whisky. Anna befriended me in law school and affirmed during those years that I didn't have to stop being myself just because I was in a setting that wasn't quite the right fit for me. And in St. Louis, Irene, Ashley, Jenny, and Celia have lit up the hours with conversation and music and bonfires, those most ancient of storytelling inspirations.